MISCHIEF

ED McBAIN

MISCHIEF

AVON BOOKS ◆ NEW YORK

AVON BOOKS
A division of
The Hearst Corporation
1350 Avenue of the Americas
New York, New York 10019

Copyright © 1993 by HUI Corporation
Inside cover author photograph by Mary Vann Hunter
Published by arrangement with the author
Library of Congress Catalog Card Number: 93-10404
ISBN: 0-380-71384-5

Published in hardcover by William Morrow and Company, Inc.; for information address Permissions Department, William Morrow and Company, Inc., 1350 Avenue of the Americas, New York, New York 10019.

First Avon Books Printing: June 1994
First Avon Books International Printing: May 1994

AVON TRADEMARK REG. U.S. PAT. OFF. AND IN OTHER COUNTRIES, MARCA REGISTRADA, HECHO EN U.S.A.

Printed in the U.S.A.

RA 10 9 8 7 6 5 4 3 2 1

*This is for
Judy and Michel Cornier*

The city in these pages is imaginary.
The people, the places are all fictitious.
Only the police routine is based on
established investigatory technique.

1.

The luminous dial of his watch showed ten minutes past two in the morning. The rain had tapered off at about midnight. He would not have come out if it'd still been raining. These *writers* didn't work in the rain. Didn't want to get their spray cans all wet. Some writers. *Scribblers* was more like it. Each one scribbling right over the one before him. Kept on scribbling and scribbling till all there was left of a clean white wall was a barbed-wire tangle of words and names you couldn't even read.

The wall he'd chosen tonight was a new one.

You could almost smell the fresh cement.

New walls attracted these writers the way honey did bears. Put up a new wall or a new fence, wouldn't be ten minutes before they were out spraying it. Gave them some kind of thrill, he supposed. He'd once read something about burglars defecating in people's shoes while they were in an apartment stealing things. Added insult to injury. Wasn't enough they were in there taking a man's possessions, they had to go and soil his belongings besides, let him know what contempt they had for him. This was the same thing. Person sprayed his paint scribbles on a wall or a fence, he was telling the citizens of this city he was *shitting* on them.

He hoped it wouldn't start raining again.

There were lightning flashes in the distance, rumbles of thunder, but he didn't think the rain was moving any closer to where he was standing here waiting for someone to show up.

This was a two-lane street here running under the highway.

Your writers never sprayed where their work wouldn't be seen, they always picked a street or a road with traffic on it, so every time you went by you could ooh and aah over the terrific mess they'd made of the wall. There weren't any leaves on the trees yet, no protection that way, nothing to create any kind of shadow, just these naked branches reaching up toward the parkway where every now and again a car's headlights drilled the blackness of the night. Spring was slow coming this year. This was the twenty-third of March, a dreary Monday morning. Even though spring had arrived officially three days earlier, it had been raining on and off ever since. Cold, too. Walking in the cold dank rain, he had worked out his plan.

Tonight would be the first of them.

If anybody showed.

If not, he'd do it tomorrow night.

No rush at all.

Get it done in time enough.

Three of them altogether, one plus one plus one.

He figured these writers had to do their dirty work at night, didn't they, you never saw any of them doing it during the daytime. Probably scouted a new wall or fence during the day, came back at night to mess it up. If anybody showed tonight, he'd wait till they did some messing up before he did a little messing of his own. Catch 'em in the act, *bam*! The gun in the pocket of his coat was a .38 caliber Smith & Wesson.

Lightning way way off in the distance now.

Low growl of thunder far far away.

On the highway overhead, a car's tires hissed on the still-wet roadway. There was a penetrating chill on the air, made a man wish he was home in his own bed, instead of out here waiting for some jackass who didn't know what he was in for.

Well, come *on*, he thought. Can't stand out here all *night*, can I? Catch pneumonia out here, night like this one. He never had much cared for the month of March, his own time of year was the fall. Something about the fall always reached him. Nothing uncertain about the fall, you knew where you stood. March, April, forget it. Third day of spring, you'd think it was still the dead of winter, chill out here working its way clear into a man's bones. His gloved hand in the pocket of his coat felt warm around the walnut grip of the pistol.

One plus one plus one again.

Then retire.

Thing was, he was beginning to realize this might take longer than he'd figured. No way of telling when or even *if* anybody would show, he could be standing out here all night long and nobody'd come and he'd just have to do it all over again each time out, night after night. Wait in the dark till—

Hold it.

Coming up the street. Hands in his pockets. Kid of seventeen, eighteen, looking this way and that, had to be up to some kind of mischief. He moved deeper into the shadow cast by the highway overhead. Lightning again in the distance. Not even the sound of thunder this time, too far away. Another car sped by overhead, tires hissing, headlights casting fallout into the naked branches of the trees. He pulled still farther back into the shadows.

The kid was wearing jeans and a black leather jacket. High-topped sneakers. Turned to look over his shoulder. Turned back again, looked left and right, looked dead ahead, then stopped under the highway, and took a flashlight from his pocket. Light splashed onto the new cement wall. His face cracked into a grin, as if he were looking at a beautiful naked woman. Stood there with the flashlight playing on the wall, moving the flashlight over the wall, inch by inch, raping the clean empty wall with his eyes and the beam of the light. Then he reached inside his jacket and took out a spray can of paint and stood back from the wall a moment, studying it, the flashlight in his left hand, the spray can in his right, deciding where he should start his masterpiece.

He was spraying red paint onto the wall, spraying an *S*, and then a *P*, and then an *I*, and then a *D*, when he heard movement behind him, and turned sharply and saw a man wearing a black wide-brimmed hat pulled low over his eyes, a dark coat with the collar pulled up high on his neck, a gun in his hand.

"Here," the man said.

And shot him twice in the face.

The boy lay still and silent on the ground under the highway, his life's blood oozing out of his face, the spray can lying beside him. He shot the boy one more time, in the chest this time, and then he reached down to pick up the can in his gloved hand, and pressed the button on top of the can, and squirted red paint all over the boy's face oozing blood, his chest oozing blood, red paint and red blood mingling while overhead another car pierced the night with its headlights and sped off into the distance where now there was no lightning at all.

During the empty hours of the night, the rain had changed to snow; it was that kind of spring. At nine o'clock that morning, it was still snowing.

"I remember, Easter *Sunday* once, it was snowing," Parker said. "This is nothing unusual."

"March twenty-third, it's unusual to be snowing," Kling said.

"Not if it could snow on Easter," Parker said.

"I remember once," Meyer said, "Passover and Easter Sunday fell on the very same day."

"That happens all the time," Carella said.

"That's because the Jews stole Passover from Easter," Parker said, blithely unaware.

Meyer didn't even bother.

The snow kept falling from the dull gray March sky. Beyond the grilled-mesh windows that protected the squad room from the brickbats of society, the day was blustery and bleak.

Andy Parker was looking over the report the graveyard shift had filed on the dead graffiti writer. The paper told him Baker

One had found the kid early this morning, under the River Highway on North Eleventh. Kid's name was Alfredo Herrera, street
name Spider. That's what he was probably trying to write on the
wall, SPIDER, when somebody pumped two into his face and
another in his chest and painted him red for good measure. Served
him right, Parker thought, fuckin writer. But didn't say. Meanwhile, the city had to spend time and money trying to find out
who done it, when who gave a shit, really?

"We supposed to inform next of kin on this, or what?" he
asked no one.

"Unless they already did," Carella said.

"That's what I'm askin," Parker said. "Willis typed this up,
did he already call whoever, or what?"

"What does it say there?"

"It doesn't say anything."

"Is a next of kin listed?"

"I don't see any."

"How'd they make I.D.?"

"Driver's license."

"Well, there must've been an address on the license."

"I don't have the *license* here," Parker said testily, "I only
have Willis's *report* here, where it says they *made* him from the
license."

"Better call the Property Clerk's Office," Kling suggested.
"See if they've got the license there."

"Why don't I just call *Willis*, ask him did he notify the parents,
or what?"

"He's probably asleep by now," Meyer suggested tactfully.

"So fuck him," Parker said. "He leaves this shit on my desk
to follow up, he should've also left a note telling me did he
notify next of kin. Who's got his number?"

"Got enough spit?" Kling asked, but looked up the number
in his notebook and read it off to Parker, who began dialing
immediately.

Willis picked up on the fourth ring. It was obvious he'd been sleeping. Parker plunged ahead regardless. Willis told him the motorized blues had found the body at a little past six this morning, that it had been removed to the morgue, and that no one had had time to notify next of kin before the shift was relieved. Parker asked him if he knew where the kid's driver's license was. Willis was awake now and getting irritable.

"Why do you need the license?" he asked.

"So I can get an address for him."

"His address is on the report," Willis said. "I typed it in from the driver's license."

"Oh," Parker said.

"Right under his name. Do you see where it says address?" he asked testily. "That's where I typed it in."

"Yeah, I see it now," Parker said.

"Why didn't you see it in the first place," Willis said, "wake a man up he just fell asleep."

"Yeah, I should've," Parker said, and looked at the phone receiver when he heard what sounded like an angry click on the other end of the line. Shrugging, he turned to Carella. "The address was right here all along," he said. "You want to see if there's a phone number for him?"

"Don't you know how to look up a phone number?" Carella asked.

"I hate to call some kid's mother, tell her he's dead."

"Yeah, well, learn how to do it," Carella said.

"Thanks a whole fuckin *lot*," Parker said, and opened his desk drawer and pulled out a worn telephone directory. "Probably be ten thousand people named Herrera, this city," he said to the phone book, and shook his head.

Almost everything Parker said bordered on the thin edge of open bigotry. Everything else he said *was* open bigotry. It depended on who was in his immediate presence. He knew that someone like Meyer, for example, might possibly take offense if he called him a chiseling kike bastard, so instead he merely mentioned that the Jews had ripped off Easter Sunday. And whereas Carella wasn't Hispanic, he had a name full of vowels and he might get on his high horse if Parker suggested that the city was overrun by spics, so he'd simply addressed his comment to the telephone book instead.

As it turned out, he was mistaken.

There were not ten thousand Herreras in the book, there were only a hundred and forty-six. But that was in *this* section of the city alone. There were four *other* sections to this bustling metropolis, and just because the dead writer had been found here didn't mean he lived here. All Parker knew was that he was right now looking at a hundred and forty-six fuckin names that would take him all fuckin day to call all of them. For what? To tell some lady who couldn't speak English that her shithead son was dead, which it served him right, anyway?

Sometimes he wished he wasn't so dedicated.

He hit pay dirt on the forty-fourth number he tried. He considered this fortunate. This was now close to twelve noon and he wanted to go out to lunch.

The woman's name was Catalina Herrera. When he asked her if she had a son named Alfredo Herrera, she said, "Yes, I have. Who is this calling, please?"

Heavy Spanish accent. Naturally.

"This is Detective Andrew Parker of the Eighty-Seventh Precinct," he said. "Is your son eighteen years old?"

"Eighteen, yes. Is something . . . ?"

"Birth date September fourteenth?"

"Yes? What . . . ?"

"He's dead," Parker said.

He told her where the body was, asked her if she could meet him there later to make positive identification, and then told the other detectives he was heading out for lunch.

"Nice bedside manner you got there," Carella said.

"Thanks," Parker said, and went out smiling.

"There's this ship in the middle of the Pacific," Meyer said. "This is World War II. The loudspeaker goes off and the chief bosun's voice says, 'All hands, fall to on the quarterdeck. All hands, fall to on the quarterdeck.'"

"I think I heard this story," Kling said.

"Seaman Shavorsky?" Meyer asked.

"No."

"Well, all the sailors gather on the quarterdeck, and the bosun says, 'At ease, we just got a radio message from the States. Seaman O'Neill, your mother is dead.' Well, the captain overhears this, and he calls the bosun into his cabin, and he says, 'That's no way to break news of this sort. These men are a long way from home, you've got to be more considerate if anything like this happens again.' The bosun salutes and says, 'Yes, sir, I'm sorry, sir, I certainly will be more careful next time if there is a next time, sir.'"

"Are you sure I didn't hear this?" Kling asked.

"How should I know if you heard it or not? Anyway, a couple of months later, the bosun's voice comes over the speaker again, 'All hands, fall to on the quarterdeck, all hands fall to on the quarterdeck,' and all the sailors gather again, and the bosun says, 'We just got a radio message from the States. All you men whose mothers are still living, take one step forw—*not* so fast, Seaman Shavorsky!'"

Carella burst out laughing.

"I don't get it," Kling said.

"Maybe cause you heard it already," Meyer said.

"No, I don't think I ever heard it. I just don't get it."

"It has to do with Parker and the dead kid's mother," Meyer said.

"Is that the dead kid's name? Shavorsky?"

"Forget it," Meyer said.

"I thought it was a Latino name."

"Forget it," Meyer said again, and went to answer the telephone ringing on his desk.

"Shavorsky doesn't sound Latino at *all*," Kling said, and winked at Carella.

"Forget it, forget it," Meyer said, and picked up the receiver. "Eighty-Seventh Squad, Detective Meyer," he said. He listened, nodded, said, "Just a second, please," and then, "For you, Steve. On four."

Carella hit the four button on his desk extension, and picked up the receiver.

"Detective Carella," he said.

"Good morning," a pleasant voice said. "Or is it afternoon already?"

"Twenty past twelve, sir," Carella answered, glancing up at the wall clock. "How can I help you?"

"You'll have to speak louder," the voice said. "I'm a little hard of hearing."

Detective-Lieutenant Peter Byrnes told the three of them they'd *already* spent too damn much time on it.

"I don't care if it's the Deaf Man again, or the Deaf Man's *brother*, I don't want another minute wasted on his damn tom-foolery. Man thinks he can call this squadroom anytime he— what time *did* he call?"

"Around noon," Carella said.

The three detectives were standing in a casual semicircle around Byrnes's desk. The snow had stopped and faint sunlight peeped tentatively through the lieutenant's corner windows, lending a promise of vernal cheer to the little law-enforcement tableau: Detective/Second Grade Steve Carella looking like a ballplayer sans chewing tobacco, tall and rangy, with dark hair and brown eyes somewhat slanted to give him a slightly Oriental appearance; Detective/Second Grade Meyer Meyer, an inch or so taller than Carella, burly and bald and blue-eyed, a look of infinite patience on his round face; Bert Kling, the baby of the squad, with blond hair and hazel eyes and the look of a cornfed

bumpkin though he, too, had known his share of the big bad
city. All of them thirtysomething, give or take, nobody was
counting. All of them thinking the Deaf Man was back and the
lieutenant was brushing him off.

"What'd he say?" Byrnes asked.

"He said he missed us," Carella said.

"Missed us," Byrnes repeated blankly, and shook his head.
At the age of fiftysomething—but again, who was counting?—
the lieutenant was beginning to get a bit crotchety. Years ago,
he might have welcomed the appearance of the Deaf Man as a
lively diversion in an otherwise tiresome and predictable routine.
But now . . . well, the Deaf Man might *still* represent challenge
and provocation—if only his infrequent appearances didn't cause
the lieutenant's men to behave like a band of bumbling buffoons.
Whenever he arrived on the scene, they seemed unable to predict
what he was planning even though he gifted them with lavish
clues. Fumble-fingered and flat-footed, they stood by foolishly
while his latest escapade took place, helpless to stop it no matter
how hard they tried. In fact, were it not for the sheerest accidental
good fortune, the Deaf Man could have stolen the city from
under their noses each and every time, murdering half its population in the bargain.

His very name seemed to render the squad inoperative.
Whether he signed himself L. Sordo (for *El Sordo,* which meant
the Deaf Man in Spanish) or Taubman (for *Der taube mann,*
which meant the Deaf Man in German) or Dennis Dove, familiarly known as Den Dove (for *den döve,* which meant the Deaf
Man in Swedish), his very presence turned the men of the Eight-
Seven into inept constabularies incapable of functioning as anything more effective than clumsy Keystone Kops.

"What else did he say?" Byrnes asked, suspecting he was
beginning to get sucked in despite his best intentions. Sitting
behind his desk in a wedge of sunlight, he looked like a man
who could beat anyone in a barroom fight, his body small and
compact, his face craggy, his hands thick and capable, his hair

more white than gray now, his eyes a flinty blue that glistened in the sun, betraying a secret glint of curiosity even though he was trying to convince his men he was not the slightest bit interested in this damn deaf person.

"He said it had been a long time . . ."

"Mmm," Byrnes said, and nodded sourly.

". . . but he knew how much we loved him . . ."

"Sure."

". . . and he knew we would welcome him back with a song in our hearts."

"Oh, no question."

"He also said we wouldn't have to wait too long to make fools of ourselves this time."

"Mmm. What'd the CID show?"

He was referring to the Caller Identification equipment that had been installed on every desk in the squadroom not two weeks ago. Before then, the detectives had seen the instrument only on television, in dramatized commercials where an obscene caller would be informed by his female victim that she already *knew* his telephone number and—lo and behold!—there it *was,* right there on the phone's display panel. Now the equipment was standard in the squadroom. No need to trace a call anymore, you knew the caller's number at a glance.

"Out-of-state number," Meyer said. "We checked it with Information, it's a cellular phone listed to a woman named Mary Callendar."

"Did you try the number? Never mind, I don't want to know."

"I tried it," Carella said. "Got a message saying the mobile customer had left the vehicle and traveled beyond the service area."

"Meaning he'd turned off the power. How about the woman? Mary *what*?"

"Callendar. Information gave me a listing for her home phone," Carella said. "When I spoke to her she told me the cellular had been stolen from her car yesterday."

"Naturally. So he's using a stolen phone."

"Used it *once,* anyway. He'll probably use a different one next time he calls."

"I don't want you answering."

"How can we not ans . . . ?"

"Then hang up the minute you know it's him."

"Then we'll never get him, Pete."

"I don't *care* if we get him. I don't want anything to do with him. What else did he say?"

"That's all he said."

"Didn't he tell you his name?" Byrnes asked, thinking he was making a little joke.

"Yes, he did," Carella said.

"He gave you his *name*?"

"I said, 'Who's this?' and he . . ."

"He gave you his *name*?" Byrnes said, still astonished.

"He said, 'You can call me Sanson.' "

"Samson?"

"*Sanson.* With an *n.* He spelled it out for me. S-A-N-S-O-N."

"Sanson," Byrnes said. "Look it up."

"We did," Kling said.

"All five directories," Meyer said.

"There are twelve Sansons in the . . ."

"No," Byrnes said. "*No,* damn it, I *won't* have you tracking down these people! This is another goddamn game he's playing, only this time we're not falling for it! Get back to whatever the hell you were doing before he called. And if he calls again, hang up!"

"I was just thinking," Carella said.

"I don't want to hear it."

"Okay, Loot."

"What were you thinking?"

"The first of April is only nine days away."

"So?"

"April Fools' Day," Carella said.

The man standing on the bow of the thirty-two-foot Chris-Craft was tall and blond and suntanned and there was a hearing aid in his right ear. He had chartered the boat under the name Harry Gimperde, pronouncing the last syllable of the surname—*perde*—to rhyme with *merde,* in the French manner. Harry Gim-*perde*. The *Gim,* on the other hand, was pronounced like the beginning of *gimlet* or the end of *begin.* Harry Gimperde. Say it over and over again—Harry Gimperde, Harry Gimperde, Harry Gimperde, Harry Gimperde—and it became Hearing Impaired.

The woman who'd filled out the papers at Dockside Charters never once suspected that the blond man wearing the hearing aid was creating a little meaningless entertainment for himself, something to lend a touch of humor to the otherwise boring but essential task that lay ahead. The girl accompanying Mr. Gimperde served much the same purpose; she would add a little spice to the outing once the task was completed. The girl thought the Deaf Man's name was *really* Harry Gimperde. She thought he must be very rich to be able to afford a cellular telephone and to rent a boat this size—not that she'd been on any boat of any size ever in her life before now. She only wished the weather was nicer. She was beginning to think that the best thing about boats was watching them from the shore. She was also beginning to feel a bit neglected, even though the man she thought was Harry Gimperde had poured her a glass of French champagne and had made her comfortable in the back of the boat—what he called the stern—on a bunch of pillows with the bottle sitting in an ice cooler an inch from her elbow, while he went up front to look at the shoreline.

The building the Deaf Man was watching was close to Isola's northern shore, a structure shaped somewhat like a very large

Quonset hut constructed of concrete rather than tin. In essence, the building consisted of two parts, a rectangular bottom and an arched top, wedded to create a not-unpleasant whole. Affixed to the top of the rectangle facing the river, just where the base of the arch joined it, were the stainless-steel letters

DEPARTMENT OF SANITATION

The facility had been opened in January; it still looked spanking clean even though smoke was billowing out of two tall chimneys on the side of the building farthest from the river. The currents were strong out here on the water. The boat kept bobbing on the heavy chop, causing the building to move in and out of range on the binoculars. Patiently, the Deaf Man kept watching.

He had begun watching the building on the fifteenth of January, shortly after the facility was officially opened. He had watched it steadily for a solid week, trying to determine if anything but sanitation-department personnel and vehicles would be here on any days but the first Saturday of each month. During all that time he had seen nothing but the spruce-green uniforms of the department's employees and the hulking trucks they used for moving garbage. He had begun his surveillance again on the twenty-eighth of that same month, and had seen only the same employees and the same trucks each and every day until the first Saturday in February, when at last he was rewarded with the sight of police department vehicles and blue police uniforms.

On that first day of February, at ten minutes past twelve in the afternoon—while the Deaf Man watched from a different chartered boat with a different girl sitting bundled in deck robes and drinking champagne in the stern—a blue-and-white van with the words POLICE DEPARTMENT lettered on its sides pulled into the parking lot on the river side of the building. Three uniformed policemen got out of the van. Lower-level personnel from the looks of them, silver shields on uniforms sporting neither stripes nor braid. Mere patrolmen. Some five minutes later, an unmarked Lincoln Continental pulled into the parking lot, and three policemen of a higher rank stepped out into the wintry sunshine, the brass on their uniforms catching whatever pale light reflected off the water.

The Deaf Man kept watching through the binoculars.

In a little while three blue-and-white radio motor patrol cars came down the ramp from the River Highway, and made the right turn into the parking lot. Two patrolmen got out of the first car. A patrolman and a sergeant got out of the second car. A sergeant and a captain got out of the third car. Each of the patrol cars was marked on its side with the blue lettering 87TH PCT. In the next half hour or so, a television van and several unmarked cars drove into the parking lot. The media and the press. All here to record for posterity this first public spectacle at the spanking-new facility. By five minutes to one on that first day of February, the Deaf Man figured that everyone who was going to be there was already there.

Today was the twenty-third day of March.

Across the choppy waters of the River Harb, the building sat on the edge of the shore, uniformed men walking in and out of it, but none of them wearing police uniforms. These were sanitation engineers, if one wished to be politically correct. To the Deaf Man, they were garbage men. The police would not assemble again for their little monthly ritual until the fourth of April.

In February, the commissioner himself had attended the festive little gathering here on the water's edge. He had not been present at the March seventh meeting. Also present at that first event had been two high-ranking police officers the Deaf Man recognized as Chief of Detectives Louis Fremont and Chief Inspector Curtis Fleet. They were not there in March. Neither were two deputy inspectors whom the Deaf Man had been unable to identify at the February conclave. No one from the media or the press showed up in March. Like everything else in America, only the first time was novelty. Even *Desert Storm*, that fine miniseries concocted for television, would have become boring if it had lasted a moment longer. *Sic transit gloria mundi*. The Deaf Man was not expecting much of a crowd on the fourth of April. Just enough policemen to supervise the job and to record the happening.

He took the binoculars from his eyes.

He would check the facility once again next week, to ensure that the routine was, in fact, unchanging. Then, on April fourth, he would be here for the monthly festivities. Until then, there was much to do.

Smiling, he went to the stern of the boat, where the girl was pouring herself another glass of champagne.

"Here, let me do that," he said.

"Thank you," she said. "Are you all finished with whatever it was you were doing?"

"The coastal survey, yes," he said.

She had a tiny breathless Marilyn Monroe voice and eyes the color of emeralds. He had advised her to wear rubber-soled shoes and to dress for what might turn out to be inclement weather. She had taken this to mean white sneakers without socks, short white shorts and a white T-shirt, a yellow rain slicker, and a yellow nor'wester pulled down over her long blond hair. She sat now with the coat open and the champagne glass in one hand, her long legs crossed, watching him as he poured. He guessed she was twenty-three years old, twenty-four at most.

"There we are," he said, topping off her glass, and then pouring one for himself.

"Thank you, Harry," she said. She had never liked the name Harry, but on him it was kind of cute. On him, *any* name would be kind of cute.

He lifted his glass in a toast.

"To you," he said.

"Thank you," she said.

"And to me," he said.

"Okay," she said, and smiled.

"And to the beautiful music we'll make together."

She nodded, but said nothing. No need to make him feel too confident. They clinked glasses. They sipped champagne as the boat bobbed on the water and a raw wind blew in off the river, tearing the clouds to tatters, allowing the sunshine to break through at last.

"There's a CD player below," he said.

"Is there?"

Emerald eyes wide in interest.

"Do you think you might like to go down there?"

"What *else* is down there?"

Champagne glass poised near her generous mouth. Lips slightly parted. One sneakered foot jiggling.

"A double bed . . ."

"Oh my."

"And more champagne."

"Mmm."

"And me," he said, and leaned over to kiss her.

She felt suddenly dizzy, and wondered if he'd put something in the champagne. And then she realized it was only the way he was kissing her that made her so dizzy, and she thought Oh boy am I in trouble. He lifted her from the banquette. Carried her across the bobbing deck to where there was an open doorway leading downstairs. Carried her down the stairway, a ladder she guessed you called it, into what looked like a small kitchen, a galley she guessed you called it, carried her up front, up *forward,* to where there was a double bed—which was the only possible thing you *could* call it.

As he lowered her gently to the bed, he said, "I'm going to fuck you senseless, Gail."

Which was her name.

And which she guessed he just might.

2.

"What I don't like about what I'm seeing here is this is a freebie gig we're doing and it's only twelve days away and we're gettin no coverage at *all* on it, *that's* what I don't like about it," Jeeb said.

Jeeb was the lead rapper in the group. There were four of them altogether, Jeeb and Silver and the two girls, one of them named Sophie and the other named Grass. The group called itself Spit Shine. It was Jeeb who'd thought up the name. This was when they were still rapping on street corners in Diamondback and calling themselves Four-Q, which was certainly appropriate for the kind of music they were making, but which Jeeb figured might not go down too well in the big time, which was where they planned to *go,* man, straight to the top, man.

Jeeb remembered his grandfather telling him they used to use the word "shine" to describe people of color back in the old days, though he didn't know where the word had come from, maybe it had something to do with black folks's skin looking shiny, was what his grandpa told him. Anyway, it was an expression in common use back then, shine. Jeeb figured it'd be good to throw that word right back in Whitey's face—shine, huh?—but attach the word *spit* to it so it came out *spit* shine, like a black man snarling and spitting, which is what their music was all about, anyway. The girls thought the new name was terrific. Silver thought it sucked. Silver thought it was cool somebody came up to you, ast you what the name of this crew was, you

tole him, "Four-Q." Silver thought that was real cool, man.
Jeeb told him it would put off a record producer, he'd think you
were tellin him to go fuck himself. Silver said that was ex-*actly*
the attitude they should be tryin'a project here, man, you don't
like what we're tellin you, then Four-Q, man.

The girls said they were embarrassed to tell they mamas Four-
Q. Grass, especially, who was only fourteen back then when
they were rapping for nickels and dimes on street corners, she
was ashamed to say the name of the band out loud, her mother'd
hit her one upside the head if'n she did. Grass was the only
virgin Jeeb knew at the time. He respected her opinion because
he felt there was something pure about her. He couldn't understand why she didn't mind *rapping* the word *fuck* but was
ashamed of *saying* Four-Q, he couldn't understand that at all.
He knew in his heart, though, that Spit Shine was a better name
than the one they had, and he also knew it wouldn't pay to get
all huffy with Silver, tell him Hey, man, *I'm* the leader of this
crew, so you know what you can do, man, don't you? That
wouldn't work with Silver, who had more pride than anyone
Jeeb knew. So he just took him aside one day and reasoned with
him and then told him it'd be great could Silver write a new
song for them called "Spit Shine," spellin it all out for anybody
out there wasn't gettin the message. Silver liked that idea. He
wrote the best lyrics of any rapper in the business, wasn't anything he liked better than writing. He took that name Spit Shine
and turned it into a rap that shook thunder from the sky.

> Shine what you call me,
> Shine what I am,
> Spit in your eye, *man*,
> Shine that I am . . .

Was Spit Shine the *song* that flew off their first album and
right onto the singles chart. Was Spit Shine the *song* that made
a household name of Spit Shine the *crew*. Silver never let Jeeb
forget it was *him* who'd written that song. Silver never let any-

body forget *anything*. Only thing he was willing to forget was
the name he was born with, Sylvester. Sylvester Cummings.
Hated that name like poison, said it made him sound like some
pansy served dinner and helped you get dressed. The girls told
him Sylvester Stallone wasn't no pansy, and Silver said Stallone
didn't call himself *Sylvester*, you might've noticed, he called
himself *Sly*. So whyn't you call *your*self Sly, Sophie asked him,
and he said, Whyn't you call *your*self *Slit,* which was a reference
to the fact that Sophie had been a hooker before she'd joined the
crew.

That was four years ago.

Sophie was now twenty-two years old, and Grass (whose real
name was Grace) was now eighteen and no longer a virgin thanks
to Jeeb, whose real name was James Edward Beeson, which he'd
shortened to Jeeb, and Spit Shine was now famous enough to
do a free concert in Grover Park, sponsored by a chain of citywide
banks that now called itself FirstBank although *its* original name
was First National City Bank.

Sophie was still Sophie.

"I agree with Jeeb," she said. "The bank gets a free ride and
tons of publicity but so far the gig's almost here and there's still
nothing but a trickle about *us* performing."

"Other crews gettin all the splash," Silver said.

He was twenty-three years old, the senior member in the
crew, lanky and handsome, with eyes as dark as river mud, a
nose like a Roman centurion's, and dreadlocks that could scare
away a witch. He was wearing jeans and a black T-shirt with
the name of the crew in neon yellow across the front of it, SPIT
SHINE.

Actually, he didn't have his mind completely on what they
were talking about here. He'd recently come across an album of
calypso songs written by a singer who'd been murdered some
years back, and one of the songs had stuck in his mind as a good
example of early rap, though it was set to a calypso beat. He'd

rapped the song for Sophie, skipped the tune entirely, just rapped out Chadderton's lyrics—that was the singer's name, George Chadderton, he used to bill himself as King George. The songs had been discovered in a notebook he'd kept before he got killed and a singer who did a pretty good Belafonte imitation had recorded them for an obscure label in L.A.

Sophie hadn't much liked the song, which was titled "Sister Woman," but that was because the song was about hookers and she thought Silver was tryin'a dis her about the days when she'd earned her money walking the streets. As she argued back and forth with Jeeb now about ways they could get more publicity out of their forthcoming concert, Silver went over the Chadderton lyrics in his mind one more time:

Sister woman, black woman, sister woman mine,
Why she wearin them clothes showin half her behine?
Why she walking the street, why she working the line?
Do the white man dollar make her feel that fine?
Ain't she got no brains, ain't she got no pride,
Letting white man dollar turn her cheap inside?
Takin white man dollar, lettin he inside?

Sister woman, black woman, why she do this way?
On her back, on her knees, for the white man pay?
She a slave, sister woman, she a slave this way,
On her knees, on her back, for the white man pay.
On her knees, sister woman, is the time to pray,
Never mind what the white man he got to say,
Let the white girl do what the white man say.

Sister woman, black woman, on her knees give head
To a man like he like to see her dead
Can't she see, don't she see, can't she read in his head?
She a slave to his will, and the man want her dead.
She a nigger for sure, she a slave still in chains,
And the white man'll whip her an keep her in chains.

Sister woman, black woman, won't she hear my song?
What she doin this way surely got to be wrong.
Lift her head, raise her eyes, sing the words out strong,
Sister woman, black woman . . .

"What do *you* think, Sil?"

Jeeb's voice, cutting through the lyrics that were sliggeding through Silver's head. Good hip-hop, for sure. The album sleeve had credited copyright to Chloe Productions, Inc. He wondered who the hell *that* was.

"Silver? You with us."

"I say we call FirstBank an' tell 'em we're outta this thing entirely 'less they take a big ad headlinin us."

Grass, who had been silent until now, very softly said, "That's the onliest way, Silver, the man dissin us like that."

And smiled at him.

Jeeb all at once wondered if something was going on between these two.

Catalina Herrera was in the waiting room of the Morehouse General Hospital morgue when Parker joined her. This was now two o'clock on that afternoon of March twenty-third. The sun was shining, but the temperature was still somewhere down there in the low-to-mid-thirties and more rain was expected tonight, some spring *this* was.

Catalina was in her late twenties, early thirties, Parker guessed, a diminutive woman with large brown eyes, dark hair, and the major hooters you found on all these spics. He guessed she'd got knocked up with young Alfredo when she was twelve, thirteen years old, they matured early down there in the tropics and it was difficult for all those macho caballeros down there to keep their hands off all those ripe boobs under the palms in the sand. Catalina's eyes were luminous with tears. He was here only to ascertain that the dead kid in there was, in fact, Alfredo Herrera and not somebody who'd copped his I.D. Sobbingly, she told Parker that the kid on the slab in there was her son.

"He was a good boy," she said.

Which is what they all said. Looked you straight in the eye after their kid had killed his grandmother, his four-year-old sister, his pet beagle, and his three goldfish, and told you without flinching, "He was a good boy." Parker had already done a computer run on the late Alfredo Herrera and had come up with zilch. The kid was clean, albeit dead. Parker wondered if his mother knew how handy he'd been with a spray can. He also wondered if she knew whether or not her son had been into anything that might have invited two big ones in the face and another one in the chest. He decided to ask her to have a cup of coffee with him in the hospital coffee shop. He was thinking he might try taking her to bed, those boobs. Parker thought women found him irresistible.

In the coffee shop, with doctors and nurses sitting at tables all around them—some of them in green surgical gowns ostentatiously spattered with blood, green surgical masks hanging down around their throats like they'd just come from some tremendous lifesaving operation mere mortals couldn't appreciate— Parker asked Catalina if she knew what her son was doing out in the middle of the night last night, which was presumably when he'd got shot.

"I don' know wha' he wass doing," she said.

Thick Spanish accent that Parker found attractive on these Latino women but disgusting on the men, who should for Christ's sake learn how to speak English.

"When's the last time you saw him?" he asked, and ended the sentence there, without adding the word *alive*, thereby rescuing himself from another Seaman Shavorskyism.

"When I come home," she said. "I was out."

"What time was that?"

"Siss, siss-t'irty," she said.

Very charming. Made him think of guitars and black lace, languid breezes playing. Made him think of fucking her, too.

"We ha' supper together."

Lilting to the ear. Lovely. You got used to it after a while, it almost sounded accent-free. He wondered if she'd ever made love in English. He almost asked her. Instead he said, "What'd you talk about during dinner?"

"Oh, I don't know," she said. "Many things."

"Like what?"

"He told me he wanted to buy a car."

"Does he have money to buy a car?"

Parker immediately thought dope. Eighteen-year-old kid tells his mother he's thinking of buying a car, where's he gonna get the bread for the car? Dope, right? Besides, he was Hispanic. On Parker's block, that meant he was into dope.

"His grandmother left him money when she died," Catalina said.

"I'm sorry to hear that."

"It was my husband's mother," she said, dismissing the woman with a shrug.

She's got a husband, Parker thought.

"What sort of work does your husband do?"

"We're divorced, I don't know what he does anymore. He went back to Santo Domingo. I haven't seen him in maybe six months."

But still counting, Parker thought.

"What time did your son leave the house last night?" he asked.

"I don't know. I left before him."

"Where'd you go?"

A boyfriend, Parker thought.

"To a movie," she said.

She likes movies, he thought.

"Alone?" he asked.

She looked at him. He realized all at once that she thought he was asking her for an alibi, trying to make sure she hadn't dusted her own kid and then painted him red afterward, which of course was a possibility, wet eyes or not.

"With a girlfriend," she said.

He wondered if he should ask her to go to a movie with him tonight.

"What time did you get back?"

"Around midnight."

"And he was gone."

"He was gone," she said, and burst into tears again.

Parker watched her.

Everywhere around them, all these medical people were discussing anything but medicine. It was as if there was an unwritten rule in the coffee shop that you didn't talk about appendectomies or catheters or loose bowel movements or anything that had to do with work. This was break time, and you didn't let blood and pus interfere with the enjoyment of your cheese Danish. Parker was a little embarrassed that some of the nurses had turned to look at Catalina crying. The doctors couldn't care less, they were in a universe of their own, but some of the nurses had turned to stare at this tiny, very attractive brunette who was crying her eyes out, and Parker was afraid they might think *he* was the one who'd made her cry, not that he gave a shit. Besides, this was a hospital, there were people dying here every ten minutes, the nurses should've been used to seeing somebody crying, it wasn't such a big deal. Still, it made him feel uncomfortable, the two or three nurses who turned to look at them, one of them wearing a green O.R. gown, she'd probably just come from looking inside somebody's stomach or chest.

Awkwardly, he watched her.

"He was a good boy," she said again, this time into her damp handkerchief.

He waited.

"I'm sorry," she said.

"No, hey," he said. He didn't feel comfortable comforting people. He wanted to ask her if she'd ever seen any spray cans around the house, but he figured he'd better wait till she stopped crying. He also wanted to ask her if her son had been in any serious fights or arguments with anybody in the neighborhood recently, like somebody who might want to pump three shots into him because of it, and then paint him red besides. But she was still crying.

He kept waiting.

At last the crying stopped, sort of. She still kept dabbing at a stray tear every now and then, but the real storm had passed, she was in control of herself again. He asked her if she'd like another cup of coffee, and she looked at her watch, and it suddenly occurred to him that perhaps there was a job she had to get to, her son's murder had consumed the major part of her day so far. But he'd reached her at home this morning, and that had been before lunchtime. He wondered if her husband in the Dominican Republic was paying alimony.

"More coffee?" he said again.

"I would like to, but . . ."

Another look at her watch. Tears welling in her eyes again. So frail, so beautiful.

"Do you have to get to work or something?" he asked.

"I work at home," she said.

"Oh. What do you do?"

"Typing."

"Ahh," he said.

"Yes. But today . . . I want to help you. I want you to find whoever . . ."

And burst into tears again.

Jesus, he thought.

He signaled to one of the volunteer pink-lady waitresses and ordered two more cups of coffee, trying to disassociate himself from this woman bawling across the table from him, people looking at him now like he was a wife-beater or something. He felt like taking out the little leather fob holding his shield, flash the tin, let them know he was a fucking *police* officer here doing a job, trying to get some information from this woman here, whose dumb spic son went around writing on walls. Again, he waited. He was beginning to get a little irritated with her, busting into tears every thirty seconds.

"I'm sorry," she said again, into the very wet handkerchief now.

"Hey, no," he said again, but without as much conviction as last time.

The coffee came. He watched as she spooned four teaspoons of sugar into it, they had sweet tooths, these Latinos. Just a dollop of milk, she liked it dark. She was under control again. He hoped that this time he could get some answers from her before she turned on the tears again.

"Did he belong to a gang?" he asked.

Flat out. Get to it. Get it over and done with.

"No," she said.

"Anybody putting any pressure on him to join one?"

"Not that I know about."

"I have to ask this, was he into dope?"

"What do you mean? Using dope? No, Alfredo never . . ."

"Using it, dealing it, I have to ask. Was he in any way connected with narcotics?"

"No."

"You're sure about that?"

"Positive."

Brown eyes flashing something very close to anger now.

"Did you know he was a wall-writer?"

"No. A what? What's that, a wall-writer?"

"A graffiti artist. A person who sprays graffiti on walls. With paint."

"No, I didn't know that."

"We're pretty sure that's what he was doing when he got shot. Unless somebody went to a lot of trouble putting his fingerprints on the spray can, your son's. Ever see him leaving the house with a spray can?''

"No."

"Ever see any spray cans around the house? This one was red, ever see any red spray cans around? These cans that spray paint?''

"No, never."

"Ever hear the name Spider?''

"No."

"Do you know that's what your son was called on the street?''

"No."

"But you say he didn't belong to a gang.''

"He did not belong to a gang.''

"I'll take your word for it.''

Her eyes said You better.

"Will you need help with funeral arrangements?'' he asked.

For Christ's sake, don't bust out crying again, he thought.

"I'll give you a hand with that, you need help,'' he said.

"Por favor," she said, and lowered her head to hide the tears that were brimming in her eyes again.

Parker felt something like genuine sympathy.

This was a city on the thin edge of explosion.

Everywhere you looked, you saw anger seething just below the surface.

The Deaf Man liked that.

One out of every two teenagers in this city owned a handgun. You saw some kids up to some kind of mischief in the street, you didn't tell them to behave themselves, you had to be crazy to do that because if there were four of them, two of them might be the ones packing the guns. You had to be very careful about people getting angry in this city.

You hailed a taxicab in this city, and you didn't see the guy standing on the corner with his hand raised to call the same cab, and the cab stopped for you instead of him, and the guy came running over yelling, "You fucking asshole, didn't you see I had my hand up?" and when you told him, "Hey, I'm sorry, I didn't see you, take the cab," he said, "Don't lie to me, you fucking asshole, you saw me all the time," not happy with your giving him the cab, not happy with your apology, wanting to extend the argument, wanting to get *even* somehow for something you didn't even do, *hurt* you somehow for some imagined offense you hadn't committed.

This was a city waiting to erupt.

Good, the Deaf Man thought.

You're waiting on a street corner for the light to change, and finally the signal turns to WALK and you start across the street and a limo makes a left turn into the block, almost knocking you over when he's supposed to stop for a pedestrian crossing with the light and you raise your eyebrows and spread your hands as if to say Hey, come on, gimme a break, willya, and he leans over the seat and yells through the window on the passenger side, "What the fuck you *want* me to do, you cocksucker, drive up on the sidewalk?"—but it's best not to argue. He's not a teenager, he's maybe thirty-three, thirty-four years old, but the anger is there and who knows whether or not *he's* got a gun in the glove compartment, teenager or not.

Ready to flare.

Ready to take offense.

Ready to strike out.

The Deaf Man liked all that.

That night, as the temperature began to drop again, two kids were larking around under the lamppost on the corner of Mason and Sixth. One of the kids was eleven years old. The other was twelve. They were just clowning around, making a little mischief on a night at the beginning of spring, you know how kids are. The guns they were packing were made of plastic, super squirt guns with a capacity of two gallons, capable of shooting water fifty feet or more. The kids were running around the lamppost, squirting water at each other, their breaths feathering out of their mouths on the frosty air. It was a cold night, but spring was already three days old, and the sap was beginning to run someplace in America, so they were running around having a good time, what the hell. Giggling as they ran around the lamppost squirting each other with water, these huge jets of water gushing out of the plastic guns every time they squeezed the trigger, yelling and screaming like Indians surrounding the cavalry in the days of the Wild West. But this wasn't the Wild West, this was the big bad city. And there was anger in this city.

The man who happened to be walking by had his hands in his pockets and his head was bent and he wasn't paying any attention to the kids and their game because he had problems of his own. The first he even knew they existed was when some drops of water splashed onto his sleeve. He turned with an angry scowl on his face, started to say "What the fuck . . . ?" and that was when the second jet of water hit him in the face. He turned at once, furiously screaming "You fuckin little shits," and a gun came out of his jacket pocket. This gun was not made of plastic, this gun was made of steel, this gun was a Colt .45 caliber automatic, and he fired it three times, killing the eleven-year-old on the spot, and shooting the twelve-year-old through the left lung.

He ran off into the night while the kid who was still alive twisted on the sidewalk, gasping for breath and coughing up blood and crying for his mama.

Out on the Spit, there'd been lightning, and the old lady in the backseat had begun whimpering each time the lightning flashed. Here in the city, there wasn't any lightning at all, but she was still mewling back there. Rocking back and forth where she sat against the window on the right-hand side of the car, keening like a widow at an Irish wake, but softly and weakly, as if she didn't have the strength to let out a real cry of terror. He kept his eye on her in the rearview mirror, alternating his gaze from the road ahead to where she sat whimpering and looking bewildered.

"You don't have to worry," he told her. "Nobody's going to hurt you. This is for your own good."

The old lady said nothing, just kept whimpering in that soft weak way, rocking, rocking.

"This is an act of love," he told her.

Whimpering. Whimpering.

"That's why I'm doing this. You'll be better off, wait and see."

Fuck am I trying to explain anything to her, he thought. She doesn't even know her own *name* anymore. Still, she had to understand this wasn't an act of cruelty. He wouldn't do anything cruel to her or anyone else. Wasn't in his nature to do anything cruel or even thoughtless. This was a merciful act here, what he was doing.

"This is a merciful act," he told her.

"Where are we?"

Her words came out of the blackness behind him, as startling as a gunshot explosion, surprisingly strong and clear and demanding.

"If I told you, would you know?" he asked, and grinned into the rearview mirror.

"Tell me," she said.

"You familiar with the city?"

"No," she said. "Who are you?"

"Would you remember if I told you?" he said, and grinned into the mirror again.

"Do I know you? Are you my grandson?"

"You remember your grandson, huh?" he said.

"Buddy," she said, and nodded.

"You remember Buddy, huh?"

"Or Ralph. Are you Ralph?"

"That's a dog's name, Ralph. Here, Ralph," he said, and laughed aloud.

"You must be Buddy then," she said.

"Whatever you say, Grandma. We're almost there now, so you just take it easy, don't trouble your head with anything at all. This is something good I'm doing for you, you'll thank me later on, you'll see."

"Ralph wasn't a dog," she said.

"Here, Ralph," he said, and laughed again.

"I think he drowned," she said.

"Maybe so."

"I wish I could remember things."

"I wish I could *forget* things," he said. "You don't know how lucky you are. People who love you, who are willing to do this for you, make life comfortable for you, you don't know how lucky, really."

"I *am* lucky," she said.

"I know, Grandma. What have I been telling you? I know you're lucky."

"I am."

"Almost there now. I've got a nice blanket here on the seat beside me, I'll wrap it around you later, keep you nice and warm. Spring's never coming this year, is it?"

"Did I say good night to Polly?"

"I don't remember."

"*I'm* the one who can't remember," she said, and began chuckling. He laughed with her. Together, as the car moved through the empty hours of the night, they laughed together in the dark.

The railroad station at two in the morning was deserted and dark except for a single light that burned inside the locked and empty waiting room. He had reconnoitered the station and he knew that the waiting room was locked from 10:30 P.M. to 4:30

A.M., fifteen minutes before the first morning train came through. He also knew there was a Mickey Mouse lock on the door—well, nothing to *steal* in there, why bother with anything fancier than a simple spring bolt? There were three cars parked in the lot adjacent to the station. He found a spot close to the waiting room, parked near the meter there, opened the driver's side door, told her, "I'll be right back," and stepped out of the car. He debated whether he should put a quarter in the meter, and decided he'd better just in case some cop happened to cruise by while he was inside the waiting room. He deposited the quarter, twisted the knob, nodded, and then walked up the steps to the platform and around to where there was a door facing the tracks. There was another door on the other side of the waiting room, but it was visible from the street, and he didn't want anyone spotting him while he worked the lock. Wouldn't be any trains coming through this time of night, he'd checked the schedule. Swiftly, silently, he loided the lock with his American Express credit card, opened the door, and left it ajar.

She was sitting in the backseat where he'd left her. She was whimpering again. He opened the front door on the passenger side, took the plaid blanket from the seat, draped it over his arm, and then opened the door where she was sitting.

"Time to go, Grandma," he said.

She didn't say anything as he lifted her from the seat and into his arms, so frail, almost weightless, rested her head against his shoulder as he carried her up the steps to the platform, whimpering into his shoulder. He moved swiftly to where he'd left the door ajar, carried her into the waiting room, and gently kicked the door shut behind him.

"Nice and warm in here," he said.

She kept whimpering.

"Nothing to be afraid of," he said.

He carried her to the bench along the streetside wall of the room, the far end of the bench where there was a little nook formed by the armrest, and he lowered her to the seat and said,

"You'll be comfortable here. There'll be a light burning all night long, nothing for you to be afraid of here, someone'll be in around four, they'll take good care of you, don't worry."

She just kept whimpering.

"So I'll be running along now," he said.

Whimpering.

"Goodbye, Grandma," he said, and left her alone in the room with the dimly burning light.

Old Chancery Hospital—familiarly called the Chancery, or sometimes the *Last* Chancery—was on Old Chancery Road, three blocks from the Whitcomb Avenue Station on the Harb Valley line, which ran all the way upstate to Castleview. Two radio motor patrol cops from the Eight-Six had responded to a call from the stationmaster at 4:35 this morning. They had picked up the old lady and—on the orders of their sergeant—had dropped her off at the Chancery's emergency room some ten minutes later. It was now five o'clock on this early Tuesday morning, the twenty-fourth of March. The doctors who stood around the bed in the old lady's room on the third floor of the hospital were trying to elicit some answers that would get her off their hands and back where she belonged, wher*ever* that might be.

Granny dumping was not a new problem for them. It had started at the Chancery some ten years ago, when the first of the elderly victims had shown up sitting in a wheelchair outside the emergency room, an unsigned, hand-lettered note pinned to her chest: I AM ABIGAIL. I HAVE ALZHEIMER'S DISEASE. PLEASE HELP ME. During that first year, five to ten elderly people were abandoned at the hospital each and every month, a trend that peaked some three years later, after which the number dropped to two or three a month.

"Do you know your name?" Frank Haggerty asked.

He was the hospital's Chief of Staff, one of the two medical men who stood around the bed, a man some sixty-three years old with a mane of white hair, riveting blue eyes, and a skin prematurely wrinkled by years of indifferent exposure to the sun. With him in the old lady's room were his E.R. Chief and his Director of Social Services. This was the sixth case of abandonment the hospital had experienced in the past month, up from four the month before. Granny dumping was back—with a vengeance. Haggerty couldn't afford any more of these incidents; the city had cut its hospital budget by thirty-five percent last year and the Chancery was a city hospital. It was now working with a skeleton staff more appropriate to a clinic in Zagreb than to a hospital in one of the world's largest and most influential cities.

"Ma'am?" he said. "Can you tell us your name?"

The old woman shook her head.

She'd been carrying no identification. All of the labels had been cut out of her clothes: the nightgown and robe she was wearing, the panties underneath those, even her diaper.

"Do you know where you live?" Max Elman asked.

The other doctor, E.R. Chief, forty-seven years old, brown eyes, black hair, dark complexion, looking more like one of the Indian residents working under him than he did an American Jew. His wife was a doctor, too, working at a hospital in Calm's Point. The only way they really got to see each other was to retreat to the little farmhouse they'd bought in Maine; they particularly liked it during the winter months, go ask.

"With Polly," the woman said.

"Who's Polly?" the third man asked.

He was the only civilian in the room, even though, like the two others, his title was *Doctor*. Dr. Gregory Sloane, whose master's had come from the USC School of Social Work, and whose doctorate in Social Medicine had come from Ramsey University, right here in the city. At thirty-eight, he was the youngest of the three men, twice divorced and going bald, a not-unrelated physical phenomenon; his hair had begun falling out when his first wife, Sheila, left him for a man who scouted ballplayers for a major-league team. He guessed that along about now, she'd be with him in some backwater town someplace, watching would-be stars shagging pop flies. Buck, his name was. The scout.

"Polly," the old lady said. "That's who."

"Is she your daughter?"

"Don't have any."

"No daughters?" Sloane asked.

"You deaf?" she said.

Four out of five American families were caring at home for their sick or elderly parents. Women constituted seventy-five percent of these caretakers, who sometimes got stuck with aging uncles or aunts as well, relatives who'd been dumped on them when a spouse died or a son suddenly ran off to Outer Mongolia. Millions of American women who'd once thought they might begin pursuing their own lives once their children were grown and out of the nest now discovered they'd been sadly mistaken: They were doomed to care for their parents even longer than they'd had to care for the children. Which was why they'd asked if Polly was a daughter.

"How about sons?" Elman asked. "Have you got any sons, ma'am?"

"I can't remember," she said.

"Any grandchildren? Would you remember any grandchildren?" Haggerty asked.

"Ralph," she said.

"Ralph wha . . . ?"

"That's not a dog's name," she said.

"Ralph what, would you remember?"

"Here, Ralph," she said.

"What's his last name, do you know?"

"I can't remember," she said. "He drowned."

"Any other grandchildren? Any boys or girls you can . . . ?"

"Buddy," she said.

"Buddy what? What's his last name?"

"I can't remember. Where am I?"

"Old Chancery Hospital," Haggerty told her.

There were four million Alzheimer's sufferers in the United States of America. This number was expected to triple within the next twenty-five years. But not all cases of abandonment were Alzheimer's victims; some of them were suffering from other chronic illnesses, some of them were merely old and frail. The woman seemed to be an Alzheimer's victim. The care of an Alzheimer's patient was at best trying on a family, at worst debilitating, a round-the-clock regimen of incessant attention that more often than not led to stress, despair, burnout, and eventual physical, emotional, and financial breakdown. It was easy for these men to understand why Polly—or whoever—had wanted out.

Two of these men were doctors.

They had taken the Hippocratic oath.

But what were they to do when someone requiring extensive testing and exhaustive personal care was dropped off on their doorstep with no one in sight to pay the bills?

"Can you tell us anything at all about yourself?" Sloane asked.

"I always wet the bed," the woman said. "Polly doesn't like it."

Haggerty sighed.

"Let's call Missing Persons," he said. "Maybe she wandered over to that railroad station all by herself. Maybe somebody's out there looking for her."

Sloane doubted it. Besides, wouldn't the people at the Eight-Six have called Missing Persons *before* bringing her here? Actually, he doubted that, too. This was a pass-the-buck society.

"Couldn't hurt," he said.

But he was thinking they were stuck with her.

The frozen-yogurt place was on Stemmler and North Fifth, not too distant from the Eight-Seven's station house. This was now only nine in the morning. The teenage kid working the counter had just opened the place when the man walked in, and stood there for a while, looking at the chart, and finally told the kid that what he wanted was the no-fat chocolate on a cone. Then, so he'd have his hands free when the kid served him, he said, "How much will that be? So I can get the money out now."

The kid said, "Depends what size you want."

His wallet already in his hand now, the man said, "What *are* the different sizes?"

"There's the small and the large," the kid said.

"What's the difference between them?"

"The small is about this high," the kid said, holding the palm of his hand some three inches above the top of the cone, "and the large is about *this* high," he said, raising his palm a few inches higher.

"I'll take the small," the man said.

"Okay," the kid said, and pulled a lever and began swirling yogurt onto the cone.

"So how much will that be?" the man asked, ready to take from his wallet the bill or the several bills or whatever it would cost to pay for the yogurt before he was unable to handle cone and wallet at the same time.

"I have no idea," the kid said. "I just started . . ."

"Excuse me," the man said, his wallet still in his hand, "but didn't you just tell me the price depended on the size?"

"Yeah, but . . ."

"So I ordered the small, you're making me a small right there, so what's this you got no idea what the price'll be?"

"What it is . . ."

"You tryin'a be a wise guy?" the man said.

"No, sir, it's just . . ."

"You tryin'a make a fuckin fool outta me?"

"Sir, today's my first . . ."

"You don't know what the fuckin *price* is, huh? You know what *this* is?" the man said and the kid found himself standing there with a no-fat chocolate on a cone looking into the barrel of a gun. The kid began shaking. The man said, ''Never mind, I don't *want* the fuckin thing no more,'' and shot the kid in the chest.

It was the city's first shooting that day.

Another one would take place fifteen hours later.

3.

"We were beginning to wonder when you'd put in an appearance," Parker said.

"Sure, sure," Monoghan said.

"Sure," Monroe said.

"This is now getting to be worthy of Homicide's close attention, am I right?" Parker said. "A serial sprayer?"

"Sure, sure," Monoghan said.

"Which is why we're graced with your company, am I right?" Parker said, and winked at Kling.

"Yeah, bullshit," Monroe said.

He and his partner were dressed identically, and they now waved away Parker's wise-ass remarks in unison. As the forecasters had promised, it had begun raining a few hours ago. Now, at seven in the morning, the four men were standing—or trying to stand—under an overhang that might have accommodated only two of them if neither was as wide of girth as the two Homicide cops. Monoghan and Monroe were wearing belted black trench coats, in keeping with an unwritten rule they had formulated for themselves, which dictated that they dress in basic black since they considered the color, or lack of it, fashionable. In truth, they sometimes *did* look dapper, though not as dapper as they *thought,* and certainly not today, standing under the dripping overhang in wet and rumpled raincoats. They looked, in fact, like some dark stout seabirds that had just swum ashore in a foul climate somewhere. Both of them kept trying to shoulder

Parker and Kling out from under the slim protection of the over-hang and onto the sidewalk where the dead man lay all covered with paint and blood.

The rain was relentless.

It washed away the blood, but not the paint.

The dead man had been painted in two metallic tones, gold and silver all over his face and his hands and the front of his T-shirt and barn jacket. He looked like a robot whose wires had been pulled, lying there on the sidewalk all limp and gilded in front of the graffiti-sprayed wall.

"Those are designer jeans he's wearing," Monoghan said.

He himself wasn't feeling quite as sartorially elegant as he preferred looking. That was because he hadn't wanted to get his black bowler all wet in the rain and had left it home in his closet. Whenever he wore his bowler, Monoghan felt very British. Whenever he and Monroe were out together in their identical bowlers, they called each other "Inspector." Wot say you, In-spector Monroe? *Cheer*-ee-oh, Inspector Monoghan. And so on. Actually, they were *not* inspectors, but mere detectives/first grade—as distinguished from first-grade detectives. No one in the police department—or in his right mind, for that matter—would have called either of them a first-grade detective. In fact, their roles were merely supervisory at best, intrusive at worst.

Monoghan and Monroe frequently showed up at homicide crime scenes even though they never actively investigated a case; that was the job of whichever precinct detectives happened to catch the squeal. Later on, you sent Homicide the paperwork and they'd make a few calls to see how you were doing, but most of the time they stayed out of your way unless you were taking forever to come up with a lead on a case that was making newspaper and television headlines. The murder of the first graf-fiti artist had captured the attention of the television newscasters because it had been a very pictorial crime, what with all the red letters scribbled on the wall behind the Herrera kid. Also, every-body in this city hated graffiti writers, and was silently cheering on the killer, hoping he would wipe out every fucking one of them. So Monoghan and Monroe had decided to drop in this morning, see how things were coming along now that they had a second victim painted all silver and gold and bleeding from three holes in his forehead.

"How old you think he is?" Monroe asked.

"Thirty-five, forty," Monoghan said.

"I didn't think they came that old, these writers," Monroe said.

"They come in all ages," Parker said. "The one the other night was only eighteen."

"This one looks a lot older than that," Monroe said.

"You know how old Paul McCartney is?" Monoghan asked.

"What's that got to do with graffiti writers?" Monroe said.

"I'm saying graffiti writers came along around the same time the Beatles did. So you get some of these veteran writers, they could be the same age as McCartney."

"What's McCartney? Forty, in there?"

"He's got to be forty-five, forty-six years old, you could have graffiti writers that old, too," Monoghan said. "Is what I'm saying."

"Fifty," Kling said.

"Fifty? Who?"

"At least."

"McCartney? Come on. Then how old is Ringo?"

"Even older," Kling said.

"Come on, willya?" Monoghan said.

"Anyway, this guy don't look no fifty," Monroe said.

"What I'm saying, he could be McCartney's age, though McCartney's no fifty, that's for sure," Monoghan said, and glared at Kling.

"Thirty-five, forty is what this guy looks," Monroe said, also shooting Kling a dirty look. "Which, you ask me, is old for one of these punks."

The assistant medical examiner arrived some five minutes

later. He was smoking a cigarette when he got out of his car. He coughed, spit up some phlegm, shook his head, ground out the cigarette under the sole of his shoe, and went over to where the men were trying to keep out of the rain, standing against the graffiti-covered wall under the overhang.

"Anybody touch him?" the M.E. asked.

"Yeah, we had our hands all over him," Monroe said.

"Don't laugh," the M.E. said. "I had one last month, the blues went through his pockets before anybody else got there."

"You had another writer last *month*?"

"No, just this person got stabbed."

"This one got shot," Monoghan said.

"Who's the doctor here?" the M.E. said testily, and lighted another cigarette. Coughing, he knelt beside the painted body on the sidewalk and began his examination.

The rain kept falling.

"Rain makes some people cranky," Monroe observed.

The M.E. didn't even look up.

"You think this guy's gonna go through every writer in the city?" Monoghan asked.

"We don't catch him, he will," Monroe said.

"What you mean *we*, Kimosabe?" Parker said, and Monroe looked at him blankly.

Kling was staring at the falling rain.

"Did a nice job on his face, didn't he?" Monroe said.

"You mean the holes in it, or the artwork?"

"Both. He blended the artwork nice around the holes, you notice? Made like gold and silver circles coming out from the holes. Like ripples? In a river? When you throw in a stone? That's hard to do with a spray can."

"The Stones are even older," Monoghan said, reminded again. "Mick Jagger must be sixty, sixty-five."

"What was he spraying?" Kling asked suddenly.

"What do you *think* he was spraying? The face, the chest, the hands, the guy's clothes. He went *crazy* with the two spray cans.''

"I mean the writer.''

"Huh?''

"I don't see any gold or silver paint on the wall here.''

They all looked at the wall.

The graffiti artists had been busy here forever. Markers and tags fought for space with your color-blended burners, and your two-tone and even 3-D pieces. But Kling was right. There wasn't any gold or silver paint on the wall. Nor did there seem to be *any* fresh paint at all.

"Musta caught him before he got started,'' Monroe said.

"The Herrera kid was writing when the killer done him,'' Parker said, picking up on Kling's thought.

"Don't mean anything,'' Monoghan assured him. "You get these guys doing missionary murders, they don't necessarily follow any set M.O.''

"*Missionary* murders?'' Monroe said.

"Yeah, these guys on a mission.''

"I thought you meant the fuckin stiff was a *priest* or something.''

"A *quest*,'' Monoghan said. "Shooting all the fuckin writers in the city, is what I mean. Like a *quest*. Like the fuckin impossible *dream*, you understand what I'm saying?''

"Sure.''

"A man on a *mission*, a *missionary* murderer, he doesn't *need* an M.O., he just shoots and sprays, or sprays and shoots, there doesn't *have* to be a pattern.''

"Even so,'' Parker said, and shrugged. "The Herrera kid was doing his fuckin masterpiece when the killer done him.''

"Don't mean a thing,'' Monoghan said.

"Cause of death is gunshot wounds to the head,'' the M.E. said, and lighted another cigarette.

* * *

The person sitting with the Deaf Man was called Florry Paradise. This was the name he'd used when he was the lead guitarist in a rock group called the Meteors, not too prophetic in that it never *did* achieve any measure of fame, its streak across the stratosphere being confined to the single gig it played in the local high school gymnasium. The rest of the time, the group spent rehearsing in their parents' garages. This was when Florry was eighteen years old and there was a rock group rehearsing in every garage in America.

Florry's legacy from those days was threefold.

He had always hated the name Fiorello Paradiso, which he felt had been foisted upon him at birth rather than offered to him as a matter of choice. Everything in America these days was either pro-choice or no-choice and it seemed to him that a person should at least have the right to choose his own fucking *name*, which he'd done when he was eighteen and which, at the age of forty-two, he still had: Florry Paradise. That was the first thing he'd inherited from those joyous days with the unmeteoric Meteors.

The second thing was a little bit of deafness primarily due to keeping the volume controls up so loud when the group was practicing and due secondarily to listening to rock stations on the radio with the volume turned up to the same decibels. Florry shared this same slight loss of hearing with anyone who back then had learned three guitar chords and talked their parents into buying them twenty-thousand dollars' worth of amplifiers and speakers for which they needed only one *other* cord (his father was fond of saying) to plug into an electric outlet, har, har, har, Dad.

But all this fiddling around with expensive and very heavy-to-carry paraphernalia had inadvertently provided the former Fiorello Paradiso with a vast knowledge of electronics that years later enabled him to open and operate a shop specializing in sound systems and equipment. The name of Florry's business, of which he was the president and sole stockholder, was Meteor

Sound Systems, Inc., a nod in the direction of the old group, which was also responsible for him having met his wife, though back then she wore granny gowns and beads and no bra and flowers in her hair. Maggie Paradise used to be the band's female vocalist, her name back then being Margaret Riley, Irish to the core and fair as a summer morn. He did not, however, think of her as another Meteor legacy; three of those were quite enough, and besides she was now fat and forty and Florry was screwing the firm's bookkeeper, whose name was Clarice like the woman in *Silence of the Lambs,* the movie, only with bigger tits, usually after hours while the speakers in his shop blared the Stones' "Lady Jane." Florry was fascinated by anything that transported or amplified or modified or enhanced sound, the Deaf Man's hearing aid included. He was thinking of getting one for himself, though he would never in the world admit to anyone—not even his wife and *especially* not Clarice—that he sometimes couldn't hear exactly everything a person was saying.

He heard everything the Deaf Man was saying now; he guessed the acoustics in this apartment were exceptionally fine. The apartment itself was on Grover Avenue, overlooking Grover Park, which was where the concert would be taking place. The Deaf Man had given Florry a map of the park, and he referred to that now as he listened to what would be needed from him, looking up at the Deaf Man's lips every now and then because no matter *how* good the acoustics were, you could sometimes miss a word or two, hmm?

"Do you see the largest patch of blue on the map?" the Deaf Man asked.

"Yes, I do," Florry said.

"It's called the Swan. It's an artificial lake."

"I see that," he said, and looked at the map again.

"Just below that is an area tinted green. That's called the Cow Pasture. It's the largest grassy area in the park."

"Uh-huh."

"That's where the concert will be held."

"That's where they do all the outdoor theater stuff, too, isn't it?"

"Yes. It's a beautiful spot. The lake in the background to the east, the buildings lining Grover Avenue to the north—well, you can see it from here," he said, and walked to the wide expanse of windows lining the southern wall of the apartment. Florry went to stand beside him. Both men looked down the twelve stories to the park across the street.

There was the faintest hint of green on trees moving into timid leaf, but nothing was flowering yet, neither forsythia nor cornelian cherry shrub added touches of yellow or pink to the panorama below. Yet even in the rain, at three in the afternoon, there was a simple beauty to the starkness of naked trees against a gray and solemn sky. The lawn itself looked patchy and brown from above, but if the intermittent rains persisted, it would be green enough in time for the concert. And, of course, the lake beyond looked magnificent from this viewpoint, a dark patch of blue spreading amoebalike between the Cow Pasture to the west and the tennis courts to the east. Both men looked down appreciatively. There were still some things that could be enjoyed in this city—if only from a distance.

"They're estimating a crowd of some two hundred thousand people," the Deaf Man said.

"Be quite a bash," Florry said. "Did you go to Woodstock that time?"

"No," the Deaf Man said.

"August of 1969? You didn't go that time? Man, you really missed something. There were *four* hundred thousand people there that time. What a thing that was! I got laid *eight* times in two days! *Eight* different girls! What a thing!"

"This won't be like that," the Deaf Man said.

"Oh, I *know*. Nothing could be like Woodstock. Ever again. Nothing."

The Deaf Man suddenly wondered if he'd chosen the wrong man for the job. Would an anachronistic hippie be capable of shouldering such a huge responsibility? And yet, he had come highly recommended, a man who possessed not only the skills the Deaf Man required but who, in addition, held the quaint precepts of the law in rightful contempt. According to what the Deaf Man had learned, Florry—on thirteen separate occasions and for compensation far more generous than what Meteor Sound Systems, Inc. could ever provide—had been *instrumental,* one might say, in circumventing some rather elaborate alarm systems, thereby enabling easy access to the people who'd hired him. Since all of these burglaries—a round baker's dozen, so to speak—had been committed in dwellings during the nighttime, this made Florry an accomplice to precisely thirteen committed Burg Ones, for which he could have been sentenced to a good long time in a state penitentiary if ever he were caught and convicted.

The Deaf Man's source had worked with Florry on four break-ins over the past six months, and he'd told the Deaf Man that Florry knew everything there was to know about sound systems, that he worked well under pressure, and could also recite the names of all the hit songs and albums of every rock group there'd been for the past thirty years. The Deaf Man had been impressed—but he hadn't realized then that Florry Paradise would still be wearing beads and a ponytail and a fringed deerskin vest while he reminisced about the good old days at Woodstock.

"I need an enormously sophisticated system," he said.

"What are we talking about?" Florry asked. "Rap or real music?"

"Voice," the Deaf Man said.

"You mean rap? This is for amplifying *rap* music?"

"No. It's for amplifying a *voice.*"

"Well, that's what rap *is,* am I right? Voices and drums, am I right? Like in the jungle."

"Yes, but this won't be rap. This will be a recorded *voice.* I'd need you to make the recording. . . ."

"On tape? Or do we burn an EPROM?"

"I don't know what that is," the Deaf Man admitted. Nor did he know how you burned one.

"It's an electronic chip. We'd digitally store the voice on it."

"Well, whatever you think best."

"But this won't be rap, huh?"

The Deaf Man was ready to strangle him.

"Because this is a *rap* concert, am I right?" Florry said. "The one coming up in the park?"

"Rap *and* rock."

"How big is that lawn?"

"A bit over ten acres."

"They'll be using stuff'll blow away everything in sight. Woodstock, they didn't even have any delay towers. You weren't there, you really missed something. I got laid eight times in two days, did I tell you? The sound system there was primitive compared to what we got today. The stuff they'll be using in the park'll carry sound all over those ten acres and then some. You want this voice to go out over the speakers, is that it?"

"I want to drown out anything else that's going on at the time. When we start the tape, or the chip, or whatever . . ."

"Will this be a delayed start, or what?"

"Yes, that's what I'd like. I don't want to be anywhere near the lawn when the tape starts."

"That's easy enough, I can rig that for you. You know . . . well, it depends, of course."

"What were you about to say?"

"If you really want to do this right, let's just knock out their signal and substitute yours for it."

"That would be perfect."

"But this would have to be after all their equipment is in place, you understand."

"Yes."

"They'll probably be placing the stage, two, three days before the event. Do their equipment check the day before. What kind of fuzz will I have to worry about?"

"There shouldn't be any additional police presence in the days preceding the concert. There'll be a larger presence on the day itself . . ."

"Naturally."

". . . but the only thing we'll have to worry about then is getting the tape started on cue. . . ."

"That'll be automatic."

"Good."

"So how many cops while I'm in there messing around?"

"I have no idea. My guess is you'll have to worry more about private security guards. But I don't think anyone will bother you. It's been my experience that if a workman simply goes about his business, no one will bother him."

"Mine, too. But these various groups, their own people might like challenge me, you know? Who're you, man? What're you doing here, man?"

"Tell them you're with the parks department, setting up some noise-monitoring equipment for the parks commissioner. Tell them anything you like, I don't think you'll have any trouble, truly."

"Just so they don't go running to the cops, hey, there's this honkie settin up shit here, he don't belong to none of our groups."

"That won't happen."

"Cause then, all of a sudden, I got fuzz wanting to know who I am and what I'm doing and I'm standin there with like my finger up my ass."

"Would you like me to arrange some false identification for you?"

"A laminate would be terrific."

"What's a laminate?"

"Like a card covered with plastic, you wear it around your neck at these events, nobody bothers you."

"Where would I get such a thing?"

"The promoter's usually in charge of handing them out, they're valuable as gold. Anybody asts you anything, you flash the laminate, they say Pass, friend, I go about my work. That's *if* anybody asts me anything. Otherwise, I mind my own business, like you said, I don't look for no trouble, I don't get none.''

"I'll see what I can do."

"A laminate should be easy."

"Maybe," the Deaf Man said. He wasn't at all sure it would be that easy. "Is there anything else you'll need?"

"Yeah," Florry said. "Money. We haven't discussed money yet."

"For wiring the job, fifty thousand."

"That sounds low. In fact, that sounds *very* low, all the risks."

"I don't see any risks. If I can get the laminate for you . . ."

"Even with the laminate, I still see there could be risks. I'm in there working into these other guys' shit, I can see risks."

"You understand that the fifty is just for the wiring. On the day of the concert . . ."

"It's still low for the wiring. Cause frankly, that's the most exposure, when I'm out there placing the stuff. The day of the concert, I'm with you and the others, we're like mutual protection. But when I'm placing the stuff and there're cops wandering around looking over the progress of the work and whatnot, this is when there's exposure, and exposure is risk. So I don't know how much you had in mind for the day of the concert . . ."

"I had thirty in mind."

He really had fifty in mind.

"Thirty's fine for what has to be done that day," Florry said, "if it's as simple as you say it's gonna be, but for the rigging beforehand I'd need at least another eighty."

"Sixty is as high as I can go," the Deaf Man said.

"Seventy-five's my bottom line."

"Let's compromise at seventy and we've got a deal."

"Seventy for the rigging plus thirty for later on."

"A hundred altogether, yes."

"Okay, we've got a deal at a hundred."

Which was what the Deaf Man had planned to pay all along.

"When do you want to burn the EPROM?"

"The sooner the better."

"Then let's get it out of the way tomorrow sometime, okay? Can you stop by the shop like around eleven?"

"Eleven sounds fine."

"Bring me ten K in cash," Florry said, "the rest payable right after the gig. I should actually charge you more up front, cause that's where the biggest risk is, when I'm in there fuckin up their work. But I'm being a good guy cause I think I'm gonna enjoy the challenge."

"Thanks," the Deaf Man said.

Dryly.

At six P.M. on that rainy evening of March twenty-fifth, Sylvester Cummings, otherwise and preferably known as Silver Cummings, met the most beautiful woman he had ever seen in his life.

Her name was Chloe Chadderton.

They sat in a bar atop one of the city's more elegant midtown hotels, Silver's agent having made the reservation, thereby paving the way for his appearance. Otherwise, the headwaiter might not have admitted a young black man wearing dreadlocks and what looked like carpenter's overalls over a red T-shirt, not to mention footwear that had the appearance of used combat boots.

Chloe was more appropriately attired, wearing a simple brown woolen dress—this was springtime, yes, but the weather outside warranted clothing more suited to Scotland in the month of January—high-heeled brown pumps to match, a heavy gold bracelet on her right wrist, and a dangling gold medallion that nestled in the hollow of her throat. If Silver had been pressed to say what color she was, he would have said "Uptown ripe," what the slave owners down South used to call "high yeller," which exact words he had used in one of his songs to pillory modern-day bigots *wherever* they lived. Silver's own color was a rich chocolate brown, which he hoped Chloe found attractive because thirty seconds after they'd met he was madly in love.

The one thing a rapper could never be accused of was being tongue-tied. He was close to that now.

"It was really nice of me to . . . of *you* to come meet me," he said.

Chloe thought he was sort of cute, stammering and lowering his head that way, like a schoolboy. She figured him for twenty-three, twenty-four years old, some four or five years younger than she was—but since George's death, she'd dated men who were even younger than that. On the phone Silver had sounded very businesslike. Introduced himself as the writer for Spit Shine, which group she'd heard of, told her he was interested in acquiring the rights to one of George Chadderton's songs, who should he talk to up there at Chloe Productions, Inc.? She'd told him she was George Chadderton's widow, and she was the person he should talk to, and he suggested that they meet for a drink, he'd tell her what he had in mind.

Reason he had asked her to have a drink with him instead of going up there to her office was he didn't know how she'd take to the idea of a rap crew doing only her late husband's *lyrics* and throwing his music in the garbage can. He *still* didn't know how she'd react. But the lyrics were all he wanted, never mind that calypso shit.

Rain snakes slithered down the long window beside their table. Sunset wasn't due for another fifteen minutes yet, but the city already looked dark and forbidding and there were lights on in all the office and apartment buildings. Chloe was drinking a Johnny Walker Black on the rocks, Silver was drinking a Perrier and lime. Needed to keep his head clear. He really wanted that song, wanted to get it in rehearsal for the concert coming up.

"The song I'm interested in," he said, "is 'Sister Woman.'"

"Good song," she said. "George wrote it just before he got killed. Well, the lyrics, anyway."

He could've jumped on this at once, this business about the

lyrics, but instead he said, "I'm sorry, I didn't know there'd been that kind of trouble."

"Well, it's a long story," she said. "Some crazy woman was keeping his brother prisoner . . . it was really too weird. Anyway, he left this notebook full of lyrics, and I thought something could be done with them. So I hired this person to put some calypso music to them. . . ."

"There's no composer listed on the . . ."

"I paid him outright. A thousand bucks."

Smart lady, he thought.

"Copyrighted it all under the name of Chloe Productions. Wrapped an album deal that netted me three."

Well, *not* so smart, he thought.

"Not enough to retire on, but it got me through a long cold winter. How much did you plan to pay for using the song?"

Straight to the point. Had it been another long cold winter? Even so, spring was here. Wasn't it?

"We'd only want to use the lyrics," he said. "Spit Shine. We're a rap group. . . ,"

"Yes, I know."

"We don't do calypso stuff."

"I didn't think you did."

"So all we'd want would be the lyrics. Cause they make the kind of point we're int'rested in makin."

"Um-huh. So how much would these lyrics be worth to you? Did you plan to record this, or just perform it live?"

"We'd use it in the concert first—we're doin a concert on the fourth, though you'd never know it."

"The Fourth of July?" she said. Eyes opening wide. Gorgeous sloe eyes the color of coal. Narrow oval face. Good firm breasts in the fitted brown dress. Medallion hanging in the hollow of her throat. Long, graceful neck, he wanted to kiss her behind each ear.

"No, no," he said. "Next month. The fourth."

"So there's some kind of urgency," she said.

"Well, we'd have to put it together, rehearse it . . ."

"Put it together how?"

"As rap," he said. "Give it the rhythms rap needs. This isn't just a matter of *talkin* the lyrics, you know, they got to be paced, they got to be skittered."

"Where's this going to be?" she asked. "The concert."

"In the park here. Grover Park."

"Be a lot of people?"

"It's a free concert," he said, figuring he'd cut her off at the pass before she got any grandiose ideas.

"You want the song *free* then?" she asked. "Because it's a free *concert*?"

"No, we'd pay you for the use."

"How much?"

He figured he was dealing small time here. The lady needed money, that was the long and the short of it. He didn't know she was in fact dead broke and considering a life not dissimilar to the one Sister Woman lived in the song.

The music company aside—it was virtually defunct, anyway—Chloe was still doing what she'd been doing at the time of her husband's murder, dancing almost naked on bartops, men tucking dollar bills into her G-string, sometimes five, rarely more than that unless you went in the back room with them. In the back, you danced naked for them, you let them touch your breasts, kiss your nipples, slide their hands up your legs to your garters, all this was a simple step above performing forty-dollar hand jobs behind the plastic greenery, which she had never done because she knew that once you crossed the Rubicon into performing an actual sex act, the progression after that—and the justification for it—was easy. Massage parlor work, escort work, outright prostitution. She had girlfriends who'd gone that route, girls who used to dance alongside her on the bar. They told her she was dumb not doing it herself. She had considered it. She was still considering it. But here was a man interested in her dead husband's work. . . .

"What about the other songs on the album?" she said.

"Not interested in anything but the hooker song," he said, and shook his head. "I'd like to put it in the group's li'berry."

"Say it was yours?"

"No, no."

"Say you wrote it?"

"No, I wouldn't rip it. We'd give your husband credit."

"Fuck my husband," she said, startling him. "All I'm interested in is what'll bring the most money. You want to buy the copyright, fine, say the song is yours, that's fine, too, the lyrics are yours, whatever you *want,* but that'll cost you. You want to perform it one time, that's another matter. Then you'd have to come back to me next time you want to do it. I'll level with you, Mr. Cummings. . . ."

"Silver," he corrected.

"Sounds like the Lone Ranger's horse," she said.

He flared for a moment. And then burst out laughing. She watched him. Even white teeth, strong jaw, he really was quite attractive.

"Make it Sil then," he said, still laughing. "That's what all my friends call me."

"Sil," she said, "I need some real cash. I want to keep this apartment I'm in, but the lease runs out the end of April and I know they plan to raise the rent, and the truth is I'm still doing the kind of work I was doing when my husband got killed, but I don't much . . ."

"What kind of work *do* you do?" he asked.

She looked him dead in the eye.

"I'm a dancer," she said.

But didn't tell him she danced naked for men who touched her breasts and her legs, and even kissed her nipples. . . .

"But I'm not enjoying it . . ."

Which was the truth.

". . . so I'd like to start my own business, open a beauty salon in Diamondback, there's always room for another beauty salon."

"I would guess you know a great deal about beauty," he said, intending a compliment and hoping she took it as such, relieved when she said, "Why, thank you, Sil," sounding enormously surprised.

"A great deal," he repeated, like a politician emphasizing key words in his speech.

"Thank you," she said, "but I need cash if I'm going to go out on my own, do you understand what I mean?"

She did not say that some of her girlfriends were pulling down five, six hundred dollars a day, five days a week, twenty-five hundred to three thousand a week, something like a hundred and fifty thousand a year, she did not tell him that. Nor did she tell him how tempted she was lately, or how trapped she was beginning to feel. She did not want to become a whore. She did not.

Outside the windows, night had already claimed the city.

"How much are you looking for?" he asked.

"Twenty thousand," she said.

Which was outrageous.

"You've got it," he said.

The two police officers in Adam One were taking another quick run at the sector before they parked awhile to fool around a little. Necking on the job, not to mention reciprocal masturbation, was specifically forbidden by police-department regulations, but boys will be boys and girls will be girls, and the police officers in Adam One were respectively named Adam O'Hare, no relation to the car, and Josie Ruggiero, and they had been playing around on the job and running around on their respective spouses for the past month and a half now. Their burgeoning affair had started with a little hand-holding on the front seat, the walkie-talkie squawking between them, and had rapidly progressed to a little kissy-facey and then a little touchy-feely, and it would be merely a matter of time now before they found themselves a deserted stretch of turf on the graveyard shift and went "all the way," as such mischief was known in the trade.

It was now a quarter past five on this rainy morning. It would be dark until six A.M., and they were not due back at the Eight-Seven till a quarter of eight, at which time they would turn in the car and be relieved by the next shift. Relief of quite another sort was what they had in mind at the moment, however. As soon as they completed this routine pass at the sector, they would drive over to the posted Quiet Zone surrounding St. Sebastian's Hospital. Considering what their present separate but identical states of mind were urgently demanding, the dark, tree-lined streets there would perfectly serve their needs. Rarely if ever, and certainly not at this hour of the morning, was the area frequented by through traffic; the posted speed limit was ten miles per hour and there were traffic lights on every corner, blinking to the deserted streets. Park in the empty visitors' parking lot, douse the headlights, anyone saw a patrol car sitting there in the rain, they'd think it was a radar speed trap instead of two horny cops unzipping each other's flies.

O'Hare wished they'd let Josie wear a skirt to work, make life so much simpler. Josie wished her husband never found out what Adam and she had been doing every night on the job since the middle of February. Her husband was a sergeant who worked out of Narcotics and he was six feet two inches tall and he weighed two hundred and ten pounds and he had been known to bust a few heads in his lifetime. Adam, on the other hand, was five feet eight inches tall, and he weighed a hundred and fifty-four pounds, although when it came to size he was adequately compensated elsewhere.

"Wanna park awhile?" he asked now.

"Mmm, yeah," she said.

Adam nodded. He was already outrageously erect inside his blue uniform trousers, and he couldn't wait to have her hands on him again. Adam's wife, Susan, was seven months pregnant and there wasn't much activity at home for him these days.

Susan—like every other cop's wife in this city—didn't like the
idea of him being partnered with a woman, no less a dark-haired
beauty like Josie Ruggiero, *Italian* in the bargain, whom she'd
met at the Policemen's Benevolent Association Ball this past
Christmas, before anything had started between her husband and
his new partner. His *old* partner had been killed on the job. Susan
told Adam that if he ever so much as looked cockeyed at Josie,
his *new* partner would be killed also, though not necessarily on
the job. Adam, too. There would be a double homicide there in
the old Eight-Seven, and no judge in his right mind would ever
blame Susan.

Adam rationalized his actions by telling himself a stiff cock
had no conscience.

Josie rationalized hers by telling herself she was gloriously in
love.

Either way, they were consenting adults who knew exactly
what they were doing and who looked forward to ever-escalating
ecstasy night after night after night.

What they *weren't* looking forward to on this early morning
of March twenty-sixth, the very *last* thing they wanted this morning as they drove into the Quiet Zone, each one separately en-
tertaining high hopes and great expectations of secret steamy
congress in the snugness of their blue-and-white cocoon, the
surprise they definitely had not anticipated and did not now expect
to find in the middle of the parking lot was a little old man sitting
in a wheelchair in the rain.

The intern in the emergency room at St. Sebastian's Hospital
was telling Meyer Meyer that someone had dumped an old man
in the hospital's parking lot sometime early this morning, and
he was wondering now if the police had any missing-persons
reports that might describe the man, his name was Charlie. That
was all they were able to get from him, Charlie. This was now
a little after eight o'clock in the morning. The day shift had

relieved some twenty minutes ago, and Meyer was now having his breakfast—a cup of coffee and a toasted English muffin—at his desk.

"Charlie what?" he asked.

"I just told you," the intern said. "Charlie is all we got from him."

"That isn't much to go on," Meyer said, "just Charlie."

"I can give you a description," the intern said. "He's got to be at least seventy-five years old. . . . "

"Is that a guess, or did he tell you?"

"No. All he knows is his first name."

"Then you're just *guessing* he's seventy-five."

"Educated guess."

"Seventy-five, right. Color of his eyes?"

"Blue."

"Hair?"

"Fringe of white around the ears. Otherwise, he's bald."

Like me, Meyer thought.

"I'll check Missing Persons," he said, "see if they have anything."

There were currently two hospitals within the confines of the 87th Precinct's geographical boundaries, both of them lousy. Morehouse General was considered one of the worst hospitals in the city, but St. Sab's—as it was familiarly known—ran a close second. Cops knew where all the good hospitals were; whenever a cop got shot, a radio car raced him to the nearest good hospital, siren screaming. The Old Chancery in the Eight-Six was another wonderful hospital to be avoided at all costs. Buenavista was a good one, and there were several others to which you could quickly transport a wounded cop if you were hitting the hammer and riding hell-bent for leather.

Meyer and Hawes went over to St. Sab's at a little past nine that morning. They made an interesting-looking pair of cops,

Meyer standing some two inches shorter than Hawes, both men
burly and tall, but Meyer completely bald whereas Hawes had
flaming red hair with a white streak over the left temple. Meyer
wondered what the politically correct term for "bald" was. De-
pilated? Non-hirsute? He also wondered why you didn't see as
many bald women as you saw bald men. He had, in fact, seen
only one bald woman in his entire lifetime, and she had drowned
in a bathtub full of soapy water, a lady almost ninety years old
and too weak to get herself out of the tub, drowned while she
was probably calling weakly for help all day long. There was a
blonde wig on a stand in the bathroom, alongside the sink. Meyer
wondered what that old lady had looked like when she was young
and had her own blonde hair. Bald and emaciated, she had looked
like a concentration-camp survivor.

Meyer thought about that little old bald lady for months after
they'd found her in her apartment in that soapy bathtub. Sometimes he would wake up in the middle of the night thinking about
her. About how she'd looked Jewish to him. Because it was one
thing to be a Jew who thought of Israel as a foreign country and
it was another thing to be a Jew who put up a Christmas tree
every year and who hadn't been inside a synagogue since the
time he was investigating the murder of a dead rabbi, years and
years ago, but it was quite another thing to know that what had
happened to the Jews in Germany had happened only because
they *were* Jews like himself. The little old lady with her blonde
wig on a bathroom stand caused Meyer to weep for every Jew
in the world—even though it turned out she wasn't Jewish at all;
her name in fact was Kelly.

He guessed he was thinking about her now because the man
named Charlie looked a lot older than the seventy-five years the
intern had estimated. Sitting up in bed, he seemed totally out of
it, a frail old man peering out of a face with skin as transparent
as parchment, his eyes as blue as chicory blooms.

"How you doing, sir?" Hawes asked.

The old man nodded.

Charlie.

Charlie is all we got from him.

Labels cut out of all his clothes. Wrapped in a blanket, sitting in a wheelchair in the rain.

"We've run some tests," the intern said now. "He's diabetic and anemic, he's got high blood pressure, rheumatoid arthritis, and cataracts on both eyes. The memory loss could be Alzheimer's, but who can tell?"

"Does he know how he got here?" Hawes asked.

"Do you know how you got here, sir?" Meyer asked.

"In a car," Charlie said.

"Who was driving the car, do you know?"

"A man," Charlie said.

"Do you know who he was?"

"No."

"Do you know his name?"

"No."

His voice was shaky. So were his hands. Meyer wondered if he also had Parkinson's. The intern hadn't mentioned anything about Parkinson's. The intern's name—his last name, anyway, and an initial for his first name—was lettered onto a little plastic tag pinned to his tunic. DR. J. MOOKHERJI. Indian, Meyer guessed. There were more Indian doctors training in this city than there were Indian snake charmers in all Calcutta. If you were admitted to an emergency room in this city, chances were the doctor treating you had a mother in Delhi.

"How'd you get in his car?" Hawes asked.

"Carried me out to it. Put me on the front seat with him."

"When was this?"

"Last night."

"Where?"

"From the house."

"Where would that be, sir?"

"The house," he said again, and shrugged.

"He doesn't know where he lives," Mookherji said. "I've already asked."

"What time was this, sir?" Hawes asked. "When the man carried you out to the . . . ?"

"If he ever knew how to tell time, he doesn't anymore," Mookherji said.

"What did the man look like?" Meyer asked.

He wasn't hoping for much. Some of these people, they could remember something had happened to them when they were four years old, but they couldn't recall where they'd put their hat three minutes ago.

"He was forty, forty-five years old," Charlie said, "about five feet ten inches tall, with brown eyes and dark hair. Wearing jeans and a brown leather jacket with a yellow shirt under it, no hat."

Meyer was impressed. So was Hawes.

"Was he white or black?" Meyer asked.

"White."

"Anything else you can remember about him?"

"He was nice to me," Charlie said.

"Did you contact Missing Persons?" Mookherji asked.

"No one answering his description," Meyer said. He did not mention that the detective he'd spoken to had asked, "What is this, a fuckin epidemic?"

"Did he drive you straight here from the house?" Hawes asked.

"Don't know," Charlie said.

"My guess is he was bedridden," Mookherji said. "He's got bedsores all over him. We'd really like to locate his people, whoever they are, whoever dumped him here." Hospital personnel had picked up the media expression. Hardly anyone in a hospital called it abandonment. It was dumping, plain and simple. Like dumping your garbage. Only these were human beings.

"How long were you in the car, do you know?" Hawes asked.

"He has no concept of time," Mookherji said.

"Twenty months," Charlie said.

"Did he say anything to you?"

"He knew my name."

"Knew you were Charlie?"

"Called me Charlie, knew my name."

"Charlie what?"

"Don't know."

"Did he say anything to you when he left you here?"

"Said I'd be all right."

"Anything else?"

"Said there were people who loved me," Charlie said, and looked into Meyer's face, and said, "Do you love me?" and began weeping.

4.

At a little past ten o'clock that Thursday morning, the telephone on Carella's desk rang. He picked up the receiver, said, "Eighty-Seventh Squad, Carella," and glanced at the LED display of the caller's number.

"Don't bother with a trace," the Deaf Man said. "I'm using a stolen mobile phone."

"Okay," Carella said, but he jotted down the number, anyway.

"And it's not the same phone I used the other day."

"I didn't think it would be."

"I love modern technology, don't you? Are you looking at a CID?"

"Yes. The area code is for Elsinore County, but I don't suppose you're calling from there, are you?"

"No, I'm not. In fact, I'm right across the street. In the park."

"Mm-huh."

"You don't believe me, do you?"

"I don't know where you are. Or what you want. I'm pretty busy here, though, so if you've got a crime to report . . ."

"I want to tell you what I plan to do."

"Mm-huh."

"That's a nasty little tic you're developing. The mm-huh. Makes you sound somewhat skeptical."

"Mm."

"Even in its abbreviated form."

"Look, if you have something to say . . ."

"Patience, patie . . ."

Carella hung up.

Arthur Brown was just walking in, easing a man in handcuffs through the gate in the slatted rail divider that separated the squadroom from the corridor outside. Both men were black, an inappropriate bit of labeling in that Brown was actually the color of his surname, and the handcuffed man with him was the color of sand. African-Americans would have been a misnomer, too; the man with Brown had been born in Haiti, and Brown had been born right here in the good old U.S. of A., which made him a native son and not a hyphenate of any stripe or persuasion.

Yankee Doodle Brown was what he was, six feet four inches tall, weighing two hundred and twenty-four pounds—this morning, anyway—and looking high, wide, and handsome in a trench coat he'd worn because it had still been raining when he'd left the house this morning. The man with him was five-six, five-seven, in there, wearing green polyester slacks, a matching green windbreaker, and scuffed black loafers with white socks. His eyes were green; lots of French blood in him, Brown guessed. So far, the man had spoken only French, which Brown didn't understand at all.

"What've you got?" Carella asked.

"Don't know yet," Brown said. "Man was turning a Korean grocery store upside down, throwing fruit and vegetables all over the place, I just happened to be passing by in my car."

"Lucky you," Carella said.

"Oh, don't I know it?" Brown said, and took off the man's handcuffs.

"*Eux, ils sont débiles,*" the Haitian said.

"Empty your pockets," Brown told him. "Everything on the desk here."

"Doesn't he speak any English?" Carella asked.

"Not to me he doesn't. Your pockets," Brown said, and demonstrated by reaching into his right-hand pocket and taking from it his keys and some change, and putting these on the desk, and then pulling the pocket inside out. "Empty your pockets on the desk here. Understand?"

Being a police officer was getting to be very difficult in this city. Years ago, most of your foreigners coming to live in this city were white Europeans; for the most part, the only foreign languages you had to contend with were Italian, Spanish, Yiddish, and German. Nowadays, the immigrants were mostly black, Hispanic, and Asian. Back then, if you booked anyone Hispanic, nine times out of ten he was from Puerto Rico. Nowadays, anyone with a Puerto Rican heritage was usually a second- or third-generation American who spoke English without a trace of accent. The ones with the heavy Spanish accents were the newcomers, most of them from the Dominican Republic or Colombia. Well, that wasn't such a problem; a lot of working cops had picked up at least a little Spanish over the years, and besides there were hundreds of cops on the force whose grandparents had come here from Guayama or San Juan and you could always count on them translating what some guy was machine-gunning in his native tongue.

But what'd you do when you came up against somebody speaking *French*, the way this Haitian guy was? Brown had no idea whether this was pure French or bastardized French or even the patois some of them spoke, which not even a Parisian could understand. All he knew was that he couldn't make out a word the guy was saying. He was used to not understanding what half the people they dragged in here were saying. What were you supposed to do, for example, when you got somebody in here from Guyana? In the old days you chatted up a black man, you found out he had people in Georgia or Mississippi or South Carolina, he'd been "down home" for the holidays, or to see his sister in a hospital in Mobile, Alabama, whatever. Nowadays, you talked to a black man, you found out *his* relatives were in New Amsterdam or Georgetown, and he spoke a kind of English you could hardly understand, anyway. One out of every four blacks in this city was foreign-born. One out of every four. Count 'em. You got some of them from Guyana, they didn't talk English at *all*, they spoke a Creole patois it was impossible to decipher. You got some of those East *Indians* from Guyana, they spoke either Hindi or Urdu, who the hell on the police force could understand *those* languages? Not to mention the Koreans and the Chinese and the Vietnamese, who they might just as well have been speaking Martian.

You took the number-seven subway train from Majesta into the city proper, you saw a third-world country on it every morning. The host on one of the city's nighttime talk shows dubbed the number seven "The UN Express." The immigrants riding that train didn't know what the hell he meant. The mayor said on the radio that the city's dramatic population change could be considered a glorious experiment in the racial forces of manifold coexistence in a continually changing kaleidoscope of cross-cultural opportunity. The people he was talking about didn't know what the hell *he* meant, either. Not even Brown knew what the mayor meant.

All Brown knew was that in the old days, a person came here from a foreign country, he planned to *stay* here, earn a living here, raise a family here, learn the language they spoke here, become a citizen—in short, make some kind of *investment* in this city and this nation. Nowadays, the immigrants you got from Latin America and the Caribbean preferred remaining citizens of their native lands, shuttling back and forth like diplomats between countries, supporting nuclear families here and extended families in their homelands. This meant that the city's *largest* immigrant groups were showing little if any interest in joining the mainstream of American society. Shoot a dope dealer in a neighborhood composed largely of immigrants from Santo Domingo, and the flags that came out in protest were red, white, and blue, all right, but they weren't the Stars and Stripes, they were the flags of the Dominican Republic. No wonder so many walls in this city were covered with graffiti. If it ain't our city, then fuck it.

The man from Haiti was carrying a green card that identified him as Jean-Pierre Chandron. Brown wondered if the card was a phony. You could buy any kind of card you needed for twenty-five bucks, sometimes less. You could also buy a bag of heroin for a mere five bucks these days and a puff of crack for seventy-five *cents*! The Six-Bit Hit, it was called. You couldn't buy a *candy* bar for six bits anymore, but you could start frying your brain for that amount of cash anytime you took a notion. What they did, they passed the crack pipe through a slot in a locked door after you dropped in your cash in quarters or even in nickels and dimes. Only thing they wouldn't accept was pennies cause they were too bulky; otherwise, money was money.

In much the same way that big manufacturers dumped their merchandise at ridiculously low prices in order to infiltrate new markets, the dope peddlers in this city were now dangling their bait to the uninitiated. Lookee here, man, you can fly to the moon for a scant six bits, wanna try, wanna buy, wanna fly? Or if you prefer heroin, we now have shit so pure you'd think it was virgin. You can snort it off a mirror, man, same as you do with coke, it's that pure. You don't have to worry about no needle, man, no fear of getting the old HIV, you can *inhale* this shit, man, and it's only a nickel a bag, how can you refuse? The days of the dime bag are dead and gone, come join the party! The nickel bag is back, man, rejoice and carouse!

"Why'd you go berserk in that store?" Brown asked the Haitian.

The telephone rang.

"Eighty-Seventh Squad, Car . . ."

"Please don't hang up again," the Deaf Man said. "I'm trying to be of assistance here."

"I'll just bet you are."

"I'm trying to prevent a catastrophe of gigantic proportions."

The same CID number was showing on the display panel. Carella wondered if he really was calling from the park. Although knowing him, he'd already moved his location. He was beginning to think the lieutenant was right, though. Just ignore the son of a bitch and . . .

"I'll make it easy for you," he said.

"Thanks," Carella said.

"No song and dance this time."

"I'm listening."

"The title of the novel is *The Fear and the Fury*. It's science fiction. Do you like science fiction?"

"Sometimes I think *you're* science fiction," Carella said.

"I don't particularly admire the genre," the Deaf Man said, "but I thought its simplicity might appeal to you. The author is a Bolivian named Arturo Rivera. The chapter you'll want to read is the very first one in the book. It's called 'The Rites of Spring.' I think you may find it interesting."

"Why should I . . . ?"

This time the Deaf Man hung up.

"Does anybody around here speak French?" Brown asked the four walls.

"Va te faire foutre," the Haitian told him.

Meyer and Hawes were just coming through the gate in the railing.

"You speak French?" Brown asked them.

"Oui," Hawes said.

"Then talk to this guy, willya?"

"That's my entire vocabulary," Hawes said.

"How about you?"

"My wife speaks French," Meyer said.

"Lotta help that is."

Meyer went to the phone and dialed the Missing Persons Bureau, and asked to talk to Detective Hastings, the man he'd called earlier this morning. Behind him, Carella was trying some Italian on the Haitian, and Hawes was trying some Spanish, and Brown was trying to raise the patrol sergeant to see if any of his blues spoke French. Meyer waited.

"Hastings," a voice said.

"Hi, this is Meyer at the Eight-Seven again, I called you around eight this morning, do you remember? To ask if you had anything on a John Doe named Charlie, guy around . . ."

"I can hardly remember my *own* name that early in the morning," Hastings said.

"Guy around seventy-five years old, you remember we talked about it?"

"Yeah, what about it? We *still* don't have anything on anybody named Charlie."

"You mentioned something about an epidemic, though, do you remember?"

"No, I don't."

"What'd you mean? About an epidemic."

"I got no idea."

"Well, why'd you use the word *epidemic*?"

"Maybe cause it's *always* an epidemic here. There are times I think everybody in this fuckin *city* is slowly disappearing from the face of the earth."

"But when I mentioned this guy Charlie was maybe seventy-five years old, you said, 'What is this, an epidemic?' Do you remember that?"

"Vaguely."

"Well, why'd you say it? Did you have another seventy-five-year-old John Doe?"

"Yeah, that's right, now I remember."

"Another John Doe?"

"A *Jane*."

"What about her?"

"Some blues from the Eight-Six found this old lady in the waiting room of the Whitcomb Avenue Station, took her over to the Chancery. I spoke to a doctor there wanted to know we had anything on her."

"When was this?"

"Early Tuesday morning, musta been. Everybody calls first thing in the morning, why *is* that? I'm tryin'a have my coffee, the phone starts ringing off the hook."

"So Tuesday this old lady gets dumped," Meyer said, "and today it's this guy Charlie. So that's what you meant by an epidemic?"

"Of *dumping*, yeah. Not of missing persons. Missing persons, it's *always* an epidemic."

"Do you remember who you spoke to at the Chancery?"

"I've got it here someplace, hold on," Hastings said.

At eleven-fifteen that morning, there were only three patients in the emergency room at Old Chancery Hospital. One of these was a pregnant woman who'd been shoved down a flight of steps by her boyfriend. The other two were heroin users who'd shot up on the new stuff coming in from Asia and Colombia and were suffering the toxic aftereffects of "pure" fixes. Actually, nothing sold on the street was ever *truly* pure; the more the drug was stepped on, the more profit there was for everyone down the line. But the new stuff was decidedly more potent than what the city's estimated 200,000 heroin addicts were used to, and these two old needle buddies in the E.R. had been scared half to death by sudden symptoms of heroin poisoning. One of them had already begun to turn blue before they both decided in their infinite wisdom that it was time to seek medical assistance. Elman left them in the capable hands of his team of Indian interns and led Meyer upstairs to talk to the Jane Doe the hospital had inherited two days earlier. Elman planned to leave for Maine at four o'clock tomorrow afternoon, before the start of the weekend rush of bruised and bleeding bodies. Meanwhile, here was a miraculously interested detective who might just possibly help them find out who the hell she was.

"She keeps talking about somebody named Polly," Elman

said. "Doesn't have any daughters, or so she says, which leads us to believe this Polly person may be a nurse of some sort. All the labels were cut out of her clothes, which may indicate they could have identified a nursing home, do you see what I mean?"

"Yes, I do," Meyer said.

But if she was missing from a nursing home, why hadn't someone notified the police?

"She's diabetic, by the way. Whoever dumped her probably didn't know that. Or maybe didn't give a damn."

"How do you mean?"

"No medication on her. Nothing in her pockets, that is. She wasn't carrying a handbag."

"What *was* she wearing?" Meyer asked.

"Nightgown, slippers, panties, diaper, and robe."

"Labels removed from the slippers, too?"

"Yes."

"Sometimes they overlook that."

"Not this time. Here we are."

Elman entered the room the way doctors always entered a hospital room, never bothering to knock, just barging in without a by-your-leave. Never mind whether the patient might be moving his bowels or picking his nose, a sick person lost all privacy the moment he was admitted to a hospital.

The woman who didn't know her own name was sitting in a chair beside the bed, watching a soap opera on television. Daytime serials, they called them. Everything politically correct in this country. Meyer still wondered what the politically correct word for *bald* was. This woman had hair. Lots of it. All of it white. She did not turn from the television set when they walked in.

"Excuse me," Elman said, not because he'd walked in uninvited but because he wanted her attention. When she still didn't turn from the set, he picked up the remote-control unit and clicked off the picture. She turned to him angrily, seemed about to protest, and then sighed heavily and sank back into

her chair. In that instant, Meyer saw in her eyes the helpless resignation of an old woman accustomed to intrusions and
commands.

"There's a police officer here who'd like to talk to you,"
Elman said without apology. "Detective Meyer. From the
Eighty-Seventh Precinct."

"How do you do, ma'am?" Meyer said.

The woman nodded.

"There are a few questions I'd like to ask you, if you don't
mind," he said.

"Sure," she said.

Looking him over.

"Who's Polly?" he asked.

Straight out. Sometimes if you took them by surprise, they
blurted out a memory they didn't even know they possessed.

"She takes care of me," the woman said.

"Where?"

"Home."

But was she referring to home as in *house*, or home as in
nursing?

"Where's that?" he asked. "Home?"

"I don't know."

"Who brought you here, ma'am?"

"Policemen."

"Where'd they find you?"

"I don't know."

Bewildered look on her face. Eighty, eighty-five years old,
Meyer guessed. Too many new things happening to her all at
once. Confused. Sitting there wanting to watch her TV show,
which was something she knew and understood, but instead she
had to talk to this person asking her questions she couldn't
answer.

"Do you remember a railroad station?"

"No."

"Do you remember someone taking you to a railroad station?"

"No. I remember lightning."

"If I described a man to you, would that help you remember?"

"Maybe. It's hard," she said. "Remembering."

"He would've been forty or forty-five years old," Meyer said, repeating what Charlie had told him this morning. "About five feet ten, with brown eyes and dark hair."

"Buddy," she said.

"She's mentioned that name before," Elman said. "Buddy. We think he's a grandson."

"Buddy what, ma'am?" Meyer asked. "Can you tell me his last name?"

"I don't remember it."

"Was he wearing blue jeans and a brown jack . . . ?"

"I don't remember what he was wearing."

"Yellow shirt . . ."

"I told you I don't *remember*," she said. Getting angry with herself. Getting angry with not being able to *remember* things.

"Ma'am, do you know whether the railroad station is close to home?"

"I was in a car," she said suddenly.

"Driving in a car with someone?"

"Yes. Lightning."

"Driving from home?"

"Yes."

"Where's that, ma'am?"

"I don't remember," she said.

She was about to start crying. Frustration and anger were building tears behind her eyes. He did not want her to cry.

"Thank you, ma'am," he said, "I'm sorry we bothered you," and picked up the remote-control unit and turned on her television show again. In the corridor outside, he asked Elman if he could have a look at the woman's clothes. Elman took him downstairs to what Meyer guessed was the equivalent of the police department's Property Clerk's Office, asked the female attendant there to bring Mr. Meyer the clothing the Jane Doe in 305 had been

wearing when the police brought her in, and then excused himself
and went back to the emergency room.

Sometimes a nursing home stenciled its name into the garments
its patients wore, for identification when the clothes were sent
out to be laundered. There were neither stencil marks nor laundry
marks in the woman's robe or nightgown, nothing in her panties,
nothing in the diaper except a dried urine stain. The corner edges
of labels were still stitched to each article of clothing, but the
empty space between them indicated where the labels had been
scissored out. In each of the bedroom slippers a sticky rectan-
gular-shaped residue showed where the labels had been torn from
the inner soles.

For all intents and purposes, the woman was still anonymous.

The name of the second victim's wife was Debra Wilkins.

She was a petite blonde with green eyes and a Dutchboy bob,
in her mid-thirties, they guessed. The driver's license in her
husband's wallet had given Parker and Kling a name and an
address; the telephone directory had given them a phone number.
When they'd called her at a little before nine yesterday morning,
she'd just been leaving for an exercise class. Instead, she came
to meet them at the hospital morgue. They hadn't been able to
get much from her yesterday when she'd sobbingly—uncon-
trollably, in fact—identified the remains of her husband, Peter
Wilkins.

They sat now in the living room of the Wilkinses' three-story
brownstone on Albermarle Way, a cul-de-sac off Silvermine
Road, on the northernmost edge of the precinct territory. Through
the living-room windows, they had a clear shot of the River Harb
as dusk settled on the water. It was time to get down to business.

"Mrs. Wilkins," Kling said, cautiously taking the lead, "I
know this is a difficult time for you, but there are some questions
we have to ask."

"I'm all right now," she said. "I'm sorry about yesterday."

She'd just got back from the funeral home. Parker was thinking that her hysterics yesterday had given the killer a healthy lead. Couldn't *talk* to the goddamn woman. Every time they mentioned her husband, she'd begun wailing like a banshee. She seemed pretty much in control now. Sitting there in a simple blue suit, blue pantyhose, French-heeled blue pumps. Eyes rimmed with red, all those tears. Waiting attentively for Kling's first question.

"Mrs. Wilkins," he said, "your husband was found near the . . ."

Her lip began trembling.

Careful, Kling thought.

"Near the Reed entrance to the River Highway," he said. "In front of an abandoned building at 1227 Harlow. That's about a mile from here. Coroner's Office has estimated the time of death . . ."

He cleared his throat, kept his eye on that trembling lip. He didn't want her to go to pieces again.

". . . at around midnight Tuesday. It was raining all that night, and it was still raining yesterday morning when we got to the scene. Ma'am, if you could tell us when you saw him last, and what he said to you before he left here, whether he gave you any . . ."

"The last time I saw him was after dinner on Tuesday night. He left the apartment at around eight-thirty. There was a movie he wanted to see. Something that didn't interest me at all. A cop movie," she said.

"What time did you expect him home?"

"Eleven, eleven-thirty."

"But he didn't come home."

"No. He didn't come home."

Turning her head away.

"That's why I called the police."

Kling looked at Parker. Parker nodded. It was possible.

"When was this?" he asked.

"At midnight. I was really worried by then. I knew it was

raining, but the movie theater's only a few blocks from here, on Stemmler, and he could've walked it in ten minutes. And Peter isn't the . . . wasn't the sort of man who'd stop in a bar or anything on the way home. So I . . . I was worried. I called nine-one-one and described him and . . . and what he was wearing . . . and I told them he should have been home by then. I don't know what they did about it.''

What they'd have done, they'd have alerted the local precinct, which in this case was the Eight-Seven, where there wouldn't have been a chance in hell that the patrol sergeant would instruct his blues to keep an eye out for a husband who was half an hour late getting home.

"When you called yesterday morning,'' Debra said, ''I thought it . . . I thought you might have some news. I wasn't expec . . . expecting what you . . . told me. That he was dead. I wasn't expecting that.''

Controlling herself. Biting down hard on her lower lip again. She would not cry. She would help them. Kling admired that. Parker wondered if it was an act. In many respects, Parker and Kling were the perfect good cop/bad cop team. That was because neither of them had to act a part; Parker really was a bad cop and Kling really was a good one.

"What was he wearing when he left here, can you tell us?'' Kling asked.

"Blue jeans. A T-shirt. A barn jacket. From J. Crew.''

Exactly what he'd been wearing when they'd found him painted all silver and gold with three holes in his head.

"Did he go to the movie alone?'' Parker asked.

"Yes?''

Question mark at the end of her answer, asking *him* the significance of such a question. Was he suggesting . . . ?

"Didn't go with a *friend* or anything, huh?'' Parker asked, skirting close to the edge of another Shavorskyism.

"Alone,'' Debra said.

"Do you keep a car here in the city?'' Kling asked.

"No. We rent one when we need one."

"I was wondering how he ended up a mile from here. The rain and all."

"Didn't go with a buddy or anything, did he?" Parker asked, getting back to it. "To the movie, I mean."

"No. He went alone."

"Lots of people don't like going to the movies alone," Parker said. "They go with a boyfriend," he said, and paused. "Or a girlfriend," he added, and looked at her.

"He went *alone*," she said again.

"Your husband ever do any artwork around the house?" Parker said.

"*Art*work?"

"Yeah. Lettering? Painting? Anything like that?"

"No."

"He's not a sign painter or anything, is he?"

"He's a lawyer," Debra said.

Until now, Parker thought he'd heard everything there ever *was* to hear about lawyers. But a lawyer who sprayed paint on walls?

"Did he ever go out alone at night when he *wasn't* going to a movie?" Parker asked.

"We had separate interests. He sometimes went out alone, yes."

"Like what? What separate interests?"

"He liked basketball, I didn't. He liked poetry readings, I didn't. Sometimes, he'd have dinner with a client. Naturally, I didn't go along on those . . ."

"Did he ever leave the house late at night to pursue these separate interests?" Parker asked.

"Never."

"But he sometimes got home late, didn't he?"

"Sometimes."

"Did you ever see him carrying a spray can when he left the house?"

"A what?"

"A spray can. That you spray paint with."

"No. A *spray* can? What on earth would he be doing with . . . ?"

"Mrs. Wilkins, would it be all right if we looked around the apartment a little?"

"Why would you want to do that?"

"Look at some of his things."

"Why?"

"See if we can't get a bead on why somebody would've wanted to kill him."

"I don't see how . . ."

"My partner means like his appointment calendar, his diary, anything that . . ."

"He didn't keep . . ."

"No, I meant . . ."

". . . a diary."

". . . like his *closet*."

Debra looked him dead in the eye.

"Officer," she said at last, "are you aware that *Peter* was the one who got killed here? Are you aware that my husband was the *victim*?"

"Yes, ma'am, all I'm . . ."

"Then why do you want to look at some of *his* things? Why don't you go look at the goddamn *killer's* things? Why aren't you out there in the street looking for the goddamn *killer*?"

"Ma'am," Parker said, unperturbed, "your husband is the second graffiti writer who got . . ."

"My husband was *not* a graffiti writer," she said. "He was a *lawyer*."

"All I'm saying," Parker said, "if there's anything in his pockets or on his shelves or in his dresser or wherever that would give us some idea what took him over to that wall last night, then maybe we can find out whether somebody he *knew* was a graffiti writer, is all I'm saying. Ma'am, there's got to be a connection here, two people found dead with paint sprayed all over them, I'm sure you can see that.''

"My husband was *not* a graffiti writer," she said.

"Well," Parker said and shrugged as if to say Look, you want us to find who killed your fuckin husband, or you don't?

She looked at him.

She looked at Kling.

"I'll show you where he kept his things," she said curtly, and led them into the bedroom.

On the top shelf of his closet, they found twenty-two cans of spray paint in various colors of the rainbow.

Before there was Detective Stephen Louis Carella in her life, there was *her* life.

Theodora Franklin.

Teddy Franklin.

Four fifths Irish with a fifth of Scotch thrown in, as her father was fond of telling her. Signed this to her with his hands, emphasized the joke with his wide expressive face, exaggerated the words on his lips so that she could read them while his fingers formed them, all of this because his one and only beloved daughter had been born deaf and dumb—or hearing- and speech-impaired as they said in this enlightened day and age, where a blind man was no longer blind but merely sight-impaired. Teddy felt that the word "impaired" was more heavily freighted than either "deaf" *or* "dumb," more heavily burdened with derogatory meaning than even the simple designation "deaf mute"—but who was she to comment, being merely deaf *and* mute since birth?

But, truly, didn't "impaired" mean *defective*, wasn't that the dictionary definition of impaired? And didn't "defective" mean *damaged*, or *flawed*, or *imperfect*? And didn't *all* of these imply

deficient, or—worse yet—somehow *bad.* She did not want to
think of herself as impaired. For too long a time, she had thought
of herself in exactly that way.

Before Carella, there'd been only one "hearing" man in her
life. Well, a boy, actually. Back then, most hearing-impaired
people went to schools for the so-called deaf, but she was fortunate—perhaps—in that her Riverhead neighborhood had a high
school offering special classes for people like her. People with
hearing problems. Speech problems. Four of them actually. The
other kids in the class were what they called "retarded" back
then. Mentally deficient. Until Salvatore Di Napoli asked her
out, the only boys she'd ever dated were the ones with hearing
problems, the ones in the special class.

The faculty adviser of the cheerleading squad saw nothing
wrong with putting Teddy on it, even though she had no voice.
She was prettier than any of the other girls, with raven-black
hair and expressive brown eyes and breasts that looked terrific
in the white sweater with the letter on its front and legs that
looked spectacular in the short pleated skirt, not inconsiderable
assets for a cheerleader, so why not? It didn't matter that she
couldn't *yell* out the cheers. She could certainly mouth them and
dramatize them, and that was all that mattered. In a shouting
crowd, no one is speechless. In a roaring crowd, it doesn't matter
if you can't hear because nobody else can, either.

She caught Salvatore Di Napoli's eye at one of the football
games.

"Would you like to go to a movie or something?" he
asked her.

This was in the hallway on the Monday after the game.

He had pale blue eyes and long slender fingers. He played the
violin. Everyone called him Salvie. He confessed to her one
night that he hated the name Salvatore and that when he was old
enough—he was sixteen then, a year younger than she was—he
would change it legally. He would pick a good WASP name that

would make him feel more at home in America, even though he had been born here of parents who had also been born here.

"I might call myself Steve," he said.

At the time, she didn't think there was anything remarkable about what he'd said. The name he'd chosen. Steve. She didn't even think it was a particularly WASPy name. She knew a lot of Irish Catholics named Steve, and she didn't think they considered themselves WASPs.

His voice faltered, his fingers fumbled, the first time he asked her to go to bed with him.

"Do you . . . is it possible . . . could we . . . do you think . . . is there a chance we might . . . ?"

She kissed him and guided his long slender fingers to the buttons on her blouse.

She went steady with him until her graduation a year later. He was in his junior year at the time. She was eighteen—what her father called "a young woman"—and Salvie was seventeen. While she was still debating whether or not she wanted to go to college, he transferred to a school specializing in music and drama, and the next time she saw him he was completely changed. He had new friends now, new pursuits, new encouraged ambitions. And although in high school he had professed his undying love for her, she now had the feeling he considered her a person from another life, a *deaf* person he had once known only casually.

She learned much later that he had finally changed his name. Not to Steve. To Sam. Sam Knapp. For Di Napoli. Samuel Knapp. Who'd written a musical that was being performed in Chicago, and who was dating the blonde (*and* hearing) actress playing the lead role. Teddy remembered that once, long ago, when they were in high school together, he had taken her to see *La Traviata*.

When she was twenty . . .

Quite out of the blue . . .

Steve Carella entered her life.

On the fifth day of February that winter, a Sunday, someone burglarized the offices where she worked, and on Monday morning the sixth, a detective named Stephen Louis Carella came around to ask questions.

She thought it was . . . well, *odd* . . . him having the very first name Salvie Di Napoli would have chosen for himself, although he'd finally ended up with Sam Knapp, dating a cute little blonde and hearing actress in the Second City.

Steve Carella.

She had already decided by then that there were two separate worlds, the world of the hearing and the world of those who could not hear. Or speak. And she had pretty much decided that she didn't want to have anything more to do with any man in that *other* world, the *hearing* world, because Sam Knapp had in the long run made her feel hopelessly and helplessly *defective*. She did not want to feel *defective* ever again in her life. Ever.

The second time he came to the office, he brought along a police interpreter. This was two days after the burglary. Tuesday, the seventh of February. The name of the firm for which she'd been working was Endicott Mail Order, Inc., she still remembered it after all these years. She used to address envelopes for them, a not unimportant job in that most of their business was conducted by mail—well, Endicott *Mail* Order, would they have used carrier pigeons? He had already asked everyone in the office a lot of questions, and now he was back with an interpreter who knew how to sign, and she immediately figured he considered her a prime suspect.

"I thought we could save some time if I brought along an interpreter," he said, and she thought He doesn't think I'm a suspect, thank God, he only thinks I'm a *dummy*.

But he didn't think that, either.

What he wanted to know was whether any of the people who made deliveries or pickups at the office might have had access to the key to the front door.

"Because you see," he said, and waited for the interpreter to translate, "there are no marks on the door or around the keyway. There doesn't seem to have been any forced entry, you see. So I've got to think someone got in with a key."

Watching the interpreter's flying fingers.

There are lots of people making pickups and deliveries, Teddy signed.

"What'd she say?" Carella asked.

"Lots of pickups and deliveries," the interpreter said.

"Names," Carella said, keeping it short, figuring it'd be easier that way. "Can she give me names?"

The interpreter's fingers flashed.

She watched. Big brown eyes. Brownest eyes Carella had ever seen in his life.

I know a few of them by name, she signed. *But usually I know them by their companies.*

"She only knows the company names," the interpreter said.

She had been watching his lips.

She shook her head.

I know some of the messengers' *names, too*, she signed, *but not all of them*.

The interpreter shrugged.

"What'd she say?" Carella asked.

"She said she knows *some* of the messengers' names."

"So why didn't you translate it?"

"I did," he said, and shrugged again.

"I want to hear *everything* she has to say."

"Sure," the interpreter said. His look said Fuck you.

"Ask her to write them down for me. All the company names, all the individual names."

Teddy began writing.

"Does the key always hang in that same place?" Carella asked.

She looked up. The interpreter translated.

Yes, she signed. *Because we keep the front door locked, and*

*when anyone goes to the bathroom he has to take the door key
with him, too. To get back in.*

The lock on the door was a spring bolt. The key to it hung
on a rack behind Teddy's desk, alongside a key to the men's
room and a key to the ladies' room. An experienced burglar
wouldn't have had to steal a key to get into the place. He'd have
loided the lock with a credit card. Actually, the burglar who'd
done the job here had only *borrowed* the key and replaced it
before he'd left the premises. Throw the police off the scent, he
probably figured. Brilliant burglar making no attempt to conceal
the absence of forced entry, but hangs the key back up before
he leaves. A rocket scientist, this burglar. Carella was willing
to bet a week's salary that he was one of the kids who made
deliveries or pickups here. Two weeks' salary.

He watched her as she completed the list.

Short list.

This one would be a piece of cake.

"Ask her if that's all of them," he said to the interpreter.

She had read his lips, she knew the question before it formed
on the interpreter's hands, answered it before he signed the first
word.

Yes, she signed. *That's all I can remember.*

"Ask her if she'd like to have dinner with me tomorrow
night," Carella said.

"What?" the interpreter said.

"Ask her."

The interpreter shrugged. His fingers moved. She watched his
hands. She turned to look at Carella, surprised. Her own fingers
moved. Briefly.

"She wants to know why?" the interpreter said.

"Tell her I think she's beautiful."

He signed it to her. Teddy signed back.

"She says she knows she's beautiful."

"Tell her I'd like to get to know her better."

Tell him I'm busy tomorrow night.

"She's busy tomorrow night."

"Then how about lunch the next day?"

I'm busy then, too.

"She's busy then, too."

"Then how about dinner that night? Friday night. How about dinner?"

I'm busy for dinner Friday, too.

"She's busy all day Friday."

Carella put his face very close to hers.

"Listen to me," he said. "Watch my lips." Slowly and distinctly, he said, "How about breakfast Saturday morning?"

She watched his lips.

He said it again.

"Breakfast. Saturday morning. Okay?"

He smiled.

She shook her head.

Carella turned to the interpreter.

"Did she say *no*?" he asked.

"That's what she said, pal."

Carella looked at her.

"No?" he said incredulously.

She shook her head again.

And then spelled the word out with her right hand, letter by letter, so there'd be no mistake.

N . . .

O . . .

No.

He caught the burglar three days later. A kid who delivered lunch to the office from the local deli, got grandiose ideas about how much money the firm had to be making, concocted his brilliant caper, stole the key, and sneaked in one night to score a big two hundred and twelve dollars that would net him at least three years on a Burg Two. Eighteen years old, he'd be out of jail when he was twenty-one. Maybe.

He came to the office again on that Friday, the eleventh day of February—she remembered all these dates accurately and precisely because they all led to the beginning. Coming out of Mr. Endicott's office where he'd just reported the results of his investigation, he stopped at Teddy's desk to repeat the story. She listened without an interpreter this time. Studied his mouth as he spoke, his lips.

"Why won't you go out with me?" he asked abruptly.

She shrugged.

"Tell me."

She shook her head.

"Please," he said.

She touched her lips.

She touched her ears.

She shook her head again.

"What's *that* got to do with anything?" he asked.

She sighed heavily, spread her arms helplessly. Her face said *It has everything to do with everything*.

He read this on her face and in her eyes, and he said, "No, Teddy, it doesn't. It doesn't mean a damn thing."

She nodded.

Yes, her face said. Her eyes said *Yes, it does.*

He kept looking at her.

"I don't understand," he said. "Haven't you ever dated men who . . . well, who can *hear*?"

She nodded.

"And speak?"

She nodded again.

"You *have*?"

She nodded again. Yes, I have.

Once, she thought.

"Well, good," he said, "I was beginning to think . . ."

She pointed at him.

Shook her head.

Wagged her finger *No*.

"Why not?" he said.

She shrugged.

"I mean . . . why *not*?"

She turned away.

"Well . . ." he said.

She did not turn to face him again. She was no longer listening.

"See you around," he said, which she didn't hear or see. And left the office.

She had not told him she was afraid of what might happen if she started seeing this handsome detective with the slanted brown Chinese eyes and the easy smile and the long rangy look of an athlete. Never again, she thought. I will never again fall in love with a *hearing* man, I will never again even allow myself the *opportunity* . . . never grant myself even the *possibility* of it happening ever again.

But on Valentine's Day that year . . .

A Monday.

It was snowing that Monday. She took the bus home from work, and walked up the street to her building, the air swirling with snowflakes, the ground underfoot white and clean, the air sharp, a spot of red up ahead in the overwhelming white, she squinted through the flying flakes and saw someone sitting on the front stoop of her building, and recognized him as Detective Stephen Louis Carella.

Steve.

His face was windblown and his hair blowing in the wind was covered with snow, and the spot of color in his gloveless hand was a single red rose.

"Change your mind," he said, and extended the rose to her.

She hesitated.

The rose still in his hand, its petals moving in the wind.

Extended to her.

He raised the other hand.

Slowly his fingers formed the single letter *O*.

And then the letter *K*.

OK?

"Change your mind," he said again.

And raised his eyebrows plaintively, and she found herself nodding, perhaps because he had taken the trouble to learn how to sign those two letters, *O* and *K*, OK, Okay, change your mind, okay? Or perhaps because she saw in those Chinese eyes an honesty she had never seen on the face of any man she'd ever known. She knew in that instant that this man would never hurt her. This man could be trusted with her very life.

Still nodding, she accepted the rose.

He sat across the room now, in the big easy chair before the imitation Tiffany floor lamp they'd bought when they were first furnishing the house. He was reading, his brow furrowed in concentration. He must have felt her steady gaze upon him. He lifted his eyes. From across the room, she smiled and signed *I love you*. He returned the smile. Returned the words. Mouthed them and signed them. *I love you*. And went back to the book.

She had not yet told him what she planned to do tomorrow morning.

The first chapter of the book was thirty-five pages long. He had read it through once after dinner, and was now reading it for the second time, and he *still* didn't understand why the Deaf Man had asked him to look at it. Well, The Rites of Spring, sure. He was planning a spring surprise of some sort. Planning to *spring* a surprise, so to speak. But that was too obvious, since spring was already here. And obviousness simply wasn't the Deaf Man's way. Direction by indirection was more his style. Tell them exactly what he planned to do but in a way that made it all seem unfathomable.

The book had originally been published in South America.

Carella had no way of knowing whether the English translation was any worse than the Spanish original had been. To him, the book seemed atrocious, but then again he wasn't used to reading science fiction, if that's what this was. The novel's opening chapter began with the premise that the creatures on a planet named Obadon feared nothing more than the approach of the planting season. Rivera then went on to explain how this fear of the magic of growth led the entire population of the planet to gather on a wide open plain every year, to participate in what for time immemorial had been called The Festivities.

"Here on this dusty red plain ringed by the mountains of Kahnara, here beneath the four glistening moons of the season, the Obadons gathered to shout and to chant and to stamp their feet against the swollen soil . . ."

God, this is awful, Carella thought.

". . . so that their timeless fear of the magic of growth could once more be exorcized by a magic of their own, a magic born of ecstatic fury, presaging the moment when the plains would run red with water turned muddy and nascent."

Carella read the paragraph again.

What the hell was the Deaf Man trying to tell him?

There weren't any real writers anymore in this city, not what you could call genuine artists, there were only guys writing gang shit or dope shit, it was disgusting the way things had disintegrated the past twenty years. Nowadays, you did a whole subway car, the fuckin transit police had it acid-cleaned the very next day, it hardly paid getting the name out anymore.

Timmo considered himself one of the last great writers.

Way he put up his tag it was TMO, wrote it in one quick motion, index finger on the spray can button, paint jetting out, so it looked like:

Everybody knew this was Timmo writing.

Back in the old days, when he was doing maybe two, three trains a week—not a whole *car,* man, that took time—but doing a piece with the three letters TMO or sometimes a top-to-bottom with the same tag, writing in a style that was instantly recognizable by other experienced writers and also by the newer writers coming along, what you called toys. People biting his style was kind of flattering, Timmo guessed, but it always pissed him off, made him want to go find the guy stealing from him, look in his face, tell him you want to bite my style, man, come bite *this.* I see anything you throw up, I go over it, man, I cross it out, you dig? You get a background payback, man, each and every time.

That was in the old days.

That was when you went in a train yard with four, five other writers, you did a whole car that night, brought along a suitcase full of paint and something to eat and drink, some pot, gloves because it could get messy. You looked for a coalminer, one of the older cars that were harder to clean afterward, instead of the stainless-steel dingdongs. You looked for a yard that wasn't hot, it became a communal kind of thing, three, four writers working on the same car, you each threw up your tag when the car was finished, you sometimes waited till the sun came up so you could see what you'd done during the night, it was satisfying. It was making a thing of beauty out of a rusting piece of shit.

There was one yard they all stayed away from back then, this was the yard they called the Screamer because there was supposed to be the ghost of a writer there who stepped on the third rail and died screaming in the night. Nobody wanted to go anywhere near that yard even though there were coalminers laid up all over the place there and all you had to do to get in was climb over this cyclone fence had no razor wire on it. His style back then was a combo of Bubble and Calm's Point, what he called Bubble Point, and what a lot of writers bit from him cause it was an easy style to imitate, he guessed, though it had taken him a while to evolve. The style was easily adaptable to two-tone pieces, color-blended burners, 3-D pieces, you threw up your marker in the corner afterward, everybody knew your name.

His style nowadays was more a wild style, he wasn't interested in anything but getting the name up, TMO, spray it all over the city so they'd know he was still out here, man. He'd racked up the paints he was carrying tonight, some of the old traditions were still alive, any writer didn't *steal* his paints wasn't a writer worth shit. Your experienced writer was an experienced racker, too. That didn't make him one of these *gang* assholes whose main occupation was dealing dope and beating up people and spraying walls to mark their territory. Like, man, you are now entering **DEADLY SAVAGE** turf! Or **Killer Psycho Tribe** territory, whatever dumb names they called themselves. You saw MM21 sprayed on a wall or markered on a train, no style at all, you knew it stood for the Macho Men from Twenty-first Street, they were telling you beware, man, this is the land of the super assholes! Cross out a gang tag, you were in serious trouble. Dealers, too. Dealers used their tags to mark drug territory. Don't come sellin' your shit on this corner, it belongs to Taco, you see the tag, man? No place left for a genuine writer to go anymore, no place at all.

Except that in the night . . .

Night like tonight . . .

You could still feel free and easy in the night.

Find yourself a wall wasn't too crowded, take your time doing a two-tone burner in Bubble Point. Be like old times. Free and easy in the empty hours of the night, smoke a little, drink a little, look over the piece, define it, refine it, and sign it TMO. For Timmo. Yeah.

The wall he had in mind was one he'd passed by late yesterday afternoon, almost virgin. Three or four bubble tags on it, no gang markers. He'd racked up a can of blue and a can of yellow, which when you put them close together you got a greenish look he favored. He had two rolled joints in the bag with the paint, and a ham sandwich he'd bought in the deli on Culver and Tenth, and a can of Coke, he was like set, man.

Five minutes later, he was like dead, man.

5.

Her alarm clock had a two-position switch. The first position caused the bedside lamp to flash when the alarm went off. The second position flashed the lamp and simultaneously turned on a vibrator under her pillow. Normally, the flashing lamp was enough to awaken her, but this morning she was taking no chances; the switch was set to the second position. The combination of flashing lamp and vibrating pillow woke her up in five seconds flat. She hit the OFF button before all that shaking and blinking woke up Carella, who grunted, muttered something unintelligible, and rolled away from the light an instant before it quit.

The LED display on the clock read 3:01 A.M.

It was still dark an hour later, when she left the house and began walking to the elevated subway station four blocks away. She was thinking that this section of Riverhead was still relatively safe, but she wasn't used to being abroad alone—or even a broad alone, she thought, and smiled—at this hour of the night. She walked as fast as she could, somehow comforted by the lights burning in the surrounding apartment buildings, even at this ungodly hour. People were awake. People were preparing to start the day. I'm *not* alone, she thought, even though she hadn't been out of the house at this hour since her high school prom, which she'd attended with the former Salvatore Di Napoli.

She expected the platform to be empty, but there were several other men and women standing on it waiting for the next train to come in, some of them wearing what she had been advised to wear, blue jeans and sneakers, and—at least in the case of one woman whose coat was hanging open—a blue T-shirt like the one the clinic had given Teddy yesterday, and which she was also wearing today. Lettered onto the front of the shirt were the words: PRO-CHOICE. She unbuttoned her coat now, revealing the shirt, and smiled at the woman in greeting. The woman smiled back. Both of them looked up the track for any sign of an incoming train. Nothing yet. Teddy figured the ride downtown would take about forty-five minutes, most of it on elevated tracks before the train plunged underground at the Grady Street station in lower Riverhead. She was due at the clinic at five sharp.

There was a scene in the movie *Viva Zapata!* that Teddy never tired of seeing, even though the musical accompaniment that was an integral part of it was lost on her. It was the long passage where Zapata and his brother are marching to the capital, or wherever they're going, this was Marlon Brando when he was young and handsome and Anthony Quinn when he was young and possibly even more handsome. And as they march along with a straggling little band of followers, both of them looking fiercely determined, peasants keep coming out of the hills to join them, and all of the peasants are wearing white trousers and shirts and big sombreros, and they keep pouring down out of the hills with machetes in their hands, joining this straggling little band of maybe ten, twenty people until finally there's an army of ten *thousand* behind them, all of them in those identifying white trousers and shirts.

It was like that on the subway this morning.

As the train rattled its way through the dark on the overhead tracks, the cars began filling with people on their way to work, yes, but they also began filling with people wearing the clinic's blue shirt with the PRO-CHOICE lettering on its front. Men and women alike, all of them wearing the shirt, until the little band of stragglers who had boarded the train at Teddy's stop became an army in uniform by the time the train reached the College

Street station on Isola's Upper South Side. Well, not an army the size of *Zapata's*, not *that* overwhelming mass of white flowing down out of the hills to join him, no, nothing quite that grand or impressive, but impressive enough to Teddy's eyes; at least a hundred people came up out of the College Street kiosk that morning, emerging from the dimness of the underground tunnel into the pale promising light of morngloam.

Sunrise was still an hour away as they gathered at the clinic to await the onslaught of the most fanatic faction of the anti-abortion movement, a self-styled "rescue" group funded by reactionaries and led by a pair of Catholic priests who in the past several years had been jailed far more often than they'd offered the host. Their tactics had been explained to Teddy yesterday at the last of the training and orientation meetings. As she assembled with the others, she felt totally prepared for anything that might come today.

She was wrong.

"Did your son know anyone named Timothy O'Laughlin?" Parker asked.

That was the name of the dead writer the blues had found at three o'clock this morning, just about when Teddy's alarm was starting to blink and shake her awake. It was now a little past eight, and Catalina Herrera was trying to get back to her typewriter. Her son had been buried yesterday, and it was time now to begin attacking the pile of manuscripts and correspondence that had accumulated on the small desk she'd set up near the kitchen window. Barefoot and wearing a black skirt and a white blouse recklessly unbuttoned some four buttons down from the top to expose the slopes of her generous breasts, she stood silhouetted in the window that now streamed early morning sunlight. It looked as if spring might actually have arrived at last. It was time to get on with her work. Time to try to get on with living her life again.

"No, I don' know thees name," she said.

"Timmo?" he said. "Does that ring a bell?"

"No, I don't know thees, too," she said.

The charming Spanish accent. Parker loved it. Listening to her voice, he smiled—though a third victim was certainly nothing to smile about.

He and Kling had been called at home at twenty minutes past three this morning because the guy lying on the sidewalk near the graffiti-covered wall of what used to be the Municipal Fish Market in the northeast corner of the precinct had been shot twice in the head and once through the hand and then spray-painted afterward. The bullet through the hand was probably the result of his having thrown it up in self-defense, thinking perhaps he was Superman and could stop speeding bullets. Whether or not *three* shots had been fired or merely *two*—with the same bullet going through the hand and then the upper lip—was a matter of conjecture. As had been the case with the previous two victims, there hadn't been any spent cartridges or bullets recovered at the scene, so nobody knew what kind of gun had been used except that it definitely wasn't an automatic, which would have spewed cartridge cases like cherry pits. Each of the victims had been shot at close range. The bullets had gone right on through, so either the techs weren't doing their jobs right or else the shooter had picked up after himself, like a conscientious citizen scooping up dog doo. Gathering bullets *and* cartridge cases if the gun had been an auto, bullets alone if it had been a revolver. A hunter and gatherer was the Graffiti Killer, as the tabloids had begun calling him.

"Mrs. Herrera," Parker said, "we now have . . . do you mind if I call you Catalina?" he said, pronouncing it "Cat-uh-leen-uh" and not the way she herself would have pronounced it, "Cah-tah-leen-ah."

"Cathy," she said, surprising Kling.

Parker blinked.

"My friends call me Cathy," she said.

"Cathy, good," Parker said, and nodded. "What I was saying, Cathy, is that we now have three victims of this person, including your son, which by the way I'm sorry I couldn't get to the funeral yesterday."

"*De nada*," she said.

So damn cute, the way they talked, he thought. The women.

"But we were busy trying to get a line on the second one," he said, "who doesn't seem to fit the picture, although we found cans of spray paint in his house. I never heard of a *closet* graffiti writer, did you, Bert?" Parker asked, pulling him into it, showing with a grin what a jovial and well-meaning fellow he was, unlike other police detectives Cathy may have known. Kling did not enjoy being an accomplice. Parker wanted to hit on the woman, let him do it on his own time.

"We found the paint in his *closet*," you see, Parker explained, though Kling guessed little Cathy here didn't know what a closet *anything* was, no less a closet graffiti writer. Still, Parker had explained his little joke, which showed his heart was in the right place. "But the guy's a lawyer, the second one, *was* a lawyer, thirty-eight years old, it turned out, with a wife thirty-five. You don't expect a person like that to be writing graffiti, do you?"

"Of cours' nah," Cathy said.

Holmes to Watson, Kling thought. Watson agreeing with the master sleuth's theory. In an accent you could slice with a machete.

"Your son never mentioned *his* name, did he happen to?"

"Wha' *wass* hees name?"

God, Parker loved the way she talked.

"Peter Wilkins," he said.

"No. I never heard this name before."

He was beginning to get bilingual, understanding every word she spoke. He wondered what she spoke in bed. He hoped she spoke Spanish. He wanted her to tell him all sorts of things in Spanish. Like how much she loved his cock in her Spanish mouth.

"So your son never mentioned *either* of them, is that right? What we're looking for, Catalina, *Cathy,* is some kind of connection between the three of them, someplace we can hang our hats, is what we call it in police work," he said, and smiled again.

Jee-sus! Kling thought.

"I don't know anything to help," she said.

It seemed clear to Kling that the woman had nothing further to contribute along these lines. The possibility was less than remote that her son had known *either* of the other two victims, one of them a lawyer, the other a veteran writer with a Criminal Mischief record. That's what writing graffiti was called in the law books—Criminal Mischief. Three degrees of it.

Crim Mis *One* was defined as: *With intent to do so and having no right to do so nor any reasonable ground to believe that one has such right, damaging property of another: 1. In an amount exceeding $1,500; OR 2. by means of an explosive.* This was a Class-D felony punishable by sentences ranging from a one-year minimum in prison to a seven-year max, unless you happened to be a sixteen-to-twenty-one-year-old toddler, in which case you could be sent to a reformatory instead.

The other two degrees of Criminal Mischief were determined by the value of the property damaged, more than $250 in the case of Crim Mis *Two,* a Class-E felony, and less than $250 in the case of Crim Mis *Three,* a mere Class-A misdemeanor. A Class-E felony was punishable by a min of one and a max of four with the same reformatory provision for so-called minors. A Class-A misdemeanor was punishable by no more than a year in prison or a thousand-dollar fine.

Kling was thinking that signs advising graffiti writers of the prison sentences they faced should be posted all over town.

Parker was saying, "What I'd like you to do, Cathy—when you finish your work here, I don't want to interfere with your work, I see you have a lot of work to do—I want you to make a list for me of all of your son's friends, so I can look them up and see whether there's a possibility here of one of them being the person responsible."

Kling was thinking that this was a dead end here. The Herrera kid seemed to be at the bottom of the pecking order, a simple "toy" in the hierarchy of graffiti writers. Timmo, on the other hand, had been a well-known writer back in the days when subway cars were being decorated top to bottom. God alone knew where the lawyer fit into the scheme of things. Was he some kind of nut who filed briefs during the daytime and then put on a Batman costume and went around spraying buildings at night? Either way, Kling figured the killer for some vigilante type choosing his victims at random.

"I'm working today and tomorrow, but I've got all day Sunday off," Parker said, and smiled into Cathy's open blouse. "We can spend the whole day together, if you like, going over the list. Do you think you'd like to do that? Cathy?"

And to Kling's everlasting surprise, she said, "Yes, I think that would be very nice, thank you, what time should I expect you?"

Charlie's clothes told the same story.

Or rather, they didn't tell any story at all.

Dr. Mookherji at St. Sebastian's Hospital had told Meyer that all the labels had been cut out of the old man's clothes, and Meyer had accepted the observation at face value. But Mookherji wasn't a cop, and Meyer was still looking for a place to hang his hat—as Parker might have put it—which was what took him back to St. Sab's that Friday.

True to Mookherji's word, the labels had been cut out of everything, including Charlie's bathrobe, his pajamas, and his bedroom slippers. Somebody had gone to a lot of trouble to make certain that neither of these two old people would be identified. Meyer had no real reason to believe that the dumpings were related, of course, except for the fact that he'd got an immediate response from the old woman when he'd described the man who'd dropped Charlie—"Buddy," she'd said at once. Not to mention the remarkably similar M.O.'s, guy drives off with each of them, dumps them in the middle of the night. . . .

"The slippers, too," he told the woman behind the counter, and sighed heavily. "Which wasn't easy, getting the labels out."

The woman nodded. She was thinking she'd have to refold all these clothes when he got through with them. Put them back in their proper bin.

"Well, thanks a lot," Meyer said, and gave the countertop a little farewell pat. "I appreciate your help."

"Did you want to see his blanket, too?" the woman asked.

They had told her the "rescue" workers would try to chain the doors of the clinic shut, looping a Kryptonite chain through the door handles, if that's the way the doors were constructed, and then fastening the links with a Kryptonite lock. If the doors were fashioned differently—say a simple flush metal door with a dead-bolt keyway in it, or possibly a metal door with a wire-embedded glass panel in the upper half—they would try other ways to bar access to the clinic. They would chain themselves together, for example, and lie down in the walk leading to the entrance door so that if the police tried to remove them, they would be struggling with lifting or dragging twelve bodies chained together instead of a single body.

The idea was to make certain no one got in or out. Not the doctors who were murdering babies inside there, and not the girls or women who were carrying unwanted babies and who were seeking medical assistance to terminate their pregnancies—as was their right under the law of the land. The rescue group gathered outside the clinic this morning had deliberately chosen this location only three blocks from the Claremore College for Girls. Their strategy was to bring home the fact that many of the so-called *women* seeking abortions weren't women at all but were, in fact, merely uninformed *girls*. These girls had to be taught that they were not exercising a right concerning their own bodies but were instead usurping a fundamental right of another human being—the fetus in the womb—trampling upon that right in the most fundamental way, terminating the *life* of that human being, *murdering* that human being. Once this was made clear to the young girls in this country, why, then and only then could the slaughter of the unborn innocent be stopped.

None of these rescuers seemed to realize that abortion was *legal*, that they were attempting to stop people from doing something that was entirely *legal*. In their interference and harassment, they had been supported by a president who—though sworn to uphold the laws of the land—had given succor to them by telephoning whenever they were disrupting a clinic and telling them how much he admired their position. To Teddy's way of thinking, this was akin to the Commissioner of Police calling a bank robber while he was inside a bank holding hostages and telling him how much he respected the courageous stand he was taking.

They usually hit the clinics before dawn.

Chained the doors shut, nailed them shut, anything to prevent access, anything to make it more difficult for someone in desperate need of help. Sometimes they got inside the clinics and chained themselves to radiators or heavy pieces of furniture, the better to disrupt the entirely legal activities within. Mischief was the name of the game. Do their mischief, create their havoc, make it so difficult to pursue a legal right that eventually the right would erode and the small minority of people hoping to destroy it would have triumphed.

Frequently, their mischief was illegal.

Targeting a doctor who performed abortions, telephoning him and screaming the word "Murderer!" into his ear was considered a crime in most states of the union. In this state, it was called Aggravated Harassment, and it was a Class-A misdemeanor, punishable by the same year in prison and/or thousand-dollar fine a graffiti writer could get for vandalizing a building. Calling that same doctor, reeling off the names of his children, and asking how they were feeling today, was the sort of veiled threat many states considered the crime of Coercion—which in this state was a Class-D felony, three to seven in the slammer, correct. Printing posters with an innocent doctor's name and picture and the words WANTED FOR MURDER on them was in most states called "libel," which, while not a crime, was a tort for which a person could seek punitive damages in court.

That morning at twenty minutes past ten, a man demonstrating outside the abortion clinic committed *two* crimes in rapid succession—*three* if you counted the fact that he had ignored the court order prohibiting him from coming any closer than fifteen feet of the police barricade.

The first crime was called simple Harassment, as opposed to the *aggravated* kind. This was a mere violation, for which all the perpetrator could expect was fifteen days in jail. This was defined as "engaging in a course of conduct or repeatedly committing acts which alarm or seriously annoy another person and which serve no legitimate purpose." The specific action in which the man was engaged happened to be repeatedly shouting the word "Murderer!" into a woman's face from six inches away.

The second crime was more serious.

It consisted of hurling a bag of blood into that same woman's face from six inches away.

The woman was Teddy Carella.

The man was wearing a black suit, and a black shirt, and a white collar.

He called himself a priest.

Tossing the blood still might have been simple harassment had it not damaged *property*. As it was, the blood drenched not only Teddy's face and her hair and her neck but it *also* soaked the front of the PRO-CHOICE T-shirt—$6.99 including the lettering when purchased in bulk, but property nonetheless—and this escalated the crime into a Crim Mis Three and the penalty to a possible year behind bars. The priest who threw the open plastic bag of blood at Teddy may not have known this, or might not have cared. He simply shouted, "Suffer the blood of the children!" and tossed the blood into her face. Teddy was totally unprepared for the sudden splash of foul-smelling stuff and for a moment thought this was actually *human* blood, and then correctly deduced that it couldn't possibly be human blood, it had to be some kind of animal blood that had been allowed to sit unrefrigerated in order to achieve its present odious stench, dripping from her hair and down her face, and tasting vile where it touched her lips.

She had removed her coat and left it inside the clinic because the day had turned sunny and bright and mild, spring *was* truly here at last, though no one might have guessed from the anger roiling outside this place. The PRO-CHOICE T-shirt was short-sleeved, so there was nothing she could immediately use to wipe the blood from her face. As she fumbled for a possible tissue in the back pocket of her jeans, the priest put his face close to hers again and began screaming what sounded like a litany, flecks of spittle flying from his lips to mingle with the blood on her face.

"Taste the blood of the children!" he shouted. "Taste the blood of the innocent children, *murderer* who would slaughter them! Taste the blood of the unborn innocent, *murderer* who would pluck them from their mothers' sacred wombs! Taste the blood of the defenseless progeny, slain by the *murderers* who would deny them birth! Drink the blood of the blessed unborn, fruit of the mother whose holy vessel the *murderers* would violate! Taste of the blood, drink of the blood, drown the *murderers'* evil quest in the innocent blood of the issue torn from the sanctity and purity of all womankind! *Murderers*, give the children *life*! *Murderers*, give the children *life*! *Murderers*, give the children *life*!"

And now a handful of anti-abortion protesters formed behind their frocked leader in a tight semicircle, the focal point of which was Teddy, for she was the one streaming blood, she was the one they'd singled out to drench in blood, to target as the symbolic murderer of innocent children, she was the focus of their chanting now, eight of them standing shoulder to shoulder, pointing fingers in accusation and shouting in unison, *"Murderers, give the children life! Murderers, give the children life! Murderers, give the children life! Murderers, give the children life!"*

She could find no tissue in her pocket.

The blood kept streaming down her face.

Sonny Sanson was what he'd told Carter his name was, but Carter didn't believe it for a minute. Big tall guy, blond, with a hearing aid in his ear, he'd make a good leading man if only he wasn't deaf—*hearing*-impaired, excuse me, everything had to be so politically *correct* these days. It sometimes drove Carter crazy, trying to remember what was acceptable and what wasn't; fuckin *broads,* it was all their fault. When he was in the slammer, a deaf man was a *deaf* man, period.

"The trouble with these uniforms you rent from costume supply houses," the deaf man was saying, "is they all look fake."

Carter tended to agree with him.

Carter didn't like the idea to begin with—going in as a *garbage* man, which is what he gathered this was going to be—but he tended to agree that the stuff you rented always looked like it was for a summer-stock production of *My Sister Eileen* or *Arsenic and Old Lace* or *The Price* or *Guys and Dolls* or *West Side Story,* none of which had *garbage* men in them. Carter knew. Before he'd got caught dealing dope—on a very minor level, by the way—he used to be an actor. In fact, he'd played Officer Krupke in *West Side Story* and Officer Brophy in *Arsenic and Old Lace,* and he'd been up for the role of the cop brother in the Miller play, he couldn't recall the name of the character, for a production they were doing at the Provincetown Playhouse, if he remembered correctly. It just went to show, you could play a hundred cops on the stage, it didn't make a fuckin difference if they decided to bust you.

This deaf man here—Sanson, whatever his name was—knew that Carter had done time—for such a lowball operation, too, selling dope to the kids in *Sound of Music*—and he also knew that Carter had done some acting, which is what Carter supposed had caught his attention in the first place, the fact that he'd had acting experience—well, singing, too, for that matter. From what Carter could gather, the deaf man's scheme had something to do with impersonating *garbage* men. Which was why he needed the uniforms. And this probably involved eyeball-to-eyeball contact, like theater in the round, which was why the uniforms couldn't look fake. Carter was waiting to hear more about it, saying nothing for the moment, just listening. He had learned that the best actors in the world were also the best listeners.

"Which is why we'll have to *steal* them," the deaf man said. "The uniforms."

"You plan to steal sanitation-department uniforms," Carter said.

Deadpan delivery, like a take in itself, he'd learned that a long time ago. You just blankly repeated a man's words, it made them sound preposterous.

"Yes," Sonny said. "Or rather, I was hoping *you'd* steal them for me."

"You want me to steal sanitation-department uniforms," Carter said.

No emphasis on any of the words, just repeating the man's statement flat out, deadpanned and dead-eyed, you want me to steal sanitation-department uniforms, like a *double* take this time.

"Yes," the deaf man said.

"From off the backs of garbage men?" Carter asked, and smiled, making a little joke, heh-heh.

"If that's what it requires, yes."

"Must be some other way to get them," Carter said.

"I'm not too sure about that."

"Without stealing them."

"Stealing is sometimes the easiest way."

"Stealing could also fuck up a job from minute one. You do something stupid like stealing *garbage* man uniforms, it could make the whole thing explode in your face. Which I don't suppose you want to happen."

"No."

"So how many uniforms will you need?"

"Four of us will be going in."

"Who are these four people? Cause I'll need sizes, you realize."

"Of course."

"So who are they?"

"You, me, a man named Florry Paradise . . ."

"Florry Paradise."

Same deadpan delivery.

"Yes, and another man yet to be selected."

"How risky is this thing going to be?" Carter asked and gave him The Look. He had cultivated The Look when he was playing a small-time drug dealer in an episode of *Miami Vice;* this was before he himself became a real-life small-time drug dealer and got sent away on a five-and-dime, reduced to two-and-a-half for good behavior and an Academy Award performance before the parole board during which he convinced them that acting was a legitimate form of making a worthwhile contribution to society. Actually, he hadn't acted a lick since he'd got out six years ago. Actually, he'd drifted into burglary was what he'd done, the things a man can learn in prison if only he pays attention. The Look said I am a reasonable man, so don't fuck with me.

"*Because,*" he said, still wearing The Look, "the riskier this is, the more money I want for the part, the uh participation."

"That's understandable," the deaf man said. "So suppose I tell you up front exactly what I'll need from you, and then you can tell me whether or not you feel the risk is worth whatever it is I'm willing to pay for your participation, isn't that the word you used?"

"Yes," Carter said.

He had the feeling he was being put on, the fuckin hearing-impaired jackass.

"So tell me what you need," he said.

"First the uniforms. Four in all. I don't care if you buy them or steal them or find them under a rock. You know your own size, I'll give you mine and Florry's, and I'll have the other one for you by the end of the week."

"What are you thinking here? A wheel man and three to go in?"

"Something like that."

"Cause I know a good wheel man, if you need one. Guy I met in the joint. Very good. Hands like a brain surgeon. He can drive you in and out of a pay toilet without putting in a quarter."

"Can he drive a garbage truck?"

"A what?"

"A garbage truck."

"What kind of heist *is* this, anyway?"

"A very big one."

"With just four men involved?"

"That's all it'll take."

"What kind of security are we talking about?"

"Virtually none."

"Like what? What does virtually none mean?"

"A handful of policemen at most."

"Does this involve taking out cops? Cause I have to tell you, I draw the line at doing cops. Except on the English-speaking stage, if you follow me."

"I don't plan on injuring any policemen."

"But does the possibility exist?"

"Yes, it does. If things go *very* very wrong. But I don't . . ."

"That's what I . . ."

". . . expect anything . . ."

". . . meant. Taking out a cop . . ."

". . . to go wrong."

"Well, you never know. And what I'm trying to say, you box

a cop, you never get the bastards off your back. They'll hound you till you're old and gray, those bastards. They stick up for their own, it's like a fuckin *tribe* they've got."

"I recognize the risks."

"I'm glad you do. I don't mean the uniforms. For all I know you can walk in some store and buy them right off the rack. It's not like a police uniform, where it could mean trouble if the wrong person got hold of it. Who the hell would want to wear a *garbage* man's uniform except a *garbage* man?"

"Me," the deaf man said, and smiled.

"And me, apparently. And two *other* guys."

"Correct."

"One on the wheel . . ."

"Yes, and another on the front seat beside him."

"And the other two?"

"Hanging off the truck. The way garbage men do."

"We're going to ride a garbage truck to a bank stickup, right?"

"No, we're not going to stick up a bank. This is so much simpler. But yes, we'll be using a garbage truck."

"Where are we going to *get* this garbage truck?"

"I'm afraid you'll have to steal one."

"Here we go with the risk element again," Carter said. "The uniforms, I'm not too worried about. A garbage truck is another thing again. You can't just walk off with a fuckin *garbage* truck. That's taking a very big risk, ripping off something as big as a garbage truck. In *size*, I mean."

"But I heard you're very good."

"Sure, breaking into an apartment, opening a wall safe, like that. But the biggest thing I ever stole—I'm talking about *size* now, physical *size*, not value—the biggest thing was a bronze lamp supposed to come from some Egyptian museum, it turned out it was as queer as a turnip, it brought me twenty bucks from my fence. This big bronze thing like an elephant. Twenty bucks, can you believe it? I nearly got a hernia carrying it out. But a garbage truck? I never stole a garbage truck in my life."

"Maybe you can just borrow one."

Another smile. Big fuckin joke here, stealing a garbage truck.

"Big risk, a garbage truck," Carter said, and gave him The Look again.

"Yes. That's why I'm willing to pay you fifty thousand dollars for this part of the job alone."

Carter swallowed.

"What does the *rest* of the job entail?" he asked.

Fox Hill was a town in Elsinore County on Sands Spit, some sixty-odd miles outside the city. The town had originally been named Vauxhall by the British, after the district of that name in the borough of Lambeth in London, but over the years the name had become Americanized—some might say bastardized—to its present form. The county had also been named by a British colonist well versed in the works of his most illustrious countryman. Nobody knew who had named Sands Spit.

Fox Hill had been a sleepy little fishing village until as recently as forty years ago, when an enterprising gentleman from Los Angeles came east to open what was then called the Fox Hill Inn, a huge rambling waterfront hotel that had since fallen into different hands and been renamed the Fox Hill Arms. The building of the hotel had also been responsible for the building of a town around it, rather the way a frontier fort in the dear, dead days eventually led to a settlement around it. Fox Hill was now a community of some forty thousand people, thirty thousand of them year-round residents, ten thousand known alternately as "the summer people" or, less affectionately, "the Sea Gulls."

Herman Friedlich was a year-round resident.

At five forty-five P.M. on that Friday, the twenty-seventh day of March, Friedlich called the Fox Hill Police Department to say that he'd left his 1987 smoky-blue Acura Legend coupe outside the Grand Union supermarket while he went inside for a bottle of milk, and when he came out the car was gone.

The police officer to whom he'd reported this was Detective Sergeant Andrew Budd.

"Was the car locked?" Budd asked.

"No, I was just going in for a minute," Friedlich said. "I got caught on the damn checkout line."

You jackass, Budd thought.

6.

Thing Sil liked to do best was work by the window. Sit by the window, look down at the street, watch the people going by, write his words about the people. He still lived in Diamondback, better apartment than he used to live in with his mother and three sisters when he was just coming along. Close to the uptown edge of the park here. Look out the window, watch the people, write about the people. Difference between a rock group, no matter how lofty they played, and a rap crew was that the rapper was a social commentator, the rapper was writing about the people, telling the people what it was like to be *black*. You got some of your white rappers, they *tried*, man, they got the beat right and they got the words *almost* right, but the protest was plastic, man, they didn't know what it was *like*.

If you weren't black, you didn't know what it was *like* to be black, you couldn't even begin to *imagine* what it was like. So whatever you wrote sympathetic about being black, why this was suspect, man, because without the pain thing you just didn't grab the *main* thing. Being black was all about pain. Striving to rise above the daily pain. Or giving in to the pain, letting it take over, letting it lead you to ways that were unpro*duct*ive, man, the choice was always there. This was what he tried to write in his songs, how the people had inside them the power to rise above the pain, *be* something. So when he wrote something like . . .

> *Dig the pig, man . . .*
> *Dig the big pig, man . . .*
> *See how he strut, man . . .*
> *Kickin yo butt, man.*
> *Wanna be a pig, man?*
> *Wanna join the force, man?*
> *Wanna take the life force outta yo own*
>   *force?*
> *Wanna kick some butt, man, wanna kiss*
>   *some butt, man?*
> *Go put on the blue, man, cover up the black,*
>   *man, fo' get that you a black man, juss go*
>   *be a pig, man . . .*

When he wrote something like that, he wasn't saying the police were no good, he was only saying that for a black man to join the police was for the *black* man to become a traitor to his own people because it was the police holding down the people, it was the police looking the other way while the dealers did their thing on every street corner in every black hood in this city, looking the other way while the kids got poisoned and the fat fuckin wops in Sicily and the fat fuckin spics in Colombia got richer and fatter doing their thing.

Wasn't a law-enforcement officer in the world didn't know how this thing worked. More cocaine in America now than there was vanilla ice cream, the nation's *favorite* flavor . . .

> *You dig vanilla?*
> *Now ain't that a killer!*
> *You say you hate chocolate?*
> *I say you juss thoughtless.*
> *Cause chocolate is the color*
> *Of the Lord's first children*
> *Juss go ask the diggers . . .*
> *The men who find the bones*
> *Go ask them 'bout chocolate . . .*
> *Go ask them 'bout niggers . . .*

That was another one of his songs. Got up to seventeen on the charts, never went higher because they didn't understand the archeo*log*ical shit in it, the proof that the first man on earth was a black man, standing tall and proud a hundred light years from a gorilla. You got your kids dropping out of school in the seventh grade, the fuck they knew about scientists digging up the bones of the first man and he's a black African like you and me.

No pain back then.

Just went around doing your thing, hunted, fished, picked berries from the bushes and plants from the ground, moved with your group from place to place, living off the land, no drug dealer standing on a street corner offering you goodies cheap, this was before pain was invented. Wasn't a law-enforcement officer alive who didn't know how the triangle worked. America was saturated with cocaine now, there was hardly room for anybody else to snort even another tiny little *speck* of cocaine up his nose or inhale another puff of crack, which was base cocaine, as if you didn't know, man. Everybody *wanting* to do coke was *already* doing coke, just ask your kid sister. That's why you could get a six-bit hit now, try to get new customers that way. He sometimes thought the entire country was one big fuckin crack house spreading from New York to L.A. and every place in between. Which is where the triangle came in. The Colombians needed new markets for their goods, so what better place to go than Europe? Spit Shine played a gig in London at the Palladium last fall, Sil asked one of the other musicians—a brother who lived in Bloomsbury, wherever *that* was—asked him if there was any crack in London, the brother said the police here had *heard* of it but they'd never actually *seen* it. The brother was on hashish. Heroin, man. Hoss was still the big thing in Europe.

So that was the arrangement, that was the triangle. The Mafia was bringing in opium from the East and turning it into heroin, and the Colombian cartel was growing the coca plant and turning it into cocaine. So down the line all these ships arrive in Sicily and they offload cocaine and onload heroin. In Europe,

the cocaine is turned into crack—look what *we* got, kiddies,
a whole new thing for you to try along with democracy! And
in the United States, a bag of H is sold for five slim ones,
reviving a market that had begun to die when crack became
all the rage. In no time at all, brothers and sisters would be
begging for it all over again. Unless someone like Sil explained
in his words that the only thing the wops and the spics had
to offer the black man was contempt. The same contempt the
Jew had for anyone who wasn't lily-white vanilla. Sil wouldn't
be surprised if when they got to the bottom of the triangulation,
it turned out a Jew was running the whole show. Try to tell
any white man about a black man's pain. Try even explaining
it to somebody black as you were, but with a name like Gomez
or Sanchez, which took the curse off it, made it sound like
you were descended from Spanish nobility instead of somebody
carried here in chains on a slave ship. The pain. Try to explain
it. Write about it.

He wrote on a lined yellow pad, looking out his window. It
was another sunny day like yesterday. Saturday morning, lots
of people out there enjoying the sun, heading out to do their
chores . . .

Dealer standing there on the corner of Ainsley where it joined
the park . . .

People jogging or cycling in the park . . .

Not too many whites ventured this far uptown in the park.

His pencil was poised over the pad.

He saw a black woman in jogging shorts and a tank top walk
into the park and then begin running the moment she was inside
the wall, almost as if a starter's pistol had been fired.

He began writing:

Black woman, black woman, oh yo eyes so black,
Tho yo skin wants color, why is that, tell me that.
Why is that, black woman, don't confuse me tonight . . .

* * *

They had buried Peter Wilkins at ten-thirty this morning, and now the funeral party was back in the three-story brownstone on Albermarle Street, partaking of the coffee, sandwiches, and cakes that relatives and neighbors had set out on the long dining-room table. There were perhaps two dozen people gathered in the living room when Kling arrived at a little before noon. He located Debra Wilkins standing in a circle of several other people, one of whom he determined was the minister who'd delivered the graveside eulogy and who was now modestly accepting compliments on how wonderful it had been.

Debra's green eyes were streaked with red, and her eyelids were swollen. She stood listening to the others, nodding, a pained, numbed look on her face. Kling caught her eye. Recognizing him, she came to him at once.

"Have you . . . has there been any . . . ?" she started, and he told her immediately that there hadn't been any significant developments in the case, and he knew this was a bad time, but there were some questions he would like to ask her, if that was all right with her. Otherwise, he could come back some other time. She said now would be fine, and asked him if he would like a cup of coffee, something to eat. He told her No, thanks, this would just take a few minutes. They sat on chairs that had been arranged against the wall at the far end of the room. Everywhere around them there was the hushed conversation peculiar to these ritual gatherings. The people in this room were here less to honor the dead than to pay tribute to the living. Life goes on, these tribal meetings said. That was their essence and their importance. But the voices here were not raised in celebration; they were simply lowered in recognition. Kling, too, lowered his voice.

"Mrs. Wilkins," he said, "when I called you yesterday, you told me you'd never heard the name Timothy O'Laughlin, and you were positive he wasn't anyone your husband had known. I'm beginning to think there *is* no link between the victims, they were simply chosen at random, which is why I'd like to know a little more about where your husband actually *went* the night he was killed.''

Debra nodded. This was still very difficult for her. He hated having to talk to her just now, but time was rushing by, and whoever had killed three people was still out there someplace.

''You said he was going to a movie . . .''

''Yes.''

''Told you he was going to a movie . . .''

''Yes.''

''I checked the schedule for the theater you gave us, and the show he would have caught—if he left here at eight-thirty—the next show would have been at nine, and it would've let out at eleven. Coroner's Office has estimated the postmortem interval . . . they have ways of determining the time of death, you see, I don't even know how they figure it myself, and I've been a cop for a long time now. I hate to be talking about this, Mrs. Wilkins, but I have to, I hope you understand that.''

''Yes, please don't worry. I want to help in any way I can.''

''Well, thank you, I appreciate that. But they can't be *exact* about how many hours elapse since the time of death, even though they usually come pretty close. So when they say the time of death was around midnight, it could just as easily have been eleven, when the movie let out. The thing that keeps bothering me is why he went all the way over to Harlow Street, over there near the parkway. I asked the coroner if the body might have been moved . . . yes, they can determine that, too, in some instances,'' he said, ''don't ask me how. It has something to do with the position of the body, the way the blood gathers in certain parts of the body, which—if the body is then *moved* and placed in another position—the earlier lividity, I think they call it, wouldn't jibe with the new position. I'm not a doctor, I'm sorry, I just take for granted whatever they tell me on the autopsy report.''

''I understand.''

"But in this case, they weren't able to tell whether the murder had taken place where your husband was found or whether he was transported there. There wasn't much blood on the sidewalk, which there would've been if that was where he'd been shot, but it was raining all night, and it could've got washed away. In any case, they don't know if that was the murder scene or not. The coroner couldn't tell from just the autopsy, and the techs didn't find anything at the scene that would have indicated the body was moved. So we've got to assume that's where the murder was committed, which brings me back to why he went all the way over there to Harlow Street from Stemmler Avenue—in the pouring rain, no less."

"I can't understand it," she said.

"He wasn't carrying any paint when he left the apartment, was he?"

"Honestly, I didn't notice. I was in the bathtub when he left."

"Ah," Kling said.

"He poked his head in, said he'd be back a little after eleven, and I said okay, see you later, something like that, and he was gone. I was getting ready for bed, you see. I usually take a bath around eight-thirty, nine o'clock, and then get in bed and read till the news comes on at ten. I'm usually asleep by eleven."

"But not that night."

"Pardon?"

"You told us you called the police at midnight. . . ."

"Yes, when Peter hadn't come home."

"Were you waiting up for him?"

"Yes. That is, I was in bed, but I knew he'd be coming home, so I wasn't *sleeping,* if that's what you mean."

"Yes, I meant awake. I didn't mean sitting up in the living room or anything."

"I was awake, yes," she said. "But in bed."

"And when he *didn't* come home, you called the police."

"Yes."

"At around midnight, you said."

"I think it was *exactly* midnight. The clock was bonging. The one in the living room."

"Did you ever see those cans of paint in his closet? I mean, before we found them the other day."

"Never."

"Do you have your own closet?"

"Yes.'

"Never hung anything in his closet? Put anything in his closet?"

"Never."

"So those cans were as much a surprise to you as they were to us."

"A total surprise."

"He wasn't working on any art project of any kind, was he?"

"No. He didn't have any inclinations along those lines."

"Or a woodworking project. Something he might have planned to paint later on."

"No, nothing like that."

"I'll tell you," Kling said, "it's hard to believe your husband was one of these writers . . . these graffiti writers . . . but I can't think of anything else that would have taken him over to Harlow Street. You don't have any *friends* on Harlow Street, do you?"

"No."

"I didn't think so. That stretch near the highway approach isn't a particularly nice area." He thought for a moment, looked at her, and said, "Mrs. Wilkins, I know my partner was a little clumsy about this the other day, but it's something I have to ask you now. Do you have any reason to believe your husband might have been involved with another woman?"

"A woman who lives on *Harlow* Street?" she asked, beginning to bristle.

"A woman who lives anywhere," Kling said levelly.

"I have no reason to believe that," Debra said.

"Do you have any idea at *all* as to why he would have gone over to that wall on Harlow Street?"

"None."

"A *graffiti*-covered wall."

"I don't know why he went there."

"In the rain."

"In the rain," she repeated. "He told me he'd be coming home straight after the movie. He told me he'd be home a little after eleven. I don't know how he ended up dead . . . in the rain . . . on that street. I just don't know," she said, and began crying.

Kling waited.

"I'm sorry," she said.

"That's okay," he said. "I know how difficult . . ."

"Debra?"

The voice was soft, polite, seemingly unwilling to intrude. Kling turned. He saw a slender man some five feet eleven inches tall, wearing a brown suit and brown shoes, a white button-down shirt, and a striped gold-and-brown tie. Some thirty-five years old, Kling guessed. Unhandsome, his plain, craggy face somehow conveying a sense of dependability. He had a mustache, and he was wearing eyeglasses. Behind the glasses, his eyes were the color of the dark suit. It looked as if he, too, might have been crying. The look in his eyes certainly gave that impression. There was ineffable sadness there, unbearable grief. When he spoke again, it was in that same soft voice, as if he were whispering in church.

"I have to go now, Debra," he said.

He extended both hands to her. Took her hands in his.

"You know how sorry I am," he said.

She nodded.

They embraced.

She was crying again.

"I don't know what we'll do without him," he said, and clutched her to him. She nodded into his shoulder, the tears flowing freely down her face. "Call me if you need anything," he said, holding her at arm's length now, looking down into her tearful face. "All right?"

"Yes," she said. "Thank you, Jeff."

"Call me," he said again, and patted her hand, and then nodded to Kling in farewell, and worked his way through the crowd of mourners to the front door.

"My husband's partner," she said. "Jeff Colbert. I don't know what I'd have done without him. He's been marvelous."

"Mrs. Wilkins," Kling said, "I'll say the same thing he said. Call me. If you think of anything, however unimportant it may seem, call me." He took out his wallet, found a card, handed it to her. "Any time of the day or night," he said. "The message will get to me."

"Thank you," she said.

"Either my partner or I will stay in touch," he said, and wondered where the hell Parker was.

Teddy hadn't seen Eileen Burke since she'd begun therapy, and the change in her now was virtually miraculous. Where earlier there had been a troubled police detective who couldn't seem to reconcile her professional life with her personal life, there was now a woman who seemed in complete control of both. Wearing blue jeans and a green blazer that matched the color of her eyes, Eileen sat opposite her in the Chinese restaurant they'd chosen, her hands flashing across the table. She had learned to sign a little.

For you, she signed. *Because we're friends.*

The signing was shaky, but well intentioned. Moreover, like many people learning a foreign language—which, in a sense, signing was—Eileen could understand it better than she could speak it. Teddy was grateful for that; she had a lot to tell her.

The two women would have attracted attention even if they hadn't been signing. Neither of them would ever have thought this of herself, but each was startlingly beautiful in her own Irish way, Eileen with her fair complexion and fiery red hair, Teddy with her dark eyes and black hair. But the fact that they were signing to each other across the table, their fingers excitedly flying—well, Eileen's weren't quite *soaring*, but she was trying—captured the interest of the largely Chinese clientele lunching here.

Teddy was telling her what had happened outside the clinic yesterday. Eileen watched her fingers. She was signing more slowly than she might have with her husband or her children, but the fire in her eyes conveyed the excitement she felt in recalling the incident. Teddy was saying that the people planning the clinic defense had briefed them against engaging in any physical or verbal dialogue, or any other conduct that would escalate the potential for violence. She signed the words now: *Verbal dialogue*.

The irony had not been lost on her, nor was it lost on Eileen now. Teddy could not have answered the taunts hurled at her even if she'd chosen to.

I stood there with the blood running down my face, she signed . . .

. . . running down her neck and her shoulders and into the crew neck of the T-shirt, her eyes locked with the priest's eyes for he was the one leading the verbal assault, he was the one directing the chanting as though conducting a church choir, seeing the hurtful words on his lips, the contorted faces of the others, the sheer *volume* of the attack lost on her, but this they did not know. Their words were literally falling on deaf ears.

She would neither yield nor bend.

The men and women who had come here today to defend the clinic stood shoulder to shoulder with her, and turned their smoldering eyes onto the nine whose frenzy seemed to rise in direct proportion to the silence Teddy would have kept in any event, but which she was incapable of breaking then or any other time. Her gaze fixed, her mouth set, she stared directly into the face

of the priest who'd thrown the blood. Behind him, the sky was
bluer than any there'd been so far this spring—"*Murderers*, give
the children *life*! *Murderers*, give the children . . ."

"The sons of bitches," Eileen said, and tried to sign it, but
Teddy had already read her lips.

Her own fingers were moving again.

For twenty minutes they . . .

. . . tried to provoke a response from her, nine of them in a
tight semicircle, raping her with their taunting shouts while the
blood caked around her eyes and in the curves and ridges of her
unhearing ears and at the corners of her mouth. The PRO-CHOICE
shirt was sticky with blood, its blue turned purple from the
infusion of red.

She kept staring into the priest's dark eyes.

It was such a beautiful spring day, she signed now.

Eileen looked at her. Green eyes wide in expectation.

So? she signed.

This she knew how to sign.

Simple word.

So?

Teddy opened her eyes as wide as Eileen's, and raised her
eyebrows and her shoulders in remembered surprise.

They simply left! she signed.

"Good," Eileen whispered, and nodded. She clumsily signed
You did it, girl, and reached across the table to take Teddy's
hands in her own.

Teddy smiled.

Yep, the smile said.

She didn't even have to sign it.

The woman who opened the door of the white clapboard house
on Merriwether Lane was in her seventies, Budd guessed. White-
haired and stooped, wearing absurdly large eyeglasses whose
frames glittered with what appeared to be sequins, she peered at

his detective shield and I.D. card, and then said, "Yes, sir, how can I help you?"

"This is my partner," he said, "Detective Dellarosa."

"Yes?"

Somewhat impatiently. Seventy fuckin years old, Budd thought, in a big hurry to go someplace.

"May we come in, please?" he asked.

"What's this about?" she asked.

"Does a man named Rubin Shanks live here?"

"He does."

"We'd like to ask him a few questions, please."

"My husband isn't fit to answer any questions," she said.

"Can you tell me *your* name, ma'am?"

"Margaret Shanks."

"Mrs. Shanks, we've been talking to the man runs the Shell station downtown on Laker? He says he gave your husband a lift back here two days ago. . . ."

"Yes?"

"Did he?"

"What's this about?" she said again.

"It's about your husband leaving a blue 1987 Acura Legend coupe at that Shell station yesterday."

"I don't know anything about that," she said.

"Man there says the car was pushed in cause your husband couldn't get it started. He left it there with his keys and the man drove him home. Is that right, ma'am?"

"We don't own a blue car."

"What kind of car *do* you own, ma'am?"

"A black one."

"What year and make, ma'am?"

"I don't know what this is all about."

"What year and make, ma'am?"

"A 1987 Acura."

"Would it be a Legend, ma'am?"

"Yes."

"A coupe?"

"Yes."

"Can you tell me where that car is now?"

"Right here in the garage."

"Ma'am, we'd really like to talk to your husband, if that's okay with you."

"I told you, my husband isn't..."

"Who's that, Meg?"

The detectives looked past her to where a white-haired, balding man appeared behind her left shoulder. He, too, was wearing eyeglasses. He seemed older than the woman, closer to eighty, Budd guessed.

"It's no one," she said. "Go back to your television."

"Well, who is it?" he insisted.

Tall, brawny man, must've been a bruiser when he was young. Looking out at them now from behind the thick-lensed glasses, puzzled look on his face.

"Fox Hill Police," Dellarosa said. "Okay to come in, sir?"

"I told you he..."

"Sure, come on in. Something happen? Was there an accident?"

"He really can't..."

"Come on in, have some coffee," he said, and the cops stepped past Mrs. Shanks and into the house. Absent the invitation, they'd have needed a warrant. Now they were legal.

The house was simply furnished. Little development house that must've cost them twenty thousand dollars when they'd bought it forty, fifty years ago, worth a hundred grand or more now. The television set was going. One of the soap operas. Big heads talking sexual innuendo. America in the daytime.

"Are you Rubin Shanks?" Budd asked.

The man blinked. His eyes behind the glasses looked totally bewildered.

"Meg?" he said.

"You're Rubin Shanks," she told him.

He didn't seem convinced. Blinked again behind his eye-glasses, looked to her for confirmation. She nodded *Yes,* patiently but irritably.

"Mr. Shanks," Budd said, "do you know the Shell station downtown on Laker Street?"

"I certainly do," Shanks said. "Meg, would you bring these fellers some coffee? How do you take your coffee, fellers?"

"There isn't any coffee," she said.

"Why don't you make some coffee for them, hon? Take a few minutes, fellers, if you don't mind wai . . ."

"Thank you, but that's okay, Mr. Shanks, we just want to ask you a few questions," Budd said.

"What about?"

"Did you push a car into that service station yesterday afternoon?"

"What service station?"

"The one on Laker."

"Laker?"

"Laker Street. Downtown."

"Oh. Oh. Yesterday. Was I downtown yesterday, Meg?"

"You were downtown," she said.

"Right, right," he said, "it was two young fellers who pushed me. Right. I couldn't get it started. They helped me get it to the service station."

"Car wouldn't start for you, is that it?" Budd asked.

"*Key* wouldn't turn," Shanks said, and shrugged. "Couldn't get it to turn at the station, neither, they figured there was something wrong with where you put the key in. What do you call that, Meg? Where you put the key in?"

"The ignition," she said.

"Figured it was frozen or something."

"Uh-huh," Budd said, and looked at his partner.

"What were you doing in town?" Dellarosa asked.

"Went to see my buddies down the Parade."

"The Parade Bar? Down there on Laker?"

"Yessir. Stopped in to say hello to some of my old navy buddies."

"Were you drinking, Mr. Shanks?"

"Nossir, I was not. Just drove downtown to say hello to some of my buddies, is all."

"He drive that car all the time, ma'am?" Budd asked.

"I tell him not to," she said. "He won't listen."

"Been driving since I was sixteen," Shanks said.

"When you went to that bar, sir, do you remember where you parked your car?"

"What bar?"

"The Parade, sir. Where you said you went yesterday."

"Is that where I went, Meg?"

"That's what you told them, Rubin."

"So where'd I park the car?"

"That's what they want to know."

"Must've been right where I found it later. Front of the Grand Union. But it wouldn't start. Key wouldn't turn in the . . . what'd you call it, Meg?"

"The ignition."

"How'd your car get back here, sir?"

Shanks looked at his wife. The same bewildered, lost look again.

"Meg?" he said. "How'd it get back here?"

"I drove it back," she said.

"Where'd you find it, ma'am?"

"Is he going to get in trouble?"

"Where'd you find it, can you tell us?"

"Near the movie theater."

"No, Meg," Shanks said, "it was in front of the Grand Union. Right where I left it."

"Rubin," she said, "you *forgot* where you left it."

"No, I didn't. It was right there where I left it. I got in, put the key in the ig . . ."

"Rubin, you got in the *wrong* car."

"No," he said. "No, I didn't, Meg."

"Rubin, that wasn't *our* car. That was somebody *else's* car."

"It was?" he said, and looked at the detectives. "How could it have been somebody else's car?" he said. "I know my own car, don't I?"

"Mr. Shanks," Budd said, "a man named Herman Friedlich was on the jitney going to the city this morning when he looked out the window and saw his car sitting there at that Shell station. He got off the bus, ran over there, put his key in the ignition, and was starting the car when the owner ran out and told him to get out of his customer's car. Mr. Friedlich told him it was *his* car, and that it'd been stolen yesterday."

"Stolen?" Shanks said, and looked at his wife.

"Yes, sir, it was reported stolen at five-forty-five P.M. yesterday. When Mr. Friedlich called us, he said he'd left the car unlocked . . ."

"He did?" Shanks said.

"Yes, sir, because he was just going in the Grand Union for a bottle of milk. When he came out, the car was gone."

"Should've locked it," Shanks said. "Nowadays."

"Yes, sir, he should've."

"But what's that got to do with *me*?"

"You got in the wrong *car*, Rubin," his wife said impatiently, and then turned to Budd. "I'm sorry," she said, "he forgets."

"Ma'am . . . didn't the garage call last night to tell you your husband had left the wrong key?"

"Yes, they did."

"And didn't you go down there with your son . . . your son lives here in Fox Hill, too, doesn't he?"

"Yes."

"Didn't he drive you to the garage, and didn't you tell the owner—a man named Jake Sutton—didn't you ask him to give you the keys he had and you'd look for the other ones when you got home?"

"Yes. Because . . ."

"Because when you saw that blue car sitting there, you knew right off it wasn't yours, didn't you? You knew your husband had taken another man's car and . . ."

"I was afraid he'd get in trouble."

"So they gave you back the keys to *your* car . . ."

"Yes."

"And then your son must've driven you around town . . ."

"Yes, looking for the car."

"And when you found it, you drove it back here to your garage."

"I didn't want him to get in trouble."

"Even though you must've realized he'd got in another man's car, had the thing pushed all the way to the Shell station . . ."

"Young fellers saw I was having trouble," Shanks said, "asked if I wanted a push."

"You're a goddamn *fool*," his wife said.

"Margaret," he said, "I behaved in the proper manner. The key wouldn't turn, so I took the car in to have it looked at. Who are these people? Are they saying I stole somebody's car?"

His wife sighed heavily.

"What now?" she asked. "Are you going to arrest him?"

"Arrest me?" Shanks said. "What for? What'd I do?"

"How long has he been this way?" Dellarosa asked.

"Too long," Margaret said, and sighed again.

The stenciled black lettering read:

DSS TEMPLE

This was not the name of a synagogue.

The DSS stood for Department of Social Services. The Temple stood for Temple Street Armory. Yesterday afternoon, Meyer had gone back to the Old Chancery for yet another visit, this time to check the stenciling on the blanket that had been wrapped around Jane Doe when she was dropped off at the railroad station. The stenciling was, in fact, identical to what he'd seen lettered in one corner of Charlie's blanket. But while he was there, Dr. Elman had informed him of something more important.

During the night, Jane Doe had died of cardiac arrest. It was Dr. Elman's theory that the woman may have had a history of ventricular arrhythmia. If she'd been taking medication for the ailment, something like Quinidine three times a day in 320 mg doses, and then was suddenly *deprived* of the drug, abandoned *without* the drug and unable to tell anyone she'd *been* on the drug . . . well, the results were inevitable. Was what Dr. Elman had theorized. Which was why Meyer was here at the Temple Street Shelter today. Or maybe he'd have been here, anyway. Maybe tracking down whoever had dumped those two old people was terribly important to him. Maybe he thought too often of the little old lady who'd drowned in her own bathtub after putting her wig on a stand across the room.

He had called the shelter the moment Elman gave him the news, and was told that the supervisor had left for the day and wouldn't be in again till sometime after noon Saturday, nice hours supervisors kept. So here was Meyer now—on his day off, no less—talking to a man named Harold Laughton, who immediately told him that the reason he'd left so early yesterday was that he'd had to go to the dentist to get a tooth pulled and his dentist had warned him beforehand that there might be some pain the morning after, in which case he might want to take it a bit easy, which was why he'd left word that he might not be in till after noon sometime. So here *he* was, too, even though his mouth was killing him. So what did Meyer want, anyway?

Meyer wanted to know if Mr. Laughton recognized either of these blankets.

Mr. Laughton certainly did.

"Those blankets belong to my shelter," he said.

They were talking in Laughton's jerry-built office at the rear of the old brick building on Temple Street. There was a wooden desk in the office and a wooden coatrack and two wooden chairs. One wall of the office had a plate-glass panel that started at about waist high and overlooked the armory's drill floor, furnished now with hundreds of cots crammed head to toe from brick wall to brick wall. At the foot of each cot was a khaki-colored blanket identical to the ones Meyer had placed on Laughton's desk.

"Where'd you get these?" Laughton asked.

Meyer told him where he'd got them.

"If one of them was wrapped around a woman, she's not one of my people," Laughton said. "My shelter's exclusively for men. Nine hundred and twenty cots out there, all for men."

With nine hundred and twenty blankets on them, Meyer thought.

"I run one of the best shelters in this city," Laughton said. "Other shelters, you have rats running across the floor all night long, keeping the men awake, biting them. Not here at Temple. I run a good shelter."

"I'm sure you do," Meyer said.

"Other shelters, you have men getting beaten at night, other men using pipes on them, or sawed-off broomstick handles, but not here, not in my shelter. The guards I have here make certain that nothing like that happens to the men here. I have a top-notch psychiatrist assigned here. The social workers I have here are among the best in the city. This is more than just three hots and a cot here, this is a shelter with a heart. I'm very proud of my shelter here."

"Any idea how these blankets got on those two people?" Meyer asked.

Laughton looked at him as if he'd just made a disparaging remark about this shelter he was very proud of here. He was a man in his late forties, Meyer guessed, virtually as bald as Meyer himself, but with a ferocious-looking handlebar mustache compensating for the lack of hair anywhere else on his head. Some five feet eight inches tall, give or take. His jaw swollen where the tooth had been pulled. Fierce blue eyes studying Meyer now, trying to decide whether the police were here to make some kind of trouble for him.

"We *do* have occasional thefts," he said. "The men here aren't the cream of society, you know. They come and go. Some of them—*many* of them—have criminal records. Things occasionally stick to their fingers. Anything that isn't nailed down, in fact. Mind you, we don't have a security problem as such—as I told you, the guards here are very good—but occasionally things *will* disappear."

"Blankets?"

"Blankets, yes. Occasionally. In fact, *some* homeless people come in here *just* to steal blankets. And bedding. Especially during the wintertime. And spring's been so late coming this year."

"Yes."

"So, yes, we've had blankets stolen. Occasionally."

"Assuming these blankets *were* stolen . . ."

"Well, how else would they have left the premises?"

"Assuming that to be the case then . . ."

"Yes?"

Impatiently.

Meyer was taking up too much of his time, and besides he had a goddamn toothache.

Patiently, Meyer said, "Is there any way you can tell *when* these blankets might have been stolen?"

"No."

"Nothing about them that would distinguish . . ."

"Nothing."

"Have you had any blanket thefts *recently*?"

"I wouldn't know. We take inventory at the beginning of each month. We won't be taking inventory again until the first of April."

"What did your inventory show at the beginning of March?"

"We'd lost something like fourteen blankets the month before."

"Fourteen blankets were stolen . . ."

"Or lost . . ."

"During February alone?"

"Yes. *New* blankets, too."

"Are *these* blankets . . .?"

"That figure is low, by the way, when you compare it with other shelters in the city. But excuse me, Detective Meyer, why are you . . . ?"

"Excuse *me*, but are *these* blankets new?"

"Yes, I would expect so."

"You can *tell* they're new?"

"Yes, of course."

"What do you mean by new?"

"We received an allotment at the beginning of the year."

"Then there *is* a way of determining when they were stolen. Or lost."

"Well, yes, I suppose . . ."

"When in January did you receive your allotment?"

"Around the fifteenth."

"How many blankets?"

"Fifty. To replace what had been stolen in the past quarter."

"Fifty blankets had been stolen in the previous three months?"

"Roughly that many. I put in for fifty in replacement. That was a round number."

"So you'd lost . . . what would you say . . . approximately sixteen, seventeen blankets a month."

"About that many, yes."

"And the city sent you fifty new blankets to replace them."

"Yes."

"How many of those blankets do you have left now?"

"I told you. We don't take inventory till the first of each month."

"How many blankets were stolen . . . or lost . . . in January, would you remember?"

"Twelve."

"And fourteen in February, you said."

"Fourteen, yes."

"Twenty-six altogether."

"Yes."

"A little less than it was in the last quarter."

"I suppose it is, actually."

"Well, it's only thirteen a month so far . . ."

"That's right, actually, yes."

"So there's been a drop from the previous quarter."

"Yes, it would seem so."

"Even though spring's been a long time coming."

"We can't prevent the occasional theft, you know," Laughton said. "There are nine hundred and twenty cots in this shelter, and our security is second to none. But our main concern, security-wise, is keeping the shelter drug-free, and protecting the men who come to us for help. But . . . excuse me, Mr. Meyer. Surely the theft of a few blankets isn't worth all this time, is it? And these two people who were abandoned . . . well, surely this is an everyday occurrence."

"Not if one of them dies," Meyer said.

When the telephone rang at four o'clock the next morning, Eileen was dead asleep. She fumbled for the phone in the darkness, lifted the receiver, turned on the bedside light, and saw snow falling outside her window. *Snow* again?

"Burke?"

"Yes, sir."

Deputy Inspector Brady on the other end.

"Meet me at three-ten South Cumberland," he said. "Hit the hammer."

"Yes, sir," she said.

He knew she didn't have a siren in her personal car, he was merely expressing the urgency of the situation, hit the hammer. There was no traffic, anyway, at this hour on a Sunday morning, she made it to the scene in ten minutes flat. A crowd of police personnel was standing in the falling snow near the emergency service truck and the dozen or more motor patrol cars angled in against the curb. Inspector Brady was nowhere in sight. She spotted Tony Pellegrino among the mass of black rain slickers and hoods, short and wiry and wearing jeans and a blue windbreaker with the word POLICE lettered across its back in white. She walked over to him and asked him what the situation was.

She was dressed much as Pellegrino was, jeans and the blue uniform windbreaker with the identifying word across the back, no hat, red hair glowing in the light of the overhead street lamp. You weren't supposed to try kidding a hostage taker into believing you were anything but a cop. The word POLICE across the back of the jacket let the taker know exactly where he stood; this wasn't a game here, this was all about people who were being held captive, there were lives at stake here.

The situation here involved *two* lives, if you counted the taker's. The team's motto was Nobody Gets Hurt; the taker's life was as important to them as was the life of any hostage. Pellegrino told Eileen that what had happened here, the taker was this guy who lived with his brother and the brother's wife . . . the sister-in-law . . . and slept in the room next door to theirs, just down the hall. What happened was he woke up in the middle of the night to go take a pee, and all at once he went bananas and pulled a gun and threatened to kill both his brother *and* the wife . . . the sister-in-law . . . if the brother didn't leave the apartment right that minute.

"The brother went out of there like a shot," Pellegrino said. "Called nine-one-one from the phone booth on the corner. The

Boss is in the building already, working the door. He said you should go up the minute you got here."

The Boss was Inspector Brady.

"What apartment?" she asked.

"Four-oh-nine. You can't miss it. There's a hundred cops in the hallway."

"Thanks, Tony," she said, and walked away from him through the lightly falling snow. She found Brady on the fourth floor, just coming away from the door as she moved through the knot of uniformed emergency service cops. Brady had turned fifty-four last month, a tall trim man with bright blue eyes, a fringe of white hair circling his otherwise bald head. His nose was a bit too prominent for his otherwise small features; it gave his face a cleaving appearance. Like a ship under sail, parting the wave of blue uniforms in his path, he came toward Eileen and said at once, "A bad one."

"Tony filled me in," she said, nodding.

"Guy's got the hots for his sister-in-law, plain and simple," Brady said. "He heard them making love during the night and that set him off. Now the brother's out of the apartment, he'll either rape her or shoot her or both."

"Older brother, younger, what? The taker."

"Older. He's thirty-two, the brother's twenty."

"How old's the woman?"

"If you can call her that," Brady said. "She's only seventeen."

Eileen nodded.

"Want to try the door?" he asked. "Be very careful. He may be on something, it's hard to tell."

"What's his name?"

"Jimmy."

"How far'd you get with him?"

"Nowhere," Brady said.

This was a big admission for him. In the eight months since she'd begun working for Brady, nothing had changed her opinion

of him as an egotistical sexist who used women on the door only
when he felt a situation absolutely demanded it. For all his bullshit about hoping to expand the team so that it would one day
include more than the two women now on it, he kept replacing
burned-out male negotiators with new male negotiators, and
when Martha Halsted flunked out the first time she had a real
shot at the door, he began training not another woman but a
man. The way Eileen saw it, Brady felt nobody did the job as
well as he did, male *or* female. But he normally put a woman
on the door only when the taker inside was *another* woman. It
was rare that he trusted a woman to negotiate with a *male* taker.
So why Eileen today? Was it because there was a potential rape
victim in the apartment? Or was it because Jimmy had a hard-
on and Brady was tossing him a juicy redhead? Some things in
the police department never changed. She'd started the job as a
decoy with Special Forces, and sometimes she felt like a decoy
all over again. Nowadays, the guys on the job didn't piss in a
female cop's locker anymore, but—

   "Hello," she said, "I'm Detective Eileen Burke, I'm a police-
department negotiator."

7.

The letter from the Deaf Man had been delivered to the squad-room the day before, but Carella didn't get to see it till eight A.M. that Sunday morning, when a uniformed cop from downstairs dropped it on his desk together with a lot of other stuff, including an announcement for the Detectives' Benevolent Association's Easter Ball. Carella wished that all he had on his mind was Easter, with spring just here and the streets covered with slush.

The letter was addressed to him.

Plain white envelope, no return address front or back. *Detective Stephen Louis Carella* typed on the front of the envelope, and then *87th Detective Squad* and the Grover Avenue address. It was postmarked Friday, March 27. He knew who had sent the letter even before he tore open the envelope flap.

There was a typewritten note attached to a single sheet of paper. The note read:

```
Dear Steve:
To make it easier for you.
              Love,
              Sanson
              P.S. More later.
```

The sheet of paper clipped to the note had obviously been photocopied from the book the Deaf Man had earlier recommended. It read:

> "I FEAR AN explosion," Tikona said. "I fear the jostling of the feet will awaken the earth too soon. I fear the voices of the multitude will anger the sleeping rain god and cause him to unleash his watery fury before the fear has been vanquished. I fear the fury of the multitude may not be contained."
>
> "I, too, share this terrible fear, my son," Okino said. "But The Plain is vast, and though the multitude multiplies, it can know no boundaries here, it cannot be restrained by walls. Such was the reason The Plain was chosen by the elders for these yearly rites of spring."

"I know you haven't read the book," Carella told Brown, "well, the first chapter, actually, is all he recommended . . ."

"Our local friendly librarian," Brown said.

"It's all about these rites of spring, the first chapter. And what he says is that there are . . ."

"Who's this you're talking about?" Brown asked. "The Deaf Man or the author?"

His shoes were wet from having trudged through the slush from the subway station to the precinct. His mother had told him that when your feet got wet and cold you felt cold all over. He didn't feel cold all over, he just felt wet in the *feet*, and that made him irritated. When he was irritated, he scowled like a bear. He was not scowling at Carella, he was merely scowling at his wet shoes and his wet feet and this dumb weather for the end of March. Hadn't come *in* like any damn lamb, either.

"The author," Carella said. "Arturo Rivera."

"And he says?"

"He says that this *multitude* gathers on this big open plain ringed by mountains. . . ."

"We don't have any mountains, this city," Brown said.

"I know. This is another planet."

"Another planet, huh? Sometimes I think this city *is* another planet."

"What I think is he may be calling our attention to a *crowd,* you know?" Carella said. "A multitude?"

"The Deaf Man, you mean?"

"Yeah. Using Rivera as his spokesman."

"So you think he's planning something that has to do with a crowd."

"Yeah, in an open space," Carella said. "This vast *plain,* you know?"

"No *plains* in this city, either," Brown said. His wet feet were beginning to irritate him more and more. He wondered if he had a pair of clean socks in his locker. "What was that business about an explosion?"

"He fears an explosion."

"Who, the Deaf Man?"

"No, no . . ."

"Then who? Rivera?"

"No, this guy Tikona."

"Read that part out loud, will you?" Brown said.

Carella cleared his throat and began reading.

" 'I fear an explosion,' Tikona said. 'I fear the jostling of the feet will awaken the earth too soon. I fear the voices of the multitude will anger the sleeping rain god and cause him to unleash his watery fury before the fear has been vanquished. I fear the fury of the multitude may not be contained.' "

"He fears an explosion 'cause the crowd's getting too big, right?"

"The multitude, right."

"So all we got to do is *find* this multitude."

"This whole damn *city* is a multitude," Carella said.

"Find the multitude," Brown said, "and then stop him from doing whatever it is he plans to *do* with the multitude."

"Yeah," Carella said glumly.

"Nobody said he'd make it easy," Brown said.

"He himself said so."

"No, Steve. He only said *easier*. Not *easy*. With him, nothing's ever easy. What size socks do you wear?"

"I recognize your obvious qualifications," the Deaf Man was saying, "but the problem is you're a woman."

"Some people might consider that a sexist attitude," Gloria said.

"It's just that I've never seen a female garbage man."

"What's garbage got to do with a good wheel man? I'm either a good wheel man, or I'm *not* a good wheel man. You knew I was a woman when you asked me to come for the interview. So I come here at nine o'clock on a Sunday morning, when *most* people are in church, for Christ's sake, and you tell me . . ."

"I was expecting a different *sort* of woman," he said.

He had not been expecting a thirty-two-year-old blonde with eyes the color of seaweed, some five feet nine inches tall and looking tall and slender and firm in a jump suit and high-heeled pumps. Sitting on the couch in his living room, facing Grover Park and a gunmetal sky. Oh to be in England, he thought, now that spring is here.

"What *sort* of woman were you expecting?" Gloria asked, raising one eyebrow and hitting the word hard.

"Someone more masculine," he said. "Someone who might possibly pass for a man. I suppose I should have asked for a description on the phone, but fair employment practices seemed to preclude that," he said, and smiled charmingly.

He's so full of shit, Gloria thought.

But she wanted the job.

"Someone more masculine, huh?" she said.

"Someone who could pass for a truck driver," he said. "Someone . . . beefier. With less refined features . . ."

"Thank you," she said.

"Shorter hair . . ."

"I can cut my hair."

"Yes, but you can't gain forty pounds in the next six days."

"Is that when it's going down?"

"The fourth of April, yes."

"A Saturday," she said, and nodded.

"How do you happen to know that?"

"I have this trick I do," she said.

"What trick?" he asked, his interest immediately captured.

"You give me any date, and I can tell you what day of the week it falls on."

"How can you do that?"

"Secret," she said, and smiled. "Have you got a calendar?"

"Yes?"

"Go get it."

"Sure," he said, and walked over to his desk and opened the drawer over the kneehole, and took from it a leather-bound appointment calendar. Without opening it, he said, "Christmas. December twenty-fifth."

"Oh, come on," she said, "give me a hard one."

"Do Christmas first."

"This year?"

"Sure."

"It'll fall on a Friday. Check it."

He checked it.

"Friday is right," he said. "How about May seventeenth? *Next* year."

"Easy," she said. "A Monday."

He checked it. She was right.

"Have you got an almanac?" she asked.

"No."

"Too bad. I could give you the day of the week for any date since we went on the Gregorian calendar."

"How do you do it?" he asked.

"Do I get the job?"

"Gloria," he said, "believe me, everything you've told me about yourself . . ."

"Damn right," she said. "I've been driving since I was twelve, did my first wheel job when I was only sixteen. I've got the surest pair of hands in the business and the calmest nerves. I can drive through the eye of a needle with one eye shut. I can drive a racing car or a ten-wheeler, and I can outdrive any man in the business. You want me to cut my hair, I'll cut my hair. You want me to gain a hundred pounds, I'll gain a hundred pounds. You want me to be a garbage man, I'll be a garbage man. I need this job. I'll do anything to get this job."

"Anything?" the Deaf Man asked.

"*Anything*," she said, and looked him dead in the eye.

"Tell me how you do the date trick," he said.

"Tell me I have the job."

"Don't you want to know what it pays?"

"I have a house on the Spit that's about ready to fall into the Atlantic Ocean," she said. "It's gonna cost me a coupla grand at *least* to have them shore up the pilings or whatever it is they have to do. I usually work for a percentage of the take. . . ."

"That's out of the question here," he said.

"That's the usual wheel-man fee."

"Yes, but . . ."

"A good wheel man always gets a piece of the action. You know that."

"Sometimes."

"Any job I ever worked. The beach house cost me half a million. That was my end on a bank job we did in Boston. What I'm saying is I don't know how much this job is expected to gross, but let's say the wheel man is worth at *least* ten percent of that. So if this is a two-million-dollar job, I'd expect, say, two hundred grand. Which will keep my house from floating off to Europe. If it's bigger than that, I'd expect more. That's my fee. That's what any good wheel man would expect."

"Too bad you're not a wheel *man*," he said, and smiled again.

"Right, I'm a wheel *woman*. What do you want me to do? Suck your cock?"

"I don't pay women for sex," he said.

"Good. Cause I don't suck cocks for money."

But she was the one who'd first raised it. He would remind her of that later. When she was tied to the bed and begging for it.

"Cut your hair and put on at least twenty pounds," he said.

"Okay," she said.

"A flat hundred grand for all the run-throughs and the actual job."

"Make it a hundred and fifty. In case they find cockroaches or dry rot when they open up my house."

"A hundred is all I can pay."

"Why? Because I'm a woman?"

"No. Because a hundred is what I'm paying everyone else."

"When do we start?" she said.

"How do you do that trick?" he asked.

After five hours of working the door, Eileen now knew that the girl inside there—she couldn't bring herself to call a seventeen-year-old girl a *woman*, even if she was married, and even if it meant agreeing with Brady's terminology—the *girl* was named Lisa. She also knew that Jimmy had handcuffed her to the bed in his room, the one adjacent to the one where Lisa slept with his brother, Tom. Jimmy, Lisa, and Tom, nice little family triangle here that had erupted in the middle of the night and that could, if she wasn't careful, end with somebody getting hurt. She didn't want the girl to get hurt, and she didn't want Jimmy to get hurt, either, but most of all she didn't want herself to get hurt. She'd been hurt once on the job, hurt very badly, and she didn't want that to happen ever again.

"Where'd you get the handcuffs?" she asked casually.

"Bought them," Jimmy said.

The door was open some three inches, held by a safety chain. She was standing to the left of the door, unwilling to afford him a clear shot until she knew which way he might go. She couldn't see him and he couldn't see her. So far, they were still two disembodied voices, but dialogue was what negotiation was all about. Nobody gets hurt. We talk.

"You're not a cop or anything, are you?" she asked.

"Shit, no," he said.

"I didn't know anybody but cops could buy handcuffs," she said.

Just talking. Just keeping him engaged. They'd worked up a profile from what the brother had told them, and she knew damn well Jimmy wasn't a cop. She also knew you could buy handcuffs in any one of a hundred sex shops in the city, and in any number of antiques shops selling junk from your grandmother's attic. She was just talking. Just trying to get him to talk back. Trying to get his mind off hurting anybody. Raping the girl. Or shooting her. He had threatened to shoot the girl if they didn't leave him alone here.

"Where can you buy handcuffs?" she asked.

"I don't remember where I bought them," he said. "Where are *your* handcuffs?"

"I don't have any with me," she said.

The truth.

"I told you I'm not armed . . ."

Also true.

". . . and I'm not carrying handcuffs, either. You're the only one has handcuffs and a gun."

Not *quite* true.

All the E.S. cops in the hallway were wearing ceramic vests and they were armed with riot guns. One shot from that apartment and they'd storm the door. You played the game only so far. Then you sent in the bombers. Basic contradiction there, but she figured she could live with it if it worked more often than not—which it did.

"Still snowing outside," she said. "Do you like snow?"

"Listen," he said. Edge to his voice. "What are you tryin'a do here, huh? I told you I'll *kill* Lisa if you fuckin guys don't leave me alone! So leave me *alone*! Get the fuck *outta* here!"

But he didn't close the door.

"Well, you don't *really* want to kill her, do you?" Eileen said.

"Never mind what I *want* to do. You're the ones are *forcing* me to do it."

"All we're interested in is making sure nobody gets hurt."

"Sure, you give a shit I get hurt or not."

"We do."

"Then whyn't *you* come in here take Lisa's place? I han'cuff *you* to the bed, I let her come out, how's that?"

"No, I can't make that kind of deal."

"Why not? You're so inner'ested in nobody gettin hurt, you come on in here, take her place."

"I'd have to be crazy to do that," Eileen said.

"How come? Big brave cop, you come on in."

"I promised you *nobody* gets hurt," she said. "That includes me. All we want to do is help you, Jimmy. Why don't you take that chain off the door so we can talk a little more easily?"

"We can talk fine just the way we are," he said. "Anyway, there's nothin to talk about. You get the fuck outta here, Lisa's got nothin to worry about. You hang around, she gets hurt. You think you can unner'stan that?"

"How do I know you haven't hurt her already? I told my boss she's okay, but he's . . ."

"She *is* okay, I told you that."

"That's just what I reported to him. But he's going to lose patience with me if he thinks I'm lying to him."

"Who's your boss, anyway? The bald-headed guy was talking to me before?"

"Yes. Deputy Inspector Brady. He's in charge of the unit."

"So go tell him to get everybody the fuck outta here."

"Well, I can't give *him* orders, he's my boss. You know how bosses are. Don't you have a boss?"

"Tommy's my boss."

Something there. Something in his voice. She let it sit for a minute.

"Your brother, do you mean?"

"Yeah. He owns a plumbing-supply store. I work for him."

Older brother working for the younger brother. Younger brother married to a seventeen-year-old girl. Older brother living in the same apartment with them.

"Do you like your job?" she asked.

"I don't wanna talk about it."

"What would you like to talk about, Jimmy?"

"Nothing. I want you to leave me the fuck alone, is what I . . ."

"Have you had anything to eat this morning?"

"I'm not hungry."

"How about Lisa? She might be hungry."

There was silence beyond the crack in the door.

"Jimmy? How about Lisa? Do you think she might like something to eat?"

"I don't know."

"Why don't you go ask her?"

"I leave the door, you'll try to break it down."

"I promise I won't."

"There are guys out there in the hallway with you, they'll break down the door."

"No, I'll ask my boss to make sure they won't. You go find out if Lisa wants something to eat, okay? Maybe we can get her something to eat. If she's hungry. You must be hungry, too, you've been up half the night. Maybe I can . . ."

"I'm not hungry."

"Then go see if Lisa is, okay?"

"You promise me nobody's gonna break down this door?"

"Jimmy, if that's what we wanted to do, we'd've done it already."

"Not with me standin here with this gun in my hand."

"The men out here are wearing bulletproof vests. They could break down the door if they wanted to, Jimmy. That's not what we want to do. What we want is to make sure nobody gets hurt. Not us, not you, not Lisa. I'm sure you don't want Lisa to get hurt. . . ."

"I don't."

"I know that."

"You *better* know it. Why the fuck you think I'm *doin* this?"

"I don't know why, Jimmy. Can you tell me why?"

"To *keep* her from gettin hurt, why do you think?"

"How do you . . . ?"

"Why do you think I chased him outta the fuckin apartment?"

"Your brother, do you mean?"

"Tommy, Tommy, who do you *think* I mean? He was beatin the shit out of her last night, I told him to leave her alone or I'd blow his fuckin brains out. I told him to get outta here and never come back. That's why I got her handcuffed to the bed. For her own good. She lets him beat her black and blue and then they fuck all night long, I'm tryin'a *protect* her, for Christ's sake!"

"Is that what woke you up last night? Him beating her?"

"*Every* night, the son of a bitch."

"We'll make sure that doesn't happen anymore, Jimmy."

"Sure, how you gonna do that?"

"There are city agencies your sister-in-law can talk to. There are ways to restrain your brother from . . ."

"I just can't stand it no more. She's no bigger than a nickel, he's always beatin the shit out of her."

"We'll put a stop to that, Jimmy. Meanwhile, go ask her if she wants something to eat, okay?"

"I'll go ask her," he said, and hesitated. "But I'm gonna close the door and lock it."

"I'd rather you didn't, Jimmy."

"Who the fuck cares *what* you want? I'm the one has the gun."

"That's why I'd rather you left the door unlocked. I don't want anyone to get hurt, Jimmy. I don't want any accidents to happen here."

"Fuck you and what you want," he said, and slammed the door shut.

In the silence of the hallway, she heard the deafening click of the lock tumblers turning.

"What I thought was we do something new and startlin for the gig," Silver said.

"New and startlin like *what*?" Jeeb said.

He never liked it when Sil came up with these new and *startlin* ideas of his. Like the time he come up with the notion just the two girls rappin in *falsetto*, their voices weren't high enough already, right? Sil goes Nobody ever done this before, man, two girls singin falsetto, gonna send chills up ever'body's spine. Jeeb told him never mind the chills, people don't like to hear things that'll *startle* 'em, they want to hear the same stuff every time out, man, the same beat, the same voices doin the rappin, they don't want to be no kind of *startled*, man. Only things enjoy gettin startled is *pigeons*, man, they get a *kick* out of being startled. You go *whoooooo* to a bunch of pigeons in the park, they like to wet their pants with joy being startled like that and making them flap up in the air. But *people* don't *like* to be startled, Jeeb told him. People hear a coupla chicks rappin in falsetto, they'll think it's a police siren or somethin, an *air*-raid siren, they'll run for cover, man.

Turned out Sil was right, though, son of a bitch was *always* right. Next gig they done—this was in Philadelphia—Grass and Sophie done this song in falsetto, like the song was called "China Doll" and it was about dope comin in from the Orient and pollutin the black youth of our cities, and they rapped it in these high falsetto voices like supposed to be comin from Chinese chicks, you know, these high singsongy voices comin from these two gorgeous black chicks, the crowd went wild. Sil didn't say I tole you so, though he could've. Was *Grass* did all the I tole yous, cause she was the one sided with Sil from the beginning. More he thought about it, Jeeb figured there was somethin goin on between her and Sil. That was gratitude for you. He's the one taught the girl everythin she knew about *any*thin, and she ends up beamin at every word Sil utters. Sheer gratitude.

"What's this new and startlin idea?" Sophie asked.

"Tell us, Sil."

This from Grass. Beamin at him fore he even opened his mouth. He was prolly gonna ask the girls to sing bass this time. Drop they voices down in they shoes, bust all the woofers. Tell us all about it, Sil. Grass lookin at him adoringly. Tell us your new *startlin* and brilliant idea so we can all fall down dead at your feet.

"Before we go into that," Jeeb said, "I want to tell you 'bout this conversation I had with Ackerman. I tole him there's been three ads in the papers so far, an none of them mentioned Spit Shine as prominent as the other headliners. This thing's gonna run for two straight days, he's booked an even dozen groups, all kinds of rap and all kinds of rock, some of them nobody ever heard of but they mothers. He's the fuckin puh-*motor*, how come we gettin dissed like that? He goes Look, fair is fair, Jeeb, only *some* of the headliners got bigger mention in the ads. So I go Look, Mort, maybe you don't *realize* how many times we *topped* the charts this past year, and he goes Anyway, *I'm* not the one placin the ads, it ain't Windows Entertainment takin the ads, it's the *bank*, it's FirstBank. I go Come on, Mort, you're the fuckin puh-motor, what does the bank know about rock or rap or any-thing but *elevator* music, for Christ's sake! He says he's tellin me the God's honest truth, but he appreciates what I'm sayin, and he'll go to the bank, the guy at the bank who's feedin the

ads to the papers, and tell him he's had complaints from some
of the artists . . ."

"Who *else* complained?" Sophie asked.

"Group named Double Damn."

"Never heard of them."

"I tole Ackerman some unknown group gets its name in the
ads same size an prominence as Spit Shine, he's gonna have an
hour an a half, two hours of dead air on that stage, time we're
supposed to be performin. Cause we just won't show, man, he
can let Double *Damn* open the fuckin concert!"

"I'm not even sure I *like* that opening spot," Sophie said.
"Biggest crowds'll be there at night, we ought to be next to
ciosin on Sunday."

"Sunday'd be bad," Grass said. "People got to get up early,
go to work the next day."

"Who's got next to closin *Saturday* night?" Sil asked.

"Guess."

"Yeah," Sil said.

"Anyway, Ackerman's gonna let us know what the bank has
to say. I tole him to remind the bank that *we're* the ones doin
the gig *free*, it don't reflect too kindly when a fucking *bank* sticks
up somebody instead of the other way around. He said he'd tell
them. He better."

"We'll get the ad," Sophie said. "Don't worry."

"We better," Jeeb said. "So far, they headlined three other
groups, and *we* get a half-inch near the bottom with groups like
Moses Roses."

"Who's Moses Roses?" Sophie asked.

"Who the fuck knows?"

"We get the right ad or we walk," Silver said, "plain and
simple."

"That's the onliest way, Sil," Grass agreed, as if it was *his*
thought and not Jeeb's. Man.

"Tell us your new idea," she said, and grinned at him, all eyes.

"We do a love song," Sil said.

* * *

The place Parker decided to take Cathy Herrera to brunch was
a steak joint frequented by high-ranking police officers, very few
of whom Parker knew. But he thought he would impress her by
suggesting that he hobnobbed with rank.

Yesterday, the city's two tabloids had both done a number on
the spray-paint killer, one in its morning edition, the other in its
afternoon edition. The morning paper had zeroed in on Peter
Wilkins, the dead lawyer, with the headline:

SECRET
SPRAYER

. . which related to the page-four profile they did on the successful litigator who went around at night spraying graffiti on
the walls of buildings.

The afternoon paper's headline read:

SPRAYER
PREY
BETTER
PRAY
(...who's next?)

The inside story was subtitled **DESTINY WITH DEATH.** A lame
journalistic exercise, it attempted to show how three people of
diverse backgrounds—an attorney, a veteran graffiti writer, and
an immigrant novice—had met the same fate at the hands of
someone the newspaper called "an obsessed vigilante." In ad-

dition, several men and women in the street had been interviewed regarding the prevalence of graffiti in the city, the question posed to them being: *What should we do about graffiti writers?* These expert criminologists—a telephone operator, a letter carrier, a construction worker, an obstetrician, and a woman protesting pornography in magazines—had varying views.

The telephone operator said that if they got caught, they should be forced to wear uniforms with stenciling that read I AM A VANDAL while publicly and under guard they cleaned off all the walls in the city.

The obstetrician said that like Norman Mailer, he considered graffiti an art form with macho qualities, and aesthetic and political values. Besides, what ever happened to free speech in this country?

The woman protesting pornography said that graffiti was a mild abuse when compared to the millions of women who became the victims of rape and other forms of sexual assault inspired by pornographic magazines.

The construction worker said that anybody caught spraying buildings *should* be shot.

The letter carrier said he had work to do.

Parker agreed with the construction worker, but he couldn't very well say this to Cathy because, after all, her son *had* been shot while spraying a building. He wasn't even sure she had seen the afternoon paper, which painted a somewhat unflattering picture of young Alfredo Herrera, intimating that because he and his mother had come from a town called Francisco de Macoris— a place with a reputation for exporting drug dealers to this city and importing dope money back to the Dominican Republic— why then wasn't it possible that Herrera himself had been part of the notorious Los Cubanos drug ring? Parker tended to agree that all spics were in some way related to the drug trade, but he couldn't say this, either, because after all Catalina Herrera was herself a spic, even if she called herself Cathy.

He decided instead to wave over at a man he'd met only briefly in court once when they were both testifying on the same case, a deputy inspector sitting in full regalia with three suits who looked important, too, all of them digging into the huge portions of steak and eggs before them.

"Inspector," Parker said, and nodded chummily, and the inspector looked back sort of bewildered, but returned the nod, and Parker said to Cathy, "Good friend of mine," and then, "Would you care for something to drink before lunch?"

Eileen kept waiting for the door to open again.

She was still standing in the hallway outside apartment 409, just to the left of the doorframe. Inspector Brady had figured out a plan to get the girl out of the apartment. Once she was out, they would talk to Jimmy about putting down the gun. Meanwhile, the important thing was to get her out of there safely. Jimmy's feelings about her seemed ambivalent at best; Michael Goodman, the negotiating team's psychiatrist, figured he could jump either way. Tom, the younger brother, had vehemently denied ever having laid a hand on his wife; Brady was inclined to believe him. More likely was his story that the sounds of their lovemaking had infuriated Jimmy. If this was true, Goodman was fearful that Jimmy would act out the fantasy he himself had created, that of his sister-in-law as the victim of physical abuse. The girl was handcuffed to the bed in there and no one knew how long it would be before Jimmy moved into action, one way or another. Goodman felt rape was a distinct possibility.

Eileen just wished she thought better of Brady's plan.

He had asked her to tell Jimmy—if and when he opened the damn door again—that her boss wanted only to protect the girl at all costs, which he was sure Jimmy *also* wanted. Toward that end, he was willing to recommend an investigation of possible assault by the brother, and to turn young Lisa over to a social agency that would help her to construct a healthful way of dealing with the battered-wife syndrome. In the meantime, because

Jimmy had embarked upon this present course of action—the
inspector's exact words—only to protect his sister-in-law from
further abuse, Brady would recommend dropping any charges
against him.

All of this was premised on the wife abuse being a reality. If,
instead and in fact, Jimmy had been lusting for young Lisa all
along and had finally been driven over the edge by the sounds
of passion next door—which both Brady *and* Goodman believed
to be the actual case—then why would Jimmy come out of that
apartment, why would he now be willing to release the object
of his desire? None of it made any sense to Eileen.

Jimmy had made no demands of them. He hadn't asked for a
limo to the airport and a jet plane to Rio, he hadn't even asked
for a cheeseburger and a bottle of beer. He wanted nothing more
than to be left alone with the girl. This they were denying him.
He had threatened to kill the girl if they did not leave him alone
with her. She doubted if he really planned to do this; he was,
after all, still talking to them. But she couldn't see how the
inspector's offer in any way jibed with *Jimmy's* stated wishes.
Wouldn't it be better, not to mention safer, if they offered to
leave him alone with the girl once she was *out* of the apartment?
Promise him the honeymoon suite at the nearest hotel, just get
them both the hell out of there.

You weren't supposed to lie to them, you weren't supposed
to say I'll get you this or that and then not deliver while there
were still hostages in there. But this would be different—or so
she told herself—this would be saying, Look, you come out of
there with the girl, we'll deliver you in a limo to such and such
a luxury hotel, where a room's been reserved for you and Lisa,
you can go there to talk this over, work something out, what do
you say? Nab him the minute he walked out of the apartment.
Provided he first put down the gun. That had to be part of the
deal. First you put down the gun. Then you come out with the
girl. Nobody gets hurt. We leave you alone with her to work it

out. No gun. That's what you want, anyway, isn't it? To be left alone with the girl?

Georgia Mowbry was coming down the hall toward her. Brady's top female negotiator, on the job long before Eileen joined the team. Was he pulling her from the door? Turn it over to someone more experienced? She hoped not. Georgia was a big rangy woman who'd recently frizzed and bleached her hair a sort of honey-blonde color. She was wearing jeans and the same blue department jacket Eileen was wearing. Stopping to say hello to one of the E.S. men, she exchanged a few words with him, and then continued down the hall to where the door to 409 was still adamantly closed.

"Lieutenant wants to know if you need anything," she said.

"No, I'm fine."

"Cup of coffee, anything?"

"Thanks, I'm okay, Georgia."

"How about the ladies' room? You want to go down the hall, I can . . ."

Both women heard the click of the lock. They both turned toward the door. It opened a crack. The night chain caught it. What happened next happened so quickly that neither of them even had time to catch her breath. There was suddenly the blunt muzzle of a pistol in the crack between door and jamb, and then there was a sudden flash of yellow at the muzzle, and the shocking sound of the gun's explosion, and the bullet took Georgia in the right eye and sent her flying backward into the corridor. Moments later, unconscious, she began vomiting.

The police department's deputy chief surgeon was a woman named Sharyn Cooke. The unfortunate spelling of her name was due to the fact that her then sixteen-year-old, unwed mother didn't know how to spell Sharon. This same mother later put Sharyn through college and then medical school on money earned scrubbing floors in white men's offices after dark. Sharyn Cooke was black, the first woman of her color ever to be appointed to the job she now held.

Her skin was the color of burnt almond, her eyes the color of loam. She wore her black hair in a modified Afro, her high cheekbones and generous mouth giving her the look of a proud Masai woman. She had turned forty this past October fifteenth, birth date of great men—and women, too—and was still getting accustomed to the fact. At five-nine, she always felt cramped in the new compact automobile she'd bought, and was constantly adjusting the front seat to accommodate her long legs. She was fiddling with the seat again on her way home from church that Sunday at twelve-twenty, when the police radio erupted with the words "Cop shot, cop down, confirmed shooting, going to Buenavista!" She hit the hammer and slammed her foot down on the accelerator. A moment later, her beeper went off. She lifted it from the seat, glanced at the number calling, punched it into her car phone, hit the SEND button and—still racing through the streets of Isola at seventy miles an hour—got Deputy Inspector Brady.

"Yes, hello, Inspector," she said.

"Doc," he said. "I've got a cop shot."

It was common knowledge in the department that the commander of the hostage negotiating team had lost his very first female negotiator to a woman who was wielding a meat cleaver. There'd been a hell of a fuss downtown over the fatal string of events—one of the taker's kids dead even before the negotiating team got there, then a police officer killed, and then the taker herself killed when the E.S. stormed the door. For a while, the entire program was in jeopardy, all the hard work Chief McCleary had done getting it started, all the advances Brady had made when he took over, everything almost went up the chimney in smoke. Took Brady a long time to get over it. Even when he felt confident that the program wouldn't be scratched, it was forever before he put another woman on the team. There were two women working for him now, an old pro—well, thirty-six years old—named Georgia Mowbry, and Eileen Burke, a new addition.

What had happened in the building at 310 South Cumberland was almost a replay of what had happened all those years back when Brady lost Julie Gunnison to a murderer with a cleaver in her hands. The E.S. cops had rushed the door the moment the guy inside fired at Georgia. They asked no questions. They knocked the door off its hinges and then six of them opened fire simultaneously with their heavy-caliber guns, blowing the guy halfway across the apartment. In the bedroom, they found his seventeen-year-old sister-in-law handcuffed to the bed and bleeding from two bullet wounds in her chest. She was dead. Probably had been dead long before the negotiating team even got there.

Hostage dead, taker dead, police officer critically wounded.

Almost a replay.

Except that back then, the police officer had died, too.

Brady didn't want to lose Georgia Mowbry now.

He told Sharyn to make damn sure they didn't lose her.

Sharyn told him she'd make sure everybody did the best job possible. She herself was a board-certified surgeon—which meant she'd gone through four years of medical school, and then five years as a resident surgeon in a hospital, after which she'd been approved for board certification by the American College of Surgeons. She still had her own private practice, but as a uniformed one-star chief she worked fifteen to eighteen hours a week in the Chief Surgeon's Office for an annual salary of $68,000. In this city, some twenty to thirty police officers were shot every year. Part of Sharyn's job was to make certain these injured officers received the best possible hospital care.

Georgia was in coma when Sharyn arrived at Buenavista Hospital at twelve-thirty-two that afternoon. She strode into the emergency room, identified herself, and then asked, "Who's in charge?"—the way she always did. The brass hadn't yet assembled. They would be here later, she knew, everyone from the Commish on down if this turned out to be a serious one. For now, there was a battery of nurses, the trauma team, a doctor named Harold Adderley, who introduced himself as the chief resident surgeon, and a junior resident surgeon named Anthony Bonifacio.

Adderley told her that Detective Mowbry had been shot in the right eye, the bullet exiting on the right lateral side of the skull. X rays showed bullet fragments in the brain and fracture on the right side of the skull. She'd been sedated with phenobarbital, and they were administering Decadron intravenously to prevent brain swelling. They were now waiting for her blood pressure and vital signs to stabilize before they did a CAT scan. Adderley expected this would be in the next ten to fifteen minutes.

"Is the O.R. ready for her?" Sharyn asked.

"We'll move her in as soon as we get the results."

"Who's standing by?"

"Pair of neurosurgeons, an ophthalmologist, and a plastic surgeon."

"How does the eye look?" Sharyn asked.

"Bad," Adderley said.

Bert Kling was sitting in his pajamas at the small round table in his tiny kitchen, eating bran flakes with strawberries that had cost him an arm and a leg at the Korean market around the corner, listening to music on the radio, when the news came on at one o'clock that Sunday afternoon. An announcer said that a police officer had been seriously wounded not half an hour ago . . .

Kling glanced up from his bowl of cereal.

. . . and was now in critical condition at Buenavista Hospital

He looked at the radio.

"The officer, a member of the hostage negotiating team . . ."

He put down his spoon.

". . . was shot in the head while negotiating with a man inside an apartment on Cumberland Avenue."

Eileen, Kling thought.

Don't let it be her, he thought.

"In Majesta this morning," the announcer said, "two young men flying pigeons on a rooftop . . ."

He got up from the table at once, turned off the radio, went into the bedroom, picked up the receiver from the bedside phone, and immediately dialed Buenavista, the best hospital in the vicinity of Cumberland. They'd have taken her there in a patrol car with the siren screaming, a radioed 10-13 alerting any other car or beat officer on the route to block traffic, expedite transport to the hospital, and provide a motor escort where possible. Nobody knew how to take care of their own like cops.

"Buenavista Hospital, good afternoon," a woman said.

"This is Detective Bert Kling," he said, "Eighty-Seventh Precinct. A shooting victim was just brought in, an officer on the hostage negotiating . . ."

"One moment, please."

He waited.

"Emergency Room," a man's voice said.

"Yes, this is Detective Bert Kling, I'm looking for information on the shooting victim that was just brought in."

"Which shooting victim did you want?" the man asked, making it sound as if a *dozen* of them were lying around there.

"This one's a police negotiator," Kling said.

"You'll have to talk to your own people about that," the man said abruptly, and hung up.

Kling looked at the phone receiver. He put it back on its cradle, took off his pajamas, and—without bothering to shower or shave—pulled on a pair of Jockey shorts, jeans, a T-shirt that had the words 87TH PRECINCT SOFTBALL TEAM lettered on the front in green, a pair of loafers without socks, and an overcoat, and then immediately left the apartment.

The first person he saw when he walked into the waiting room was Eileen Burke. He went to her at once.

"Hi," he said.

"Hi," she said.

In that brief exchange, any bystander would have known immediately that these two had once been lovers.

"I thought it was you," he said. "I came right over."

Confirming it.

"Georgia Mowbry," she said.

"How bad is it?"

"I think it's pretty bad."

There were other police officers in the waiting room. First Deputy Commissioner Anderson and Chief of Detectives Fremont were standing near the nurse's station, talking earnestly to Inspector Brady. The First Dep was wondering out loud what they should put out to the media. He was concerned because the injured police officer was a woman. He wanted to make certain they didn't get any negative feedback about placing female officers in extremely dangerous situations. After recent disclosures of what had happened to women members of the armed forces during Desert Storm, everybody was suddenly wondering whether women could cut the mustard. This was why they hadn't yet released the officer's name. Georgia Mowbry was a wife and a mother. If the department wasn't careful, the media would have a field day with this one. They were still wondering what to do when Adderley came into the room, Sharyn at his side. He didn't have to signal for attention. All eyes turned to him the moment he made his entrance.

"Gentlemen," he said, and then, seeing that there were women present as well, "ladies, we now have the results of the CAT scan, and I'd like to pass those on to you. There's a bullet wound and concomitant skull fracture in the right temporoparietal region. The orbit of the eye was blown out, there's orbit fracture and hematoma in the orbit. The eye itself has collapsed. At the moment, it's hanging by the optic nerve and some minor blood vessels in the canal. The scan gave us

a good blueprint, and Detective Mowbry will be moved into
the operating room for craniotomy as soon as she's been
prepped. I think that's everything, unless Dr. Cooke has something to add."

"I just wanted to say that Dr. Adderley and I will be joining
the others in the O.R. as soon as we're finished with the briefing
here," Sharyn said. "I must caution you," she said, and hesitated. "This is a hazardous procedure, it might be touch and go
all the way."

Touch and go, Eileen thought.

"How long will the operation take?" Brady asked.

"Depends," Sharyn said. "Five, six hours, wouldn't you
say?" she asked Adderley.

"At least," Adderley said.

"What are her chances?" the First Dep asked.

"In a trauma of this sort, all bets are off," Adderley said.

"Let me put it this way," Sharyn said. "*Without* the surgery,
her chances are nil."

Kling was staring at her.

POLICE DEPARTMENT

SICK DESK REPORT OF UNUSUAL OCCURRENCE INCIDENT

Incident reported by:	Dep Insp William Cullen Brady

TYPE OF INCIDENT (CHECK OFF ONE)

(x) Member of service shot/stabbed or seriously injured

( ) Suspect shot/killed	( ) Suspect shot/wounded
( ) Shots fired/no injury	( ) Accidental Discharge
( ) Animal/dog shot	( ) Forced ingestion of narcotics
( ) Officer witnessed traumatic incident	(x) MOS admitted to hospital
( ) Other (describe)	

DESCRIPTION OF INCIDENT REPORTED

Date March 29	Time: 1217 hours	Precinct 26th

Location: 310 South Cumberland Avenue

BRIEF DETAILS:

At T/P/O below-named officer was shot one time in
the face, through the right eye. MOS was removed
to Buenavista Hospital and Medi-Vac to Buenavista
where she is undergoing brain surgery.

**Use other side of sheet to list additional information

ACTION(S) DIRECTED:

(x) Referred to trauma unit   ( ) On call psychologist to respond

(x) On call surgeon to respond   ( ) Other action(s) taken:

MEMBER(S) OF SERVICE IDENTIFIED AS INVOLVED:

Rank	Name	Command	Tax #
Det 2/Gr	Georgia Mowbry	HNT	347-831-2

SICK DESK SUPERVISOR PREPARING REPORT:

Sergeant Olivia Nelson Giordano
**1416 hours. Deputy Chief Cooke advises that
Detective Mowbry is still in surgery for GSW.
VS stable.

T/P/O meant Time and Place of Occurrence.

MOS meant Member of the Service.

GSW meant Gun Shot Wound.

VS meant Vital Signs.

By the time this report was filed, Georgia Mowbry had already
been on the operating table for three hours.

They had removed a portion of her skull to allow for expansion
of the brain. The pistol Jimmy had used first on his sister-in-
law and next on Georgia was a .22 caliber Llama. It could
have been worse; he could have used a .357 Magnum. But
the trauma was severe nonetheless, and in all such cases blood

rushes to the injured area, causing swelling that, if it is not decompressed, can result either in death or irreparable damage to the brain. This was one of the risks Adderley hadn't been willing to discuss.

As Sharyn had told the gathered cops, the procedure was hazardous; but it was nonetheless commonplace: You went in, you stopped the bleeding, and you repaired the damage. But a big vein was open, and it took a long time to clip it, and tie it, and control the major bleeding, by which time Georgia's pulse rate had dropped to forty, and then thirty, and her blood pressure had fallen alarmingly. When her vital signs were stable again, the surgeons were confronted with the choice of either digging for the bullet fragments in the brain or else leaving them in, and decided that probing for them presented the greater risk. They chose, however, to try getting the dead bone out rather than chancing possible later abscess and infection. They had lowered the temperature of the brain with a cold saline solution; the swelling seemed to be under control.

The eye presented problems of its own.

The bullet had punctured it and caused the gel to leak out, collapsing the eye like a deflated balloon. Blown back into the skull, it now hung precariously in the canal, waiting for the eye surgeon's decision. He determined that the eye was completely destroyed and therefore unsalvageable; there was nothing to do but sever the connecting nerve and blood vessels and surgically remove it. The plastic surgeon was there to reinforce the back of the orbit and to patch the broken bones around the eye and the zygoma, the bone supporting the cheek.

All of this was painstaking, delicate, risky, and time-consuming work. At twenty minutes past midnight, some twelve hours after she'd been shot, Georgia, in a barbiturate-induced coma, was wheeled into the recovery room. She had been on the table for more than ten hours. Now there was an oxygen tube in her mouth to help her breathe, and a tube in her nose to draw out stomach contents, and a catheter going to her bladder, and tubes and lines feeding her intravenously and monitoring all her vital signs.

Early on the morning of March thirtieth, another note was added to the sick-desk report:

```
**0515 hours. Dep Ch Cooke advises MOS in recovery
room listed as Critical/Stable. Prognosis guarded
for recovery.
```

8.

The pair of them were waiting outside the hospital when Sharyn came out at six-thirty that morning. Big blond guy who looked like Kansas, beautiful redheaded woman with him. Sharyn figured them for relatives of the cop who'd got shot.

"Dr. Cooke?" the redhead said. "I'm Detective Burke? I work with Georgia? Detective Mowbry? We're on the hostage negotiating . . ."

"Yes, how are you?" Sharyn said warmly, and extended her hand.

"Detective Kling," the blond one said, and extended his hand in turn. They both seemed extremely nervous. Sharyn guessed they were anticipating bad news they didn't really want to hear.

"How is she?"

This from the blond one.

"She should be all right," Sharyn said.

"Would . . . you like a cup of coffee or something?" This from the redhead. . . . "I was standing right next to her when she got shot, I'd really like to . . ."

"Of course," Sharyn said.

The redhead's first name was Eileen.

The blond was Bert.

They were on a first-name basis and apparently knew each other well. Although Sharyn was a one-star chief, she never wore the uniform and didn't much go for the paramilitary bullshit of the police force. As they walked to the diner, she asked them to please call her Sharyn.

Kling thought he'd heard Sharon.

In his mind, he registered her name as Sharon.

The diner at seven A.M. that Monday morning was packed when the three of them walked in. It was starting out to be a nice day, the sun shining, all traces of yesterday's snow and rain gone, the temperature still quite low, though, considering that spring was already ten days old. Forty-two degrees Fahrenheit didn't feel like spring, even if the sun *was* shining. Neither did five or six degrees above zero centigrade.

Sharyn and Kling were wearing overcoats. No mufflers, no gloves, just the overcoats they'd worn in yesterday's miserable rain and snow, looking a bit rumpled now. Eileen was wearing the jeans and blue jacket she'd been wearing when Georgia got hit, the big word POLICE across the back of the jacket in white letters. All three of them looked somewhat tired and drawn as they found a leatherette booth toward the rear of the diner, the only one available, too close to the kitchen and the men's room. They took off their coats, hung them on wall hooks where they could keep an eye on them.

Kling ordered eggs over easy with home fries and bacon. Eileen ordered a Western omelet with the fries and country sausages. Sharyn ordered the Belgian waffles. All three of them ordered coffee.

"We've been getting calls all night long," Sharyn said. "She has a lot of friends."

"How is she?" Eileen asked. "*Really.*"

"Well . . . we won't *really* know for a few days yet. She'll be in the recovery room for the better part of the week, we'll be watching her carefully all that time. If there's the slightest sign that anything's wrong . . ."

"Is anything wrong *now*?" Kling asked.

He kept staring at Sharyn intently, but she assumed that was because he was so interested in what she had to tell them about Georgia Mowbry.

"Her condition is stable at the moment," she said.

"But she's in coma, isn't she?" Eileen asked. "Isn't that bad?"

"*Induced* coma," Sharyn said. "To reduce brain activity. This was a very serious injury, you know, the trauma was severe. She's lost the eye. . . ."

"Oh Jesus," Eileen said.

"There was nothing we could do for it."

Eileen nodded.

"How long will she be in the recovery room?" Kling asked.

"Better part of the week, I'd say. As soon as she comes around, we'll move her into . . ."

"*Will* she come around?" Eileen asked.

"That's our expectation. As I'm sure you know, the gun was fired at relatively close range. . . ."

"How close?" Kling asked.

"Four to five feet," Eileen said.

"No tattooing or burn marks," Sharyn said. "Not much bleeding."

"What kind of gun?" Kling asked.

"Twenty-two caliber Llama," Sharyn said. "I'll be honest with you, in cases such as this . . . skull injury, severe trauma, hemorrhaging . . ."

"I thought you said there wasn't much bleeding," Eileen said.

"At the site of the wound. But when we went in, we found an open vein in the brain. What I'm saying is we're lucky she made it alive to the hospital. That she survived the initial shock— the forcible entry of the missile, the shattering of bone, the brain penetration . . . well, that in itself is impressive. But until we know how severe the damage to the brain was . . . well."

Brain damage, Eileen thought. Jesus.

"The Commish is a bit sensitive about this one," Sharyn said. "He had to acknowledge what happened on Cumberland—there was a television truck at the scene, covering the hostage situation—but he didn't want anyone to know that the wounded cop was a woman, shot in the *eye*, no less. He wouldn't let me release her name till this morning. Brady's been calling, too . . . Inspector Brady, commander of . . .''

''Yes.''

''. . . been calling every ten minutes. I don't know which he's more worried about, her or his program. He lost a female negotiator some time back. . . .''

''Yes,'' Eileen said.

''Well, you know then.''

''Yes. Dr. Cooke . . .''

''Sharyn, please.''

''Sharyn . . . what's the prognosis?''

''I don't know. Not yet.''

''When will you know?'' Kling asked.

''When she comes around. When we can make some tests.''

''We don't want to lose her,'' Eileen said.

''Neither does anyone, believe me,'' Sharyn said. ''That's why I'm here.''

That night at twenty minutes to eleven—some thirty-five hours after Georgia was shot—the nurse who came into her room for a routine check noticed that she was having difficulty breathing, this despite the fact that she was on a respirator. Alarmed, she reported this to the resident, who examined her briefly and then asked one of his superiors to come have a look at her.

An hour later, just as the midnight shift was coming on, it was concluded that Georgia had contracted aspiration pneumonia. It was the doctors' surmise that she had breathed vomit into her lungs sometime during the first few minutes after the shooting. The vomiting had been an involuntary reaction to a bullet penetrating the brain. She had undoubtedly sucked in a deep breath, pulling vomit into her nostrils and subsequently into

her lungs. The vomit contained stomach acids, which were cor-
rosive. Chemical pneumonia had inevitably and swiftly led to
bacterial pneumonia.

They sucked the vomit out of her lungs mechanically.

They began treating her with antibiotics, and they put her on
the Positive End Expirator Pressure machine, familiarly called
the PEEP and designed to keep the lungs slightly expanded under
pressure.

Georgia Mowbry's postoperative problems were just beginning.

The meeting had started at ten P.M., but this was a matter of life
or death to them, and so the writers were still talking and arguing
at ten minutes past midnight.

The writers called themselves an "alliance."

The Park Place Writers Alliance.

Park Place was the street on which they met, a little cul-de-
sac off Grover Park. Henry Bright, the president of the Alliance,
lived in an apartment on Park Place, which was a shitty little
street lined with tenements and spindly soot-covered trees. Henry
had decorated the walls of the apartment with spray paint. Talk
about your top to bottoms, Henry Bright's apartment was a riot
of color. Henry was twenty-two years old and knew just where
he wanted to go in this city. Where he wanted to go was to the
very top. He wanted to be known through all eternity as the
writer who'd thrown up the most tags ever.

In the old days, these writers' associations prided themselves
on the scope of their artwork. Some of them even achieved a
small measure of fame. One of them even had his work, such
as it was, hanging in museums. Although *some* people thought
it strange that a graffiti writer would be so honored, since *most*
people felt these vandals should be hanged by their thumbs in
the marketplace. But at least, back then, these writers—with a
little encouragement from writers of quite another sort—really

did consider themselves artists. So when they got together to form these writers' groups or associations or leagues or unions, as the organizations were variously called, they were doing so to protect their work.

The Park Place Writers Alliance did not use spray paint anymore. They did not throw up any big two-tone pieces or color-blended burners because nowadays either there was paint-resistant material that would cause the paint to run as if it were crying, or else the piece you worked on all night would be taken off with acid the next day, it just didn't pay anymore. Besides, paint wasn't for posterity.

What was for posterity was scratching the marker into glass. You used either a key or a ring with a hard stone, if you could afford one, and you scratched the marker into the glass or the plastic, HB for Henry Bright, if you happened to be Henry. If you were one of the *other* three guys in the Alliance, you scratched either LR or JC or EB. If you worked on a *big* plate-glass window together, all four of you in the Alliance, then in addition to throwing up your personal marker, you put in the identifying Alliance tag, PPWA, in a corner of the window. This past Saturday night, they'd done a big jewelry store window on Hall Avenue downtown, all four of them etching their markers into the glass, and then throwing up the Alliance tag in the lower right-hand corner. Replace that window, it'd cost the store thousands of dollars. Be easier to leave it there, let the people look in at the jewelry through the initials scratched into the plate glass.

Henry had called the meeting tonight—*last* night, actually, since it was already a quarter past twelve now—because he'd detected that some of the others in the Alliance were running scared. Larry especially—who was only sixteen, but who was an industrious writer, throwing up the LR marker all over town, Larry Rutherford, LR, scratching in the tag with a diamond ring his grandfather had left him—Larry seemed very scared. When, for example, Henry suggested that they all go down to Hall

Avenue again this *coming* weekend—"Do the bookstore across
the street from the big jewelry store, make it like Alliance *Alley,*
what do you think?"—all Larry said was, "And get ourselves
killed?"

What they were here discussing tonight was whether they were
going to let some fuckin lunatic stand in the way of immortality.
Because Henry didn't care how the others felt about getting the
marker out, that was a matter of their own personal aspirations
or lack of them, although some measure of Alliance pride was
also involved. But his own burning ambition was to become
famous all over this city, and then to branch out across the river
maybe, make his way west across the entire U.S. of A., throwing
up the HB marker on every piece of glass or plastic in the country.
HB. For Henry Bright. Ah, yes, the famous *writer,* do you mean?

"What I think," Ephraim said—EB was his marker, for
Ephraim Beame, the only black kid in the Alliance—"is we
should wait a while before going out again, venturing out, you
know, because I like agree with Larry that this person is really
some kind of vigilante nut who's out to get us all, eliminate us,
you know, cleanse the city, purify it, is what I think. Of writers,
that is," he added. "Cleanse it of writers."

"So suppose this guy continues for a month, two months, a
year, what*ever,*" Henry said, "are we supposed to *hide* from
him all that time? Stay *underground* all that time? I really find
that extremely chickenshit, Eph, I really do."

"Thing is," Ephraim said, "he's like going around *shooting*
people, Henry. It's one thing to take a stand for what you know
is right . . ."

"Throwing up the marker *is* right, you're damn right," Henry
said.

"Am I saying no?" Ephraim asked. "I'm saying what's right
is right, is what I'm saying. But I'm *also* saying *might* makes
right, you know, and this man is out there shooting *real* bullets.
And dead is dead," he added.

"The thing we're discussing here," Joey said . . .

Joseph Croatto, whose marker was JC, though sometimes he felt sacrilegious throwing it up.

". . . is not whether we're *brave* enough to go out there in the middle of the night to get stalked by some madman who doesn't recognize what we're trying to *accomplish* in this city . . ."

"Hear, hear," Ephraim said.

". . . but whether it's wiser to *wait* a little while *before* we continue the work."

"Hear, hear."

"Because I personally don't want to wake up with a bullet in my head, thank you," Joey said, and nodded at Larry, who nodded back.

"Here's the way I see it," Larry said.

Sixteen years old with peach fuzz on his face, bright blue eyes, cheeks like a Cabbage Patch doll.

"I think you're the only one who doesn't want to cool it awhile, Henry," he said, and hastily added, "and I *admire* that, I really do. But this man isn't playing around. And what's been happening the past week or so has been scaring other writers off the streets. So if this man is out there *looking* for writers, and there aren't any out there, wouldn't it be *dumb* of the Alliance to give him exactly what he's *looking* for? To provide him with the *targets* he wants? We go down to Hall Avenue, like you suggested . . ."

"I can *taste* that fuckin bookstore window," Henry said.

"Me, too," Larry said, "don't you think we *all* want to do that window? That window is *aching* to be done. Just across the street from the jewelry store? One of the busiest corners downtown? We do that window you're *right*, it'll be Alliance *Alley* down there, we'll be *famous*! But not *now*, Henry. Give this guy a little time to burn himself out. . . ."

"I don't see any sign of that happening," Henry said.

"Then give the *cops* time to catch him. . . ."

"Ha!"

"He's killed three people already, the cops must have *some* kind of line on him," Ephraim said.

"Just give it a little time," Joey said.

Henry shook his head and shoved his glasses up higher on his nose. Behind the glasses, his eyes expressed disappointment more than they did anger. He'd been depending on these people, hoping that their vision would match his own. As the oldest person in the Alliance, he had become their natural leader, even if he was shorter than any of the others. Short and a bit squat. In fact, with his spiky hair and his rotund shape, he somewhat resembled a startled porcupine. Sixteen-year-old Larry was taller and much handsomer than Henry was. And now it seemed that he had swayed the others into thinking the way he did.

"If you won't come with me, I'll do the window alone," he said.

They all looked at him.

"And I'm not waiting till the weekend. I'm doing it tonight."

They kept looking at him.

"So who's with me?" he asked.

No one said a word.

"Okay, the meeting's over," Henry said.

It never occurred to him that wanting to carve his name all over the world had something to do with being only five feet six inches tall.

She was right, of course, there had to be another one.

He had planned to stop at three, but as usual she was right. You stop at three, she said, they'll zero in right away. Why would anyone do three and then suddenly quit? This isn't like deciding to *retire* after you've won three Academy Awards or spent three years on the best-seller list. This is killing *graffiti* writers, don't forget. That's your *mission*, remember? And a person with a *mission* doesn't stop after the third one.

This was in bed last night.

Lying in bed talking about what they would do after the final murder. Her wondering out loud if there should be five, maybe six of them. Lying there in the purple baby-doll nightgown he'd given her for Christmas, no panties under it, one leg straight out, the other bent, lying on her side that way.

"It might be a trade-off," she said. "You do five or six of them, you run the risk of them zeroing in, anyway. But . . ."

"You don't know how scary it is out there," he said. "Middle of the night."

"I'm sure it is," she said. "But you also let them know this is a real mission, you're not just somebody fooling around out there."

"Not a dilettante," he said.

"A dilettante, right. You let them know this is a serious thing with you."

"Do you see what the papers are calling me?"

"I like that," she said, and grinned and moved her knee a little, the knee on the bent leg, just moved it slightly to the left.

He got excited just thinking about her. He was excited now, thinking about last night, about her in the short purple nightgown and the way she just sort of carelessly moved her knee back and forth so that the gown sort of fell away from her, exposing her, the grin on her face saying You want some of this, baby? Come take it, sweetheart.

Got excited all over again just thinking about it.

She wanted him to do five of these fucking vandals, he'd do five. Six, he'd do six. A dozen? Name it. Doing them was her idea to begin with. If he had to do a *hundred* of them, he'd do a hundred. If he could *find* them.

One o'clock in the morning, the streets were deserted.

It was trying to second-guess them that was difficult. Figuring out where they'd hit next. What he did was drive the car around till he found an area with a lot of graffiti on the walls, figuring this was a happy hunting ground with good buffalo, they'd be

back for more, right? Tried to find a pristine wall in a neighborhood flowering with graffiti. Figured the wall would attract
them.

Tonight he was midtown.

Not much graffiti down here, but he'd read in today's paper
about a gang scratching their names onto a plate-glass window
down here, and he thought Hmm, *this* is something new, maybe
there's opportunity here.

That was after they'd made love all night long. That purple
gown, Jesus. He'd left her early this morning, bought a newspaper in the corner candy store and read it on the taxi ride back
to his own place. The newspaper was full of stories about the
graffiti killer. One of the accompanying stories was about the
jewelry-store hit this past Saturday night, though, big initials
scratched into the plate-glass window fronting Hall Avenue, the
letters PPWA in the lower right-hand corner, whatever *that* stood
for, the police weren't speculating. The story said this was a
new wrinkle, defacing glass or plastic surfaces.

He'd thought about that in the shower, thought about it while
he was putting on fresh clothes, thought about it in the deli around
the corner from his apartment, where he had breakfast, thought
about it on the subway ride downtown.

Wouldn't the graffiti killer be attracted to this new development? he wondered.

Nip it in the bud, so to speak?

Show the world he was after *anyone* vandalizing this city in
a serious way?

Show them he was serious?

So he'd driven uptown tonight and circled the blocks looking
for anyone who seemed suspicious in any way, hoping to catch
anyone writing on a store window, stop him dead in his tracks,
blow him away while he was committing the act.

Nothing.

No one.

He'd been too successful, scared off all the punks.

Didn't want to get out of the car and walk around, this was Silk Stocking territory here, a cruising cop spotted a man alone they'd think *he* was about to carve up a goddamn shop window. So he just kept cruising. No pattern to the way he drove, drifting down Hall for a few blocks, then turning North toward Detavoner and then driving uptown and turning south again, all the way to Jefferson, watching all the while for someone standing in front of a window doing his thing.

He spotted a man on Jefferson, standing against a window, all right, but he was just taking a leak.

Nature calls, he thought, and smiled in the darkness of the automobile.

Police car up ahead. MS letters on its side. Midtown South.

He made a right turn on the next corner, heading up to Hall again, and then continued across the avenue and on to Detavoner again, Midtown *North* territory, wouldn't do to have the same police car spotting him twice in the rearview mirror, now would it?

Uptown again for six blocks, hung a right, came down to Hall again, hung a louie, and was approaching the big intersection where the jewelry store had been hit, when across the street he saw a kid with hair like a picket fence standing in front of the window of the bookstore there.

He slowed the car to a crawl.

Slid down the electric window on the passenger side, purred up the street to where the kid was busily scratching away at the plate glass.

The kid turned when he heard the car stopping.

Too late.

"Here, kid!" he said, and fired two shots into his head and another into his chest and then he fired a few into the window, too, just for good measure.

When a man tells you, quote . . .

"I run one of the best shelters in this city."

Unquote.

And he also tells you, quote . . .

"I run a good shelter."

Unquote.

And goes on to say, "Other shelters, you have men getting beaten at night, other men using pipes on them, or sawed-off broomstick handles, but not here in my shelter. . . ."

Well, one could possibly forgive an experienced cop for wondering if perhaps the gentleman didth protest too much. Especially when he went on to give you, in fits and starts, other little quotable tidbits like "Mind you, we don't have a security problem as such" and then goes on to say that fifty blankets were stolen during the last quarter of the preceding year and twenty-six stolen so far in the first two months of *this* year, but "we can't prevent the occasional theft, you know. . . ."

Wellllll . . .

Meyer was certain that Harold Laughton would forgive him for marching straight over to the Sixteenth Precinct last Saturday after his visit to the shelter. And then, since he was already there, where he felt comfortable in surroundings very much like those at the old Eight-Seven, and so it shouldn't be a total waste of time, Meyer asked the desk sergeant to check the activities log for the past several months, just on the off-chance that *maybe*— listen, who could tell, stranger things had happened—just *possibly* everything wasn't quite so kosher at DSS TEMPLE as the protesting Mr. Laughton had claimed.

And lo and behold!

It seemed that in the month of January, which was as far back as the good sergeant wished to go, the precinct had dispatched Charlie Two to the shelter a total of eight times, three of those times to investigate reported assaults, five of them to investigate emergencies that subsequently required hospitalization for rat bites and/or drug overdoses.

The activities log showed an increase in Charlie Two responses for the month of February, with a total of twelve visits to the shelter, most often in the dead of night, for causes similar if not identical to those reported in January.

For the month of March, Charlie Two—which of course was the radio car patrolling the sector in which the shelter was located—had been there only seven times, but one of those calls had been occasioned by a homicide that took place in the shelter's men's room.

In short, DSS TEMPLE was no different from any of the city's other shelters, and Harold Laughton was full of shit, so Meyer called Cotton Hawes at once and told him not to shave over the weekend. Now, at one-thirty that Tuesday morning, a tall redheaded man wearing a tattered brown sports jacket and threadbare blue jeans, his face sporting a three-day beard stubble, his hands encrusted with grime, walked into the shelter and approached the registration desk. He was carrying a duffel bag presumably containing all of his worldly belongings, and he stank so badly of booze that the admissions clerk virtually reeled when the man told him his name was Jerry Hudson and he needed a place to stay for the night.

Hawes signed the register under that name, was handed first the key to a locker and next an index card with the number 104 written on it . . .

"Lucky number," Hawes said boozily and grinned at the clerk, showing greenish-yellowish-brownish teeth.

. . . was told that 104 was the number on his cot—he'd find a cardboard thing with the number on it, hanging from the foot of the cot—and was directed to a room across the drill hall floor, where he picked up a pillow, a blanket, and a toilet kit. Contributed by Halligan Food Stores, it said on the kit's flimsy blue plastic case. Walking with the uncertain step of a drunk, the blanket and pillow clutched to his chest, the duffel hanging halfway down his back, the toilet kit dangling by its cord from his right wrist, he made his way slowly across the huge room to the battered green lockers lining one entire wall. The place echoed with the snores and groans and nocturnal mumblings of hundreds of sleeping men, resonated as well with the voices of men who were wide awake at this hour of the morning and talking loudly to themselves or to others, the drone counterpointed by the mutterings and murmurs of yet more men *trying* to sleep. He located the locker corresponding to the number on his key, unlocked the door, tossed in his duffel, locked the door again, and pulled the key's elasticized loop over his right wrist. Five minutes later, he found the cot marked 104, put the blanket at the foot of it and the pillow at the head of it, and sat down heavily on its edge. He was just about to lie down when a voice said, "*Up*, Mac."

Hawes turned.

A man shorter than he was, but brimming with more muscles than should have been allowable by law, was standing at the foot of the cot, scowling. He was wearing khaki undershorts and a khaki tank-top undershirt that Hawes guessed was regulation military gear. He was tattooed all over his muscles and in some places where there weren't any muscles, including the top of his bald head.

"I said *up*," he said. "*Off* the cot."

The last thing Hawes wanted in this place was an argument. He was here to get a line on whoever had stolen a blanket subsequently wrapped around an old lady now deceased. But people had been hurt here, some of them badly, one of them so badly that they'd had to bury him afterward. Hawes wondered if it would appear convincing for a drunk to sober up in ten seconds flat. He decided it would.

"What's the problem?" he asked.

Cold sober.

Alert to any danger.

Was the impression he hoped to create.

As an afterthought, he hiccuped.

The man with all the muscles and tattoos smiled.

"My cot," he said reasonably.

"One-oh-four," Hawes said, equally reasonably, and showed

the index card and his greenish-yellowish-brownish teeth in a
smile that would have made the lab exceedingly proud.

The repulsive coloration had been created by a dentist the lab
had called in. The dentist had first cleaned Hawes's normally
pristine teeth with polishing cups, using dental toothpaste, and
asking him to rinse afterward. The dentist had then dried off the
teeth and painted them with a weak solution of acid to take off
the shine. He had let the acid stand for some fifteen to thirty
seconds, had washed it off, and had then painted on the Taub
stains normally used to match dentures to the natural teeth in the
mouth. Discolored teeth were usually green around the gum,
brown in the middle, and yellow near the tip. He painted Hawes's
teeth accordingly, coated them with clear plastic, light-fused
them, and promised him the process could be reversed whenever
Hawes decided to give up his new profession. Hawes hoped so.
But he had to admit he looked disgusting.

"One-oh-four is *always* my cot," the man said.

Still reasonably. Smiling in return.

"My ticket," Hawes said, and again showed him the index
card with the handwritten number 104 on it.

"A mistake. They must've meant one-oh-five."

Hawes looked over at the cot on his left.

Someone was sound asleep in it.

"Man in it," he said reasonably.

"One-oh-*three* then," the man said.

Hawes looked at the cot on his right. Someone was sleeping
in that one, too. This was getting to be *Goldilocks*.

"Up," the man said again, and jerked his thumb over his
tattooed shoulder. Hawes saw the head of a dragon glaring at
him in reds, blues, and greens. He wondered if the man was a
former marine.

"Fuck off, sonny," he said.

The man blinked.

"What?"

"Or you're dead fuckin meat," Hawes said, and lay down again, and closed his eyes in dismissal.

He could hear the man's sputtering astonishment at the foot of the cot. He kept his eyes closed, tensing for an attack he hoped would not come. In a little while, he pretended to be instantly asleep and snoring.

"Fuckin asshole," the man muttered at last, and Hawes heard his bare feet padding away from the cot.

He'd slept all that day in preparation for tonight. Now, after he was sure Mr. Muscles was gone for good, he gathered up his things and went into the men's room, where the voices seemed to be loudest. Carried the blanket and the pillow with him, too, so they wouldn't be stolen.

There were half a dozen grizzled men gathered near the sinks, talking to a pair of square shields in blue uniforms. Either one of the guards could have been the man Charlie had described as driving him. One a bit shorter than the other, but each in the five-nine to five-eleven range, each in his mid-forties, with brown eyes and dark hair. The conversation stopped for just an instant when Hawes came in, and then picked up again as he went over to one of the urinals. There were no doors on any of the stalls in here, the better to keep the place as drug-free as Harold Laughton had told Meyer it was.

One of the guards was saying that some off-track betting parlors were ritzier than others. That was the exact word he used, ritzier. Hawes had never seen an OTB parlor that could be called ritzy. But the guard went on to say that the parlor he preferred over *all* the others, the *really* ritzy one, was the one on Rollins and South Fifth.

"That's where I go all the time," he said. "It attracts a much better crowd."

The half-dozen grizzled men clustered around him agreed that the parlor on Rollins and South Fifth attracted a much better crowd.

"Very ritzy," one of them said.

"Who do you like in the third tomorrow?" the other security guard asked.

"Pants on Fire," the first one said.

"You're kidding me."

"Good horse," the first guard said.

"He runs like he's got a *load* in his pants, never mind a fire."

"Liar, liar, pants on fire," one of the men chanted, and everyone laughed.

One of the other men asked the guards about something supposed to've happened here at Temple only the week before. Man named Rudy Price had gone apeshit, tried to drown himself in the toilet bowl. Stuck his head in one of the toilet bowls, tried to drown himself. The guy was asking the guards if it was true. Everybody seemed to think it was comical, man trying to drown himself in a toilet bowl. The guard who liked Pants on Fire said Yeah, it was true, they caught him just in time. One of the men said they shoulda let him do it, he was a no-good fuck, Price.

Hawes zipped up his fly, and shuffled over to the group.

"What time's breakfast?" he asked the guard.

"First time here?" one of the men asked him.

Big burly black guy with a beard like Brillo. Wearing jeans and combat boots and a beaded vest and a scarf. The vest looked as if he'd got it in India someplace.

"Yeah," Hawes said. Briefly.

"Breakfast starts at six-thirty," the guard told him.

"Yuppie commuters in here got to catch they trains," the black man said, and grinned at his own little joke. His teeth were a lot whiter than the ones the lab had given Hawes. He was tempted to smile back. He didn't.

A man wearing a blue watch cap pulled low on his forehead, coal-black eyes burning in his skull, said, "Lots of crazies here tonight."

Hawes thought he looked crazy himself.

"Keep you awake all fuckin night, their screamin," he said.

"Whyn't you guys try to get some sleep?"

This from the guard who thought Pants on Fire was a dog.

Hawes had the feeling the guards wanted these guys out of the men's room here, where they could get in trouble shooting dope, or fighting, or whatever. Didn't want to have to divide their time between here and the drill floor outside. This was a shelter with a heart, Laughton had told Meyer, but things happened here. Hawes didn't know how many square shields there were on the job—he'd seen four or five of them outside when he was collecting the blanket and stuff—but there were more than nine hundred cots out there, and it seemed just possible that more guards were needed on the floor than here in the head. Hence the eagerness to get all their chickens in one coop.

"Quieter in here than out there," the man with the crazy eyes said.

"Well, let's turn in, anyway, huh?" the guard said, gently but pointedly.

The men began moving out. The two guards walked out behind them, like shepherds nudging their sheep to pasture. The big black guy fell in beside Hawes. On the drill floor just outside the men's room, a naked man was pacing back and forth, yelling, "This is a case for the Supreme Court! I cite Wagner v. Wagner, 238 Alabama, 627, 184, South Dakota, wherein it was ruled and upheld on appeal . . ."

"More of them on the streets than there is in the hospitals," the black man said.

Hawes said nothing.

"I'm Gleason," the man said.

"Hudson," Hawes said.

The guard drifted off, walking to where two other guards were standing near the registration desk. There was still a hum in the room. Lights turned low, the room humming with the sound of hundreds of men asleep or awake.

"You dealin?" Gleason asked.

Hawes looked at him.

"Get guys in here lookin like they been through all kinds of shit, they really dealin."

"Not me," Hawes said.

"You fuzz then?"

"Sure," Hawes said and rolled his eyes.

Gleason studied him, still not certain.

"Lydia brace you yet?" he asked.

"Who the fuck's Lydia?"

"The tattooed lady."

"Guy in army undershorts?"

"Queer as a fuckin geranium."

"He told me I was in his cot."

"He *wishes*."

Hawes began walking away. Gleason fell in beside him again.

"I'm here all the time," he said. "How come I never seen you here before?"

"I like it better on the street," Hawes said.

"What street? What's your corner?"

"Lewis and North Pike."

"Then what you doin here *now*?"

"I came south for the winter."

"Too bad it's already spring, man."

"Too bad it's none of your fuckin business," Hawes said.

"You *sure* you ain't fuzz?" Gleason asked.

Hawes turned to him, looked him dead in the eye, and said, "Say it just one more time, man."

Gleason nodded.

"I think you are," he said, and walked off.

The club was called Eden's Acre.

It opened for business at twelve noon, at which time free lunch was served in what was called the Snake Pit. Chloe didn't start work till around ten each night, and then she worked straight through till four in the morning, when the club closed. On a good night, she averaged something like a hundred and fifty bucks. A lot of the girls made twice that amount. But Chloe wasn't doing hand jobs in the Pit.

The first thing you saw when you walked into Eden was a stage shaped like a half-moon on the left side of the room. Flanking the stage on either side was a giant television monitor showing pornographic movies in full color. Some ten to twelve live girls in various stages of undress were dancing on the stage. Eden claimed that a hundred girls danced for the club, which was true. A hundred girls *did* work here, but there were never a hundred girls in the place all at once. Instead, there were four shifts: noon to four, four to eight, eight to midnight, and midnight to four. The girls could work whichever shifts or combinations of shifts they wanted, three or even four shifts a day if they so chose. Usually, most of the girls worked some six hours a day, overlapping one shift into another. The busiest shift was the eight to midnight. Sometimes on the eight to midnight, there were forty or fifty girls milling around the place topless.

The club advertised itself as a totally nude club, but you never saw anyone strolling around bare-assed here. What the girls did, they tugged aside the leg holes of their panties while they were dancing, exposing their genitals to the men sitting at the bar drinking nonalcoholic drinks at five bucks a throw plus tip. In this city, you couldn't serve alcoholic drinks in a so-called totally nude club. The waitresses were quick to tell you that they worked on tips here. The dancers didn't have to tell you because you could see the bills tucked into the waistbands of their bikinis or, if the girls were wearing garter belts and sheer silk stockings, the bills were visible inside the stockings, where men tucked them while simultaneously copping a feel of sweating naked flesh.

The stage was some twenty feet deep, which gave the girls plenty of room to maneuver from back to front where the half-moon became a bartop flanked by those huge television screens flashing men and women in various compromising positions. The girls danced right onto the bar top, gyrating into the faces of the customers, shaking their silicone breasts and tugging aside their panties to show the real thing, quite often shaved. All of the dancers on the stage were available for private one-on-one sessions in the Snake Pit. Little Lucite holders spaced along the bar top advised:

> ## VISIT THE SNAKE PIT
> ### ★ ★ ★
> ### • Table Top Dancing •
> ### • Close Dancing •
> ### • Dirty Dancing •
>
> *Buy Your Tickets Beforehand*

Tickets cost ten dollars for three minutes, twenty dollars for seven minutes, and so on. For fifty dollars, you could be alone with the dancer of your choice for a full twenty minutes. The way it worked, the dancers on the bar top wiggled and jiggled in your face while you kept slipping dollar bills into their panties or stockings, and when they took their break they circulated around the room, working it, sidling up to you and saying Hi, mind if I join you, and pulling up a chair. A waitress came over very quickly, asking if you'd like to buy the lady a cocktail—they called them cocktails even though there wasn't any booze in them—and this would cost you five bucks plus the tip, of course, and the girl would climb onto your lap and wiggle around there, sipping at her drink and chatting you up for a while before she asked if you'd like to go back to the Pit with her. If you said Yeah, that sounds nice, she'd lead you over to a cash register

where you then purchased your ticket or tickets and then you
went back with her to this dimly lighted room some twenty feet
wide by thirty feet long.

One side of the room—the side on which you entered—was
entirely open except for two dozen or more plastic shrubs and
trees lined up in a double row where the wall might have been.
Through the fake leaves and fronds and stalks you could still see
the stage and the girls dancing on it and the monitors displaying
fellatio and cunnilingus and other refined sexual acts while you
were back there in the Pit enjoying your one-on-one.

In the corner to your right as you came in, a fully clothed man
and a girl wearing only a bra, panties, and spike heels sat at a
card table. The dancer you'd chosen handed your ticket or tickets
to the man—the tickets rather resembled utility bonds, though
they were longer and narrower—and he scribbled her initials on
the back of each ticket, and then she came over to you, smiling,
and took your hand again. There was plush carpeting on the floor
of the room, and the carpeting continued up from the floor to
cover the banquettes that lined the other three sides of the room.
Fastened to the floor at spaced intervals in front of the banquettes
were carpet-covered platforms some three feet square and a foot
and a half high. If you were sitting on the banquette, a girl
dancing on one of these platforms had her crotch virtually level
with your face.

For ten dollars, the girl danced on the platform for three minutes, first taking off her bra top, and then lowering her panties
for you more recklessly than she had on stage. This was the
TABLE TOP DANCING promised in the little Lucite holders outside.
Twenty dollars bought seven minutes of **CLOSE DANCING**, which
required the man at the card table to strategically place three or
four of the fake plants and trees around you and the girl on the
platform so that you could nuzzle her breasts and clutch her
buttocks and kiss her nipples if you were so moved. For twenty
minutes of **DIRTY DANCING**, you and the girl moved to the far end
of the room, where you were surrounded by a virtual *jungle* of

plastic plants that thoroughly screened you from view. You sat on the banquette, the girl sat on the platform before you, unzipped your fly, slid your penis out of your trousers, and masturbated you to climax.

So far, Chloe Chadderton hadn't done any dirty dancing, even though she knew this was where the real money was. The trouble with the three-minute or seven-minute stints was that you had to do a *lot* of them to make any money. A girl's take was half the price of the ticket. Five bucks on a ten-dollar ticket, ten bucks on a twenty-dollar ticket, and so on, all the way up the line. You did a three-minute dance, you got five bucks plus tip, which was usually a deuce, although some cheap bastards slipped you a single. But then maybe it'd be *another* half hour before some other guy wanted to go back with you, so if you made twenty, thirty bucks an hour, that was a lot.

On the other hand, if you talked some guy into the dirty dancing, you got half of the fifty, which was twenty-five first crack out of the box, plus he usually tipped another ten or sometimes even twenty, from what the girls told her, which meant in twenty minutes a girl could make something like forty bucks for a mere hand job. So even if you did only *one* of those in an hour, you multiplied that by six hours, which was how long Chloe worked each night, and you went home with close to two-fifty for a night's work, which was a hell of a lot better than the five and dime, Jimmy Dean.

Tonight, as Chloe stood on the platform doing a seven-minute close dance for a white Yuppie wearing a three-piece suit and sweating profusely as he touched her breasts and her hips and her thighs and tried to slip his hand into the panties low on her crotch, her mind was a hundred miles away. Silver had called her this afternoon, to ask her to dinner tonight. She'd told him she was busy. He'd said, "How about tomorrow night then?" She said she had another date, but maybe she could break it. She'd cornered Tony Eden né Ederoso sitting at his card table in the Pit the minute she'd come in tonight, asked him if he

ould do without her tomorrow. Most times, there were plenty
of girls ready to work the eight to midnight, but Tony didn't like
to find himself in a position where there'd be a hundred guys in
the place and only a handful of dancers. He said he'd let her
know what it looked like later on tonight. Ten minutes ago, he
told her it'd be okay.

First thing tomorrow morning, she'd call Sil, tell him it was
okay for dinner.

"And by the way," she'd say, "when do you think I'll be
getting my check?"

He'd promised her twenty thousand for the rights to "Sister
Woman," but so far she hadn't seen a nickel. The big concert
in the park was scheduled for this coming weekend. His crew
would be performing the song then, but meanwhile no bread.
Until his call asking her to have dinner with him, she'd thought
this was a strictly business thing, lawyers'd draw up the papers,
she'd sign them, the check would change hands, good luck and
goodbye. Now a dinner invitation. But still no check. She wondered if dinner was some kind of stall. But he wouldn't just do
the song without *paying* her for it, would he? Wouldn't that be
dangerous for a group as well known as Spit Shine? She'd talk
to him about the check tomorrow morning. The check was her
way out of this. Before it got too late.

"Careful, man," she told the Yuppie. "I don't dance dirty."

At six-thirty that morning, the first of the shelter's hot meals
was served. It consisted of orange juice, coffee, scrambled eggs
with bacon, two slices of white bread, and a pat of butter. The
eggs were somewhat runny, but otherwise breakfast was pretty
good. Somewhat better than jail-house grub, somewhat worse
than what Hawes used to eat when he was in the navy. The
meals were served in the big dining hall on the second floor of
the armory. Upstairs, fluorescent lighting bathed the tables and
benches. Later on in the day, the windows would stream natural

light that would be denied to the level below by the new floor
installed when the place was turned into a shelter. Once upon
time, the armory had been a wide open space where reserv
soldiers drilled. Now, it was a two-level sanctuary for the home
less. It was estimated that a third of those men and women had
mental problems. The man with the crazy eyes was sitting op
posite Hawes at the table.

"So how do you like it here?" he asked.

"Fine," Hawes said.

"Good grub, huh?"

"Yeah."

"What's your name?"

"Jerry Hudson."

"I'm Frankie. You got to be careful here, Jerry."

Hawes nodded.

"Lots going on here, you got to be careful."

"Like what?" Hawes asked.

"Dope, all kinds of shit. They look the other way. The guards.
The psychologist is crazy, did you know that? The social worker,
too. They're all crazy here."

Yep, Hawes thought.

"They got a ring here."

"Um-huh."

"They steal things," Frankie said.

"Who does?"

"The guards."

"What do they steal?"

"All kinds of things. Food. Medicine. Soap. Toothpaste.
Blankets. Everything," Frankie said.

9.

April Fools' Day came in with a spectacular sunrise over the city's rooftops, but by eight o'clock on that first day of the month, the sky was already gray and menacing, and by nine it was raining again. Some people maintained that the choice of this particular date for the playing of pranks had something to do with the vernal equinox, when Old Mother Nature impishly played *weather* tricks on mere mortals. Whatever the origin, All Fools' Day, as it was alternately called, had been celebrated for centuries all over the world—and today it was raining. Again.

And today, again, another of the Deaf Man's letters was delivered by hand to the muster desk downstairs. The messenger was a sixteen-year-old kid cutting high school classes. He told Sergeant Murchison that a tall blond guy with a hearing aid had given him ten bucks to take the envelope in here and hand it to the fat guy behind the desk. Murchison told him to get the hell out of here, and then he sent one of his patrolmen upstairs with the envelope.

Meyer and Hawes had begun a hastily conceived surveillance of the shelter the night before, some fifteen hours after the guy with the crazy eyes had told Hawes about all the nefarious goings-on there. But despite Frankie's grave warnings, they'd observed nothing out-of-the-way. No square shields leaving the building carrying heaps of blankets or cartons of soap. They planned to continue sitting the place tonight, despite the rain. There was

not a cop alive who liked surveillance, especially when it wa
raining.

Meyer was telling a joke when the patrolman walked in.

"This guy is giving a lecture on supernatural phenomena,"
he said, his blue eyes already twinkling in anticipation. "And
when he finishes the lecture he asks the crowd if any of then
have ever been in the presence of a ghost. The hands go up, and
he counts them, and he says, 'That's about right, I usually ge
a response of about fifty percent to that question. Now how many
of you who just raised your hands have ever been *touched* by
ghost?' The hands go up again, and he counts them, and says
'That's about right, too, sixteen, seventeen percent is what
usually get. Now how many of you have ever had *intercours*
with a ghost?' Well, this old guy in his nineties raises his hand
and the lecturer asks him to please come up to the stage, and
the guy dodders to the front of the auditorium, and climbs the
steps, and the lecturer says, 'Sir, this is really astonishing. I give
these lectures all over the world, and this is the first time I've
ever met anyone who's actually had *intercourse* with a ghost.
The old man says, 'What? Would you say that again, please?
And the lecturer yells, 'THIS IS THE FIRST TIME I'VE EVER
MET ANYONE WHO'S ACTUALLY HAD *INTERCOURSE*
WITH A GHOST!' and the old guy says, 'Oh, excuse me,
thought you said intercourse with a *goat*!' "

"That's a Deaf Man joke for sure," Brown said, laughing.

Which was exactly when the patrolman walked in with the
letter.

No one bothered worrying about fingerprints anymore; they'
gone that route with the Deaf Man in the past, and it was a
fruitless one. The patrolman handed the envelope to Carella, to
whom it was addressed, and then hung around to see what this
lunatic was up to this time; word was spreading around the
precinct that the Deaf Man was back. Carella tore open the flap
took out a note stapled to another sheet of paper, and read the
note first:

Dear Steve:
Try not to be fooled this time.
                    Love,
                    Sanson
                    P.S. More later.

The larger sheet of paper had obviously been photocopied from Rivera's book. It read:

FROM WHERE ANKARA stood on the rock tower erected to the gods at the far end of the vast plain, he could see the milling throng moving toward the straw figure symbolizing the failure of the crop, the frightening twisted arid thing the multitude had to destroy if it were to strangle its own fear. The crowd moved forward relentlessly, chanting, stamping, shouting, a massive beast that seemed all flailing arms and thrashing legs, eager to destroy the victim it had chosen, the common enemy, a roar rising as if from a single throat, "Kill, kill, *kill*!"

"He's gonna *kill* somebody," Brown said.

"Somebody in a *crowd*," Meyer said.

"On a vast *plain*," Carella said.

"Either that or he's trying to fool us again," Hawes said.

"Try not to be fooled this time," Carella quoted.

"You know what they call him in France, don't you?" Meyer asked.

"Who? The Deaf Man?"

"No. The person who gets fooled. On April Fools' Day. They call him *poisson d' avril*."

"I thought you didn't speak French," Brown said, remembering his Haitian.

"My wife does," Meyer said, and shrugged.

"What's that mean, anyway?" Hawes asked.

"April fish."

"You think something big's gonna happen outside today?" Brown asked. "Something with a huge crowd ready to explode?"

"A crowd ready to *kill*," Hawes said.

"Let's check the newspaper," Carella said.

"Go brush your teeth," Meyer told Hawes.

They checked the paper.

There were no advertisements for any big outdoor event happening that day.

Good thing, too.

It would have been washed out.

April Fools' Day.

Raining to beat the band.

The Romans used to celebrate something called the Festival of Hilaria, which somewhat resembled it. But that was on the twenty-fifth of March. In India, too, there was a festival called Holī, during which similar high jinks occurred before its conclusion on the thirty-first of March. Here in America, here in this city, the jokes started early.

The city for which these men worked was divided into five separate geographical sections. The center of the city, Isola, was an island, hence its name: "isola" *means* "island" in Italian. In actual practice, however, the *entire* city was casually referred to as Isola, even though the other four sections were separately and more imaginatively named.

In Isola that morning, a seventy-six-year-old priest named the Reverend Albert J. Courter of the St. Mary of Our Sorrows Church on Harrington and Morse was wearing clerical garb and waiting for the J train on the Morse Street platform when he was suddenly attacked by two men who stole his wallet, his rosary, and a medal identifying him as a member of the Order of the Blessed Sacrament Fathers.

The first of the men said, "Good morning, Father," as the priest came up the steps to the platform. The next thing the priest knew, another man grabbed him in a choke hold from behind, causing him to lose consciousness for several moments. While he was lying on the platform, they began ripping his pockets. He regained consciousness just as they were running off.

Father Courter was taken to the nearest hospital, on Harrington and Cole, where he was treated for cuts and bruises on his face before he was released. He told Lieutenant George Kagouris of the Transit Authority Police that he'd been heading downtown to visit with friends and fellow priests in the neighborhood where he'd grown up. He told the lieutenant that there'd been only twenty dollars in the wallet. He told the lieutenant that the medal and rosary beads had no real monetary value. He told the lieutenant that before his attackers ran off, the one who'd first greeted him turned with a grin and shouted, "April Fool, Father!"

The woman's name was Rebecca Bright, and she told Kling immediately that her younger brother had been a little odd even when he was a kid, and she wasn't surprised that he'd been doing graffiti or that he'd got himself killed for it.

The detectives at Midtown South—where Henry Bright's body had been found on the sidewalk outside the bookshop, the shards of the shattered plate-glass window all around him—had called Kling early this morning with an FMU request. Operations Division had informed them that detectives Parker and Kling were currently investigating the uptown murders of the three previous graffiti writers, and since this seemed obviously related, it was

a clear case of First Man Up, and should be turned over to the
Eight-Seven, not that Midtown South was trying to shirk its
responsibilities.

Kling wanted to know why they considered this a clear case
of FMU, not that *he* was trying to shirk *his* responsibilities, but
copycatting was not an unknown phenomenon in this city. For
example, had they recovered any *bullets* at the scene? This was
a trick question. There'd been no bullets or cartridge cases recovered at the scenes of any of the three previous murders. But
to Kling's great surprise, the detective calling from M.S. said,
"Yeah, we did, matter of fact, but that's not why we're turning
this over to you. We *know* you didn't find nothing previous."

"What'd you find?"

"Three bullets inside the front window. Guy must've missed
the victim first few times he fired. Anyway, the slugs went
through the plate glass, and we recovered them."

"That still doesn't add up to . . ."

"We also got a note."

"A *what*?"

"*This* time he pinned a note to the body."

"A *note*?"

"Got it right here in my hand. Nice handwritten note. What
it says is, 'I killed the three uptown.' Now does *that* sound like
FMU, or does it?"

Kling was thinking the guy wanted to get caught, leaving a
handwritten note. Only the ones who wanted to get caught left
notes. Except the Deaf Man. *He* left notes because he *didn't*
want to get caught.

Rebecca Bright was a singularly plain woman, some thirty
years old, Kling guessed, sitting in a small office at the travel
agency for which she worked. Posters of Italy and Spain covered
the walls behind her. Kling wondered what it was like in Italy
or Spain.

"Did you know your brother was writing graffiti?"

"No," she said. "But, as I told you, I'm not surprised."

"*Scratching* graffiti, actually," Kling said. "A section of the broken window had his initials on it. Scratched into the glass. An *H*, anyway, and part of a *B*. He was killed before he could finish the tag."

"The what?"

"The tag. The marker. That's what these writers call them. The graffiti writers."

"I see."

"Did you know any of your brother's friends?"

"No."

"Wouldn't know if any of them were writers then?"

"No. You mean *graffiti* writers, I take it."

"Yes."

"Far as I knew, Henry worked in the produce department of a supermarket. I had no idea what he was doing at night. Scratching his name on windows, you now tell me. Or his friends, either."

"Never met any of them, is that right?"

"Never. Henry and I didn't see much of each other. Henry was a pain in the ass, if you'll pardon my French. I didn't like him when he was a kid, and I liked him less when he grew up. *If* you can call a twenty-two-year-old who scratches his name on windows a *grown-up*."

"But you didn't know he was doing that."

"That's right. I would have liked him even *less* if I'd known."

"Would you recognize the handwriting on this note?" Kling asked, and showed her a photocopy of the note M.S. had turned over to him.

Rebecca studied it.

"No," she said. "Is *that* who killed my brother? The one I've been reading about in the papers?"

"It's a possibility," Kling said.

"He's got to be crazy, don't you think? Though, I'll tell you the truth . . ."

Kling waited.

"Sometimes I feel like killing them myself."

No one knew why brawling, boisterous Calm's Point was called that. Perhaps at one time, when the British were still there, it had indeed been a peaceful pastoral place. Nowadays, the name carried with it a touch of irony bordering on sarcasm: Calm's Point was the noisiest section of the sprawling city, and the spin its residents put on the English language was the cause of derision, amusement, and gross imitation everywhere else in the United States. Ask a native of Calm's Point where he came from, and he would proudly and unerringly tell you "Carm's Pernt."

The officers who answered the radio call had been told only to investigate a complaint of "loud music" coming from apartment 42 at 2116 Nightingale Avenue in a largely Colombian section of Calm's Point. They could hear the music blasting the moment they entered the building. They were experienced cops; it was with a sense of foreboding that they climbed the steps to the fourth floor. They knocked. They knocked again, using their batons this time. They yelled "Police!" over the blare of the Spanish music coming from inside the apartment. They banged on the door again. Then they kicked it in.

A man later identified as Escamilio Riomonte was lying on the floor with a bullet hole in the back of his head.

A woman later identified as Anita Riomonte, his wife, was found lying beside him, a bullet hole in the back of her head.

A four-month-old baby later identified as their daughter, Jewel, was found alive in her crib.

Neighbors told the responding officers that the couple sold heroin from the apartment and that the motive was probably robbery. It was later established that each of the victims had been shot once in the back of the head with a .25 caliber semiautomatic handgun. Sergeant Charles Culligan of the Six-Three Precinct remarked, "Whoever did it, looks like they done it before."

The child was removed to the Riverhead Municipal Hospital Center where it was concluded that she'd spent at least twenty-four hours in that crib before the officers discovered her. Her temperature upon admission to the hospital was recorded as a hundred and five degrees. The moment she began hyperventilating, she was moved to an intensive-care unit. Although the shooting had taken place the day before, Jewel died at 12:34 P.M. that April Fools' Day.

The newspaper ads last weekend had listed the name of the promoter as Windows Entertainment. It had also listed the names of the groups that would be performing in Grover Park this coming weekend. The Deaf Man chose one of the lesser-known groups—he *guessed* it was lesser known because its name was in smaller type than some of the others—and then placed his call to Windows.

"Hello," he said to the woman who answered the phone, "this is Sonny Sanson, I'm handling the arrangements for Spit Shine? For the gig this weekend?"

"Yes, Mr. Samson, how . . . ?"

"*San*son," he said. "S-A-*N*-S."

"I'm sorry, Mr. Sanson, how can I help you?"

"My people are worried about the laminates."

"Worried?"

"When and where do we pick them up?"

"Oh. Just a moment, please, I'll put you through to our security division."

The Deaf Man waited. He wasn't sure he wanted to talk to anyone in the security division. In the corporate world, it was always best to deal with lower-level twerps because twerps always wanted to make themselves seem important even if they had to give away the store to create the impression. Someone in Security might . . .

"Hello?" a voice said.

"This is Sonny Sanson," the Deaf Man said. "Who am I speaking to, please?"

"Ronnie Hemmler."

"Mr. Hemmler, I'm handling the arrangements here in the city for Spit Shine? For the weekend gig? My people are wondering about the laminates. Would you know what the plans are?"

"Plans for what?" Hemmler asked.

Note of suspicion in his voice, not for nothing was he a Security person.

"For picking them up. My people are getting nervous."

"What people?"

"Spit Shine?" the Deaf Man said patiently. "The group?"

"Yeah?"

"We want to pick up our laminates."

"Didn't you get anything in the mail on this?"

"Not yet."

"Something went out on this last week."

"From you?"

"No, no, it would've come from Artco."

"Artco? Is that another company?"

"No, it's a department here. Artists Coordination. They're in charge of things like that."

"Who do I talk to there?"

"Just a second," Hemmler said.

The Deaf Man waited.

When Hemmler came back on, he said, "Sonny?"

He hated it when people who didn't know him called him by his first name—even if it wasn't his *real* name.

"Yes?" he said, not having to feign irritation this time.

"You can try Larry Palmer up there, I'll give you his extension number."

"Can't you just switch me?"

"I'll try, but it doesn't always work. Let me give you the extension in case you get cut off."

"Thank you," the Deaf Man said.

Hemmler gave him the extension number and said, "Now hang on."

The Deaf Man listened while Hemmler told the operator to transfer the call to three-nine-four, and then he waited again, certain he would be disconnected and surprised when a woman's voice said, "Artco."

"Larry Palmer, please," he said.

"May I ask who's calling?"

"Sonny Sanson. Ronnie Hemmler in Security asked me to call."

"Just one moment, please."

He waited again.

"Larry Palmer."

The Deaf Man went through the whole drill yet another time. Palmer listened patiently.

"So what is it you want to know?" he asked.

"We haven't got our laminates yet. My people . . ."

"You'll get those at the site. You managing Spit Shine?"

"No, I'm just smoothing the way for them while they're here."

"Well, when they get to the park . . . they'll want to do a sound check, I guess, make sure everything's the way they want it . . ."

"Oh, sure."

"So just have your road manager stop in the trailer, let them know who he wants around the act. In the stage area, you know? How many people he wants there. They'll give him the laminates he needs."

"What trailer would that be?" the Deaf Man asked.

"The production trailer," Palmer said, sounding somewhat surprised. "On the site. Windows'll have a stage manager in there."

"Who do we talk to if the stage manager's out to lunch?" he asked, smiling, keeping his tone light.

"Well, there'll be a secretary in the trailer, two or three assistants, you know how these things work."

"Sure. What's a good time to stop by?"

"Once they start setting up, they'll be going day and night."

"When will that be?"

"Listen, don't you *know* all this?"

"There was a foul-up," the Deaf Man said.

"What kind of foul-up?"

"Long story," he said. "I *still* don't know when we'll be setting up, or when we can do our sound checks, or . . ."

"Well, the unions'll be loading in at six tomorrow morning, but you won't want to pick up your laminates then, there'll be a mob scene at the trailer. You won't need them till your act gets there, anyway, so what's the hurry?"

"No hurry at all," the Deaf Man said. "Thanks a lot."

"No sweat, Sonny," Palmer said, and hung up.

In Riverhead early that afternoon . . .

The name Riverhead came from the Dutch, though not directly. The land up there had once been owned by a patroon named Ryerhurt, and it had been called Ryerhurt's Farms, which eventually became abbreviated and bastardized to Riverhead. Over the years, this section of the city had been inhabited sequentially by Jews, Italians, blacks, Puerto Ricans, and—most recently—Koreans, Colombians, and Dominicans. If ever there was a melting pot, Riverhead was it. The only trouble was that the melting pot had never come to a boil.

In Riverhead early that afternoon, two young men crouched behind the stairs in the ground floor hallway of the parole office on Edgerley Avenue, whispering in their native tongue about April Fools' Day. In Colombia, April Fools' Day was called *el día de engañabobos*, and whoever was made a fool of on this day was called *un inocente*. Today, the two young men planned to make a fool of a parole officer named Allen Maguire. The way they planned to do this was to kill him.

In this city, killing someone wasn't such a big deal. In the first quarter of the year, for example, five hundred and forty-six murders were committed, which might have sounded like a lot when you compared it to the mere fifty blankets stolen from DSS TEMPLE in three months last year, but all it really came to was a scant nine murders a day, not bad when you considered all the guns out there. Sixty-one percent of all the murders in this city were committed by firearms, but that was no reason to take guns away from people, was it? After all, in *eight* percent of this city's murders, feet or fists were the weapons, but did anybody suggest *amputation* as a means of control? Of course not.

The two men planning to kill the parole officer did not plan to use their fists or their feet. They were both armed with Intratec nine-millimeter semiautomatic pistols capable of laying down a barrage of fire at the rate of five or six rounds a second. The Intratecs were part of the April Fools' Day joke. The two Colombians had been hired by a Riverhead drug dealer named Flavio (Fat Boy) Garcia, who'd been convicted two months ago for a parole violation, namely for having in his possession a firearm, namely an Intratec nine. Maguire was the person who'd brought the parole violation charges after Garcia's arrest, and now Fat Boy was languishing upstate in a delightful little cell at Castleview Penitentiary, from which he'd ordered the two Colombians to "seriously injure" the parole officer. They took this to mean kill him.

They had not been instructed to kill him on April Fools' Day, however, nor had they been instructed to use Intratecs on him, but they both felt that since an Intratec had been the instrument of Garcia's embarrassment, it should now be the instrument of his revenge. They were quite looking forward to doing the parole officer, not the least because Garcia had promised to give both of them promotions if they succeeded in carrying out his instructions. At the moment, they were both clockers, who were low-level people who sold cocaine on street corners. A clocker in the drug world was somewhat higher in status than a toy in the world of graffiti writers. Manuel and Marco planned to change their status within the next twenty minutes.

It only took fifteen.

At precisely seven minutes past two that afternoon, Allen Maguire came back from lunch and stepped into the building on Edgerley, only to see two young men step from behind the staircase with pistols in their hands. He turned to run, but he was too late. One of them yelled, *"Inocente! Inocente!"* and then both of them opened fire. Maguire was dead twenty times over when they stepped over his bleeding body, giggling, and ran out of the building into the rain.

The man who stopped at the 87th Precinct's muster desk at two-thirty that afternoon said he wanted to talk to the detectives investigating the Wilkins case. Sergeant Murchison took his name, called upstairs, told Kling who was here, and then asked the man to go up to the detective division on the second floor, he'd see the signs.

The man introduced himself as David Wilkins.

"Peter was my brother," he said.

Thirty-four, thirty-five years old, Kling guessed. Brown eyes, reddish hair, reddish mustache. Slender and fit-looking; Kling supposed he exercised regularly. He was sporting a tan, in fact. Had he just come back from a vacation in the sun someplace?

"The reason I'm here," Wilkins said, "is I went to Surrogate's Court this morning to see what it said in my brother's will, and they told me a will hadn't been filed."

"Yes?" Kling said.

"I feel certain there's a will."

"Yes?"

"So why hasn't it been filed yet?"

"Well, it sometimes takes a while to get papers to court," Kling said. "Two, three months sometimes. It's still early to be . . ."

"I think I'm *in* that will," Wilkins said. "I think *that's* why it hasn't been filed yet."

"What makes you think you're in it?"

"Little things my brother said. Hints. We were very close."

Kling wanted to ask him if he'd known his brother was a closet graffiti writer. Those twenty-two cans of paint in the closet still bothered him. Debra Wilkins as surprised to see them as the detectives were. No idea her husband was hoarding paint for his nocturnal forays.

"I think Debra *knows* I'm in the will, and is trying to hide it from me," Wilkins said.

"Have you *asked* her if you're in it?"

"We don't speak to each other."

"Oh."

Kling was suddenly interested. Detectives liked nothing better than family disputes. Family disputes provided motives. But an unfiled will? A *hidden* will? That was the stuff of paperback mysteries. In police work there were no mysteries. There were only crimes and the motives for those crimes.

"Haven't spoken to each other since the wedding," Wilkins said. "That was three years ago. She threw a glass of champagne in my face."

"Why'd she do that, Mr. Wilkins?"

Seeming only mildly interested, but this was a family dispute and he was listening intently.

"I called her a whore."

Kling all ears now. This was turning into a Southern Gothic.

"Why'd you do that, Mr. Wilkins?"

"Because she *is* one," he said, and shrugged.

"You don't mean that literally," Kling said, prodding.

"No, but you know what I mean."

"No, what *do* you mean?"

"A cock tease," Wilkins said.

Good thing you didn't call her *that*, Kling thought. She'd have broken the whole *bottle* of champagne over your head.

"Ever mention this to your brother?" he asked.

"Of course not," Wilkins said. "I figured he made his bed, let him lie in it."

But now he's dead, Kling thought.

"And you think she's hiding the will from you, is that it?"

"I'm *sure* she's hiding it. What I want is for you to go in her house with a search warrant . . ."

"Well, we can't do that, Mr. Wilkins."

"Why not?"

"I don't think a judge would grant one. Not to go in and search for a will. Not without some reason to believe it would constitute evidence in a crime."

"If she's keeping money from me, it *is* a crime."

"Well, we don't know if there *is* a will, you see, or if you're in it, if there is one. And if there is, how do you know it's in her house? Have you ever *seen* this will?"

"No, but . . ."

"So how can I ask for a court order to search for a will that may not exist? The judge would throw me out."

"So she just gets away with it, huh? Hiding the will from me?"

"Well . . . what you *can* do . . . I'm not a lawyer, and I don't want to advise you. But if you *went* to see a lawyer . . ."

"*Lawyers!*" Wilkins said.

" . . . I'm sure he could write a letter to your sister-in-law . . ."

"*That* bitch!"

" . . . asking her if there is a will, and if so, when does she plan to petition the court for probate. Then if she doesn't answer in a reasonable amount of time, he can take it from there."

"Take it *where* from there?"

"Go to court for you, I guess."

"What you're saying is it's going to cost me money to get whatever money my brother left me."

If he left you any, Kling thought.

"What I'm saying," Kling said, "is that this isn't a police matter."

But maybe it was.

This was the Old City.

The ocean-battered seawall still stood where the Dutch had built it centuries ago, the massive cannons atop it seeming even now to control the approach from the Atlantic though their barrels had long ago been filled with cement. If you looked out over the wall at the very tip of the island, you could watch the Dix and the Harb churning with crosscurrents where the two rivers met. The wind howled in fiercely here, ripping through streets that had once accommodated horse-drawn carts but that were now too narrow to allow the passage of more than a single automobile. Where once there had been two-story wooden taverns, a precious few of which still survived, there were now concrete buildings soaring high into the sky, infested redundantly with lawyers and financiers. The firm of Osborne, Wilkins, Promontori and Colbert was in one of those buildings.

"I love the view from up here," Parker said. "This part of the city."

They were strolling down the hallway toward a huge floor-to-ceiling window through which they could see towering skyscrapers succumbing to dusk. It was close to five o'clock. They hadn't called ahead, and Kling was wondering now if they should have. But Parker had told him he liked to surprise people. Parker thought he was full of surprises. Maybe he was. His surprise for today was that he hadn't shaved. Kling wondered if it was wise to go into a fancy lawyer's office without either an appointment or a shave.

The receptionist asked them who they were.

Parker flashed the tin and told her they wanted to talk to Mr. Colbert, please, if he could spare them a minute. Neither of them particularly liked lawyers. Aside from district attorneys, their entire experience with lawyers was with *defense* lawyers, many of whom had once *been* D.A.'s, all of whom were determined to impeach them as witnesses and cast them as brutes, racists, and perjurers. But Peter Wilkins had been a lawyer, and he was dead. And this morning his brother had raised the question of a will that might or might not exist, in which he might or might not have been named as a beneficiary. So they were here to talk to yet *another* lawyer, who happened to have been Peter Wilkins's partner, and who now came out of his office to greet them personally.

Kling recognized the man he'd met at the wake. Thirty-five years old or thereabouts, plain, craggy face, dark eyes, mustache, eyeglasses. Wearing the same brown suit he'd been wearing when they'd met the first time. Button-down collar, striped tie. Tall and angular. Hand extended in greeting.

"Gentlemen," he said, "come in, please, have you learned anything?"

"No, not yet," Kling said.

"Few questions we'd like to ask you, though," Parker said, "if that's all right with you."

"Yes, please," he said, ushering them into his private office and closing the door behind them. They were facing a window wall that offered a breathtaking view of the skyline. Big wooden desk covered with papers in blue binders. Bookshelves sagging with heavy legal tomes. Framed university degrees on the walls. Colbert sat behind his desk, the window wall behind him.

"So," he said. "How can I help you?"

"I got a visit this morning from a man named David Wilkins," Kling said. "Do you know him?"

"Peter's brother. Yes. I know him."

"I understand he and Mrs. Wilkins don't get along."

"That's putting it mildly," Colbert said, and smiled.

"Threw champagne in her face, that right?" Parker asked.

"And shouted obscenities at her. At her own wedding reception, mind you. I've never seen her so angry."

"You were there?"

"Oh, yes. The three of us have been friends . . ." He shook his head. "I'm sorry, I still can't get used to the idea of Peter being gone." He sighed, shook his head again, and said, "Yes, I was there. I was Peter's best man, in fact."

"Wilkins seems to think his brother left a will," Kling said.

Colbert said nothing.

"And that he's in it," Parker said.

Colbert still said nothing.

"Would you know if there's such a will?" Kling asked.

"Why do you want to know this?" Colbert said.

"Well . . . there's been a murder committed," Kling said, "and we like to cover all the . . ."

"What my partner's trying to say," Parker said, "is that it has been known in the annals of crime for people to *kill* other people in order to inherit money. Is what I think he's trying to say."

"I see. So you think . . ."

"We don't think anything yet," Kling said. "We're trying . . ."

"What we *think*," Parker said, "is that Wilkins sounds like a flake goes around insulting the bride at her own wedding and now thinks he's named in his brother's will, is what we think. Which could have some bearing on the case."

"So *is* there such a will?" Kling asked.

"By *such* a will, do you mean a will in which David Wilkins is named as a beneficiary? Or merely a will Peter Wilkins left?"

"Take your choice," Parker said.

"Peter Wilkins left a will, yes," Colbert said. "Hasn't Debra told you this?"

"We didn't ask her," Parker said. "Do you have a copy of that will, Mr. Colbert?"

"I have the original," Colbert said.

"May we see that will, please?" Kling asked.

"Why?" Colbert said.

"As my partner explained, it might have some bearing if Wilkins was named as . . ."

"Yes, I understand. But the will hasn't yet been probated, hasn't been made a public document. If I showed it to you, I'd be violating the privacy . . ."

"Mr. Colbert," Parker said, "your partner was killed. We're trying to find out who did it."

"I recognize that. But I don't think I can show you his will." Parker looked at him.

"I'm sorry," Colbert said.

"Can you tell us if David Wilkins is a beneficiary in the will?" Kling asked.

"Suppose I say he is? Will you then want to know what the *conditions* of the will are, what the *terms* of the will are, what . . ."

"Can't you just give us a simple yes or no?" Parker said.

"Can't you wait till the will is probated? The man was *buried* only last week, I would think . . ."

"Let me put it to you this way, Mr. Colbert," Parker said. "Suppose this nutty brother of his who loses his head at weddings discovers he's going to inherit a million bucks when his brother dies. And suppose he sees in the newspaper that a person was killed spraying a wall, and suppose he decides it would be a good idea to kill his brother and make it look like the same person did it so he can collect his mil and run off to the South Pacific, do you think *then* you could understand why we might want to know if this guy's *really* going to inherit?"

"Yes, but . . ."

"So give us a break, willya?" Parker said.

Colbert smiled.

"I suppose I can disclose a negative," he said. "No, David Wilkins is not named as a beneficiary in his brother's will."

"Thank you," Parker said. "Can you tell us who *is* named?"

"That would be a positive," Colbert said, and smiled again. "I'm sorry, really, but I couldn't reveal that without first asking Debra Wilkins's permission."

"It'll be a matter of public record the minute she files for probate," Kling said.

"Yes, but it's not a matter of public record yet."

"Do you know *when* she plans to file?"

"I have no idea."

"Hasn't said anything to you about . . ."

"She's given me no instructions. Her husband was just killed, Mr. Kling. I'm sure the *last* thing on her mind is filing his will."

Kling nodded.

Parker nodded, too.

"Well, thanks a lot," he said, "we appreciate your time."

"Happy to be of help," Colbert said, and came from behind his desk to show them to the door. "If you like," he said, "I'll give Debra a call, ask if it's okay to supply the information you're looking for."

"Yeah, we'd appreciate that," Parker said, and handed him his card.

"Thanks again," Kling said.

In the hallway outside, as they walked toward the elevators, Parker said, "Did you see those diplomas on his wall? The guy went to *Harvard*!"

"Why'd he wait till we were on our way out?" Kling asked.

"Wait for *what*?" Parker said. "Sometimes you've very fucking mysterious, you know that?"

"Wait to make his offer. About calling the wife."

"Let me tell you what that's called, okay? It's called lawyer-client confidentiality, and it means you don't call your client while somebody is with you who can hear the conversation. Got it?"

"I'm gonna ask her about that will," Kling said. "I don't see what the big *secret* is about a will that's gonna be probated anyway."

"It'll wait till tomorrow," Parker said. "You bucking for commissioner or what?"

Kling looked at his watch.

"It'll wait till tomorrow," Parker said again.

Kling nodded. "Wanna grab a burger?" he asked.

"Yeah," Parker said, and grinned. "But not with you."

Chloe thought it was an April Fools' Day joke at first, Sil handing her the check over the table. He'd told her on the phone this morning that it might take a few days yet for the group's business manager to cut the check, but here he was handing it to her, nice pretty yellow check, his fingers to her fingers over the table. The first thing she saw was the six zeros, four of them in front of the decimal point and another two after it. Then she saw the two, and sure enough, she was looking at a check for twenty thousand dollars.

"I should have asked for it in singles," she said, and rolled her eyes.

"How about quarters?" Sil said. "Wheelbarrow full of quarters."

"This won't bounce, will it?" she asked.

"Better not," he said, and raised his wineglass.

She put the check in her handbag and snapped the bag shut before she lifted her glass.

"Here's to the first Spit Shine performance of 'Sister Woman' this Saturday," he said.

"Here's to it," she said, and they both drank.

"Will you come hear us?" he asked. "I'll get you a laminate, you can sit right on the stage with us."

"What's a laminate?"

"A pass. Get you through security."

"What time Saturday?" she asked.

"We're opening the whole thing," he said. "Only better spot would be the closing one. Usually, your headliner's the last act on stage. But Grass thinks *next* to closing would be better for a Sunday. The thing's running two full days, you know. Starts at one o'clock Saturday, ends midnight Sunday."

"Who's Grass?" Chloe asked.

"Girl in the crew."

The way he said it, so offhandedly like that, she figured there was something going on between them. Looked away, too, something going on there for sure.

"There'll be ten groups altogether, five on Saturday, another five on Sunday. Figure an hour onstage for each of us, maybe even an hour and a half, depending on how it's going. Then, when you figure in your dead time . . ."

"Dead time?"

"Yeah, the next act placing they instruments and setting up they own mikes and amps, that all takes time. Sometimes your dead time can be an hour between each act, depending how fussy the group wants t'be. What I'm saying is it'll be a full day, if you want to go the whole route. I'd be happy t'stay with you, you want to stick around after we're through performing. Or we can go someplace else, if you like, spend the day together. If you like," he said.

"I haven't yet said I was coming," she said.

"Well, *if* you come. I thought you might like to hear us do 'Sister Woman,' is all. We've been rehearsing it, I think it'll go down real fine."

"It's a good song."

"Oh yeah."

"When will you be doing it? I mean, where in the act?"

"We're opening with it. Usually, you open with something familiar, give 'em time to settle down while they listen to one of your hits. This time, we're jumpin right in with both feet, givin 'em a new one. *Then* we'll do one of our hits . . . you familiar with 'Hate'?''

"No, I'm sorry."

"You got a date with hate, at the Devil's gate," he rapped, beating out the rhythm on the tabletop, "you gotta *hate* the ofay . . . you don't know it, huh? Big hit. Anyway, we do that after 'Sister Woman' and then we've got a big surprise planned for later on, I was hoping you'd stay for it. Something unusual for us. Chloe, I'd . . . be very disappointed if you didn't come Saturday. I was looking forward to your coming. It'd be very special for me if you was to come."

She had promised Tony she'd work all day Saturday—which was supposed to be her day off—to make up for tonight. Now that she had the check, she could tell Tony things had changed. Tell him she didn't need the job anymore. Though she knew people who'd won more than twenty on the lottery, blew it all in a month. She couldn't let that happen. Maybe she should hang on to the job till she figured what to do next. Put the money in the bank, keep dancing at Eden's till she explored the opportunities open to her. Go in this Saturday, like she said she would. Still, she *did* want to hear them do "Sister Woman." Then again, that tune was the past, man, that tune was George Chadderton, long dead and gone and scarcely missed at all. The future was *Chloe* Chadderton. But maybe the future was Sil, too.

"One o'clock, you say?"

"Get you a laminate the minute you say the word. All access, you can roam around wherever you like before the concert starts. I'll set you up on the stage where you can hear and see everything we do. Take you around later, introduce you to the other groups." He lowered his eyes again. "That'd make me very proud," he said.

"I'll see," she said.

She wasn't playing it cute, she wasn't that kind of woman,

never had been. She was still thinking it might be better to hang on to the job, go in Saturday like she'd promised Tony. Maybe Sil *was* the future, though she wasn't too sure about that, either. Men were men, and too damn many of them were alike. But future or not, the job at the Eden was the *present*. She didn't want to start living on that twenty. That twenty was her stake.

"Well, you think it over," he said, and took another sip of the wine. "I don't know too much about Italian food," he said, "except pizza on the road. There's some great pizza joints in Pennsylvania and Ohio. But I asked Mort . . . Mort Ackerman . . . what he thought the best . . ."

"Who's Mort Ackerman?"

"Promoter doing the concert. Windows Entertainment, you ever hear of them?"

"No."

"They're gigantic. Mort's the CEO. We were yellin at him about the ads, and he called today to say there'd be full-page ads in all the papers tomorrow, and Spit Shine's featured real prominent, big as any other headliner."

"I'll look for them," she said.

"Mort says this is his favorite restaurant in all the city," Sil said, and hesitated, and then said, "Romantic, too. Mort said."

"It *is* romantic," she said. "Don't you think it's romantic?"

"Oh yes, I do, yes," he said. "All these flags. Would you care for some more wine?"

"Please," she said.

He signaled to the waiter. The waiter poured.

"And whenever you're ready, sir," he said, "I'll be happy to take your order."

"In just a bit," Sil said.

He lifted his glass, looked over it into her eyes.

"Chloe," he said, "please say you'll come Saturday."

"Yes, I think I will," she said.

"Good," he said, and grinned.

She returned the smile.

She was thinking he was very cute. She was hoping he *would* turn out to be the future.

They clinked glasses.

They drank.

"I can't wait to see your face," he said.

"When you do George's song, you mean?"

"Well, that, too," he said mysteriously.

"Well, what *do* you mean?"

"You'll see."

"No, tell me."

"You'll see," he said.

Looking like the cat that swallowed the canary.

So damn cute she could eat him alive.

"I'm starving to death," he said. "Let's order."

In Majesta that Wednesday night . . .

Majesta had without question been named by the British; the cognomen rang with all the authority, grandeur, greatness, and dignity of sovereignty, its roots being in the Middle English word *maieste*, from the Old French *majesté*, from the Latin *mãjestãs*. Even the section called Port Royal had long ago been British, though by the early nineteen-hundreds it had already become an exclusively Italian community. In the forties, the Puerto Ricans started coming in. Now there were Dominicans and Chinese as well.

In Majesta that Wednesday night, in Port Royal, at seven minutes past seven, with the sun already gone for almost an hour, a fifteen-year-old girl who called herself "Italian" even though her parents and grandparents had been born in this country, sat on the front stoop of her apartment building, enjoying the sweet fresh smell of the city now that the rain had stopped. The night was mild, it seemed to Carol Girasole that spring was honestly here at last.

At eight minutes past seven, eighteen-year-old Ramón Guz-man walked up to Carol where she sat on the front stoop, bowed from the waist, said, "Haw do you do, miss?" in faintly accented English, stood up, grinned, punched her in the eye, shouted "April Fool!" and ran off.

Carol started yelling blue murder. Nothing like this had ever happened to her in her life! The nerve! A spic coming up to her and punching her for no good reason! Running off into the night, Ramón thought that what he'd just done was very comical, per-haps because he'd had a little too much to drink. He was still laughing to himself when he reached his own street and went upstairs to the apartment he lived in with his mother and three sisters. Five minutes later, he heard a great commotion down-stairs and went to the window to look out.

The girl he had punched was standing outside the building with five grown men who'd formed a sort of circle around Ger-aldo Jiminez, it looked like, and they were yelling "You the April Fool kid? You the one hit this girl?" Geraldo, who was sixteen years old, and skinny as a needle, had just got here from Santo Domingo two months ago, and he didn't speak enough English to know what "April Fool" meant, so he just kept shaking his head and saying no, not understanding what these men were so upset about, but figuring if he just shook his head and kept saying no over and over again, they'd realize there was some kind of mistake here. But the men kept yelling, "Wha'd you do, April Fool? You hit the girl here, huh?" and Geraldo said, "*No hablo inglés,*" and one of the men yelled, "Don't lie!" and someone else hit him, and then they were all hitting him and Carol said, very softly, "I don't think that's him," but they kept hitting him with their fists, yelling, "You lying spic bastard!" and "Hit a girl, huh?" and "April Fool, huh?" all the while hitting him. And then one of the men broke a bottle on his head, and when Geraldo fell to the sidewalk, they began kicking him. They kicked him everywhere, his head, his chest, his stomach, his groin, everywhere. Carol said, more softly this

time, "I don't think he's the one," but they kept kicking him
till he lay still and silent and bleeding on the sidewalk.

Ramón watched all this from his window.

Then he took off his clothes and went to sleep in his undershorts
in the room he shared with his three sisters.

In Isola at nine o'clock that night, Sharyn Cooke and three other
surgeons stood around Georgia Mowbry's bed in the recovery
room at Buenavista Hospital, talking quietly about their next
move. This was now almost forty-eight hours since she'd been
wheeled out of the operating room and she was neither responding
to verbal stimuli nor voluntarily moving any of her extremities.
At the same time, her fever stubbornly refused to drop and her
white blood-cell count continued rising. Most alarming, though,
was a significant increase in intracranial pressure, which almost
certainly indicated free bleeding and the consequent danger of a
blood clot. The surgeons could see no course except to go in
again and find whatever was causing the problem. Dr. Adderley
ordered Georgia prepped at once for emergency craniotomy.

At twenty minutes to ten, they opened her skull again.

An expanding blood clot killed her three minutes later.

Parker figured that the way to seduce a girl was to tell her how
brave you were. Let her know you'd been in some very dangerous
situations where you'd behaved courageously and fearlessly and
with good humor, and she would then equate this with the size
of your cock. So he told her first that he had flown an airplane
in the war, but he didn't bother to mention which war because
he'd never flown an airplane in his life and he didn't want her
to start asking technical questions about this or that.

Then he told her he'd joined the police force after his honorable
discharge and had made detective six months later—which was
another lie since it had taken him three years to get the gold

shield even though he'd had a rabbi in the Chief of Detectives' Office putting in the good word. He told her he loved detective work because it gave him an opportunity to help the poor and oppressed by righting wrongs and by making certain the victim-izers of this world got put behind bars where they belonged. He halfway believed this. About the victimizers, not the poor and oppressed bullshit. Far as Parker was concerned, nobody was poor and oppressed unless he *chose* to be poor and oppressed. He was saving the best part for last. The best part was the only true part.

They were sitting in the living room of her apartment on Chelsea Street, this was now almost eleven o'clock. He'd left Kling at five-thirty, later than he normally cared to work, he normally liked to quit for the day at three-forty-five on the button. But there'd been a lot of paper work to file on the new jackass got himself killed on Hall Avenue—*scratching* a window, no less. Only good thing about the new murder was it gave him an excuse to call Cathy again, ask her a few more questions on the phone and then ask her if, by the way, she'd like to grab a quick bite, nothing fancy, maybe a pizza or something—brunch on Sunday had cost him seventy-five bucks for the two of them, with nothing but a stroll in the park and a handshake after—and then catch a movie later. Cathy told him she was just finishing typing a screenplay, what a coincidence, would six o'clock be okay? The movie had let out at ten, and she'd asked him to come back here for coffee, which he figured was a very good sign. So now he was laying the groundwork.

The porcupine story was always a good one because it was true and also because it showed him in a brave and also hu-morously sympathetic light. The way the porcupine story went— he had told it to so many different women on so many different occasions that he knew it by heart and never varied the details of it, listen, if something wasn't broke, why fix it? The way it went, he was in the squadroom all alone one day when this lunatic . . .

"This was before I got transferred to the Eight-Seven. I was working out of the Six-Four in Calm's Point, a very tough precinct. I was on the graveyard shift, this was maybe three, four o'clock in the morning, still as death up there, this guy walks in with a porcupine on a leash."

He waited for her amused expression, women always thought a porcupine on a leash was something cute. Unless the thing's owner had a gun in his hand. Which this guy had in his hand. The first thing Parker wondered was how he'd got past the desk sergeant. This was before bomb threats were common in this city; there weren't patrolmen posted outside the front doors of station houses back then. But anyone walking in still had to stop at the muster desk, state his business, big sign advising them to do so. Especially a guy with a fuckin *porcupine* on a leash!

He risked the word *fuckin* with her.

Waited for her reaction.

Nothing.

He considered that a good sign.

Anyway, the guy had to've told the desk sergeant what his business was, and the sergeant had probably sent him upstairs, maybe the porcupine had rabies or something, whatever these things got. But the guy certainly hadn't told the sergeant he had a gun in his pocket, which he took out the minute he walked into the squadroom.

"So you got this picture, Cath?"

He risked using the diminutive, which sounded like a pet name. They were sitting on the couch and he had his arm around her. Her blouse unbuttoned low, which he realized was a habit with her, the better to see the boobs, my dear.

"Here's this guy with a big gun in his right hand and his left hand is holding a leash at the end of which is this porcupine looks like an attack dog with quills."

He laughed.

Cathy laughed, too.

He sort of hugged her when she laughed. Arm around her shoulders. Pulled her a little closer.

"It turns out he wants me to shoot the porcupine," Parker said. "He's nuttier than a Hershey bar, you understand . . ."

. . . keeps waving the gun in Parker's face, it's a thirty-eight, and telling him that the porcupine here is his wife's pet who shit all over the house, and he wants Parker to shoot it for him. That's why he brought the gun up here, he's got a carry license for it, he works in the diamond center, it's the only humane thing to do, shoot the fuckin porcupine. Meanwhile, the guy's eyes are getting crazier and crazier and the gun is making bigger and bigger circles on the air and Parker's afraid he's going to get shot just *talking* to this maniac. This is the police department's obligation, the guy insists, mercifully putting a wild animal to sleep who has no right running around the apartment relieving himself at will while the guy is trying to sort diamonds. Meanwhile, the porcupine at the end of the leash is relieving himself all over the squadroom while Parker is trying to sort out this little dilemma he has here, whether he should put the thing to sleep with a legal handgun or risk getting shot himself as they debate the entire matter.

At this point in his recitation, Parker slid his hand down off Cathy's shoulder and into her blouse. She didn't seem to mind. Or maybe she was too fascinated by his delightful porcupine story to notice.

"I didn't want to kill that poor animal," he said, hoping his eyes were brimming with tears, "but neither did I wish to get shot myself," undoing the buttons lower on her blouse, exposing the cones of a white bra, Cathy took a deep breath. "Besides, how did I know this was a *legal* pistol? There are many ramifications to police work, you know. So what I finally did," he said, and reached behind her to undo the bra clasp, releasing her breasts into his hands, she took another deep breath, "what I did was I said to him 'How about I take the little fella for a walk?' and I got up and held out my hand for the leash, and he put the leash in my hand, and I said, 'The gun, too, so I can do what has to be done outside,' " lowering his face to her breasts, nuzzling them with his cheeks, one against each cheek, it was a good thing he'd shaved before coming over here. His hands up under her skirt now, he said, "So I took the gun and the porcupine downstairs, and I called the ASPCA to take the thing away, and I gave the gun to the desk sergeant for him to run a make on, and it turned out the guy really did work in the diamond center and he did have a carry permit for the piece, so nobody got hurt, do you think you'd like to go in the bedroom now?" he asked as he lowered her panties.

Sometime during the next hour, while it was still April Fools' Day and after Parker had brought Cathy to orgasm several times, she told him that her dream was to become a writer. He thought she meant a graffiti writer at first, like her dumb fuckin son. But she meant a movie writer. She told him she typed movie scripts all the time and it seemed like a very easy thing to do. She also told him that her other dream was to marry a decent hardworking man one day, perhaps a man like Parker, move out of the city into a little house with a low fence around it, cook barbecue in the backyard at the end of the day when she finished writing for the day, maybe in a suburb of Los Angeles, that's where all the movie writers were. That was her dream. To marry a decent hardworking man . . .

"Like you," she whispered.

. . . and write screenplays in the L.A. area and cook barbecue in the backyard.

His hand buried between her legs again, Parker thought Dream on, fool.

10.

At two o'clock on the morning of April second, the concert site was deserted except for a lone security guard. The people working in the production trailer had turned off the lights and locked up behind themselves some twenty minutes ago. Got into the two private cars parked outside, drove off on the access road that went out of the Cow Pasture and past the big lake they called The Swan, Carter wondered why. The guard—a big fat man wearing a blue uniform with a yellow stripe on the trouser legs—had waved off the two cars and then had got into his own black-and-white car with the gold shield of the company on the side. Carter figured he would radio the home office, tell them everybody'd just left, two A.M. and all's well. Then he'd take a little nap. Carter *hoped*.

The Cow Pasture was this huge lawn, some ten-plus acres of newly cropped grass that this weekend would be covered with God alone knew how many people, all of them screaming at the stage. The stage hadn't been put up yet, nothing had been put up yet, there was only the empty lawn with the trailer sitting there all alone under the stars and the guard's car parked across the entrance drive that led in from the access road. Since there was nothing to steal out here in the open except what was inside the trailer, the car was parked with its nose *facing* the trailer. But Carter figured the guard knew there was nothing much of value in that trailer; this wasn't like sitting outside Fort Knox waiting for a big caper to happen. This was a single guard sitting here in the middle of the night and never for a minute suspecting that anyone would want to get in that trailer. But the guard was armed and Carter didn't want to get spotted fiddling with the Mickey Mouse lock on the door to the trailer; they had parked the trailer so that its back was to the lake, its entrance door clearly visible from where the guard sat behind the wheel of the car.

Carter's instructions were to get in and get out without anyone knowing he'd been there. Steal one—and *only* one—of the ALL ACCESS laminates. Didn't want anyone to know anything was missing. Just take one of the laminates and get out fast. There'd be laminates in there for specific areas, and different performing groups, but Florry had told him to look for the ones that said ALL ACCESS, that was the kind he needed. When Sanson introduced them, he said Florry knew about such things, he'd worked on the sound at Woodstock. Carter didn't know what Grover Park had to do with what *they'd* be doing come Saturday, but Sanson said not to worry about it, just get the laminate, without the laminate we might not be doing *anything* come Saturday.

The uniforms had been the easiest part so far.

For all I know you can walk in some store and buy them right off the rack, he'd told Sanson. Which turned out to be exactly the case. Well, not just *any* store. What he'd done, he'd called the Department of Sanitation and told them these guys on his bowling team were sanitation employees and they'd just won a tournament . . .

"I'm captain of the team," he said.

"Hey."

. . . and he wanted to buy them some uniform stuff as a victory gift.

"What'd you have in mind?" the guy on the other end of the line asked. Heavy Calm's Point accent. Carter visualized a fire hydrant with a cigar in its mouth.

"You know," he said, "the uniforms they wear on the garbage trucks."

"You mean the spruce-green uniforms?" the guy said.

"Yeah," Carter said, "what they wear on the truck."

"Yeah, we got those here," the guy said, "the long-sleeve shirts, the pants, the jackets and hats, whatever you need, the T-shirts. We even got sweatshirts here, you want to get some of those. Those might be nice to bowl in."

"Where are you?" Carter asked.

"Public Affairs Office. There's like a little shop here. Room 831. Just come on down, you'll find whatever you need. 335 Gold. You know where Gold Street is? Down on the Lower Platform? We're next to where the old outdoor market used to be. Room 831. Just come up, we'll take care of you. The shirts are eleven dollars, the long-sleeve shirts, and the pants are fifteen. If you want the sweatshirt . . ."

"Do you have any patches there?"

"Patches?"

"Sleeve patches, you know?"

"No, I don't. But they can get those through their supervisors."

"You can't get any for me, huh? So I can sew them on, make it like a real surprise?"

"Let me see what I can do, okay? How many you need?"

"Just four."

"When are you coming in?"

"I thought tomorrow."

"I'm off tomorrow."

"Can you leave them for me?"

"The shirts? They're right here. All you have to . . ."

"The patches."

"Oh. Sure, if I can get 'em for you. What's your name?"

"Ray Gardner."

"Okay, Ray, let me see what I can do."

"Thanks, I appreciate it."

"Hey, come on."

As easy as that.

The garbage truck would be a bit more difficult.

Sanson wanted him to steal the truck on the day of the job, take it at noon, drive straight over to the river with it. Carter had argued against this. First, it would mean a daylight heist, which increased the risk. And next, the trucks were in *use* during the day, they weren't just sitting around in empty lots all over the city the way they were at night. Cyclone fences around the lots, razor wire on top of the fences, be hard enough getting in at *night*, never mind the daytime. Sanson had listened hard—he *always* listened hard, the deaf fuck—and then he'd said Okay, but it has to be as late as possible the night before, I don't want some sanitation slob to discover the missing truck and alert the entire department. It was agreed that Carter would steal a truck from the Blatty Street garage in Riverhead sometime during the empty hours of the night before the concert.

For now, he had to get that laminate.

He could see movement in the car, Fat Boy was *never* going to sleep. One thing Carter hated was conscientious public servants. He looked over toward the trailer, wondering whether the area near the door was dark enough for him to risk it even with the guard awake. He decided it wasn't. All he needed was half a minute to pick that lock, couldn't the guy sneak forty winks for him? He waited another ten minutes, decided Fat Boy would be awake all night, and went into the woods bordering the lake. Hoping he wouldn't step on any lovers' asses in there, he circled around toward the access road, picked up a rock the size of a cantaloupe, came up behind the car, and hurled the rock at the rear window. He was back in the woods again even before Fat Boy came out of the car yelling. Took Carter three minutes to run back to the trailer. Another minute to pick the lock and open the door. Over to the left, he could hear Fat Boy chasing shadows on the access road. Still out of breath, he pulled the door shut behind him and locked the door from the inside.

Taking a Mag-Lite from his pocket, he shielded it before he

snapped it on, allowing only a pinpoint of illumination to escape
his cupped hands as he began searching the trailer. Nothing
was locked in here, nothing to steal but the laminates, and
there was a guard outside making sure *that* wouldn't happen.
He found boxes and boxes of them inside a metal cabinet at
the far end of the trailer. All of the laminates were marked in
the left-hand corner with the slightly-ajar-window logo of Windows Entertainment. They were color-coded in four different
colors: yellow, pink, pastel blue, and orange. There were laminates with the names of the various groups on them, and
laminates with big numbers on them— **1, 2, 3, 4** —and then
he found the box he needed, the ones with the laminates marked
ALL ACCESS. He didn't know which of the colors were for
which days, so he took one in each color, and grabbed a handful
of lanyards from the shelf. He doused the light and was about
to step out of the trailer again when he heard the guard's
footsteps outside.

He waited in the dark.

Fat Boy shook the knob.

Standard procedure.

Shake it, see if it's locked.

Which was why Carter had locked it from the inside.

He kept waiting.

Heard footsteps moving off.

Heard the car door opening and then closing again. Fat Boy
on the horn to the home office, Hey, somebody smashed my
fuckin *window*!

Carter stayed inside the trailer for another ten minutes. Then
he eased open the door a few inches, looked toward the car,
opened the door wider, stepped down onto the grass, and slipped
silently into the night.

The Deaf Man's next letter was delivered to the squadroom early
that Thursday morning, the second day of April. As usual, there

was a short note attached to a larger sheet of paper. The note read:

```
Dear Steve:
Getting close ?
             Love,
             Sanson
             P.S. More later.
```

The paragraph photocopied from Rivera's book read:

SISHONA'S BLOND HAIR glistened in the light of the four moons. Everywhere around them, the naked bodies twisted and the voices roared to the night.

"The multitude will destroy itself," she told Tikona. "It will turn upon itself and see in itself the olden enemy. Its fury will blind its eyes. It will know only the enmities of the Ancients."

"The river runs fast after the Rites of Spring," Tikona said.

"But the fury rises before," Sishona answered.

"I don't know what the hell he's talking about," Carella said.

"Rivera or the Deaf Man?" Brown asked.

"The *Deaf* Man," Carella said. "What's the goddamn *jackass* trying to tell us?"

"A jackass he's not," Meyer said. "In fact, maybe he's a genius."

"That's what he'd like us to believe, anyway."

"Let's go over it from the start, okay?" Meyer said. "First he tells us there's this multitude that's going to explode."

"Let me see that damn thing again," Carella said. He was beginning to get irritated. The Deaf Man always irritated him. More so because he was deaf. Or pretending to be deaf. The person Carella loved most in his life was a woman who was *really* deaf. *This* son of a bitch . . .

"Here," Hawes said.

Yesterday, the dentist had removed the stain from his teeth. He looked normal again. Or almost normal. The dentist had used a fine abrasive stone to clean off the sealant and stain, and then had polished the teeth with fine sandpaper. He told Hawes that the enamel would never come back—something they hadn't told him *before* he'd given his all for the job—but that the calcium in the teeth would remineralize them, whatever the hell *that* meant. Hawes was annoyed. As much by the Deaf Man as by the dentist.

They all looked at the first message yet another time:

66I FEAR AN explosion," Tikona said. "I fear the jostling of the feet will awaken the earth too soon. I fear the voices of the multitude will anger the sleeping rain god and cause him to unleash his watery fury before the fear has been vanquished. I fear the fury of the multitude may not be contained."

"I, too, share this terrible fear, my son," Okino said. "But The Plain is vast, and though the multitude multiplies, it can know no boundaries here, it cannot be restrained by walls. Such was the reason The Plain was chosen by the elders for these yearly rites of spring."

"A multitude on a vast plain," Kling said.

"A multitude that's *multiplying*," Brown said.

"More and more people."

"Jostling."

"Ready to explode."

"Let's see the next one," Carella said.

They all looked at the next message:

FROM WHERE ANKARA stood on the rock tower erected to the gods at the far end of the vast plain, he could see the milling throng moving toward the straw figure symbolizing the failure of the crop, the frightening twisted arid thing the multitude had to destroy if it were to strangle its own fear. The crowd moved forward relentlessly, chanting, stamping, shouting, a massive beast that seemed all flailing arms and thrashing legs, eager to destroy the victim it had chosen, the common enemy, a roar rising as if from a single throat, "Kill, kill, *kill*!"

"A *milling* crowd," Hawes said.

"A *killing* crowd."

"A crowd moving toward its victim."

"Its common enemy."

"Chanting, stamping, shouting."

"All flailing arms and thrashing legs."

"Kill, kill, *kill*!"

"I *hate* this son of a bitch," Carella said.

"Let's look at the one we got today," Kling said.

They put it on the desk beside the other two:

SISHONA'S BLOND HAIR glistened in the light of the four moons. Everywhere around them, the naked bodies twisted and the voices roared to the night.

"The multitude will destroy itself," she told Tikona. "It will turn upon itself and see in itself the olden enemy. Its fury will blind its eyes. It will know only the enmities of the Ancients."

"The river runs fast after the Rites of Spring," Tikona said.

"But the fury rises before," Sishona answered.

"Where does he get these crazy names?" Kling said. "Sishona."

"Never mind Sishona," Brown said. "What's he trying to *tell* us here?"

"Sounds like a goddamn orgy," Hawes said irritably.

"The multitude will destroy itself," Meyer said.

"Turn upon itself."

"See in itself the olden enemy."

"The enmities of the Ancients," Kling said.

They all looked at each other.

"What we have to do," Carella said, "is find this goddamn crowd."

Today was pink.

Florry had laminates in four different delightful colors, but the men walking past the security guards were all wearing pink, so he took out his pink **ALL ACCESS** pass from his pocket, hung it on the lanyard Sanson had provided with the laminate, and then looped the lanyard over his head. He had learned over the years that if you behaved as if you belonged someplace, nobody ever questioned you. The laminate helped. All pink and official-looking, the card passed him through the checkpoint without even a sideward glance from the two security guards.

The concert site was bustling with activity at nine that morning. The technicians and the work crews had begun arriving at six A.M., before it was light, picking up their laminates at the production trailer, buying early morning breakfasts from the catering tent, and then beginning to load in as morngloam tinted the sky to the east. The concert was a one-off show, which meant that everything erected here today and tomorrow would be torn down next Monday. Florry had deliberately chosen to arrive late, when the men would already be at work. Union people tended to know one another, and there were hordes of them here today. The same held true for sound technicians. All he wanted to do was blend in with the crowd. Move from space to space as if he belonged. Ask no questions. Move around, look around, get the lay of the land.

The Union, of course, was IATSE, which curt acronym stood for the very long-winded International Alliance of Theatrical Stage Employees and Moving Picture Machine Operators of the U.S. and Canada. But it was the Teamsters who had unloaded the trucks and it was the International Brotherhood of Electrical Workers who were snaking cables all over the place, and men from the Carpenters Local who were sawing and hammering away at the foundation of what would eventually become a huge stage.

The ground was still wet after all the rain this week, and the trucks and milling men had turned it into a quagmire. The sun was shining now, though, and the people from Windows Entertainment were hopeful that the ground would dry out before the crowds came in. Meanwhile, things were progressing on schedule, and there was no doubt that everything would be ready when the first of the groups was scheduled to perform.

Florry enjoyed all this activity.

There must've been close to a hundred people working here, all of them experts at what they were doing, all of them with a deadline to meet: By one o'clock this Saturday the stage and the roof over it, and the lighting hanging from it, and the speakers and amps in the sound towers on either side of it, and the delay towers with more speakers and amps, and the control tower for the house mix had to be up and ready to go, rain or shine.

Woodstock, you didn't have any delay towers, they were too unreliable back then. Now you could calibrate your delays so that the sound coming from the stage stacks was exactly in synch with what was coming from the speakers out in the audience. Back then, all you had on the stage was two giant speakers whereas nowadays it wasn't unusual to have a half-dozen stacks of speakers going at once. Back then, whenever you sent out a high signal, you distorted the mixer, and had to compensate for it by padding your mike line to reduce the signal. Today, you could correct the distortion right at the console, using your pre-amp gain control.

Still there was nothing today that could match Woodstock for excitement. Well, how could it? You did a Paul Simon concert right here in this same park, you got a crowd of 750,000 people—but that was expected. Woodstock, they were anticipating 200,000 and they got somewhere between half a million and 600,000! This weekend, nobody knew how many would show up. You got rain again, you could fold your tent and go home, even if the concert *was* free. Still, there were a couple of head-liners scheduled to appear, so if the weather was good, you could draw a tremendous crowd. Free, that was the key word. You walked in, you sat on your blanket, and you listened. Big open crowd here in the outdoors. Listening.

It was Florry's job to make sure they heard the right thing at the right time.

The right time was 1:20 P.M.

The right thing was Sanson's message.

Already burned into the chip and ready to go.

All Florry had to do was get into the console.

But the console wasn't even up yet, wouldn't be up till some-time tomorrow most likely.

For now, Florry had seen all he had to see.

He walked toward where a busy crew was erecting a cyclone fence around the backstage area. A pair of security guards were watching the fence go up. Neither of them even glanced at him as he left the construction site.

* * *

Debra Wilkins seemed to have gained control of herself. This
was now a week and a day since her husband was slain by the
person the newspapers were currently calling the Sprayer Slayer.
In America, everything needed a title because everything was a
miniseries concocted for the enjoyment of the populace. This
new miniseries was titled *The Sprayer Slayer* and Part I was
subtitled "The Hunt." If they ever caught him, Part II would
be subtitled "The Trial." But if they wanted to keep their audience, they had better catch him soon. In America, nothing
bored people more than something that went on for longer than
a week or so. Americans had very short attention spans. Maybe
this accounted for the fact that whereas Parker had taken Catalina
Herrera to bed only the night before, he was this morning giving
the widow Wilkins the eye. If they made a miniseries based on
Parker's romantic adventures, it would probably be titled *Cop
Lover*.

"As you know," he told Debra, "we now have *four* victims
of this person, and whereas until now there didn't seem to be
any definite link between the four . . ."

"*Have* you found a link?" Debra asked.

"The killer left a note at the scene of the last murder," Parker
said gravely. You had to play different women different ways.
You had to impress certain blonde and glacial types with your
sincerity. He was hoping Debra Wilkins would see him as a
dedicated professional for whom she would happily take off her
panties. "If it isn't too much trouble, Mrs. Wilkins, I wonder
if you'd take a look at the note and tell us if you recognize the
handwriting. Bert?" he said, as if prompting his presenter-partner
at the Academy Awards to hand him the envelope, please.

Kling produced the photocopy of the note Midtown South had
given him. He handed it to Parker who in turn handed it to
Debra. She studied it carefully.

"It doesn't look at all familiar," she said.

"It was written on a scrap of paper he probably picked up at
the scene," Parker said. "One of these throwaway flyers ad-

vertising a neighborhood deli. We figure the note was a spur-of-the-moment idea."

"We figure he wants to get caught," Kling said.

"How do you figure that?" she asked.

"What my partner's trying to say," Parker said, "is that *if* we can match this handwriting, then we've got him on all *four* murders. Because it was found at the scene of *one* murder, and he confesses in the note to the other *three*."

"I see. But why would he do such a stupid thing?" Debra asked.

"Like my partner says, he may *want* to get caught."

"Either that," she said, "or he's a copycat who committed only the one murder and wants to take credit for the previous ones as well."

"Now that is *very* good investigative thinking, Mrs. Wilkins," Parker said, and shook his head in appreciative wonder. "Have you ever done police work?"

"Never," she said.

Kling suddenly wondered if she was employed. The Wilkinses didn't have any children, and homemaking for a childless couple didn't seem like much of a full-time occupation. Before he could ask her, though, Debra said, "I was once a legal secretary. For a firm that mostly handled criminal cases. That's how I met Peter. He'd negotiated the divorce settlement for a woman whose husband later held up a bank. We were defending the husband in the criminal suit, and we called the former wife in for a deposition. I think he was claiming her as an alibi on the day of the robbery, I forget the exact circumstances. In any case, Peter and his partner . . ."

She turned to Kling.

"Jeffry Colbert," she said. "You met him here last Saturday."

"Yes, I remember," Kling said. "We talked to him yesterday."

"Oh?" Debra aid.

So the son of a bitch *didn't* call her like he said he would, Parker thought.

Kling was wondering if this would be a good time to bring up the will. He decided it wasn't. But he felt further explanation about why they'd gone to see Colbert . . . or *was* it necessary?

"Few questions we wanted to ask him," he said, and then, immediately, "You were telling us how you'd met your husband."

"Yes, he and Jeffry accompanied this woman to the deposition. I started dating Peter and . . . well . . . eventually we got married."

"How long ago was that?" Kling asked.

"Three years," she said.

Her lip was beginning to quiver again. Maybe she wasn't quite as much in control as Kling had earlier thought. Partly to move her away from memories of what had been a happier time, partly because the logistics were still bugging him, he said, "I've been trying to figure how your husband could have got all those paint cans into the apartment without your noticing. I gather you're not working now . . ."

"No, I'm not."

"Are you gone a lot? Out of the apartment, I mean."

"I walk a lot," she said. "I'm still learning the city, you see. I came here from Pittsburgh four years ago, but I was just beginning to know it when Peter . . . when the . . . when he . . . he got killed."

"I wonder if we can take another look at those paint cans," Kling said.

"I threw them out," she said.

"Why?" he said, surprised.

"They . . . reminded me that Peter had a secret life, something I knew nothing about. I couldn't stand looking at them any longer."

"When did you throw them out?"

"Yesterday."

"Where?"

"I left them in the basement. We have a man . . ."

She caught herself. She could no longer use the word "we" when discussing her family. Her husband was dead. Now it was the singular. I. She avoided that, too.

"A handyman comes in three times a week. We leave . . ."

It could no longer be avoided.

"I leave things down there for him to get rid of."

"To get rid of how?"

"Some things he puts out with the garbage. The rest he carts off himself."

"Where is he now? Your handyman?"

"I saw him outside just a little while ago. Working in the yard."

"I don't see what's so important about those cans," Parker said, "you should be bothering Mrs. Wilkins about them."

"I'm sorry," she said, "I didn't know you'd need them."

"Don't worry about it," Parker said. "Mrs. Wilkins, I'm going to leave you my card. If you remember anything you think we should know . . . if, for example, anything about the hand-writing rings a bell . . . we'll be leaving this with you, by the way, it's just a copy . . . you call me, okay? I'll be here in a minute," he said, and grinned like a shark.

"Thank you," Debra said, and accepted the card.

"There's just one more thing," Kling said.

She looked up from the card.

"When we saw Mr. Colbert yesterday, he mentioned that your husband had left a will. . . ."

"Yes?"

"You know about the will, do you?"

"Yes?"

"I know it hasn't been probated yet. . . ."

"Now that . . . the . . . the funeral is over and I . . ."

The lip quivering again, the eyes beginning to well with tears.

"I plan to do that tomorrow," she said.

"Then . . . if the will's going to be made public, anyway," Kling said, "can you tell us who the beneficiaries are?"

"There's only one beneficiary," she said. "I'm the sole beneficiary."

"Thank you," he said.

"You have my card," Parker said, and winked at her.

In the hallway outside, Kling said, "Let's go talk to that handyman."

"Why?" Parker said.

"She cries too much."

"For Christ's sake, her husband got *whacked* last week!"

"And she's his sole goddamn *beneficiary*."

Parker looked at him.

"How come she never saw those cans in his closet?" Kling asked.

"She told you. She didn't *go* in his closet."

"Didn't see him carrying them into the house, either, huh?"

"You heard her, she's out a lot. What are you saying, Bert? You saying *she* whacked him?"

"I'm saying *opportunity*."

"What the fuck does that mean, opportunity?"

"Do you buy Wilkins as a writer?"

"Why not? Lots of guys lead peculiar lives."

"A lawyer? Writing on *walls*?"

"Lawyers *especially* are very peculiar," Parker said.

"You don't think it's amazing she never noticed twenty-two cans of paint in her husband's closet, huh?"

Parker let this sink in.

"You're saying exactly what I said about the brother, right? She hears about this nut who killed . . ."

"Right, and opportunity knocks," Kling said. "She whacks the husband and then makes him look like one of the victims."

"You're forgetting she's the one who just now *suggested* a copycat, aren't you?"

"Which, if she killed him, was very smart of her."

Parker looked at him again.

"Okay," he said at last, "let's go find them fuckin cans."

The handyman hadn't thrown the paint cans into the garbage waiting for disposal because they looked brand-new and he figured that would be a tragic waste. At first he was reluctant to show the cans to the detectives because he was afraid they might take them away from him. Kling convinced him they only wanted to have a look at them.

On the bottom of each can, there was a little sticker that read:

```
SAV MOR
19-06-07
$2.49
```

They now knew where the paint had been purchased.

Trouble was, there were eight SavMor Hardware stores in Isola alone, and another twelve scattered all over the city.

At three o'clock that afternoon, Eileen went downtown to talk to Karin Lefkowitz. Karin was her shrink. She went to see her because she was feeling guilty about Georgia Mowbry. She told Karin that she was the one who'd been working the door and yet it was Georgia who'd been shot and killed. It didn't seem fair, she said.

People kept telling Karin that she looked a lot like Barbra Streisand playing Lowenstein in *Prince of Tides*. Karin resented this because she didn't know a single analyst who would have behaved as outrageously as that one had; in the picture, anyway; she hadn't read the book. Besides, she didn't think she looked or behaved at *all* like Barbra Streisand. Her nose *was* a trifle long, true, but she didn't have long fingernails and she didn't wear high heels to work and she didn't hire any of her patients to give her son football lessons. As a matter of fact, she didn't *have* any children, perhaps because she wasn't married. And what she wore to work was tailored suits and Reeboks. Anyway, *she'd* been here first.

"Would you rather have been the one who got shot and killed?" she asked Eileen.

"Well, no. Of course not."

"Then why do you feel guilty?"

Eileen told her all over again how Georgia had come to the door . . .

"Yes."

. . . to see if she needed anything or wanted to use the ladies' room . . .

"Yes."

"And just that minute the goddamn door opened and he shot her."

"So?"

"So I think he was firing at *me*. I think he opened that door and let loose thinking he'd be shooting *me*. Killing *me*. Because he'd already killed the girl in the apartment and I'd been the one talking to him, so maybe he figured *I* was the one responsible for what he'd done, who the hell knows *what* he was thinking, he was nuts."

"That's right, you have no way of . . ."

"But I was the target, I'm sure of that, not Georgia. He fired blind, he didn't even *know* there were two of us out there when he opened that door. He was going for *me*, Karin. And Georgia got it instead. And now Georgia's dead."

"Eileen," Karin said, "let me tell you something, okay?"

"Sure."

"This one isn't your freight."

"He wanted to kill . . ."

"You don't know *what* he wanted to do!"

"He couldn't have known Georgia was . . ."

"Eileen, I won't let you get away with this. Damn it, I *won't*. You can blame yourself for getting raped . . ."

"I *don't* blame myself for . . ."

"Not anymore you don't! And you can blame yourself for shooting a man who was coming at you with a knife . . ."

"I *don't*!"

"Well, good, maybe we're making some progress, after all," Karin said dryly. "But if you think I'm going to let you spend *another* century in here blaming yourself for *this* one, you're wrong. I won't do it. You can walk right out that door if you like, but I *won't* do it."

Eileen looked at her.

"Right," Karin said, and nodded.

"I thought you were supposed to *help* me deal with guilt," Eileen said.

"Only if it's yours," Karin said.

The library closest to the station house was on the corner of Liberty and Mason in an area that used to be called Whore Street but that now sported coffeehouses and boutiques and little shops that sold designer jewelry and antiques. The restoration attracted tourists to the Eight-Seven, and tourists attracted pickpockets and muggers. Carella and Brown liked it better when the short street was lined with houses of prostitution.

The librarian in the reference room told them that the way it worked with back newspapers, it usually took three weeks to a month to get them on microfilm. So if they wanted anything from *February,* for example, it would already be on microfilm, but if they were interested in *March's* papers, chances are they'd still be in the reference room.

Sitting at a long table overhung with green shaded lamps, both men began poring over the newspapers for the past month, trying to zero in on any announced outdoor event that might qualify for whatever mischief the Deaf Man had in mind. This was still only April, and not many producers of alfresco extravaganzas were foolish enough to bank on the weather at this time of year, but . . .

The circus had arrived on March twenty-first for a two-week run that would end this Saturday. Did a crowd in a tent qualify as a crowd without boundaries? Concerning such a crowd, Rivera had written, "it cannot be restrained by *walls*." Well, a tent didn't have walls, did it? Was it possible that the circus *was* the Deaf Man's target? If so, his proposed happening would take place all the way downtown in the Old City, where the huge tent had been pitched close to the battered seawall the Dutch had built centuries ago. *Le Cirque Magnifique* was the name of the troupe. Direct From Paris, the advertisement read. Carella was copying the information in his notebook when Brown said, "How about this one?"

Carella looked.

The ad was headlined:

Tony Bennett

—— *with* ——

The Count Basie Orchestra

plus

The Ralph Sharon Trio

There was a picture of Tony grinning out of the full-page ad, and beneath that the words:

FRI. & SAT., APR. 3 & 4 • 8 PM

The location of the event was given as the Holly Hills Arena in Majesta.

"Is an arena an open space?" Brown asked.

"Well, it has no ceiling," Carella said. "And there'll be a hell of a crowd there, that's for sure."

"But will it be an *outdoor* crowd?"

"Actually, I don't think so. He says no *boundaries*, no *walls*. An arena . . ."

"The Deaf Man?"

"No, Rivera. I'm sure a crowd in an arena wouldn't be the kind of crowd he means."

They kept searching the entertainment pages.

Liza Minnelli was scheduled to perform in the Coca-Cola Concert Series this coming Sunday night, the fifth of April. But that was at Isopera, the city's opera house, very definitely a walled space and therefore specifically excluded by Rivera's—and presumably the Deaf Man's—definition.

Peggy Lee was in town and so was Mel Tormé, each of them performing at separate clubs, again excluded by definition.

"Does it have to be in town?" Brown asked.

"Why?"

"Here's a couple over the bridge."

"I don't think he'd be alerting us if . . ."

"Yeah," Brown said.

"I mean, it *has* to be something in the city, don't you think?"

"Yeah."

"Here's something on a cruise ship," Carella said.

"What kind of cruise?"

"Around Isola. Big-name band cruise."

"Well, a ship doesn't have *walls*," Brown said. "But doesn't the *size* of the crowd mean something? He calls it a *multitude*, doesn't he? Rivera? A *multiplying* multitude. That doesn't sound like a crowd on a *ship* to me. That sounds more like . . ."

"Hey," Carella said.

He was looking at a full-page ad in today's morning newspaper. The headline on the ad read:

FirstBank Presents

—————

A Free Weekend of

ROCK & RAP

★ ★ ★

The location of the event was the Cow Pasture in Grover Park. The concert would start at one o'clock this Saturday and end at midnight on Sunday. At the bottom of the ad was a single line that read:

Produced by Windows Entertainment, INC

The way Meyer and Hawes figured this, the shifts at the Temple Street shelter were the same as those in the police department. They tried to time the stakeout, or the plant—or even the *sit* as it was called in some cities—so that they'd catch part of the four-to-midnight and also part of the graveyard shift. Their reasoning was that if people were walking out of the armory with armloads of goods paid for by the city, then they wouldn't be doing so in broad daylight, nor would they be doing it when there was a lot of activity on the street. The armory wasn't located in what you'd call a high-traffic area, but there *were* some scattered shops and restaurants in the surrounding streets, and at least some kind of activity till around ten, ten-thirty, when it started getting quiet. They pulled up across the street at ten-fifteen that Thursday night, doused the headlights, and sat back to watch the passing parade.

Hawes kept bitching about what they'd done to his teeth. He

told Meyer he was afraid to call Annie Rawles because she'd notice right off his teeth didn't have their usual sparkle. Meyer said he had to look at the bright side, making a pun Hawes didn't get.

"I don't *see* any bright side to this," he said. "I let them talk me into removing the *enamel* from my teeth, and now they tell me it'll never come back. What kind of bright side is that?"

Meyer had his eye on the big brick building across the street. He was thinking this would make the third night they'd be sitting the place and if something didn't come down soon, he was ready to call it quits. He frankly had his doubts about the reliability of Hawes's informer, the crazy Frankie with the wild eyes and the watch cap.

"How'd he know all this, anyway?" he asked.

"The dentist? He said he'd done it for the Feebs once. What I should've said is I don't want you to do anything to me you did for *them* jackasses, is what I *should've* said. Now the enamel won't grow back."

"I meant your informer," Meyer said. "Frankie."

"He said he saw them walking out with the stuff."

"When?"

"All the time, he said."

"At night, during the day? *When*, Cotton?"

"What the hell are *you* so cranky about? It's *my* goddamn teeth."

"I'm thinking we're wasting our time here, is why I'm getting a little *impatient*, let's say, not cranky."

"Meyer, it stands to reason if they're stealing the whole damn store, they're doing it at night."

"They haven't done it so far the past *two* nights," Meyer said.

"Thursday's a good night for stealing," Hawes said mysteriously.

Meyer looked at him.

"He said they're all in on it, all the square shields, they take turns divvying up the loot,'' Hawes said. ''They walk out with it a little at a time. . . .''

''Like what? A bar of soap every six months?''

''No, like half a dozen blankets, a carton of toothpaste, like that. Spaced out. So the stuff won't be missed.''

''Is Laughton in on this?''

''The supervisor? My guy didn't say.''

''Your guy,'' Meyer said.

''Yeah.''

''A guy you meet inside there in the dead of night, he's crazy as a bedbug, he's all at once your *guy*, as if he's a respected *informer*,'' Meyer said, not realizing he'd just uttered an oxymoron.

''Let's say he seemed reliable,'' Hawes said.

''Why is Thursday such a good night for stealing?'' Meyer asked.

''Is that a riddle?'' Hawes said.

''You said Thursday . . .''

''I give up,'' Hawes said. ''Why *is* Thursday such a good night for stealing?''

Someone was coming out of the shelter.

A man wearing a brown jacket and dark trousers, hatless, carrying a big cardboard carton in his arms.

''What do you think?'' Meyer asked.

''I don't think he's one of the guards.''

''You only saw the ones on the graveyard.''

''Want to take him?''

''That box looks heavy, doesn't it?''

''Let's wait till he clears the shelter. Otherwise we blow the plant.''

They waited. The man was struggling with the weight of the carton, staggering up the street with it. They kept watching him till he turned the corner, and then they got out on either side of the car, and ran to the corner. He was halfway up the block now, walking in the middle of the sidewalk, still bent with his load. They came up behind him, one on each side, flanking him.

"Police," Meyer said softly.

The guy dropped the box. Hawes wouldn't have been surprised if he'd simultaneously wet his pants. The box clattered to the sidewalk as if it contained a load of scrap iron. Meyer pulled open the flaps and looked inside.

"Where'd you get these?" Meyer asked.

He was looking at half a dozen used pots and pans.

"They're mine," the man said.

He was unshaven and unshowered and he smelled like a four-day-old flounder. The brown jacket was stiff and crusted with grime. He was wearing high-top black sneakers worn through at the big toe on each foot. His trousers were too large for him, soiled at the cuffs, baggy in the seat, torn at each knee.

At first glance, the carton seemed to contain only the cooking implements, which they guessed he'd stolen from the shelter's kitchen. But this was only the top layer. As they dug deeper into the box, they discovered a stainless-steel fork, knife, and tea-spoon, a coffee mug, a quart thermos bottle, a tiny reading lamp, three or four frayed paperback mystery novels, an umbrella, a plaid lap robe, an inflatable pillow, a folding aluminium chair with green plastic back and seat, a tattered pair of fur-lined gloves, a black leather aviator's helmet with glass goggles, a stack of paper plates, a packet of paper napkins, an alarm clock with a broken dial, a desk calendar, a red plastic egg crate, a corded stack of newspapers, three pairs of socks, one pair of Jockey shorts, a comb, a hairbrush, a bottle of Tylenol, a deo-dorant spray can, a . . .

They both realized in the same instant that they were looking into the man's home.

"Sorry to bother you," Meyer mumbled.

"It's a mistake," Hawes said.

"Sorry," Meyer said.

The man closed the flaps on the carton, picked it up again, and began walking up the street, struggling with its weight.

They almost felt like helping him.

"I wanted you to hear this without any background noise," Silver said.

Chloe figured this was like being invited up to some guy's apartment to see his etchings. He'd called her twenty minutes ago, asked if she could stop by on her way to rehearsal. He still thought she worked with some kind of dance group, she'd been pretty vague about what *kind* of dance. It was now ten-forty, she was due at the club at eleven. She hoped he hadn't picked tonight to make his move, hoped he really *did* want her to hear this song he'd written. She'd pretty much decided she'd go to bed with him sooner or later, but there were things she had to sort out first.

Like, for example, why she hadn't yet quit the job.

Why hadn't she just marched in, said So long, Tony, it was nice getting groped all these months, and thanks for the use of the hall, but I've got twenty grand in the bank now, and what I'm going to do is open a beauty parlor.

Simple thing to do, right?

So why hadn't she done it?

Something scary about it, she guessed. Going out on her own. Easier to suffer the hands on her. Easier to . . .

"Nice thing about rap, I can accompany myself," he said, and grinned.

His apartment was on a stretch of turf that used to be called Honey Lane when Diamondback was in its heyday. Lots of rich and respectable black people used to live right here on this street. The brownstones lining Honey Lane were as fancy as any you could find on the Upper South Side of Isola. Stained-glass panels set in mahogany entrance doors. Polished brass doorknobs and knockers. Sweeping carpeted stairways. This was back when

Mr. Charlie came uptown to listen to jazz and watch the high-yeller chicks strutting in their little beaded dresses. Diamondback was *the* place to go back then.

Dope hit Diamondback long before it hit the rest of America, right after the War—the *real* war, not the miniseries in the Gulf. There were many blacks—and Chloe Chadderton was one of them—who believed that dope was the white man's way of keeping the nigger in his place. Spread dope in all the black hoods, the way the British used to do when they were running China, and you subjugated the people, you made sure they *never* got any power. The fat black cats in Diamondback ran for the hills when dope came in, sold out and left for the suburbs, same as *whites* did whenever *blacks* moved in, it was kind of funny. Now Diamondback was a war zone. Half a century of indifference and you had teenagers clocking for big-time dealers and doing crack themselves.

Which was maybe why Chloe was scared of going out there on her own. In a white man's bar, on a white man's table top, with a white man's hands all over her, she sometimes felt . . . safe. Cared for. Protected. This was what they'd done to her. In the long run, she was still a slave, still afraid to take that leap into freedom.

"It's called 'Black Woman,'" Sil said.

"Takeoff on 'Sister Woman'?" she asked, and was immediately sorry.

His face fell.

"Well . . . no," he said. "'Sister Woman' is somethin else, Chloe. 'Sister Woman' was your husband's *bleat,* his way of protestin before rap was even a *dream* in anybody's head. You want to know what rap is, it's calypso without melody, straight out of the West Indies, never mind Africa. That's why 'Sister Woman' fits in so good with what we do. Spit Shine is pure *rhythm,* and your husband's lyrics got the beat of the drums in them, right up front, hell, he coulda been writin his words specially for us. But 'Black Woman' . . ."

"I didn't mean you ripped it off," she said. "I'm sorry if you . . ."

"No, no, all I'm tryin'a splain is how the two raps are different. 'Sister Woman' is a rap we got from *calypso,* but 'Black Woman' is somethin I pulled out of rhythm and blues. Well, you'll see what I mean when you hear it."

"Uh-huh," she said.

"On Saturday, we start the act with your husband's song, new rap for the group, they sit up and take notice the minute we open our mouths. Then we do 'Hate,' which was a hit they all know, and which is just what it says it is, man, it's about *hate,* pure and simple. And then we do 'Black Woman.' Which is about love. R and B is always about love. And lovers," he said.

"Uh-huh," she said again.

"Would you like to hear it?" he asked.

"Yes," she said. "But I told you, Sil, I have to be at the . . . the rehearsal starts at . . ."

"That's cool, don't worry," he said, and grinned, and sat at the table and began beating out a rhythm with the palms of his hands, the gut rhythm of rap, an intricate clickety rhythm that made her want to move her feet in response, a rhythm as immediate as a bulletin from the front. Over the beat of his hands on the tabletop, he began the rap he'd written last Saturday:

"Black woman, black woman, oh yo eyes so black,
"Tho yo skin wants some color, why is *that,* tell me that.
"Why is *that,* black woman, don't confuse me tonight,
"You confusin me, woman, you confusin me quite,
"Cause you *look* so white
"When I *know* you black."

"Black woman, black woman, is you white or black?
"Is you *quite* black, woman, don't confuse me tonight,
"You confusin me, woman, I'm a'taken aback

"Cause you *look* so white

"When I *know* you black."

"Now you know where I stand, cause you know how I look,
you been hearin my rap, you been readin my book.

"You can see in my hand all the cards I can play, you can
read in my eyes all the things I can say.

"Do you spec me to lose all them centuries past,

"Do you spec me to worship at yo lily-white ass?

"Do you spec me to love all that's white that's within you?

"Do you spec me to love all the *white* man that's in you?

"Well, I will."

"Black woman, white woman, gonna love you so,

"Be you black, be you white, even so, that is so,

"That is *that,* white woman, no confusion tonight,

"No confusion, black woman, I'm forgettin the white,

"In the night, in the night,

"All is black, all is white

"Love the black, love the white,

"Love the *woman* tonight."

His hands stopped their erratic rhythm on the tabletop. He
looked at her very solemnly.

"That's . . . lovely," she said.

"I wrote it for you," he said.

She had thought so.

"I love you," he said.

She had thought that, too.

She went into his arms. They kissed. She could feel his heart
pounding in his chest. In a little while, she would call the club
to tell Tony Eden she was quitting. There was no hurry.

* * *

At seven-thirty on the morning of April third, just as Chloe and Sil were sitting down to breakfast at the small kitchen table in his apartment facing Grover Park, a British nanny was wheeling a baby carriage into the playground near Silvermine Oval, close to the River Harb, on the northernmost edge of the 87th Precinct.

An old man was sitting on one of the benches.

He was wearing pajamas and a robe, and he was wrapped in a khaki-colored blanket.

His hair was white. It danced about his balding head in the early morning breeze. He sat staring past the playground equipment and out over the water. He was wearing thick-lensed eyeglasses. His eyes were moist with tears behind them.

The nanny went over to him, and in her polite British way, asked, "Sir, are you all right?"

The old man nodded.

"Aye, aye, sir," he said.

11.

This time, they'd made a mistake.

They'd cut all the labels out of his underwear, his pajamas, his robe, and his slippers, and they'd wrapped him in the same presumably stolen DSS TEMPLE blanket, but there was one label they could not remove, and that one was tattooed on the biceps of his left arm:

Hawes looked through his directory, found the private police number for the U.S. Navy's Discharged Personnel Center, and placed the call. The woman he spoke to was a chief petty officer named Helen Dibbs. Hawes identified himself, told her what he was looking for, and asked how long it would take her to get back.

"Is that all you've got on him?" she asked.

"That's it."

"Try to make it difficult, will you? Just the name of a *ship* with a woman's name under it?"

"A war, too, don't forget. Haven't you got World War II on your computers?"

"Sure, we do. But gimme a break, huh?"

"Just run the *Hanson* through from 1941 to 1945. See if anyone in the crew listed Meg as a next of kin."

"Sure."

"Easy, right?"

"Sure."

"When can you get back?"

"When I get back," Dibbs said, and hung up.

She got back two hours later.

"Here's the poop," she said. "The *Hanson* was a radar picket ship, named for Robert Murray Hanson, a marine hero who got shot down in the Pacific. She was commissioned in May of 1945, which made my job a little easier since I didn't have to track her all the way back to Pearl Harbor. It still wasn't a piece of cake, though; there were three hundred and fifty men and twenty officers aboard her when she sailed for the Pacific. As for Meg . . ."

Hawes held his breath.

"It's a good thing it wasn't Mary. Only five men listed Margarets or Marjories as their next of kin, and one of them was later killed in the Korean War, on a minesweep in . . ."

"I don't think Meg's a form of Marjorie," Hawes said.

"Then that leaves three. You got a pencil?"

A first-class gunner's mate named Angelo Peretti had listed his mother, Margaret, as next of kin. At the time of his discharge, Peretti's mother was living in Boston, Massachussetts.

A lieutenant j.g. named Ogden Pierce had listed his wife, Margaret, as next of kin. He'd lived with her in Baltimore, Maryland.

A seaman first class, radar striker, named Rubin Shanks had listed his wife, Margaret, as next of kin. They were living at the time of his discharge in Pittsburgh, Pennsylvania.

None of them had lived in this city.

But Meyer and Hawes hit the phone books for all five administrative units of the city, anyway, and for good measure they went through the directories for all the surrounding suburbs; both of the previous victims had been *driven* to where they'd been dumped. There was a Victor Peretti in Calm's Point; he did not know anyone named Angelo Peretti. There was a Robert Pierce in Isola; he did not know any Ogden Pierces.

In the Elsinore County directory, they found a listing for SHANKS, RUBIN on Merriwether Lane. When they called the number, a woman named Margaret Shanks said, "What did he do now?"

They asked if they could come out there to talk to her.

She said they could.

At that very moment, another letter from the Deaf Man was being delivered to the muster desk downstairs.

Dear Steve:
        Burn this!
                Love,
                Sanson

AND NOW THE rhythm reached a frantic pitch, and from where he stood on the tower built of rock, Ankara saw the swell and rise of the multitude and he knew that the fear had turned at last to fury and that the sowing would be good and the reaping plentiful. Listening to the rhythmic stamping of the feet, hearing the voices raised in joyous fury, he smiled up at the four moons and made the sign of the planting.

"Well, that's it for sure," Brown said. "He's planning something at that rock concert."

"Then why does he tell us to *burn* this one?" Carella asked.

"Maybe he's gonna start a *fire* there."

"You notice there's no 'P.S.' this time? Nothing about more coming later."

"So this is the last one."

"So it's got to be tomorrow."

"And it's got to be the concert."

"Where's that ad?" Carella said.

They looked at the ad again.

"The Cow Pasture," Brown said.

"Starts at one tomorrow."

"Ends at midnight Sunday."

"What *else* starts tomorrow?" Carella asked.

"What do you mean?"

"Well, you don't think he's *really* telling us, do you?"

"Maybe not. But even so, we'd better see what kind of security they've got at this concert."

"Windows Entertainment," Carella said, and pulled the phone directory to him.

Margaret Shanks was wearing eyeglasses that looked like the ones that British guy on television wore, whatever his name was, the guy who performed in drag. It was almost impossible to focus on anything but the glasses. Tiny woman with white hair and these big oversized glasses, asking the detectives if they'd like some coffee. This was now close to twelve noon. Sunlight was streaming through the windows in the small living room of the development house. They declined her offer, and then showed her a Polaroid picture they'd taken of the man who'd been dumped in the Silver Harb playground early that morning.

"Is that your husband?" Hawes asked.

"Yes, it is. Where is he?"

"At the moment, ma'am, he's at Morehouse General Hospital in Isola."

"Was he in an accident?"

"No, ma'am," Meyer said. "He was left in the playground early this morning. The blues who picked him up took him directly to the hospital."

"Is he all right then?"

"Yes, ma'am, he's fine."

"I worry so about him," she said, and lowered her eyes behind the outlandish glasses.

"Yes, ma'am," Meyer said. "Ma'am, do you have any idea how he might have got to that playground?"

"None at all. Last week, he drove himself into town and then forgot . . ."

"Into the city, do you mean?"

"No, right here. Fox Hill."

"And what happened?"

"He forgot where he'd parked the car. Got into another man's car by mistake, had it pushed to a service station . . . it was a terrible mess. The police came here, I had to straighten it all out, thank God nobody pressed criminal charges. But the man whose car it was said Rubin had damaged it, which he hadn't, and now he's suing us, it's terrible. I haven't let Rubin drive since, I don't know how he got into the city."

"When was this?" Hawes asked. "When he got into another man's car?"

"It was exactly a week ago."

"That would've made it . . ."

"The twenty-seventh," Meyer said, looking at the calendar in his notebook. "Last Friday."

"And you say he hasn't been driving since?" Hawes said.

"I hide the keys."

"Because you see," Meyer said, "he was in a robe and pajamas. So he couldn't have taken the train in, could he? Not dressed like that."

"I don't know how he got in," Margaret said.

"When's the last time you saw him?" Hawes asked.

Margaret hesitated.

"Last night," she said.

The hesitation had been enough for both detectives. By instinct, they closed in. Old lady or not, they closed in.

"When last night?" Meyer asked.

"When . . . he was getting ready for bed."

"Putting on his pajamas?" Hawes asked.

"Yes"

"What time was this?"

"Around ten o'clock."

"Getting ready for bed, you said."

"Yes."

"Doing what?" Meyer asked.

Working in tandem. They had done this a thousand times before, they would do it a thousand times again. There was something here. They wanted to know what it was.

"I was . . . helping him wash and . . . and brush his teeth. He can't do those . . . things too well for himself anymore."

"Could he do those things a week ago? When he drove the car into town."

"I wouldn't have let him go if I'd seen him getting in it. It's difficult to keep track, you know. He . . . you can't just keep your eye on someone day and night."

"Did you have your eye on him last night?" Hawes asked.

"Yes, I . . . try to take care of him the best I can."

"But last night he got out of the house somehow, didn't he?"

"Well, I . . . I guess he did. If he's in the city now, then I guess . . . I guess he must've . . . must've got out somehow."

"*You* didn't drive him to the city, did you?" Meyer asked.

"No."

"You're sure about that, are you?"

"Positive."

"What time did you go to bed?"

"Around ten-thirty."

"Your husband went to bed at that time, too?"

"Yes."

"Do you sleep in the same room?"

"No. He snores."

"Anybody else have a key to this house?"

"No."

"When did you learn he was missing?"

"What?"

"When did you learn he was missing, ma'am? We called you at a little past ten this morning, and you asked what he'd done this time. Did you know he was missing before we called?"

"Yes, I . . . did."

"When did you find out he was missing, ma'am?"

"When I . . . woke up this morning."

"What time was that?"

"Around seven."

"How'd you learn he was gone?"

"He wasn't in his bed."

"What'd you do then?"

"I . . ."

Her eyes were beginning to mist behind the ridiculous eyeglasses.

"What'd you do, ma'am?"

"Nothing," she said.

"You didn't call the police to report him missing?"

"I didn't want any more trouble with the police."

"So you didn't call them?"

"No."

"Your husband wasn't in his bed, he wasn't in the house, but you didn't . . ."

"You don't know what it's like," she said.

Both men fell silent.

"Day and night, living with a ghost, you don't know what

it's like. He talks to me, but he doesn't make sense, it's like
being alone. Last week, when the thing with the car happened,
at least he still knew my name. Now he doesn't even know my
name. Day by day, he forgets a little more, a little more. Last
week, he could drive the car, now he can't even tie his own
shoelaces! He gets worse and worse all the time. All the time.
I think he may have had a small stroke, I don't know, I just
don't know. I have to take him to the bathroom, I have to *wipe*
him, you don't know what it's *like*! No, I *didn't* call the police.
I didn't *want* to call the police. I didn't *want* them to find him!
Why did you have to *find* him? Why did you have to find *me*?
Why can't you leave me in *peace,* damn you!''

"Ma'am . . .''

"Leave me alone,'' she said. "Please leave me alone.''

"Ma'am,'' Meyer said, "do you know how your husband got
into the city?''

She hesitated a long time before answering.

Her eyes behind the absurd eyeglasses were wet with tears
now. She stared vacantly past the detectives into somewhere beyond, perhaps to a time when a young sailor had his wife's pet
name tattooed onto his arm, a name he could no longer remember.
Perhaps she was thinking how rotten it was to get old.

"Yes,'' she said at last, "I know how he got into the city.''

The four of them were in the car the Deaf Man had rented that
morning. Gloria was sitting with him on the front seat, behind
the wheel and fifteen pounds heavier than when he'd interviewed
her last Sunday. Carter and Florry were on the back seat. The
car was parked on Silvermine Drive, overlooking the River Highway and the Department of Sanitation facility on the water's
edge.

"The burn is set for one tomorrow,'' he said. "We go in at
twelve-thirty, secure the facility, wait for the fuzz to arrive. We

should be out of there by one-twenty latest. We'll have clear sailing all the way downtown.''

"Where do we make the transfer?" Gloria asked.

"Just off the parkway, a mile below the facility. In the boat-basin parking lot.''

"We using this same car tomorrow?" Carter asked.

"No, I've reserved four other cars.''

"Be safer that way, don't you think?''

"Yes, of course. That's why I . . .''

"I mean, in case anybody makes us today,'' Carter said, still flogging a dead horse.

"Yes, I understand,'' the Deaf Man said.

"That way, we've got *four* cars, they'll go crazy tracking us down,'' Carter insisted.

"When do we collect what's coming to us?" Florry asked, which the Deaf Man considered premature since Florry hadn't yet done anything but construct what he called his ''little black box,'' for which the Deaf Man had already paid him ten thousand as an advance against the hundred thou he'd promised. All Gloria had done so far was cut her hair and gain fifteen pounds, for which she, too, had already received ten thousand bucks. For the same amount of money, Carter had purchased the uniforms they'd be wearing, stolen the laminates, and located the garbage truck he'd be stealing early tomorrow morning. Thirty thousand bucks had been advanced thus far, against the three hundred the Deaf Man would be paying in total for their participation tomorrow. Meanwhile, the park wasn't wired, and they didn't have the garbage truck, and Gloria looked even more womanly than she had before she'd gained the weight and got her hair cut like a boy's.

"You'll all be paid the balance of your fees when we're safely across the bridge and at the motel,'' he said. "Then we all go our separate ways.''

Except Gloria, he thought. He was planning on celebrating

with her after the job tomorrow. Pay them all, send the *other* two on their merry way, and then ask Gloria to share a bottle of champagne with him in the motel room. Toot a few lines, get down to male-female basics.

He could not get over the transformation in her.

Her hair was even shorter than his now, trimmed close at the sideburns and the back of her head, a single blonde tuft combed straight back off her forehead. Last night, after they'd tried on the garbage men's uniforms, he'd sent down for pizza, and they'd all made themselves comfortable around the kitchen table. Her uniform jacket slung over the back of her chair, sitting in just the baggy green trousers and snug T-shirt, Gloria must have felt his steady gaze upon her. She turned suddenly away. He did not know whether she was embarrassed by his scrutiny, or whether she'd turned away merely to protect her job; the fact of the matter was that she'd gained weight in precisely the wrong places, transforming herself into the most voluptuous garbage man in the universe.

"You reserved a room yet?" Carter asked.

"Yes," the Deaf Man said.

"Cause otherwise, we're liable'a get there and find they're full up," he said, flogging yet another dead horse.

"The room's already been reserved," the Deaf Man said.

"Cause those motels over the bridge," Carter said, "they're riding academies, most of them, you get guys taking their bimbos there in the afternoon. We pull up with the van full of stuff, there won't be a room for us."

The Deaf Man looked at him.

"But you already reserved one," Carter said, and shrugged.

"Yes."

"Let's hope they hold it."

"For Christ's sake, go phone your mother, will you?" Gloria said testily. "Ask *her* if we've got a different *car* for tomorrow, if the *room* is reserved, if you can blow your *nose* or go take a *pee*, for Christ's sake!"

"It pays to be careful," Carter said solemnly. "When I was on the stage, even though I'd been doing the same part for weeks and of course knew my lines by heart, I always had the stage manager cue me on them every night before I went on. I never went up in all the years I was acting."

"Fine, you never went up," Gloria said, tapping her fingers impatiently on the steering wheel.

"Did I see you in anything?" Florry asked.

"You're getting on my nerves," Gloria said, "all these superfluous questions. We're here to run it through, I don't know what all these other questions have to do with anything."

"She's right," the Deaf Man said. "Let's run it."

Gloria nodded curtly and started the car.

The man they'd spoken to at SavMor's regional headquarters was a vice president named Arthur Presson. He'd told them yesterday afternoon that he would check the code numbers following the SavMor name on the pricing label and get back to them as soon as he could. He did not get back until two o'clock that Friday, almost twenty-four hours after they'd made their "urgent" request; corporate chiefs do not know from homicide investigations.

Kling took the call.

"On that pricing label," Presson said.

He sounded Yale out of Choate.

"Yes, sir," Kling said, intimidated.

"You understand that we have four hundred and thirty SavMor stores nationwide . . ."

"Yes, sir."

". . . and whereas all we sell is *hardware*, as opposed to a supermarket, say, which color-codes for frozen food, produce, dairy products, meats, and so on . . ."

"Yes, sir."

". . . we *do* need a code on our labels so that our computers can zero in immediately on the state, the specific city in that state, and the particular store in that city. The number thirty-seven, for example, would indicate . . . we have stores in each of the fifty states, you see . . .''

"I see.''

"Thirty-seven would be Georgia.''

"Yes, sir.''

"And the number four following it would mean Atlanta, as opposed to five for Macon or six for Gainesville.''

"I see.''

"And then . . . well, we have nine stores in Atlanta, so the last number in the code could be for any one of those nine stores. The coded labels are supplied to the various stores. The pricing changes for each locality. Prices are set at national headquarters. In Dallas.''

"Yes, sir.''

"The code number you read to me on the phone was 19–06–07.''

"That's the exact number,'' Kling said.

"The nineteen is for this state, and the oh-six is for this city. We have twenty stores here. The oh-seven store is in Isola. It's located on River and Marsh . . . are you familiar with the Hop-scotch area? All the way downtown?''

"I am.''

"Well, that's where it is,'' Presson said.

Which was a long way from where Peter Wilkins had lived with his wife on Albermarle Way, all the way *uptown*.

"Thank you, sir,'' Kling said, "I appreciate your time.''

"*De nada,*'' Presson said, for no good reason Kling could fathom, and then hung up.

Parker was sitting at his desk, reading the morning paper and picking his teeth. Kling told him what he had. He listened, tossed the toothpick into the metal wastebasket under his desk, folded the newspaper, put it in the bottom drawer of his desk, rose, farted, and said, "Let's go.''

* * *

River Street started on the waterfront in the oldest section of town, an area of narrow lanes and gabled houses dating back to when the Dutch were still governing. For quite some distance, it ran parallel to Goedkoop Avenue, which lay cheek by jowl with the court-houses and municipal buildings in the Chinatown Precinct, and then it crossed Marsh at the virtual hub of an area bristling with restaurants, art galleries, boutiques, bookstores, shops selling drug paraphernalia, sandals, jewelry, unpainted furniture, leather goods, lighting fixtures, herbal lotions and shampoos, Tarot cards, teas, art-deco reproductions and handcrafted items ranging from wooden whistles to whittled nudes. Here and there in the lofts along these narrow streets, a multitude of artists and photog-raphers had taken up residence, spilling over from the Quarter into Hopscotch, so-called because the first gallery to open here was on Hopper Street, overlooking the Scotch Meadows Park.

The manager of the SavMor Hardware store on the corner of River and Marsh looked at the can of paint Kling had handed him, turned it over to glance at the pricing label stuck to its bottom, said, "That's our store, all right," and then said, "How can I help you?"

"We found twenty-two cans of this stuff in a dead man's closet," Parker said, getting directly to the point. "Every color you'd care to name, twenty-two of them. Is there anything on that pricing label that'd tell you when the purchase was made?"

"No, there isn't."

"Anything at your checkouts that might help us?" Kling asked. "Mr. Presson mentioned you're computerized. Would your . . . ?"

"Yes, we are. Mr. *who*?"

"Presson. At regional headquarters. Would your computers show a sale of twenty-two cans of . . . ?"

"I thought you meant someone in the store here," the manager said. "When was this purchase made?"

"Sometime after the twenty-fourth of last month," Parker said. "That's when he got killed."

He was thinking like Kling now. If Debra had killed him, then she'd bought the paint *after* he was safely out of the way.

"*Would* your computers be able to help us?" Kling asked.

"Well, let's take a look," the manager said. "Twenty-two cans of spray paint is an unusual purchase."

It was indeed.

But on the twenty-fifth day of March—the very day Peter Wilkins was found dead on Harlow Street, the day before Parker and Kling discovered the treasure trove of cans in the Wilkins apartment—someone had in fact purchased twenty-two cans of the paint at $2.49 a can, which came to a total of $54.78 plus tax.

The girl at checkout counter number six remembered the day well.

"It was still raining," she said. "There was a lot of rain that day. This must've been around twelve, one o'clock in the afternoon, the lunch hour. We get lots of people in here during the lunch hour. He had his cart full of . . ."

"*He?*" Parker said. "It wasn't a woman?"

"Not unless she had a mustache," the girl said.

The off-track betting parlor at a little past two that afternoon was thronged with men and women waiting for the start of the fourth at Aqueduct. Meyer and Hawes had chosen this particular location because Margaret Shanks had described a man who sounded remarkably like the security guard who'd been touting Pants on Fire the night Hawes spent at the Temple Street shelter. She'd told them the man's name was Bill Hamilton. Whether he'd show here this afternoon at the parlor on Rollins and South Fifth was anybody's guess. A call to Laughton, the shelter's supervisor, had informed them that this was Hamilton's day off. A visit to the home address Laughton had supplied proved fruitless. So here they were now in the betting parlor Hamilton had called "the *really* ritzy one," rubbing elbows with a white, black, and Latino crowd both detectives might charitably have described as seedy.

There was a television monitor in each corner of the room on the wall that faced the street, the screens now showing the odds for the fourth race, which was scheduled to go off at twenty past two. The favorite, the 6F horse, was paying seven to two. The long shot, the 2B horse, was paying thirty to one. On both side walls, racing forms were posted behind glass panels, and there were posters advising the prospective gambler on how to bet in five easy steps, and other posters listing the track codes for some sixteen or seventeen tracks, AQU for Aqueduct, BEL for Belmont, SAR for Saratoga, LAU for Laurel, and so on, and yet other posters detailing the bet codes, W for Win, P for Place, S for Show, WP for Win/Place Combination, and so on.

There was a pay phone on one of the walls, with a small green sign over it asking GAMBLING PROBLEM? and then suggesting that anyone with such a problem should dial the 800 number listed below. The sign did little to dissuade the three dozen men and two women who were milling about the room, glancing up at the changing odds on the two monitors and noisily debating, in English and in Spanish, which horses to bet. Some of the gamblers were already placing their bets at any of the seven windows on the rear wall, where hanging plaques announced CASHING/SELLING and a handwritten sign cautioned NO VERBAL BETS.

The horses were being led onto the track now, the man doing the live calls from the main office downtown on Stemmler Avenue announcing each horse and rider as they came onto the screen, "The number three horse is Trumpet Vine, the rider is Fryer," or "Number six, Josie's Nose, the jockey is Mendez," or "Number nine, Golden Noose, Abbott in the saddle," and so on.

Meyer and Hawes kept watching the front door.

Some five minutes later, the man downtown announced that

betting on the fourth race would close in less than four minutes, and this caused a flurry of activity at the betting windows, people glancing over their shoulders for a last fast look at the changing odds, writing out their betting tickets with the pencils provided, paying their money, and then beginning a drift toward the television monitors as the man downtown told them betting would close on the fourth race in less than two minutes.

Hamilton came in just as the horses broke from the gate. The moment Hawes spotted him, he nudged Meyer. Hamilton wasn't wearing his security guard uniform this time around, sporting instead a brown leather jacket over blue jeans and tasseled loafers, and carrying a racing form in his right hand. He greeted someone he knew, shook hands with someone else, and was looking up at the monitor in the left-hand corner of the room when Meyer and Hawes came up to him.

"Mr. Hamilton?" Meyer said.

"Bill Hamilton?" Hawes said.

"Yeah?"

"Police," Meyer said, and flashed the tin.

On the television screens, the horses were thundering around the track, the announcer's excited voice calling the race, "Coming up on the outside, number four . . ."

"What?" Hamilton said.

"Police," Hawes said.

"Keep going!" one of the gamblers shouted.

"Pushing through on the rail, it's number nine . . ."

"Police? What is this, a joke?"

"No joke," Hawes said.

"Into the stretch, it's one and four and nine and . . ."

Not a man or woman in that place turned away from the screens as the horses galloped into the home stretch. There was a real-life drama going on behind them right here in their friendly neighborhood betting parlor, two cops in plainclothes throwing around badges and bracing a good old gambling buddy, but not a soul in the joint gave a damn. They were watching the horses. The horses were all.

"Whip him, whip him!"

"Heading for home, it's one, and nine, and three . . ."

"Is it all at once against the law to bet the ponies?" Hamilton asked, and grinned broadly, playing to the oblivious crowd.

"No, it's all at once against the law to kill little old ladies," Meyer said.

Mort Ackerman was a portly man wearing a brown suit and smoking a huge brown cigar. He looked more like a banker than a promoter, but the sign on his office door read WINDOWS ENTERTAINMENT, INC., and the posters all over his walls attested to his successful promotion of more performers than Carella or Brown knew existed.

Sitting in a black leather swivel chair, he blew out a ring of smoke and said, "I'll tell you something. An outfit crazy enough to do a show outdoors in *April,* it deserves somebody setting fire to the stage. If that's what you think's gonna happen. FirstBank has no business doing *this* thing, in *this* city, in *April,* no business at all. It isn't as if they come from Florida, these people, they don't know what the climate here is like. These are people who *know* this city, this is the only place they have their banks, is in this city. Look at the weather we've had the past few weeks. If it doesn't rain this weekend, it'll be a miracle. But if what you say is true, there's gonna be a fire . . ."

"We didn't say that, Mr. Ackerman," Brown said. "We asked you what precautions you've taken in the *event* of a fire."

"Which means you're *expecting* a fire, am I right? What I'm saying is, if there's a fire and it rains, we got nothing to worry about, am I right? The rain'll put *out* the fire."

Both detectives had seen roaring blazes that the most torrential downpours and a multitude of ladder companies had been unable to extinguish. Neither of them believed there was much opportunity for a gigantic fire in a ten-acre meadow in the middle of a huge park, but the Deaf Man had written "Burn this!"— and when the Deaf Man wrote, they listened.

"So what precautions *have* you taken?" Carella asked. "Aside from praying for rain?"

"That's very comical," Ackerman said, and took his cigar from his mouth and pointed it at Carella in recognition. "The truth is, the fire department comes around to check every time there's one of these events, indoors or out, and we always get a clean bill of health and a fare-thee-well," he said, waving his cigar in the air like a magic wand and leaving behind it a trail of smoke like glitter dust. "They don't come around till everything's set up, though, because what's the sense of inspecting an empty meadow in a park where there's hardly what you'd call a severe threat of fire on any given day of the week, am I right? So," he said, waving his magic-wand cigar again, "why don't you come back tomorrow, and that should calm your nerves about whether or not we're gonna have a holocaust in the middle of the city this weekend. How does that sound to you?"

"Why tomorrow?" Brown asked.

"Because the crews'll be finished setting up tonight, and the fire department'll do their inspection early tomorrow morning to make sure none of the wires or the portable toilets are fire hazards, and they'll give me a certificate I can show you. *That's* why tomorrow," Ackerman said.

"What time tomorrow?" Carella asked.

"You guys are really worried about this, aren't you?" Ackerman said.

He didn't know the Deaf Man.

Jeff Colbert seemed surprised to see them.

"You made good time," he said.

"Huh?" Parker said.

Colbert was standing in front of the big window in his office, the city's spectacular downtown skyline behind him.

"I called your office twenty minutes ago," he said. "Left a message with a detective named Genero?"

"We've been in the field," Kling said.

"We didn't get your message," Parker said.

"I was just calling to say Mrs. Wilkins filed Peter's will early this morning. You can have a look at it anytime you'd like."

"We already know what's in it," Kling said. "We spoke to Mrs. Wilkins yesterday."

"I wasn't aware of that," Colbert said.

"I'll bet you weren't," Parker said.

Colbert looked at him.

"Mr. Colbert," Kling said, "do you remember where you happened to be at around twelve, twelve-thirty on the afternoon of March twenty-fifth?"

"No, I don't, offhand," Colbert said. "Why do you ask?"

"Would you happen to have an appointment calendar, anything like that, could maybe *tell* you where you were?" Parker said.

"Yes, I'm sure I can check my . . ."

"Because where *we* think you were," he said, "is in the SavMor Hardware store on River and Marsh, is where *we* think you were at that time."

"Buying twenty-two cans of spray paint," Kling said.

"What makes you think that?" Colbert asked, and smiled.

"A girl who can identify you," Kling said.

"Want to meet her?" Parker asked.

He could remember a time when the chief of detectives would run a lineup downtown at headquarters every Monday through Thursday of the week. This was not for identification purposes, the way the lineup today was. Back then, two detectives from

every precinct in the city would pull lineup duty on one of those
four days, and they'd trot dutifully downtown to sit on folding
wooden chairs in the big gymnasium while felony offenders
arrested the day before were trotted onto the stage and questioned
by the chief.

The chief stood behind a microphone on a podium at the back
of the gym, and he reeled off the charges against the person
standing on the stage, and gave the circumstances of the arrest
and then kept him or her up there for five, ten minutes, however
much time he thought the offender was worth. This allowed his
rotating detectives the opportunity to *see* everyone who'd committed a felony in this fair city, the theory being that if somebody
seriously broke the law once he'd seriously break it again, and
next time the cops would be able to recognize a troublemaker
on sight. This was when law enforcement was a personal sort
of thing. Some detectives actually looked forward to pulling
lineup duty every other week. It gave them a day away from the
squadroom and it made them feel noble, seeing all those scum-
bags up there on the stage.

Nowadays, you didn't have these formal lineups anymore.
The only lineups you had were like the ones they were holding
today for the benefit of Miriam Hartman, the black girl who'd
been working SavMor's counter number six when Jeffry Colbert
presumably checked out twenty-two cans of spray paint on a
rainy Wednesday in March.

The lineup room at the Eight-Seven—or the showup room as
it was sometimes called—wasn't half so elaborate as the ones in
some of the newer, flashier precincts. Relocated in the basement
of the building, where there'd been space to build a larger stage
and to install seating for twelve behind the large sheet of one-
way plate glass, the room lacked an efficient air-conditioning
system and was sometimes suffocatingly hot during the summer
months. But this was still the beginning of April, and Miriam
Hartman seemed comfortable enough as she sat looking at the

lighted stage beyond the glass, waiting for the action to begin. If she wasn't, then fuck her, Parker thought.

For the lineup today, they had rounded up three other men with mustaches, two of them offenders they'd brought up from the holding cells, and one of them a patrolman they'd asked to change back into his street clothes. In addition, they had three men *without* mustaches, one of them from the clerical office, the other two street patrolmen, all of them wearing civvies. Including Colbert, this made seven men, four of them with mustaches, three without. Moreover, two of the men wearing mustaches were about the same height as Colbert— five-eleven, in there. All of the men were white. There would be no later opportunity for some slippery shyster to come in and say the identification process had been loaded against Colbert. This wasn't a case of him being the only tall white guy with a mustache. Miriam Hartman had her choice of *three* of them.

The seven men walked out onto the stage. With the possible exception of Colbert, all of them had been through this drill before. The two offenders they'd drafted from the holding cell came out first, followed by three policemen, and then Colbert, and then the other policeman. There were height markers on the wall behind them. The stage was well lighted, but the illumination was not blinding. None of the men had to squint into the darkened room beyond.

Parker pulled the microphone to him.

One by one, he ordered each of the men to take a step forward, to smile, and to say "Some weather, huh?" which Miriam Hartman had said were the words spoken to her by the man who'd purchased the paint. One by one, they stepped forward, smiled— somewhat ghoulishly in the case of one of the offenders—and said, "Some weather, huh?"

"Thank you, step back, please," Parker said after each man had done his little turn.

He figured later that Miriam Hartman had picked out Colbert the moment he stepped onto the stage. He was not at all surprised when she said, "That's him."

"Second from the left?" Parker asked, confirming it.

"Second from the left," she said, and nodded emphatically.

In the interrogation room upstairs, Meyer and Hawes were talking to William Harris Hamilton, which—according to his driver's license—was the shelter guard's full name.

This was going to be a tough one, and they knew it.

All they had so far was Margaret Shanks's word that she'd hired Hamilton to pick up her husband and drop him off somewhere, preferably out of her life forever. They hadn't yet been able to identify either the man known only as Charlie, or the woman who'd died of cardiac arrest after someone had left her as helpess as an infant, alone and untended in a deserted railroad station. If Hamilton was the person who'd dumped her there, they felt they could reasonably charge him with Murder in the Second Degree, a Class-A felony defined in §125.5 with the words "A person is guilty of murder in the second degree when, under circumstances evincing a depraved indifference to human life, he recklessly engages in conduct which creates a grave risk of death to another person, and thereby causes the death of another person." Failing this, they were positive a charge of Manslaughter Two—a mere Class-C—would stick. Manslaughter in the Second Degree was defined in §125.15 as "Recklessly causing the death of another person."

Hamilton told them he'd never heard of anyone named Margaret Shanks.

He told them he'd never heard of her husband Rubin Shanks, either.

"She just picked your name out of a hat, huh?" Hawes asked.

"I don't know what she did. All I know is I never heard of her," Hamilton said.

He seemed supremely confident that whatever they were after, they weren't going to get it from him. And even if they did get it, it wouldn't do them any good. They had advised him of his rights and asked him if he wanted a lawyer present while they questioned him. He'd waived his right to counsel, and now sat smoking a cigarette at the long table in the room, glancing every now and again at the one-way mirror on the wall, as if to tell them he *knew* what the thing was, and didn't give a damn if anybody was behind it watching him. At the moment, nobody was behind it. They planned to call in Margaret Shanks later, bring her face-to-face with the man she'd paid to get rid of her husband. They also planned to confront Hamilton with Rubin himself, see if the old man would recognize him as the person who'd driven him from Fox Hill to the Silver Harb playground. All in good time. Meanwhile, they went about it the way they always did.

You ask a man the same questions enough times, he'll finally run out of the pat answers he's prepared and start telling you things he didn't plan to tell you.

"Have you always done security work?" Meyer asked.

"Depends what you mean by security work."

Hawes wanted to smack him right in the mouth.

"Square-shield work," he said. "You *know* what security work is."

"I was also a prison guard. Is that security work?" Hamilton said.

Which explained why he thought he could beat the system here. Having once been in the criminal-justice business himself, more or less. Having rubbed elbows, so to speak, with all sorts of slimy bastards like himself, who'd got caught and locked up only because they were dumb. He was smarter than any of the cons he'd known, smarter too than these two jerks questioning him here, or so he thought, and which he was now trying to prove. Mr. Cool here. Grinning and smoking his cigarette. Hawes wanted to ram the cigarette down his throat.

"Which prison?" he asked.

"Castleview. Upstate."

"How long have you been working at the shelter?"

"Year and a half now."

"Hear about the blankets being stolen there?"

"No. Were some blankets stolen?"

"Lots of blankets," Meyer said. "Twenty-six so far this year."

"I don't know anything about that."

"Some of those blankets have been popping up around town."

"I don't know anything about that, either."

"One of them in the Whitcomb Avenue railroad station."

"I don't know where that is."

"Harb Valley line," Hawes said.

"Still don't know it."

"Runs all the way upstate to Castleview. You said you worked there, didn't you?"

"Yep."

"But you never heard of the Harb Valley line?"

"Sure, I have. I just don't know the Whitcomb Avenue station."

"Then you couldn't have driven this little old lady there, right?"

"Right."

"Picked her up, wherever, wrapped her in a blanket stolen from the shelter . . ."

"I don't know anything about her or about the stolen blankets, either."

"How about someone named Charlie?"

"I know a lot of people named Charlie."

"This particular Charlie gave us a pretty good description of someone who looks exactly like you."

"Oh. Really?"

"Really," Meyer said. "Forty, forty-five years old, five-ten, brown eyes and dark hair. Sounds a lot like you, doesn't it?"

"Charlie *who*, would this be?"

"You tell us."

"I told you. I know dozens of Charlies."

"Said you were wearing jeans and a brown leather jacket. Same as you're wearing now," Hawes said.

"Must be thousands of men in this city wearing the same thing right this minute."

"What are your hours at the shelter?" Hawes asked.

"They vary."

"How?"

"We work rotating shifts."

"Eight-hour shifts?"

"Yes."

"Three shifts a day?"

"Eight to four, four to midnight, midnight to eight," Hamilton said, and nodded.

"Just like us," Meyer said.

"Gee," Hamilton said.

Hawes wanted to kick him in the balls.

"Five on, two off?" he asked.

"Five on, two off, yes."

"Which days are you off?"

"Thursdays and Fridays."

"So you're off today."

"I'm off today. Which is why you found me playing the horses."

"Were you working the midnight shift on the night of March thirty-first?"

He knew Hamilton had been working that night because that was the night he'd spent there.

"I don't remember," Hamilton said.

"You don't *remember*? That was only three *nights* ago."

"Then I guess I was working the midnight shift, yeah."

"How about March twenty-fourth? You weren't working the midnight shift *that* night, were you?"

"I don't remember."

"Well, if you were working graveyard this *past* week, then the week *before* it would've been the four to midnight, isn't that right?"

"If you say so," Hamilton said.

"Well, let's look at it," Meyer said, and opened his notebook to the calendar page, and took the cap off his ballpoint pen. "You were off yesterday and you're off today . . . that's the second and third of April."

Hamilton said nothing.

"And you were working the midnight shift the five previous days, so that would've been from March twenty-eighth to April first."

"If you say so," Hamilton said again.

"Yes, I say so," Meyer said. "Then you had two days off before that—the twenty-sixth and twenty-seventh, a Thursday and Friday . . ."

Hamilton stifled a yawn.

"And you'd have worked the four-to-midnight on the five days before *that*."

"Uh-huh."

Bored to tears.

"The twenty-second to the twenty-sixth," Meyer said.

Hamilton sighed.

"So you *couldn't* have been working the midnight shift on the twenty-fourth, could you?"

"No."

"You'd have got *off* work at midnight, in fact, and then you'd have been free to roam the night, hmm?" Meyer said, and smiled pleasantly.

Hamilton looked at him.

"So do you remember where you went after work on the morning of March twenty-fourth?" he asked.

"Home to bed, I'm sure."

"You were relieved at midnight and you went straight home to bed, is that it?"

"That's what I usually do."

"But is it what you did that particular morning?"

"Yes."

"You're sure."

"Positive."

"You didn't by chance drive to the Whitcomb Avenue station, did you?"

"I told you. I'm not familiar with . . ."

"Cause that's where the woman turned up," Meyer said. "Early on the morning of March twenty-fourth."

"Am I supposed to know what you're talking about?"

"And Charlie turned up two days later, on the twenty-sixth," Hawes said. "A *Thursday* morning. Your day off."

"Charlie who? I told you, I know hundreds of Charlies."

"Would you like to meet this particular Charlie?" Meyer asked.

"Nope."

"How about Rubin Shanks?"

"Told you. I don't know him."

"Maybe they'll know you," Hawes said.

Because the interrogation room was busy, they talked to Jeffry Colbert in the relative quiet of the clerical office, the squadroom at the moment being occupied by an assortment of teenagers who'd had the bad manners and worse timing to shoot one of their classmates just as school was letting out and just as David Two was cruising past the schoolyard. They were variously screaming for their mamas or their lawyers while claiming it was really the two police officers in David car who had shot the kid in the schoolyard, not to mention the head. Their cries of innocence floated down the second-floor corridor and almost but not quite managed to batter down the door to the clerical office, where Parker and Kling now confronted Colbert with evidence even a lawyer might understand.

The moment Miriam Hartman positively identified him, they had probable cause to charge him with four counts of Murder Two, officially place him in custody, and send his fingerprints downtown. Now, at a quarter to four, they had in their possession a report from the fingerprint section, which had compared Colbert's prints against the ones the lab had lifted from the various cans delivered yesterday, after the reluctant handyman at the Wilkins building had finally turned them over to Parker and Kling when they'd threatened him with court orders and such. They asked Colbert now if he would like an attorney present while they asked him some questions, and he told them he *was* an attorney, in case they'd forgotten it. They hadn't forgotten it; they were, in fact, banking on it. But because Colbert was being such a smart-ass attorney, and because they were both such smart-ass detectives, they asked him for a waiver in writing, which Colbert—supremely confident of his own lawyerly prowess— was happy to sign.

That out of the way, Kling said, "Mr. Colbert, there are a few things we'd like to show you, and then we'd like to ask you to do something for us, and then we're going to call the District Attorney's Office, and get them to send someone here to do a Q and A. First, we want to show you this report that was just faxed to us from the fingerprint section, which positively identifies your fingerprints with the ones we lifted from the paint cans we recovered in your partner's closet, would you like to read this, please?"

Colbert read the fax.

Silently, he handed it back.

"Next, we would like you to read this signed statement from a girl, a woman, named Miriam Hartman, positively identifying you as the man who purchased those cans of paint on the afternoon of March twenty-fifth, would you care to look at this, too, please, sir?''

Colbert looked at the signed statement.

He handed it back.

''Next, sir, what we'd like you to do for us, if you will . . .''

''What we want you to *do*,'' Parker said impatiently, ''is write something on a piece of paper for us, the identical words we're going to give you, that's what we'd like you to do. *Sir,*'' he added, and shot a glance at Kling.

''I don't want to answer any further questions,'' Colbert said.

''Well, we haven't really *asked* you any questions yet, sir,'' Kling said, ''even though you waived your rights to an attorney other than yourself and said you'd be *happy* to answer whatever questions we may have. But this isn't a *question,* sir, this is a request. It's the same as if we asked you to put on your hat or touch your finger to your nose or appear in a lineup or let us take your fingerprints . . .''

''Which we already *did,* by the way,'' Parker said.

Without a fuckin peep from you, he thought.

''It's what you might call the difference between testimonial and *non*testimonial responses,'' Kling said helpfully.

''What do you want me to write?'' Colbert asked.

''Five words,'' Kling said, and eased a piece of paper and a pen across the desk to him.

Colbert picked up the pen.

''What are the words?'' he asked.

'' 'I killed the . . . ' ''

''No, I won't . . .''

'' '. . . three up . . . ' ''

''. . . write that,'' Colbert said, and put down the pen as if it had caught fire.

''I guess you know that we can get a court order forcing you to write those words for us,'' Kling said.

''Then get it,'' Colbert said.

"You want to play hardball, huh?" Parker said.

"I don't like being charged with murder. Does that surprise you?"

"Who does?" Parker agreed. "You want us to ask for a court order or not? I get on the phone, I make an oral application, a judge'll . . ."

"No judge in his right mind'll grant . . ."

"Wanna bet?"

"You can't force me to write a confession."

"Come on, Mr. Colbert," Kling said. "You know this isn't a confession. We're looking for a . . ."

"No? You want me to put in writing that I killed three . . ."

"All we're looking for is a handwriting sample, and you know it."

"Oh, that's *all*, huh?"

"We're wasting time here," Kling said. "Do we make application, or don't we? Five'll get you ten a judge signs the order in three seconds flat."

"While we're at it," Parker said, "let's ask for a warrant to toss his apartment. Find the fuckin murder weapon."

"Let's not press our luck," Kling said. "How about it, Mr. Colbert? Do we apply for a court order? Or do you write what we're asking you to write, without all the fuss and bother?"

"Get your court order," Colbert said.

Kling sighed.

12.

At four o'clock that Friday afternoon, just as Nellie Brand was trying to create some order out of the chaos on her desk so she could get out of the office by five, her beeper went off. She had tried desperately to get off the Chart today because it happened to be her wedding anniversary and she was supposed to go home and shower and make herself glamorous for a romantic candlelit evening out with her husband. The Chart was the *homicide* chart, and in this city any D.A. of quality or experience landed on it every six weeks or so, and was then on call for twenty-four hours. The number on the beeper readout was 377-8024. The Eight-Seven. She returned the call and spoke to Meyer Meyer, whom she knew, and who asked her could she get uptown right away, they had what looked like real meat on a possible Murder Two.

Nellie sighed and said, "Sure."

Hoping this would be a quick one—though none of them ever really was—she phoned Gary to tell him what had come up, and then hailed a taxi outside her building downtown on High Street.

Walking familiarly into the station house, she nodded to the desk sergeant, and then took the iron-runged steps upstairs to the second floor of the building. She was wearing a tailored blue suit, a white blouse with a stock tie, and low-heeled navy pumps. After years of wearing her hair in a breezy flying wedge, she was letting it grow out; it fell now in a sand-colored cascade that reached almost to her jawline. Meyer and Hawes were waiting in the squadroom for her.

"Let's try to make this a fast one," she said.

Meyer filled her in.

"What do you think?" he said. "Have we got a Murder Two?"

"Let's go talk to the man," Nellie said.

Hamilton had asked for a lawyer the minute they told him they'd be trotting him around town to visit hospitals hither and yon. The attorney he'd called was a man who'd handled Hamilton's daughter's divorce for her; his name was Martin Campbell, and Meyer guessed he was in his early fifties. By now, a lot of identification had taken place, and Campbell was suggesting that his client call off any further questioning. But Hamilton seemed to be enjoying all this; maybe he still felt he could beat this one; maybe he was right.

They went through all the rights business yet another time, making certain that Hamilton was still willing to answer questions, this time with a video camera going. Campbell objected to the camera, but his client had already consented to it, and he knew he was whistling in the wind. Nellie shot him a look that said Come on, counselor, let's not play games when I've got a heavy date, and Campbell harrumphed a bit about making sure the backup stenographer took down everything that was said, just in case anybody later on tried to tamper with the tape, as if anyone would.

"Mr. Hamilton," Nellie said, "I just wanted to confirm for the record that notwithstanding your attorney's advice, you are still willing to answer any questions I put to you."

"I am."

"Fine then. The police officers tell me that you've now been positively identified by three persons . . ."

"*Two* of them incompetent," Campbell said.

"Turn off that camera," Nellie ordered at once. The operator looked at her, puzzled for a moment, and then hit the OFF switch.

"Counselor," Nellie said, "this isn't a court of law, nor am I taking a deposition. Your client has consented to my questioning, has further consented to the videotaping, and I'd like to continue this without any further interruptions from you, if that's not too much of an imposition."

"For the record," Campbell said, "I merely want it noted . . ."

"This is *not* on the record," Nellie said.

"I merely want it *noted,*" Campbell repeated, "that one of the witnesses is suffering from Alzheimer's disease . . . Rubin Hanks, is that his name?"

"Shanks," Meyer supplied.

"Shanks, thank you, his wife has stated that he is an Alzheimer's victim. And the other . . ."

"His wife has *also* identified your client as . . ."

"The *other* man *also* seems to be suffering from some sort of dementia," Campbell said, "unable to tell us where he lives or who he is, other than Charlie. So if you're counting on these two *incompetent* persons to make your case, I would strongly suggest that my client be released without being charged, and I would further suggest that you pray he doesn't sue the police department for false arrest."

"Gee whiz," Nellie said. "I'll bet these detectives haven't been threatened with false arrest in a long time. I think you'll agree, however, that *Mrs.* Shanks is a competent witness, and *she* has stated that she paid your client one thousand dollars to . . ."

"You know," Campbell said, "if hearsay is being permitted on the record . . ."

"The record is the videotape," Nellie said, "all this is *off* the record. And I'd like to start the tape again, with your permission, and get on with the questioning. Or, if you think there are grounds to release your client, why don't you ask for a writ of habeas corpus, hmmm?''

"Go ahead, ask your questions," Campbell said, and waved her away with the flat of his hand.

Nellie nodded to the camera operator, who started the tape rolling again.

"Mr. Hamilton," Nellie said, "*did* Mrs. Shanks pay you a thousand . . . ?''

"No," Hamilton said.

"May I finish the question, please?''

"I never saw the woman in my life until this afternoon.''

Meyer looked at Hawes. Both men rolled their eyes.

"I hope the camera isn't picking up the faces the detectives are making at my client," Campbell said.

"Only person I'm on is the suspect," the camera operator said.

"Hold it right there!" Campbell said. "Turn that thing off! Right this minute!''

The operator looked at Nellie. Nellie nodded. The room went dead silent.

"If you plan to use that tape as later evidence, then I resent my client being called a *suspect* on it, which carries a negative connotation. I'd like to start this all over again, Mrs. Brand. Rewind that tape, and then record right over what you've got. Conduct a proper Q and A here, or by God, if I have to drag my client out of here by his coat collar I will *not* permit him to answer another question.''

"I *want* to answer their questions," Hamilton said. "They haven't got a case here, and they know it.''

"Mrs. Brand? What do you say?''

"I say absolutely *not*. The record stands from the top, the tape will *not* be rewound or erased. Moreover, counselor, I understand your *grand* scheme . . .''

"I have no grand . . .''

". . . is to destroy a Q and A to which your client has already consented *ad infinitum*. But I can tell you that if you continue to be disruptive, I'll have the police throw you out of here. Is that clear? May I now continue?''

''Sure, sure, continue,'' Campbell said.

Nellie nodded curtly.

''Start the tape,'' she said.

Q: Mr. Colbert, is there any doubt in your mind that the words you've duplicated for us . . . how many times, Andy?

A: Twenty-three times, Bert.

Q: Twenty-three times now, in accordance with the court order, the same words over and over again, 'I killed the three uptown,' is there any doubt in your mind that the handwriting on the note found at the scene of the Henry Bright murder matches your handwriting exactly?

A: I'm not a handwriting expert.

Q: Thank you for that information, Mr. Colbert. But wouldn't you agree that to a layman's eye . . .

A: I wouldn't care to speculate.

Q: Well, I can tell you that the D.A.'ll most likely bring in a handwriting expert, and he's going to tell a jury just what anyone who isn't blind can see, that the handwriting samples are a perfect match with the handwriting on the note the killer left.

A: Aren't we being a bit premature? Talking about a jury when nobody from the D.A.'s Office has even *been* here yet?

Q: Let me end the suspense for you, Mr. Colbert. We're going to call the D.A. just as soon as we finish here. And the D.A.'s gonna ask for the max on each count of Murder Two. You killed four people. You're going to spend the rest of your life behind bars.

A: That's for a jury to decide, isn't it?

Q: Who's being premature now? Let me tell you what the next step is, Mr. Colbert, now that we've got a positive handwriting match. The next step . . .

A: Please don't treat me like a child.

Q: Excuse me, I'm sure you *know* what the next step is. The next step is we're going to ask for a warrant to search your apartment for the murder weapon, which according to Ballistics was a Smith & Wesson .38. That's the next step. The court order'll be granted, Mr. Colbert, because now we've got *three* things linking you to the murders. If you want my opinion . . .

A: I don't.

Q: Take it, anyway. Gratis, and for the record. If you didn't get rid of that gun . . . if that gun, for example, is still in your apartment or your car, or wherever you're keeping it . . . then you can kiss your chances goodbye. We've got a strong case even without the murder weapon, but it'll be airtight once we recover the gun. And don't tell us again to go for a court order. You *know* we will, and you *know* it'll be granted, and you also know the gun'll wrap it tighter than Dick's hatband, *if* it's still in your possession. You're the only one who knows that, counselor. So what do you say?

A: What are you asking me?

Q: I'm asking you to tell us all about it.

A: Why should I?

Q: Make life easier for all of us.

A: How will it make *my* life easier? The way I see it, you've got a bunch of paint cans that don't link me to anything, and you've got a note that *may* or may *not* link me to the murder downtown, but that's all it does, *if* it does.

Q: It says in plain English you also killed the three *uptown*.

A: Is it signed perchance?

Q: It's in your handwriting perchance.

A: It *still* isn't signed.

Q: How about the gun, counselor?

Colbert didn't answer.

"*Are* we going to find that gun?" Kling asked.

"How would I know? Go get your search warrant. Meanwhile I suggest you take me to a judge *fast*. You've got twenty-four hours from the moment of arrest to have me arraigned—and the clock is ticking."

"Let's say we find the gun . . ."

"Let's say you do."

"We've got the bullets on the bookstore murder. If they match your gun . . ."

"Even if you find the gun, you'd have no way of proving it's mine. And no way of proving I fired it. But this is all academic. Get your search warrant, go look for the gun. Then we'll talk."

"Maybe we better step outside a minute," Parker suggested.

Kling looked at him, puzzled.

"Sure," he said.

"He knows we won't find that gun in his apartment, his car, wherever," Parker said. "And he's right. No gun, no case."

"We've got the handwriting match," Kling reminded him.

"Will that be enough to send him away on four counts of Murder Two?" Parker asked. "We get him in court, they'll put on their own handwriting expert, he'll testify *I* wrote the fuckin note."

"Wait a minute," Kling said. "If *he's* not in possession of the gun, then who *is*?"

"Some alligator down the sewer," Parker said.

"No," Kling said. "Where'd we find those paint cans?"

In a room down the hall, Assistant District Attorney Nellie Brand was having a similar conversation with Meyer and Hawes.

"Let's say we get a court order to toss his car," Nellie said.

"That's exactly what we *should* do," Meyer said. "Soon as possible."

"I agree," Nellie said. "And let's say we find some hair or skin samples that match the old lady's who died of a heart attack . . ."

"She's been buried already," Hawes said.

"We can get a court order to have the body disinterred," Nellie said.

Meyer looked at her skeptically.

"Okay, maybe not. But let's say we find fiber samples that match her robe or her nightgown or whatever. Together with the blanket, this would tie him to the old lady, and we've got either a *potential* A— skimpy but who knows?—or a positive C."

"Skimpy how? The A?"

"Samples would put her in his car, but that's all," Nellie said. "It wouldn't mean he was driving the car."

"The other two identified him as the one driving the car, the one who dumped them."

"The other two aren't dead," Nellie said.

"Not through lack of trying," Meyer said dryly.

"But even alive, we've got him cold on two good D felonies. I'll tell Campbell we're going for Murder Two with the old lady and Reckless Endangerment One on the two gents. He'll say we haven't got a case with the woman, which as a matter of fact we don't unless we come up with something from Hamilton's car, or unless the party or parties who hired him come forward, which is what I call the Fat Chance Department. So unless we come up with something in the car, I'll let Campbell talk me into dropping the old lady entirely and concentrating on the others, which he'll try to bargain down to Reckless Two, your garden-variety Class-A mis. I'll tell him No, if I forget the old lady, then it's Reckless One or nothing at all, and he'll say Okay, but his man pleads to just one count, and I'll say Come on, we've got a perfect D here, depraved indifference, guy drops off these helpless old people with just a blanket wrapped around them, grave risk of death, all that, textbook definition. He'll say Okay, he'll advise his client to plea to both D's only if I'll agree to *jail* time, *not* prison time, a bullet on each count, concurrent. I'll tell him Don't be ridiculous, I've got a good hammer here for the seven-year max on *one* D and a consecutive on the *second* D, all in the state pen. He'll say Okay, how about giving me one-to-three concurrent in a state pen, and I'll tell him No, the least I'll settle for is open D's on both counts. That'll leave the sentencing to the judge. Or, if he prefers—and if his client would rather try rolling the dice for a lifetime sentence—I'll *also* go for Murder Two on the old lady. Campbell will settle for the open D's. In court, he'll go for probation or a non-prison term, I'll go for two-and-a-third to seven consecutive in a state pen. My guess is he'll end up doing one-and-two-thirds to five consec on each count.''

"What about the old lady?" Meyer said.

"Well, if we find anything in the car, I'm ready to shoot for Murder Two.''

"And if we don't?"

"Some you win, some you lose,'' Nellie said, and shrugged. "Let's go do it. I've got to get out of here.''

Colbert was still sitting at the long table in the interrogation room when Parker and Kling got back to him at six-twenty that evening. He looked up when they walked in, grinned at Kling, and said, "Okay to go home now?"

"Few more questions, counselor,'' Kling said. "Then you can tell us everything you know about this.''

"Oh, really? This had better be good.''

"You're pretty sure we won't find that gun, aren't you?"

"I told you. Go get your warrant.''

"That's just what we plan to do. To search the premises at 1137 Albermarle Way.''

Colbert blinked.

And recovered immediately.

"Why would a judge grant such a request?''

"Oh, I think we can make a pretty strong case for tossing the Wilkins apartment," Parker said. "That's where the paint cans were. With your fingerprints all over them. Maybe the gun's there, too."

"It's no crime to buy paint. You can't link that paint to any crime."

"Unless the murder weapon is in that apartment."

"Buying paint isn't a crime."

"Murder is. Why'd you put that paint in your partner's closet? To make sure everybody thought . . . ?"

"I put it there because I didn't have room for it in my own apartment. All I have is a studio downtown."

"The day after your partner got killed . . ."

"Yes . . ."

". . . while allegedly spraying a wall with *graffiti* . . ."

"That had nothing to do with . . ."

"You run out to buy twenty-*two* cans of *spray* paint, and you store them . . ."

"I needed that paint for . . ."

"Yeah, you needed it to prove Wilkins was really a graffiti artist instead of a big-shot downtown lawyer."

"There was some furniture I wanted to . . ."

"*Is* the gun in that apartment, Mr. Colbert?"

Colbert said nothing.

"Throw her to the lions," Parker suggested.

Colbert was silent for several moments.

Then he said, "What's in it for me?"

"You talk to us, maybe we'll talk to the D.A."

"No maybes."

"We'll ask for a federal prison instead of a state pen," Parker said.

Colbert knew the code. It was as simple as black and white. And he was white.

"It was her idea," he said.

Q: Tell us how it started.

A: It started in bed. Where does anything start?

Q: Bed where?

A: In a motel across the river. The next state.

Q: When?

A: Before Christmas.

Q: You and Debra Wilkins in bed together. In a motel room.

A: Yes.

Q: How long had *that* been going on?

A: Since shortly after she married Peter.

Q: All right, what happened in that motel room?

A: She told me about his will.

Q: About her being sole beneficiary of the will?

A: Yes. I hadn't known that. She'd seen a draft copy, it hadn't yet been witnessed. Actually, several people in our office witnessed it the very next day. But she told me she stood to inherit some money. . . .

Q: How much money? Are we talking millions here, thou . . .

A: Millions? No, of course not. Thousands, yes. Maybe a few hundred thousand, something like that. The money was a secondary consideration. She was planning to leave him, anyway, you see. But this meant she'd walk out of the marriage with a little something. This wasn't money, you see. This was love.

Q: You loved each other, is that what you're saying?

A: Yes. That's why we worked out the plan.

Q: Which was?

A: To kill him.

Q: Did you, in fact, kill Peter Wilkins?

A: It was her idea.

Q: But are you the one who actually shot him?

A: Yes.

Q: And killed him.

A: He was the second one.

Q: Who was the first one?

A: The Spanish kid. I forget his name. I read his name in the paper the next day. I didn't know who he was when I shot him. I only learned his name later. Like with the others. Carrera? Was it Carerra?

Q: Herrera.

A: Whatever.

Q: When you say the others . . . ?

A: The other graffiti writers. We wanted to make it look like someone was after graffiti writers. That was Debra's idea. People hate graffiti writers, you know. It's easy for people to believe that someone would go after graffiti writers. I was in Toulouse last summer, in France. And there was graffiti on the walls there, too. Not the political slogans you *used* to see in Europe, but the same kind we have here. The markers, the tags in spray paint. It's disgusting. People hate it there, too. People hate it everywhere. Debra's idea was a very good one. We even thought people might begin *cheering* whoever was doing it. Confuse the issue even more, you see. *Really* hide what we were doing.

Q: Hide the fact that you were out to kill Peter Wilkins . . .

A: Yes.

Q: . . . so his wife would inherit under his will.

A: No, no. So she'd be free to marry *me*. I told you, this wasn't money. It was love.

Q: So her husband goes to the movies . . .

A: No, no, that was our story.

Q: He *didn't* go to the movies?

A: No, he was home. I told him I was coming over, there was a case we were working on. I killed him in the house there, and then wrapped him in a blanket, and carried him down, and drove him over to Harlow Street. Found a good wall there . . .

Q: A good wall?

A: Covered with graffiti. Dropped him in front of the wall. The idea was to make it look like someone was killing graffiti writers, you see. That's why I bought that paint the next day. Because there was all this skepticism in the papers about a lawyer being a graffiti writer, remember? I bought the paint to nail it home. That Peter was a *secret* writer. That's why I left the note when I did the one outside the bookstore. To nail the point home. To make it look like some crazy person was committing the murders.

"You succeeded," Kling said.

In the corridor outside, he said, "Even if the gun *isn't* in there . . ."

"It's in there, all right," Parker said. "Otherwise he wouldn't have told us a fuckin thing."

"But even if it *isn't,*" Kling insisted, "the apartment is where Wilkins caught it, there'll be all *kinds* of forensic evidence. The minute we find the gun, the door's wide open. We bust the wife as an accomplice and call it a day. Which'll be nice for a change, huh?"

"What do you mean?"

"That *nobody* walks," Kling said, and grinned like a schoolboy.

The garbage trucks were lined up in rows behind a cyclone fence topped with razor wire. Fifty, sixty trucks in there behind the fence. The trucks were white, the color favored by the city's sanitation department, perhaps because it represented pristine cleanliness. Unfortunately, the city's various graffiti writers had already got to the trucks, spraying them from top to bottom and creating instead an image of urban decay. At one o'clock in the morning, the lot was silent and dark.

The wire didn't bother Carter. He had no intention of climbing the fence. He wasn't going to cut a hole in it, either, because you can't drive a garbage truck though a hole in a fence. To drive the garbage truck out, Carter had to roll back the sliding gate, which was fastened to a post with a thick chain and a heavy padlock.

Carter was going for the padlock.

A padlock is merely a flat lock, and a lock is a lock, and anybody who knows how to pick one lock knows how to pick any other lock. He worked in the dark with his set of picks, jiggling and juggling, working the lock like a woman, urging her to open for him. No security here. He guessed they figured they didn't need anything but the razor wire and the big macho padlock to keep out any graffiti writers. He had the lock open in four minutes. He rolled back the gate, walked swiftly to the nearest truck all beautifully decorated with spray-paint shit, crossed the ignition wires under the hood, climbed into the cab, put the gears in reverse, made a huge turn, and then drove right on out through the gate.

He didn't turn on the headlights until he was four blocks from the lot.

By then, he was home free.

Florry was wearing his ALL ACCESS laminate in the sky-blue color of the day, but he had all the others in his jacket pocket just in case one of the security guards gave him any bullshit about the color having changed at midnight. This was now two in the morning, and the concert site was as still as a graveyard. He walked onto the site familiarly, not expecting to be stopped by the security guard at the entrance, nodding to him, in fact, but not explaining why he was there, never explain, never apologize, just march in.

Whistling softly to himself, he walked directly to the control tower some hundred and fifty feet back from the stage. This was where all the really expensive equipment was; he expected to get stopped here, and he was.

"What's up?" the guard there said, even though he could plainly see the blue laminate pinned to Florry's jacket.

"Sound," Florry said, and held up the black bag in his hand.

Keep it simple, he thought.

"Want to open it for me?" the guard said.

"Sure," Florry said pleasantly, and unzipped the bag.

The guard flashed his torch into it.

He was looking in at a black metal box some ten inches wide by fourteen inches long by two inches high.

He was looking in at tomorrow's utter confusion.

"Fuck's that?" he asked.

"Micro-amplifier," Florry said.

Which it wasn't.

"Little late, ain't it?" the guard said.

"Musicians," Florry said, and rolled his eyes.

"Okay, go on," the guard said, and watched while Florry headed straight for the console. He kept watching as Florry poked around the board here and there like somebody who knew what he was doing, and then he got bored and strolled over to where another guard was standing near the sound stack on the right side of the stage.

That was when Florry really got to work.

It took him five minutes to locate the four matrix output cables going from the console to the processing rack. It took him another five minutes to unplug the outputs from the console and patch in his black box. A minute later, he had the box snugly tucked in among the other equipment in the electronic racks.

Whistling, he waved to the two guards near the stage, said good night to the guard at the entrance, and left the site.

From a telephone booth on the corner where he'd parked his car, he phoned the Deaf Man to tell him everything was set for tomorrow.

"Thank you," the Deaf Man said.

                              *   *   *

Carella couldn't sleep.

Old songs kept running through his head, songs to which he didn't know the words, or only knew some of the words, songs he couldn't quite remember, snatches of melody blurred by time, an incessant concert he couldn't completely hear, songs from very long ago, hissing and echoing from a static-ridden radio to blend together in what he recognized was a low-key nightmare, but a nightmare nonetheless.

He couldn't believe that the concert tomorrow was the Deaf Man's real target. If he knew the man at all, and he thought he knew him pretty well, then the concert—whatever he'd planned for the concert, a fire, whatever—would only be the diversion. This was a free concert, there wasn't any box office the Deaf Man hoped to rob, his true target *had* to be somewhere else, the real thrust *had* to be elsewhere.

But where?

Big city, this one.

The songs running through his head.

Time running through his head.

The clock ticking relentlessly toward one o'clock tomorrow when the concert would start.

What else was happening at one tomorrow?

And where?

The songs kept hissing from the old radio, saxophones and trumpets, snare drum and bass, piano and trombone.

What? he wondered.

Where?

13.

The morning of April fourth dawned gray and uncertain, a lowering sky covering the city like a gunmetal lid. The crowds began gathering at eight in the morning, long before the concert site was open to the public. This was a free event, with unreserved seating, first come, first admitted. By ten o'clock, the overcast began burning off, and by a little before eleven the sun was shining brightly and the sky was as blue as a periwinkle's bloom. A fresh breeze wafted in over the River Harb, adding a briskness to the day, but no one involved with the concert in the park was complaining. For April, they could not have wished for better weather.

It must have been like this in olden times, Chloe thought, when people from miles about came to local fairs. Sil had asked her to meet him at eleven sharp, at the main entrance to the site. As she approached now, she saw at once that a crowd had gathered around him, shouting his name, waving autograph books and programs for him to sign. The moment he spotted her, he broke away from the crowd, and came to her, and took her hand. She felt enormously privileged as he ushered her quickly through security and led her toward the cyclone fence that enclosed the backstage area.

"Better put this on," he said, "let you go wherever you like." He slipped a lanyard over her head. The orange laminate hanging from it had the name of the group, Spit Shine, printed across the top, and then—in bolder lettering below it—the word

313

ARTIST. They went past the beer tent and then through the guard gates, and he helped her up the wooden steps leading to the stage. People were busily coming and going everywhere. Still holding her hand, he led her to where Jeeb was testing his sound levels. Each of the artists had one or two, sometimes three, stage monitors at his feet, enabling him to hear any other performer onstage in whichever proportions he chose. As Sil approached, Jeeb was monitoring a sample chorus from the two girls in the crew, standing some six feet away from him on either side, and rapping out the lyrics to "Hate," which would be the second song they'd be doing today.

"Jeeb," Sil said, "I'd like you to meet Chloe Chadderton. Chloe, this's Jeeb Beeson, leader of the group."

"Hey, how you doin?" Jeeb said.

"Her husband wrote 'Sister Woman,' " Sil said.

"We openin with that," Jeeb said.

"I can't wait to hear it," Chloe said.

"Girls do the main rap, me an' Silver do a kind of jungle chant behind 'em. Works real fine. Your husband wrote some fine words, Chloe."

"Thank you," she said, though George Chadderton seemed a long time ago, and Silver Cummings represented the present and, she hoped, the future as well. Six feet away, like bookends on either side of the little triangle Chloe formed with Sil and Jeeb, the girls kept rapping the lyrics to "Hate," the words angling up out of the speaker at Jeeb's feet:

"You got a date with hate . . .

"At the Devil's gate . . ."

Carella and Brown figured they'd get there by noon. Check with the security people, see if they'd seen or heard anything suspicious in the hours before the concert was scheduled to begin. But neither of them was convinced that the concert was the Deaf Man's target, so they sat now at their separate desks, poring over

newspapers and magazines, trying to pinpoint any event that
would start at one P.M. and that might or might not include fire
as part of the performance.

Neither of them realized that the event they were looking for
had been posted on the squadroom bulletin board all week long.

From: Jacques Duprès, Deputy Commissioner
      Police Department Public Information Division

... PRESS RELEASE ... PRESS RELEASE ... PRESS RELEASE ...

For Release: Immediately

On Saturday, April 4th inst. at 1:00 p.m., narcotics
seized in 6,955 arrests by the Police Department
will be destroyed at the Department of Sanitation
Incinerator on River Harb Drive at Houghton Street.
Included in the contraband to be destroyed is
24 lbs, 4 ounces and 113 grains of heroin, valued
at $24,251,875.
Cocaine valued at $3,946,406, crack cocaine
valued at $583,000, marijuana valued at $221,689,
and other drugs and equipment to administer drugs,
including LSD, opium, and hashish will also be
destroyed.

Drugs	LBS	OZ	GRAINS	EACH	VALUE
Heroin	24	4	113		$24,251,875
Cocaine	250	8	135		$3,946,406
Crack (vials)				106,000	$583,000
Opium		12	81		$84,034
Marijuana					
(Bulk)	69	10	34		$208,890
(Cigarettes)				3,657	$12,799
LSD		4	115		$908,550
Hashish	6	5	18		$63,150
Miscellaneous	51	4	257		$18,000
			Drug Total		$30,076,704

Equipment		
Syringes	996	
Eye Droppers	1,028	
Hypo Needles	7,925	$11,150
Pipes	115	125
Glue (Bags)	79	25
(Tubes)	110	30
	Equipment Total	$11,325

Total (Drugs and Equipment)   <u>$30,088,029</u>

The crowd was mostly black. The Deaf Man was counting on that. There were also whites in the crowd. The Deaf Man was counting on that as well. There were Hispanics in the crowd, and some Asians, but the Deaf Man considered them inessential to his plan. Most of the people in the crowd were young. This fit in perfectly with his scheme. Young males were quick to take offense and to seek reprisal; young girls were quick to urge mischief and to seek excitement. Fifty percent of the teenagers in this city carried guns. This was a well-publicized figure that had not escaped the Deaf Man's attention. He knew that at an event as massive as the concert, a weapons check would be unlikely if not impossible. This was not a junior high school with a security guard at the door. This was a ten-acre meadow with a makeshift entrance marked by two pylons spaced some twenty feet apart and painted in alternating red, white, and blue stripes, with a security guard standing at each pylon, smiling benignly. But even if there *was* a weapons check, even if every young male who entered the concert site was unarmed, there would be a riot anyway.

The Deaf Man was counting on it because he knew human nature and he knew it would happen.

The girls interrupted their sound check when Sil came over to introduce Chloe to them. They were wearing the same overalls and high-topped boots the men were wearing, but the bibs on theirs seemed cut a bit more narrow to reveal generous breasts in tight blue T-shirts. Sex and violence, that was what Chloe guessed rap was all about, never mind the protest crap. Protest never sold a nickel's worth of records. She'd have to tell that to Sil one day. Later. In the future.

The one named Grass, the prettier of the two, and the youngest—Chloe judged her to be no more than eighteen, nineteen—looked her up and down the way some men at the club did, gauging her, taking her measure, wondering if this was competition here, Sil holding to her hand so tight that way. Chloe figured the same as she had the night they'd had dinner together, when he'd mentioned her name so offhandedly: There was something going on between these two.

"Nice to meet you," Grass said.

Her eyes met Chloe's directly.

A challenge in them.

Little eighteen-year-old pisspants.

Chloe grabbed Sil's hand tighter.

While he waited for Brown to come out of the men's room, Carella looked over the squadroom bulletin board. Aside from the usual Wanted flyers, there were bits and scraps of everything from notices of changes in departmental rules and regulations, to a detailed reminder on how to administer the Miranda warnings; to a For Sale sign from an officer wanting to get rid of a ten-speed bike, to a flyer about aerobics and weight-lifting classes at the Headquarters Gym, to another flyer about the D.A. Easter Dance and another about the Emerald Society's Celebrity Auction, and a . . .

... PRESS RELEASE ... PRESS RELEASE ... PRESS RELEASE ...

For Release: **Immediately**

On Saturday, April 4th inst. at 1:00 p.m., narcotics seized in 6,955 arrests by the Police Department...

"Let's go," Brown said, and zipped up his fly as he came out of the men's room.

They let the crowd in at twelve noon.

The crowd streamed in between the red, white, and blue pylon markers, an orderly crowd here for a day's outing in the sun. The promoters of the event had set up concessionaire trucks around the perimeter, so that all sorts of food and soft drinks were available, but many in the crowd had brought along their own sandwiches and some of them had brought bottles of beer and soda pop in ice coolers, and some of them were sipping mixed alcoholic drinks from plastic Gatorade bottles. There was the usual mad rush to grab space near the stage area, but on the whole this was a civilized crowd intent only on enjoying the day and the music. Nobody wanted a hassle here today. Nobody wanted to fight over who got closest to the performers.

This was going to be a good, sweet, sunshine-filled day.

The chief security officer's name was Fred Bartlett. He was a burly man almost as tall and as wide as Brown, with a ruddy face and a nose that appeared to have been broken more than once. His flinty blue eyes said Don't mess with me.

"I've seen crowds at any kind of event you'd care to name," he told the detectives. "I worked security at baseball games and football games and hockey games and ice shows and pop concerts and folk concerts and rock concerts and even a concert Barbra Streisand done in her own backyard in L.A. I know when a crowd's gonna be trouble and when it ain't. I can spot a crowd gonna turn mean from the minute it comes in the place, whatever kind of place it may be, an arena, a concert hall, an ice-skating rink, or a park like this one today."

"Uh-huh," Brown said.

He was thinking the man was a blowhard.

"And I can tell you," Bartlett said, "that this crowd here today is as peaceful as any kind of crowd you'd hope for. They're all here to have a good time today. The sun don't hurt. It's about time spring really got here. That's what you can sense with this crowd. It's been a long hard winter and now spring is here and we're all gonna sit back and enjoy it."

"You haven't received any threatening phone calls, have you?" Carella asked.

"Nothing."

"Bomb scares, anything like that?" Brown said.

"Nothing," Bartlett said.

"Anybody threatening to set a fire?"

"Nothing."

Carella looked at his watch.

It was twelve-thirty sharp.

The garbage truck made a sharp turn off the street leading to the river, and then paralleled the river for several blocks, Gloria at the wheel, the Deaf Man sitting beside her. Hanging on to either side of the truck were Carter and Florry. Each of the four was wearing the sanitation department uniform: baggy spruce-green trousers, T-shirt, and jacket. Under the jackets, each of the four had tucked into the waistband of the trousers a nine-millimeter semiautomatic Uzi assault pistol. The Israeli-made weapon carried a twenty-round magazine and, because it was designed to absorb recoil, could accurately fire all twenty rounds within seconds.

They were going in with eighty rounds of ammunition.

The Deaf Man figured that would be more than enough to do the job.

*   *   *

From where Chloe Chadderton sat on a folding chair on the left-hand side of the stage, she saw someone she thought she'd known from another time, another life. The white detective who'd investigated her husband's murder all those years ago. The good-looking one with the slanted eyes that made him look like a Chink. Standing there with a brother bigger than a mountain, talking to a man in uniform almost as big. She couldn't remember the detective's name. Maybe she didn't want to.

She looked at her watch.

It was twenty minutes to one.

Gloria drove the truck in through the open gate in the cyclone fence. In the distance, puffy white clouds rode the piercing blue sky. A man was looking out over the river, where a tugboat pushed heavily against a mild chop; he was wearing the same spruce-green uniform everyone in or on the truck was wearing. He didn't even glance up as Gloria stopped the truck alongside the incinerator building.

She cut the ignition and pocketed the key.

All four of them put on the ski masks.

Something kept bothering Carella.

"What do you think?" Brown asked. "We stay awhile, or we go back to the office?"

"I think we'd better stay awhile," he said.

"Maybe he was just pulling our leg all along," Brown said.

Carella looked at him.

"Well," Brown said, and shrugged.

It was close to a shrug of defeat.

Both of them *knew* the Deaf Man hadn't been pulling their leg but neither of them had even the faintest notion of what his plan might be.

* * *

There were two Sanitation Department employees inside the incinerator building. One of them was reading a sports magazine.
The other one was eating a sausage and pepper sandwich his
wife had made him for lunch. When the front door opened, they
thought it was the cops from the Property Clerk's Office, here
to burn their dope. It was only a quarter to one, but sometimes
they got here a little early. Instead, they saw four guys in ski
masks and uniforms same as they were wearing, all four of them
holding guns.

The tallest one said, "Nice and easy."

The two garbage men knew better than to move.

From where they stood behind the stage waiting for the show to
begin, Carella and Brown could hear the voice of the crowd. It
was a single voice that vibrated with the pleasure of expectation.
At one o'clock sharp . . .

On Saturday, April 4th inst. at 1:00 P.M. . . .

. . . according to what Bartlett had told them, the concert
would open with a rap group called Spit Shine . . .

"Here's the program right here," he'd said, "you can keep
it, I've got dozens of 'em."

It was now five minutes to one, and the voice of the crowd . . .

On Saturday, April 4th inst. at 1:00 P.M. . . .

. . . hummed now with expectancy. In just five minutes, the
concert would begin. Bartlett had estimated that there were
250,000 people in the crowd. 250,000 people waiting for . . .

Explosion?

Here?

Carella could not imagine how.

* * *

At three minutes past one, just as Spit Shine began performing
the song George Chadderton had written, rapping out his words,
a van marked with the police department's seal and the words
PROPERTY CLERK'S OFFICE rolled down the ramp into the river-
front complex and parked alongside a graffiti-riddled garbage
truck near the rear of the incinerator building. A radio car came
down the ramp after it, and two officers got out of the car just
as a sergeant and another officer got out of the van. The men
exchanged greetings there at the river's edge, commented on
what a great day it was, and then the sergeant said, "Let's see
if they're ready for us," and they all walked into the building
and found themselves looking into the barrels of what appeared
to be four semiautomatic assault pistols.

The sergeant wondered why this hadn't happened long before
now, this city.

". . . why she do this way?

"On her back, on her knees, for the white man pay?

"She a slave, sister woman, she a slave this way,

"On her knees, on her back, for the white man pay . . ."

Sitting on the side of the stage, listening to the lyrics her
husband had written so long ago, Chloe realized that the group
was doing something marvelous with them, Sil and Jeeb in the
background rapping a steady insistent urgent beat, the two girls
rapping the words in a keening high-pitched wail that almost
brought Chloe to tears.

The sound was picked up by forty or fifty microphones collecting audio information on the stage and feeding it into a cable
that measured some two inches in diameter and lay on the ground
like a snake. This cable, which was in fact *called* the snake, ran
from the stage through the center of the audience in a lane flanked
by sawhorses and covered with a rubber mat, going back some
hundred and fifty feet to the control tower, where two sound
engineers sat behind the console doing a house mix by ear.

From the console, four separate feeds ran out to the delay towers and the left and right main speakers stacked on either side of the stage. There were sixteen speakers stacked in each of the delay towers, together with a dozen thousand-watt amplifiers. The system had been equalized during the days before the concert, the delays calibrated so that the sound coming from the delay towers was synchronized with the sound coming from the towers on either side of the stage, where eighty speakers in each tower were moving a hell of a lot of air.

"... won't she hear my song?

"What she doin this way surely got to be wrong.

"Lift her head, raise her eyes, sing the words out strong ...."

The only one they had to shoot was the garbage man taking the air at the river's edge. It was Gloria who shot him because she was the one standing closest to him when he turned and yelled, "Hey! What's goin on here?"

This may have been because he'd just seen four men in ski masks moving toward the police van. Gloria was thinking about the payoff on this thing, and she wasn't about to have any shitty little garbage man screw it up. She fired three shots in rapid succession, the sound dissipating instantly over the water. The shots took him full in the face and knocked him back against the cyclone fence. He slid to the ground like an oil rag.

"Nice," the Deaf Man said.

Then they all climbed into the police van, and he handed Gloria the keys he'd taken from the sergeant's belt.

The song was called "Hate."

It started at twelve minutes past one, just as Gloria turned the van's ignition key.

Jeeb was the lead rapper on this one.

Sil did backup.

The girls sneered and snarled in the background.

The Deaf Man had no prior knowledge of the program that would be performed at today's concert. He was only concerned with timing and diversion, the magician's concern. He was stealing thirty million dollars' worth of narcotics under the very noses of the police, and the only way to get away clean was to divert them.

The timer was set for one-twenty sharp.

At that time, he hoped to be transferring the contents of the police van into the rented Chevrolet already waiting in the boat-basin parking lot farther downtown.

It was pure coincidence that the song's content would aid and abet his plan. His plan was foolproof even without the song, but the song couldn't hurt; give him a little chicken soup, as the lady in the balcony once remarked. Had he been here, the Deaf Man would have been pleased by the song and the spirited performance of the group named Spit Shine.

Sitting in the audience, Carella recognized dangerous and inflammatory lyrics when he heard them, all right, but his mind kept clicking back over something he'd seen or read, something in one of the newspapers or magazines, something about . . .

Saturday, April 4th . . .

Something about . . .

April 4th inst. at 1:00 P.M. . . .

Too damn many newspapers, too damn many magazines.

". . . kick the ofay, kill the ofay, snuff the ofay, off the ofay, box the ofay, *hate* the ofay, cause the ofay hate *you*!

"Hate the ofay . . ."

His mind circled back again.

April 4th inst. at 1:00 P.M. . . .

". . . fuck the ofay, juke the ofay . . ."

Saturday, April 4th inst. at 1:00 P.M. . . .

". . . shoot the ofay, spike the ofay . . ."

Saturday, April 4th inst. at 1:00 P.M., narcotics seized in . . .

"They *burn* it!" he shouted.

". . . *do* the ofay . . ."

"What!" Brown shouted.

"The narcotics! They *burn* the stuff!"

". . . like the ofay do *you*!"

And in just that instant, Florry's timer kicked in and the Deaf Man's digitally stored voice erupted.

The way Florry had explained it to him, you had to think of it as upstream and downstream. The sound from the stage ran *downstream* to the console where it was mixed, and then it ran out of the console, back *upstream* to the speakers in the various towers. Downstream, upstream. Into the console, out of the console again.

"You've got your snake running *into* the console and then your matrix outputs running *out* of it," Florry said. "The matrix outputs are carrying the sound that came downstream and got mixed and is now running back *upstream* again. It's like a bottle-neck right there, where the mixed sound narrows down to just these four signal lines going out to the *main* speakers left and right, and the *delay* speakers left and right. You follow me so far?"

"Barely," the Deaf Man said.

"Stick with me," Florry said, and grinned. "Suppose we direct the sound going upstream into our little black box, hmm? So that instead of going straight to the speakers, it goes through the box and out of it again. Business as usual, no depredation of sound. Everything coming from the stage is mixed at the console, goes out of the console into the box, passes through the box and out of the box, and then on to the speakers. Everything still going downstream and then upstream again. Until we decide to abort it."

"How do we do that?"

"Simple," Florry said.

The way Florry did it—and the way it was working this very instant—was not, in fact, quite as simple as he'd claimed it was.

To make it easier for the Deaf Man to understand, he explained that the heart of his "little black box" was a 24-volt DC battery pack that drove all the elements necessary to abort the sound coming from the stage and to substitute for it the message the Deaf Man had recorded. In addition to the resistors, capacitors, and opamps that were the essential components of any sound circuitry, the various *other* elements in the box were:

1) A digital clock, which had been preset to go off at one-twenty sharp . . .
2) Four relays, which in effect created a two-pole switch, and . . .
3) An EPROM, the electronic chip upon which Florry had digitally stored the Deaf Man's voice.

"There are two positions in that box," Florry said. "The A position is your normal output, the mixed signal going from the console, through the box, and to the speakers. Before the timer kicks in, nobody'll even guess the signal is running through our box. That's the first position. But the instant that timer kicks in, your relays switch to the B position, which is the message on the EPROM we burned. The timer throws the switch, which kills the sound coming from the stage and sends out your voice instead. From that second on, a twenty-four-volt battery'll be running sound to every speaker in the joint! Just think of it! All those speakers in each tower, and *your* voice booming from every one of them, a goddamn box from hell!"

The Deaf Man's voice was booming from them now.

"NIGGERS EAT *SHIT*!"

If you were sitting on the stage, as Chloe was, or if you were sitting no more than fifty feet back from the stage, you might have heard the sound generated by the group's own amps and speakers, but this was almost totally overridden by the voice that thundered from the stacks of speakers the little black box was now controlling.

"*ALL* NIGGERS EAT SHIT!"

The voice was high and strident. The Deaf Man had shouted into the mike when they were burning the EPROM, and now his voice bellowed from the speakers.

"EVERY FUCKING NIGGER ON *EARTH* EATS SHIT!"

At first, the audience thought this was part of the act. Strange things sometimes happened at these concerts, and Spit Shine was still up there performing, wasn't it? Even the two men behind the console were initially confused. The board was showing input from the stage mikes, so maybe the group was just being totally outrageous. But the engineers could *see* the stage, and all at once Spit Shine stopped dead. And where an instant earlier there'd been their faintly amplified rap competing with the thunderous sound coming from all those high-powered speakers, now there was only the Deaf Man's voice, as insistent as Hitler's had been when he was exhorting his masses.

"THAT'S WHY NIGGERS ARE THE *COLOR* OF SHIT!"

The input lights on the board went out the minute Spit Shine quit.

"It's not coming from the stage," one of the engineers said.

"THAT'S WHY NIGGERS *STINK* LIKE SHIT!"

The intercom call light flashed.

The other engineer picked up.

"What's the joke?" a voice asked.

"It's not us," the engineer said.

"THAT'S WHY NIGGERS ARE *DUMB* AS SHIT!"

"Are your masters down?" the voice asked.

The first engineer slapped at the master faders.

"Nothing's going out of the console," he said.

But the shouting continued.

"NIGGERS *ARE* SHIT . . ."

"Must be somebody on the stage," the second engineer said.

"NIGGERS'LL TURN THE *WORLD* TO SHIT, NIGGERS'LL . . ."

"Let's pull all the wires," the first engineer said.

But just then the first shot was fired—and it was too late.

Carella and Brown were already in the car when the crowd exploded. On the other end of the radio Alf Miscolo in the clerical office was giving them the location of the incinerator. As an aside, he reported that Hawes and Meyer had just left the squad-room on their way to Grover Park.

"There's some kind of trouble there," he said.

The some kind of trouble was the same kind of trouble that had been eroding America's spirit for the past half-century. In an unmarked sedan speeding crosstown and downtown toward the Department of Sanitation incinerator on Houghton and the river, a white man yelled "Hit the hammer!" to a black man, and the black man flicked the siren switch and rammed the accelerator pedal to the floor. The white man and the black man in that speeding police sedan had been raised in an America that promised a melting pot, that told them stories about people from all nations living together in harmony and peace. In this land of the free and home of the brave, men and women of every religion and creed would loudly sing the praises of freedom while reaping all those amber waves of grain. The persecution, the starvation, the deprivation that had brought this human refuse to our teeming shores would be obliterated here for all time. Men and women would come to respect each other's customs and beliefs while simultaneously merging into a strong single tribe with a strong single voice, a voice distinctly American, a voice more powerful *precisely* because it was composed of so many different voices from so many different lands. Here in America, the separate parts would at last become the whole, one nation, indivisible, with liberty and justice for all.

Well, the liberty and justice for all had somehow become

liberty and justice for merely *some,* and the glorious notion of
a unified tribe had somehow become something no one ever
mentioned anymore, like a dream dreamt too often and too yearn-
ingly, until its brilliant colors faded to drab and you woke up
crying. Because the Deaf Man had realized all this, and because
he'd had not the slightest compunction about capitalizing on it,
he'd been able to instigate a riot with total certainty and absolute
ease.

Carella and Brown were well aware of the riot.

They had rushed to the car before the crowd got completely
out of hand because containing a riot was not their obligation;
catching the man who'd *caused* it was. Now there was nothing
but the riot on every police radio channel, interspersed with
dispatcher warnings to maintain total radio silence until the trouble was contained. The riot made them uncomfortable because
they were respectively a white man and a black man and the
trouble in the park was one of color. But they were a black man
and a white man acting as a team to catch the son of a bitch
responsible for the riot, the man who'd turned a promising golden
day into yet another dark and dismal gloom. Tight-lipped, they
sped downtown with the siren blaring, passing a dozen or more
radio cars racing uptown in the opposite direction.

Which was what the Deaf Man had planned all along.

"Chloe!" he shouted. "Take my hand!"

She reached for his hand.

Reached for the future.

Grasped it eagerly.

Below the stage, there was bedlam. The first shot had inspired
more shooting. When there are guns on the scene, the first gun
openly to appear encourages boldness from anyone else who's
armed. Boldness and the challenge of the Old West. High noon
in the OK Corral. All that shit. Guns are guns. Guns are weapons
of destruction. There were an estimated 250,000 people on that

lawn when the first gun came out and the first shot was fired. It was fired by a black man at a white man because the Deaf Man's baiting words were directed at blacks, and because—as Rivera had written about the multitude—"It will turn on itself and see in itself the olden enemy." Well, *this* multitude had heard the inflammatory words, and they had correctly identified the speaker of those words as white, and their single goal was to kill Whitey . . .

Its fury will blind its eyes . . .

. . . kick the ofay, kill the ofay, snuff the ofay, off the ofay, box the ofay, *hate* the ofay, cause the ofay hate *you!*

The crowd moved forward relentlessly, chanting, stamping, shouting, a massive beast that seemed all flailing arms and thrashing legs . . .

"This way!" Sil shouted. "The band trailer!"

White men and black men were shooting at each other, shoving at each other, screaming at each other, pushing at each other, kicking each other, punching each other . . .

. . . *eager to destroy the victim it had chosen, the common enemy, a roar rising as if from a single throat, "kill, kill, kill!"*

Sil threw open the trailer door, put his hands on either side of her waist, and lifted her onto the step.

The white man's bullet took Chloe in the back of her head, spattering blood and brain tissue onto the side of the trailer where the words **SPIT SHINE** were lettered in bold silver lettering edged in black, shattering her dream and killing her at once.

Outside the incinerator building, Carella and Brown found a man lying at the foot of the cyclone fence, dead. Inside the building, they found two garbage men and four police officers bound and gagged, blindfolded, and wearing ski masks for good measure.

They figured the Deaf Man had arrived in the garbage truck parked outside.

* * *

The foot patrolman walking the beat outside the boat basin saw
what looked like a police van sitting in the parking lot, close to
the river's edge. He checked it out, and sure enough it *was* a
P.D. vehicle, with Property Clerk's Office markings on its side
panels. He opened the door on the driver's side, and found a set
of keys hanging from the ignition.

Aside from that, all there was in the van was some stuff looked
like syringes and pipes and other cheap drug paraphernalia.

They had driven from the boat-basin parking lot, uptown to
the Hamilton Bridge, and then over it to the next state—Florry,
Carter, and Gloria driving their own rented cars, the Deaf Man
driving the Chevrolet he'd rented. By two-thirty that afternoon,
he'd paid all of them the remainder of their fees and had opened
several bottles of champagne in celebration. All four cars were
parked outside the motel room. The stolen narcotics were covered with a tarpaulin in the trunk of the Deaf Man's Chevy.
He had told them it would be best if they went their separate
ways in fifteen-minute intervals, Florry first, then Carter, then
Gloria. They seemed content to let him do things his way.
There'd been scarcely any fuss at all this afternoon, and they
were now all a hundred thousand dollars richer because of him.

They toasted the ease with which the job had gone down,
toasted each other's brilliance and cool, particularly toasted Gloria, who, for a woman, had displayed uncommon ballsiness in
putting away the garbage man. None of them complained about
the split. They knew—or must have known—that the narcotics
in the Chevy outside were worth a great deal more than the Deaf
Man had paid them, but he was the one who'd concocted the
scheme, and they knew in their hearts that he was entitled to the
lion's share.

So they drank their champagne like good old friends at a black tie party late in the night after everyone else had gone home, and at last Florry looked at his watch and said "Time to boogie," and went into the bathroom to change his clothes. When he came out again, he was wearing brown corduroy trousers, a green sports shirt, a tan V-necked sweater, and brown socks with brown loafers. Carter told him not to spend all his money in one place, and they all laughed and he shook hands all around and went outside, where in a minute or so they heard his car starting and driving off.

Ten minutes later, Carter sighed and said, "My friends, all good things must come to an end," and he went into the bathroom to change, shedding the spruce-green uniform and returning in a red turtleneck, gray slacks, a blue blazer, and blue socks with black shoes. He shook hands with the Deaf Man, kissed Gloria on the cheek, and went out. The moment the Deaf Man heard his car driving off, he said, "Alone at last."

Gloria arched an eyebrow.

"I have to be out of here in fifteen minutes," she said.

"You still haven't taught me that trick of yours," he said.

"That trick's a secret," she said. "I haven't taught that trick to anyone in the world."

"Know any other tricks?"

"A few."

"Want to teach me those?"

"The fifteen minutes was your idea," she said.

"But who's counting?" he said, and smiled.

He poured more champagne, and he turned on the radio that was part of the room's television set and found a station playing elevator music, soft and romantic, with a lot of strings. Gloria sat in the room's only easy chair, and he sat on the edge of the bed, and leaned over to clink his glass against hers, and they both said "Cheers" at the same moment, and then brought the glasses to their lips and sipped at the good bubbly wine. She was watching him over the rim of the glass. He considered this a good sign.

"Are you going to drive home in that garbage man's uniform?" he asked.

"No, I'll change before I leave," she said.

There was a moment's hesitation.

Then he said, "Why don't you change now?"

She looked at him for a moment. Then she put down her glass and said, "Sure."

She was in the bathroom for what seemed like a very long time. When she came out again, she was wearing a short black skirt with black pantyhose, a red silk blouse, and high-heeled black patent pumps. Through the open bathroom door, he could see all the garbage man uniforms heaped on the floor near the tub. She sat where she'd been sitting earlier, crossed her legs in the black pantyhose, picked up her champagne glass, lifted it to him in a silent toast, and drank again. He went to where she was sitting, leaned over her, and kissed her.

"The day I interviewed you," he said.

"Yes?"

Still leaning over her. Her face tilted up to his.

"You asked me what I wanted you to do, do you remember?"

"I remember."

He kissed her again.

"You have a lovely mouth," he said.

"Thank you," she said.

"You *do* remember what you said, don't you?"

"Yes, I remember."

"Do you remember what *I* said?"

"Sure."

"What did I say?"

"You said you didn't pay women for sex."

"And what'd you say to that?"

"I said, 'Good, because I don't suck cocks for money.' "

"Good," he said, "because I don't plan to *give* you any money."

"Good," she said.

"Good," he repeated, and took her hands, and helped her gently out of the chair. Lifting her into his arms, he carried her to the bed, and put her down on it, and kicked off his loafers and lay down beside her. She rolled into him to meet him, and he took her in his arms and kissed her more fiercely this time, and then his hands were under the short black skirt, easing the pantyhose down over her hips and past the blonde triangle of her pubic patch, rolling them down over the long length of her legs, until they were bunched at her ankles, holding her there like leg cuffs, the black high-heeled pumps just below them.

"I want to tie you to the bed," he said.

"Sure," she said.

With leather thongs, he tied her wrists to the headboard posts and her ankles to the footboard posts, leaving her spread-eagled and waiting on the bed while he went into the bathroom to undress. He came to her naked and hard, and kissed her again, and put his hand on her where she was spread and helpless and vulnerable below. He played games with her for an hour or more, the April afternoon drifting slowly by while he teased her first with his hands and his mouth and then with his cock and finally with the Uzi, adding a little danger to the game, the barrel of the gun cool against her thighs, Gloria writhing on the bed beside him. She was still bound when at last he entered her. He did not untie her until twenty minutes later, when they were both exhausted and sweaty and spent.

"Now you," she said.

"Oh-ho," he said.

He was lying on his back, his forearm across his eyes, his long muscular body relaxed, his cock limp.

"Sauce for the goose," she said, and gathered the leather thongs from where he'd tossed them on the floor.

She tied his hands first.

Then his ankles.

Spread-eagled on the bed, he looked at her and smiled.

"Now what?" he asked.

"Same as you did to me," she said. "Only better."

She knelt between his spread legs and took him in her mouth. He was erect again within seconds.

"Now suffer," she said, and got off the bed and put on first the pantyhose and the skirt . . .

"Reverse strip," he said, smiling.

"Yep, reverse strip," she said, and put on her brassiere and the red silk blouse and the high-heeled pumps . . .

"Come on over here," he said.

"Nope," she said, and buttoned the blouse swiftly, button by button, and tucked the blouse into the skirt . . .

"Come on, bitch."

"Beg for it," she said, and went to the dresser and picked up the Uzi.

"Uh-oh," he said, smiling.

"Yep," she said, and nodded and fired two quick shots into his chest. She turned away at once, picked up her handbag and the keys to the Chevy, looked back at him again quickly, turned away from the sight of all that blood, and left the room.

14.

They drove across the bridge in the rain because listening to the morning news on the radio, Brown had heard about a motel shooting in the town of Red Point over in the next state. Three garbage men's uniforms had been found in the motel bathroom. They called the Red Point P.D. and spoke to a detective named Roger Newcastle, who said they were welcome to come on out, but whoever'd got shot was long gone. At first, they thought he was using a euphemism, telling them the victim was dead.

But, no, when they met Newcastle at the Hamilton Motel, as it was called because of its proximity to the bridge, they learned from him that the victim—who had to've bled gallons of blood, judging from the looks of the bedclothes here—had somehow got himself loose . . .

"He must've been tied to the bed here with these here leather thongs," Newcastle said.

. . . and gone out of here leaving a trail of blood that led straight to where a car must've been parked.

"Wasn't *his* car, though, cause we got the registration on that from when he checked in. We figure it was somebody else's car, but not nobody's who was checked in at the time, cause none of them says their vehicle was stolen. So we guess it was somebody's car who was with him there in the room, maybe the person who tied him to the bed that way. Either a woman or a man, this might've been a homosexual thing, they can sometimes get kinky and fierce. There's blood all over one of the thongs, he must've made his hand bleed tryin'a work loose, like some animal gnawing off his own paw to get free of a trap."

"Find any narcotics?" Carella asked.

"Not a trace. Why? You think this was some kinda dope party?"

"Not exactly," Brown said.

"We dug out two slugs went on through and buried themselves in the wall behind the headboard," Newcastle said. "There was also a pair of nine-millimeter cartridge cases on the floor near the dresser, they're with Ballistics, too. Nobody heard any shots, this is a place guys bring girls over from the city, nobody *wants* to hear nothing. Half of them, if they *did* hear anything, they prolly got in their cars and ran for the hills. The lab's going over everything else right this minute, champagne bottles, glasses, the uniforms, who knows what they'll come up with? The car he drove in with was a Chevy, by the way, gone now, we figure whoever dusted him went off in it later on."

With thirty million dollars' worth of stolen narcotics, Carella thought.

"We checked the license-plate number he wrote on the motel registration card, it was a rented car," Newcastle said. "Hertz. Name he used when he rented it was the same one he registered under here at the motel."

Had to've shown a driver's license, Brown thought, probably a phony. Wouldn't have given him a car without a license.

"What name was that?" he asked.

"Sonny Sanson," Newcastle said. "That's not *Samson*, it's *Sanson*—with an *n*."

"Yeah," Carella said, and sighed. "We know."

In the Sunday afternoon gloom of the squadroom, they explored the possibilities.

If the person who'd been tied to that bed was whoever had been with the Deaf Man in the motel room, then the Deaf Man had done the shooting and gone on his merry way with thirty million dollars' worth of stolen narcotics.

If, on the other hand, the Deaf Man *himself* was the person who'd been tied to that bed, then whoever was with him had shot him and stolen the *already* stolen narcotics. Honor among thieves, so to speak.

Either way, the Deaf Man—or Sonny Sanson, as he'd called himself this time around—was once again gone with the wind.

"Maybe he'll turn up dead and bleeding in some ditch alongside the road," Brown said.

"Maybe," Carella said.

He did not think so.

He knew in his bones that the Deaf Man was still alive and that one day he'd be back to plague them again.

"Sarah has a theory about the name he used," Meyer said.

Sarah was his wife.

Nobody really wanted to hear Sarah's theory. Rain was pouring down outside, and the squadroom lights were on in defense against it, and all they could think was they'd lost him again. He'd made fools of them yet another time.

"She thinks it's a combination of Italian and French. She goes to Berlitz," Meyer explained. "When I retire, she wants to go live in Europe."

Rain drops trailed down the windowpanes. On the street below, there was the hiss of automobile tires on slick asphalt. It felt like the dead of winter, but it was the fifth of April and spring was here.

"She thinks the Sonny stands for '*Son'io*.' That means 'I am' in Italian. *Io sono* is the formal way of saying it. *Son'io* is more casual. That's what Sarah thinks."

Carella was listening now. So was Brown.

"So he's saying 'I am Sanson,'" Meyer said. "Or, more casually, just 'I'm Sanson.' You get it?"

"No," Brown said.

"He's telling us he's deaf," Meyer said.

"He is, huh?" Brown said.

"How does Sarah figure that?" Carella asked.

"Because of what Sanson means in French."

"What does it mean in French?"

"It means he's deaf."

"Sanson means somebody's *deaf*?" Brown asked.

"No, it's two words. That's what Sarah thinks, anyway."

"What are the two words?" Carella asked patiently.

"*Sans* and *son*. I'm not sure I'm pronouncing them right. I can call Sarah, if you like, put her on the speaker . . ."

"No, that's fine," Carella said. "What do those words *mean*?"

"*Sans* means 'without.' And *son* means 'sound.' He was saying 'I'm without sound.' He was telling us he's deaf."

Carella looked at Brown.

Brown looked back at him.

Outside, the rain kept falling.

Parker made his call from a pay phone on the locker-room wall because he wasn't so sure what kind of reception he'd get from Catalina Herrera and he didn't want any wise-ass remarks from the squadroom clowns in case he got turned down. This was Sunday, after all, and he was just now calling to report on the case they'd closed out *Friday*.

She sounded as if she'd been asleep.

"Cathy?" he said.

"*Si?*"

He wished to fuck she'd speak English.

"This is Detective Parker," he said. "Andy."

"Oh, hello, Andy."

"How you been?"

"Oh, fine."

Her voice sort of low-key. As if she was still waking up.

Either that or the rain had got to her. Not the same way it had got to him, though. Rainy days always made him horny. Which was why he was calling her.

"I guess you heard we cracked the case."

"Yes," she said. "That was good."

"Yeah, I thought so," he said. "I'm sorry I didn't call sooner, but there was a lot of paper work to do, wrap it all up, you know."

"Yes," she said.

"So how you been?"

"You didn't call since four days," she said. "Wednesday night, I saw you. This is Sunday."

"Yeah, I guess that's right," he said. "But I been out chasing the man killed your son," he reminded her. In fact, busting my *balls* trying to catch him, he wanted to say. "Which, of course, we finally done. As you know."

"Wednesday we go to bed," she said. "Sunday you call."

"Yeah, well."

There was a silence on the line.

"But I'm calling now, right?" he said.

Silence.

"I thought maybe I'd come over," he said.

The silence lengthened.

"Cathy? What do you say?"

The silence became almost unbearable.

He thought Hey, fuck you, sister, there's plenty other fish in the sea, huh? But he hung on, anyway, hoping he wouldn't have to put another fuckin quarter in the phone.

She was thinking that maybe a little house in a Los Angeles suburb wasn't for the Catalinas of this world, maybe in America, California dreaming was only for the Cathys. She was thinking that maybe Parker wasn't quite the decent hard-working man she dreamed about, the one who'd cook barbecues for her when she finished a day's work on her screenplay, maybe he wasn't that

man at all. But it was raining, and her son was dead, and she
was lonely.

"Sure, come over," she said, and hung up.

Kling made his call from a pay phone, too, and for much the
same reason Parker had. He didn't want to be turned down in a
place as public as the squadroom. He didn't want to risk possible
derision from the men with whom he worked day and night, the
men to whom he often entrusted his life. Nor did he want to
make the call from anyplace at *all* in the station house. There
were pay phones on every floor, but a police station was like a
small town, and gossip traveled fast. He did not want anyone to
overhear him fumbling for words in the event of a rejection. He
felt that rejection was a very definite possibility.

So he stood in the pouring rain a block from the station house,
at a blue plastic shell with a pay phone inside it, dialing the
number he'd got from the police directory operator, and which
he'd scribbled on a scrap of paper that was now getting soggy
in the rain. He waited while the phone rang, once, twice, three
times, four, five, and he thought She isn't home, six, sev...

"Hello?"

Her voice startled him.

"Hello, uh, Sharon?" he said. "Chief Cooke?"

"Who's this, please?"

Her voice impatient and sharp. Rain pelting down everywhere
around him. Hang up, he thought.

"This is Bert Kling?" he said.

"Who?"

The sharpness still in her voice. But edged with puzzlement
now.

"Detective Bert Kling," he said. "We...uh...met at the
hospital."

"The hospital?"

"Earlier this week. The hostage cop shooting. Georgia Mowbry."

"Yes?"

Trying to remember who he was. Unforgettable encounter, he guessed. Lasting impression.

"I was with Detective Burke," he said, ready to give up. "The redheaded hostage cop. She was with Georgia when . . ."

"Oh, yes, I remember now," Sharyn said. "How are you?"

"Fine," he said, and then very quickly, "I'm calling to tell you how sorry I am you lost her."

"That's very kind of you."

"I know I should have called earlier . . ."

"No, no, it's appreciated."

"But we were working a difficult case . . ."

"I quite understand."

Georgia Mowbry had died on Wednesday night. This was now Sunday. Sharyn suddenly wondered what this was all about. She'd been reading the papers when her phone rang. Reading all about yesterday's riot in the park. Blacks and whites rioting. Blacks and whites shooting each other, killing each other.

"So . . . uh . . . I know how difficult something like that must be," he said. "And I . . . uh . . . just thought I'd offer my . . . uh . . . sympathy."

"Thank you," she said.

There was a silence.

Then:

"Uh . . . Sharon . . ."

"By the way, it's Sharyn," she said.

"Isn't that what I'm saying?"

"You're saying Sharon."

"Right," he said.

"But it's *Sharyn*."

"I know," he said, thoroughly confused now.

"With a *y*," she said.

"Oh," he said. "Right. Thank you. I'm sorry. *Sharyn*, right."

"What's that I hear?" she asked.

"What do you mean?"

"That sound."

"Sound? Oh. It must be the rain."

"The rain? Where are you?"

"I'm calling from outside."

"From a phone booth?"

"No, not really, it's just one of these little shell things. What you're hearing is the rain hitting the plastic."

"You're standing in the rain?"

"Well, sort of."

"Isn't there a phone in the squadroom?"

"Well, yes. But . . ."

She waited.

"I . . . uh . . . didn't want anyone to hear me."

"Why not?"

"Because I . . . I didn't know how you'd feel about . . . something like this."

"Something like what?"

"My . . . asking you to have dinner with me."

Silence.

"Sharyn?"

"Yes?"

"Your being a chief and all," he said. "A deputy chief."

She blinked.

"I thought it might make a difference. That I'm just a detective/third."

"I see."

No mention of his blond hair or her black skin.

Silence.

"Does it?" he asked.

She had never dated a white man in her life.

"Does what?" she said.

"*Does* it make a difference? Your rank?"

"No."

But what about the other? she wondered. What about whites and blacks killing each other in public places? What about *that*, Detective Kling?

"Rainy day like today," he said, "I thought it'd be nice to have dinner and go to a movie."

With a white man, she thought.

Tell my mother I'm going on a date with a white man. My mother who scrubbed white men's offices on her knees.

"I'm off at four," he said. "I can go home, shower and shave, pick you up at six."

You hear this, Mom? A white man wants to pick me up at six. Take me out to dinner and a movie.

"Unless you have other plans," he said.

"Are you *really* standing in the rain?" she asked.

"Well, yes," he said. "*Do* you?"

"Do I what?"

"Have other plans?"

"No. But . . ."

Bring the subject up, she thought. Face it head on. Ask him if he knows I'm black? Tell him I've never done anything like this before. Tell him my mother'll jump off the roof. Tell him I don't need this kind of complication in my life, tell him . . .

"Well . . . uh . . . do you think you might *like* to?" he asked. "Go to a movie and have dinner?"

"Why do you want to do this?" she asked.

He hesitated a moment. She visualized him standing there in the rain, pondering the question.

"Well," he said, "I think we might enjoy each other's company, is all."

She could just see him shrugging, standing there in the rain. Calling from outside the station house because he didn't want anyone to hear him being turned down by *rank*. Never mind black, never mind white, this was detective/third and deputy chief. As simple as that. She almost smiled.

"Excuse me," he said, "but do you think you could give me some kind of answer? Cause it's sort of wet out here."

"Six o'clock is fine," she said.

"Good," he said.

"Call me when you're out of the rain, I'll give you my address."

"Good," he said again. "Good. That's good. Thank you, Sharyn. I'll call you when I get back to the squadroom. What kind of food do you like? I know a great Italian . . ."

"Get out of the rain," she said, and quickly put the phone back on the cradle.

Her heart was pounding.

God, she thought, what am I starting here?

GRITTY, SUSPENSEFUL NOVELS
BY MASTER STORYTELLERS
FROM AVON BOOKS

FORCE OF NATURE
by Stephen Solomita
70949-X/$4.95 US/$5.95 Can

"Powerful and relentlessly engaging...Tension at a riveting peak" *Publishers Weekly*

A MORNING FOR FLAMINGOS
by James Lee Burke
71360-8/$5.50 US/$6.50 Can

"No one writes better detective novels...truly astonishing"
Washington Post Book World

A TWIST OF THE KNIFE
by Stephen Solomita
70997-X/$4.95 US/$5.95 Can

"A sizzler...Wambaugh and Caunitz had better look out"
Associated Press

BLACK CHERRY BLUES
by James Lee Burke
71204-0/$5.50 US/$6.50 Can

"Remarkable...A terrific story...The plot crackles with events and suspense...Not to be missed!"
Los Angeles Times Book Review